Cortek Exiled

by Jacque Alanbery

Dedication

To Jake, without whom this story would not have been told. And to Tammy who helped make it one worth reading.

Copyright 2023 by Jacque Alanbery

Published by: Cybernet Books, LLC

ISBN 978-1-963018-01-1

Printed in the United States of America

This book is a reissue/republication of a novel originally entitled: *The Coup and the Muse* (©2021 by Jacque Alanbery)

All rights reserved. No part of this publication may be reproduced or transmitted in any form by any means, electronic or mechanical, including photocopy, recording, or any information storage and retrieval system, without permission in writing from the copyright owner.

This book is a work of fiction. Any references to historical events, real people, or real locales are used fictitiously. Other names, characters, places, and incidents are the product of the author's imagination, and any resemblance to actual events or locales or persons, living or dead, is entirely coincidental.

The Oliquin Chronicles

In the twenty-second century on Earth, inter-galactic space travel is in its infancy. On hearing a news report about the successful colonization of a distant planet, a recently retired CEO decides to sell her multi-billion-dollar corporation and fund the world's most ambitious colonization expedition to date. Many years later, the ship reaches its destination—the planet Oliquin. The colonists, along with the Earth plants and animals that made the journey, are split into groups, and four colonies are established around the planet.

Cut off from contact with Earth, and each other, and with only the most basic infrastructure, industry, and technology available to them, the colonists are set to face the challenges and tribulations of building their new life in this unfamiliar place.

This is a story from the history of Oliquin, as lived by those colonists and their descendants.

Cortek Exiled

Oath of the Cortek – Book 1

www.jacquealanbery.com

Oath of the Cortek

I solemnly swear to honor and protect the citizens of the colony to the best of my ability, and as bound by this oath.

I shall honor and keep the secrets of the Corecraft and pre-Oliquin technology except as publicly known or as sanctioned for release by the Headmaster.

I shall educate and advise the citizens of the colony and support the recording and documentation of the history of Oliquin.

I shall support Cortek factories in the production and distribution of basic materials that promote the health, safety, and well-being of the colony and its citizens.

I shall not be involved in the design, production, or distribution of weapons.

I shall not hold political office or be directly involved in political conflicts of the colony.

This oath I swear to uphold, till the end of my days, under penalty of death at the hands of my fellow Cortek.

THE COLONY OF EDYSON
EDYSON CITY
Dovetails
Meadowick
Southbrook
Casterly Lake
Sweetdale
Baytown
The Ravens
N
E
S
W

Chapter 1
Apri

Apri froze. The shuffle of boots outside her room could only mean trouble. "Damian?"

Silence.

So, not him. Her captor wasn't due back yet anyway. She picked up her sword and faced the doorway. Her fingers tingled, then flexed on the hilt. "Who is there?" she called out.

The privacy curtain whipped back, almost coming off the rod. The material wrapped around the man's hand, and he cursed, waving and flapping his hand to free it.

"Back off, Jase!" she warned, lifting the sword.

"Damian says the girl's off limits, but you," he said, blocking her exit. "He didn't make no such rule about you." He licked his lips.

She faced the intruder barefoot and wearing nothing but loose-fitting undergarments. Her sleeping cot sat on the floor between them. "Get out. Now," she ordered, her harsh, confident tone a stark contrast to her apparent vulnerability. *Why am I still here in this rat hole?* Whatever had kept her from escaping—her affair with Kendall or her fondness for Tina—it didn't matter now. She clenched her fists, a habit she'd picked up long ago to help clear her mind of useless thoughts.

"I ain't going nowhere, sweetie," he drooled. "God, you're a good-looking piece of flesh." His slurred, sluggish speech could be intentional or a result of his drunken state—she couldn't tell which. A wicked grin displayed yellow, rotting teeth. The scar on his cheek turned bright white.

And you are a repulsive fobmuck. She frowned at her use of the Edysian insult. *I have been here too long.*

Jase was among the lowest of the low-life here in the caves. He'd taken to ordering people around and stretching his authority when Damian was away. The others tolerated his cocky, overbearing attitude, unwilling to challenge him. Liquored-up or not, he was a skilled swordsman and a fierce competitor in hand-to-hand combat.

"That little poker stick of yours ain't gonna do you no good, neither."

His reach with the longsword did put her at a disadvantage. *And I am near-naked with my back against the wall. Worse yet.* "What do you want?" Her mind raced for a strategy that would get her out of this unscathed.

"You know what I want," he slurred, taking a wavering step into the room.

Definitely drunk. She'd heard that even the call girls refused Jase, finding his poor hygiene and abusive tastes not worth any price.

"All them boys talk about how all-fire brave you are. You don't look so brave to me."

I will get by him when he goes around the cot.

Jase dropped the sword and pulled a knife from his belt.

She seethed inside. *My dagger!* A gift from her trainer, Rrazmik, the kris blade had been taken from her when she first came to the caves.

He took another step toward her. Then, instead of climbing over or going around the cot, he kicked under the edge of it. As it tilted onto its side, he shoved it toward her and crushed her between it and the rock wall.

She still held her sword, but her arm was trapped and useless. The knife at her throat threatened to split her skin as he used it to hold her steady. A foul stench came from his open mouth—booze mixed with rotted teeth. It her like a punch in the face. A gag crawled up her throat and she wrenched her head to the side to breathe fresh air.

"Oh, no, sweetie, don't you turn your head from me." He licked her cheek.

Bile rose from her gut and singed her throat. She swallowed. It burned on the way back down, too. She forced herself to face him.

Strange eyes gazed at her, intensifying his hideous appearance—one muddy brown, one greenish-yellow.

"That's it, honey. You know you want it. Slide on out from behind there, now. Nice and easy."

With his weight full against the cot, he had her sandwiched between it and the stone wall of the cave. She could hardly breathe, much less move. He eased off the pressure, just so she could move a few inches and take a breath, then leaned in again. They shuffled their way together in this fashion until she neared the end of the cot.

Reaching behind it, he felt around until he found her sword and pried it out of her hand. "You come on outta there, now," he said, tossing her sword behind him. "You make one wrong move, girl, and I'll gut you like a fish."

The man was not so drunk that she could overpower him. *He will surely kill me. Sooner or later.* She slid out from behind the cot.

Jase stepped in front of her, even closer now without the bed between them.

The cot slammed to the floor with a crash.

With his free hand, he grabbed her flimsy top and tore it off, tossing it to the floor. Two-tone eyes dropped to her bare breasts. His fingers circled, then pinched her nipple. First one, then the other. She wanted to slap him or knee him in the groin. But as much as she hated the groping, with the blade pressed firmly against her neck, he would slit her throat if she tried anything.

Tina appeared in the doorway behind him dressed in a nightgown, her eyes wide with fright.

Tina! Stay quiet! Apri focused her eyes on Jase and moaned, pushing her chest into the hand that fondled her breasts.

"Oh god," Jase growled, and kissed her full on the mouth.

She moaned again. Forcing her tongue into Jase's mouth, she managed not to throw up her dinner as she projected another mental message to her friend. *Pick up the sword. Be careful!*

Apri had acquired the telepathy talent as a child. Early attempts to use the skill on others—family, friends, even strangers—usually backfired in one way or another. But with Tina, it'd been different. She'd been open to Apri from the start, and through their telepathic connection they'd developed a strong friendship.

Use two hands. You must stab him! Hard! Use all your strength! Wait till I give the word. She prayed the girl had the courage to pull it off.

Tina took a step forward, getting into position behind him.

If this doesn't work, we're both dead. That thought she kept to herself. She bit Jase's tongue, hard.

"Bitch!" Jase grabbed his mouth. Blood spilled between his fingers and ran down his chin as he stumbled away from her.

Apri sent the silent command, *Now!*

Taking two steps forward, Tina stabbed him through the back. The sword went all the way through his chest with such force that the end of the blade nicked Apri. Tina pulled the sword out, preparing to stab him again.

"That's good! You did it!" Apri said aloud.

Jase's eyes went wide. White circles surrounded the bi-colored irises. Then all expression melted away, and he fell backwards.

Tina yelped as Jase fell into her, and they tumbled to the floor together.

Apri pushed Jase's dead body off the trembling girl whose hands had drained white from her death-grip on the sword. *Good girl! Never drop your weapon.*

"Is he… dead?" Tina asked.

"Soon." Apri pried the girl's hands off the sword and helped her stand. "You saved me." She frowned. "And I am supposed to be protecting you!"

Her friend watched the man take his last breath, then looked at Apri with an unfocused gaze.

"Tina… Tina, look at me." Apri held her by the shoulders to keep her upright. She felt limp, unsteady. "Tina…"

The girl stared at Jase again.

Apri took Tina's face in her hands, forcing her eyes from the dead man. "Look at me. You are okay… Tina!"

Losing the glazed look, Tina's eyes brimmed with tears. "What are you going to do?" she asked. "I can stay with you. Explain what happened?"

"No! Do as I say. Go back to your room and clean up." Apri hated to be so harsh, so commanding. Her friend had just taken a man's life—a traumatic experience, no matter the circumstances. But Damian would be back soon, and she had no time for consolation. "Tell no one."

Tina nodded.

"I mean it, Tina. Say nothing to anyone about what happened here. No matter what. Promise?"

The girl nodded again. "I promise."

"Come along." She guided the girl into the hallway and pushed her in the direction of her own room. "Clean up and stay in there. Do not come out until morning."

Apri sighed, frowning at the dead man. Not that she cared one whit about Jase, but Damian would be furious. *Time for me to leave.*

Getting dressed in a hurry, she threw the few things she would take with her onto the cot. *Too risky to take Tina now. I'll have to come back for her.* She found the kris lodged underneath Jase, took the sheath from his belt and stuffed both in her pack along with the things on the bed.

She'd never attempted to escape before, and Damian's guards didn't keep watch on her like they had in the beginning. Even so, everyone knew she was a prisoner here. She looked around one last time to make sure she hadn't left anything important.

"Going somewhere?" Damian stood at the door. His second in command, Silas, stood beside him. Both had their swords drawn.

Her own sword still rested on top of Jase. *Damn!* "He gave me no choice," she said. "Just kept coming at me. Even when he knew I had him beat, he would not retreat."

"I doubt that," Silas said, stepping toward her.

Silas hadn't been present when she'd first encountered Damian's band of drunken, belligerent Dovetail scouts—the day she'd taken a few men out before Damian came along and stopped the fight. Like Jase, he considered accounts of that event to be greatly exaggerated. He didn't like her and took every opportunity to rebuke her in front of others.

"Stand down, Silas," Damian ordered, then addressed Apri. "Unfortunately, you leave *me* no choice." He stabbed a finger at Jase's dead body. "He didn't take that wound coming *at* you."

Apri said nothing.

"Take her to the lockup," Damian ordered.

"Lockup? I'll cut her down right now," Silas argued, continuing his advance.

Damian's face reddened. "Stand… down," he commanded again. Apri had seen Damian interact with his men enough to know he had a short fuse. And he hated his orders being challenged by anyone.

Silas sheathed his sword, and his arrogant swagger evaporated.

Damian addressed Apri. "We're taking the girl to Edyson, so you're done here anyway. I'll deal with you when I return." Then, he turned on Silas with a searing, angry glare. "Lock her up." he ordered. "And if you so much as touch a hair on her head, I'll cut you down myself. When that's done, come back here and clean this mess up." He pointed at the corpse. "I want this room cleared out and spotless. Take her things to the supply cave." The orders were given in a tone that dared his second to object. "Be ready to leave in the morning." He stormed off.

Silas said nothing.

Smart man. He wouldn't typically handle such mundane tasks. This was punishment for his insolence and disrespect. She resisted the urge to goad him about it. *No use pushing my luck.* He gripped her upper arm and shoved her out the entryway.

The lockup cell was on the opposite side of the vast cavern. She'd have to come back this way to recover her gear and weapons from the supply cave when she escaped, so she paid close attention to their route.

At the lockup cave, Silas took the key from a wall hook and opened the cell, then locked her in. Without another word, he walked out, replacing the key as he left.

Apri watched the key swing back and forth on its peg until it stopped. Shaking her head out of its trance, she inspected her surroundings. The small cave was divided in two by iron bars. Aside from the key, a three-legged stool in the far corner was the only thing on the other side of the bars. Five cots covered with thin, soiled mattresses and tattered blankets surrounded the perimeter of the cell. An empty chamber pot lay on its side. The gate held strong when she shook it, and she tested every bar to see if any were loose enough to remove. *Too easy.*

"Damn!" Cursing her frustration aloud in her native tongue, she paced around the cell and contemplated her situation. How long ago did she leave Ararat? Five months? Six? *Serves me right. I allowed this side trip to go on too long. And now Tina is in trouble, too.* She feared for her friend—the only real friend she'd made since leaving home. *Why is he taking her to the capital?*

Stuck in these caves, she could never trust her sense of time. *It must be near dawn.* Lying on the cleanest of the cots, she curled up in a ball to rest and contemplate her options for escape. *I'll get out of here.* She yawned. *Tomorrow.*

Chapter 2
Jon

Jon sat back in the saddle and pulled on the reins. "Watch out!" he shouted.

The startled pedestrian stopped, dropping his package, as Jon's horse skidded on the slick, brick-paved street.

Barely avoiding a collision, Jon dug his heel into the horse's flank, ignoring the man's obscene gesture and sharing a few choice words of his own.

The man's angry reply faded away in the clatter of hooves as Jon darted around a vendor's cart, squeezing between it and an oncoming carriage. Racing through the city at this hour, his speed bordered on perilous, yet he urged the horse on faster… faster.

Whatever interest the XLs had in visiting the Core Campus, whatever task Malcolm Covington, the reigning Legiant of Edyson, had sent them to fulfill, it wouldn't be a friendly visit. Jon's tolerance with Malcolm, his old friend—*ex-friend*—had worn thin. The longsword pounding against his back heightened his senses, like the sound of fanfare to a horse before a race.

Arriving at the campus entrance, he vaulted off the still-moving horse. The main gates were closed and barred. He entered the campus through the unlocked guard post door.

It was worse than he could have imagined.

Motionless bodies littered the usually pristine courtyard, some skewered and sliced into pieces. The brutality of the scene was reminiscent of an attack by a band of crazed forktoes. Men, women, children, old, young, none were spared. Blood, still wet and fresh, pooled around each corpse scattered about the courtyard. Two bodies floated in the pink-tinged water of the exercise pool. Jon estimated thirty dead, although with so many severed parts it could be more or less than that.

A man moaned weakly. Jon ran to him, kneeling at his side.

"Please. Tell my… my son…" The man's voice was but a harsh whisper.

Jon leaned over, hearing the man's last words—a message for his son.

The man's eyes opened. "Tell him?"

"Yes, yes, of course," he promised. There was nothing Jon could do for him. His wounds were too severe.

A woman's scream snapped Jon out of his remorse, and he bolted into a nearby building. The panic inside ranged from frantic terror to dazed and confused. *At least they're alive.*

"Get out! Now! Go!" he yelled.

Instead of going out the courtyard door, they ran down a hallway, deeper into the building. *Where are they going?*

A woman huddled on the floor attempting to console a young, hysterical child.

Jon rushed over to help them. "Are you hurt? Can you run?"

"I… I don't think so." Her whole body vibrated with fear.

Jon stopped a man from running by. "Help these two!"

The man took the child and wrapped his arm around the woman to guide her out, following the others.

There was no time to challenge their escape route. *They know this place better than me.* "Go! Go! Go!" he shouted again to fracture the shock and disorientation that gripped the rest of them.

Another scream, and another, came from the opposite direction. He sprinted toward the sound and stopped just outside the open door of a small office, risking a quick glance inside. A Cortek man lay still on the floor in a pool of blood with his head bashed in. Another sat at a table, still alive. Two women huddled in a corner.

One of the three XLs holding them hostage threatened to cut off the man's hand or finger with a dagger. The other two badgered the women for information.

Jon knew most of these XLs by crime and reputation, having been involved in their capture and conviction. They called the one hovering over the man at the desk Mute—a deaf and dumb sadist who enjoyed brutally torturing his victims.

"Which one of you two geek bitches is gonna tell us where that master of yours is hiding?"

"We don't know sir. Truly." The woman's voice trembled.

Geek. The XL's use of the age-old derogatory slur fired Jon's rage to the boiling point. He stepped inside and thrust his sword straight through the back of Mute's throat and out his mouth. Mute spoke, but his garbled, bubbly words were incoherent. Then his body jerked and went limp.

The other two scrambled behind the table with their eyes on Jon who still held his sword in the freshly-skewered Mute.

Jon's sword slipped free, and Mute fell to the floor. "Go!" he ordered the captives, as he held the XLs at bay.

One at a time, they darted out the door behind him.

"You better leave us be, fobmuck!" Lyle shouted. "The boss'll have your head."

"What do you mean, Lyle?" The other man advanced on Jon. "Won't be no need for the boss to do him in. The commander's gonna be dead soon. Just like this fella." He gestured at the man on the floor, then nodded toward the courtyard. "And all them out there."

Lyle made no move toward Jon. He just stood behind the table like a sniveling coward. "I guess we'll just have to—" Lyle's words were cut short by Jon's throwing knife, now decorating his neck like a macabre pendant. His cocky smirk disappeared, and he fell over onto the table.

Jon stepped toward the last man.

"The boss's promised a big reward for the man what brings you down," the man said then lunged forward, his axe leveled for Jon's head.

Jon stepped aside, kicking him in the knee. Unable to stop his forward momentum, the man impaled himself on Jon's sword.

Malcolm's chosen were a devious and corrupt band, but they weren't soldiers, or even competent fighters. *With one exception.* Jon kicked the still gurgling and gasping XL off his sword and grabbed the knife from Lyle's throat. He set off toward the sound of shouting and scuffling coming from behind a pair of double doors further down the hallway.

The XLs always referred to Malcolm as "boss." *So, my old friend has a price on my head now?* He wasn't surprised. It just added to the mounting evidence of how demented and delusional the man had become. *Now, even I am the enemy?*

He had to muscle the doors open to squeeze through, shoving two dead XLs across the floor. *So, these Cortek aren't completely helpless.*

More noise and commotion came from a closed door in the middle of a long, vacant hallway. The sign on the door read *Library*. Just as he reached for the doorknob, it began to turn. Jon jumped back, pressing flat against the wall.

An XL dragged a screaming woman into the hallway. "Keep on screaming, bitch. Just gets me harder."

The door closed, and Jon stepped behind him, grabbed a fistful of greasy hair, and slit the man's throat. The XL dropped, his blood pumping in measured cadence with the last few beats of his heart.

The woman lay on the floor trembling. She stared at Jon with wide, unseeing eyes.

"He can't hurt you now," Jon said, helping her stand.

Her legs wobbled unsteadily. If he let go, she would crumble to the ground. *Don't pass out on me.*

He shook her gently. "Woman!"

Her eyes were vacant and wide with fright.

"It's okay, you're okay now." He kept repeating the words, holding her upright. *Come on, girl, look at me.*

"I... am... okay... I'm okay." Bright blue eyes focused on his, fear giving over to gratitude... then determination.

"Okay?" he repeated.

She nodded.

"Go! Run!"

Pushing the library door slightly ajar, Jon peered inside. The room was lined with bookcases. A couple of unarmed Cortek men darted in and out of the aisles, tossing books and furniture—whatever they could grab—to thwart the men chasing them.

Where are you, Hill? Shifting his position to see more of the room, he spied the leader of Malcolm's band of thugs, General Thaddeus Hill, standing with his back to the door.

Jon drew his sword and eased the door open. Springing to the nearest XL, he stabbed him through the back. The man fell hard on a table, and the noise attracted the attention of the others in the room. *That's unfortunate.*

"Well, if it isn't the almighty Jon Gardner in the flesh," Hill said.

The Cortek men who'd been evading capture used the diversion to escape.

"I should've killed you when I had the chance, Hill." Jon had fought and bested Hill during the attack on the palace, when he'd led a small band of Malcolm's men to overthrow the former Legiant, Anthony Wilcox. At the time, he chose to spare the man's life when he could've ended it. The regret had plagued him since Hill's trial, where a parade of witnesses, even Hill's own men, revealed terrible details of cruelty, abuse, and violence perpetrated by the man. *And now Malcolm has released this psychopath from prison?*

"And I should've tossed you off that platform with the kid, Gardner. We both have our regrets." Hill waved at the other two XLs who circled around Jon, preparing to attack.

"The rest of your squad is dead. Do you think these two stand a chance?" Jon said.

"I don't care about these two. Or them out there, either. There's plenty more where they came from." Hill laughed.

The two men approached Jon, one on either side. The one on the left sprang first with a broad, excessive swing of his longsword.

Jon leapt toward him, then twisted around and kicked him toward the man who charged from the other side.

The two fell to the floor in a heap, and Jon thrust his sword through both men together as they thrashed about, trying to untangle themselves. He wiped the bloody sword on one of them.

Another man came out from behind Hill. He looked at Jon, then at his commander, then back at Jon. Without a word, he ran out the door, dropping his sword at Jon's feet as he went.

"Just you and me now, Gardner," Hill declared.

"You're a reeking fobmuck," Jon said.

"And you're a geek-loving bleeding heart." Hill had been Commander of the Law Squad under Wilcox, and, unlike the other XLs, was a skilled and competent fighter.

Jon steadied himself as he advanced, his eyes darting back and forth between the other man's weapons—a hooked dagger in one hand and a longsword in the other. With a quick sidestep, he spun around and clipped Hill's neck.

Wiping the blood from the fresh wound, Hill renewed his attack, lunging forward.

Ducking from the next strike, Jon body-checked Hill into a table.

The table cracked, then broke in two, taking Hill with it. His quick recovery caught Jon by surprise, and the next swing just missed Jon's head.

The two maneuvered from the remnants of the smashed table and circled each other a few times.

Jon dodged a jab from the dagger, but the hook caught him as Hill drew it back. It caught under his breastplate and ripped a deep gash in his side. He yelped in pain, grabbing at the injury as he kicked Hill away and over a chair.

Losing his balance, Hill careened into one of the bookcases. Books from the top shelves showered down on his head as the case toppled over. Then the bookcase behind that one fell, then the next. One after another they teetered and fell, until the room was littered with scrolls, books, loose pages, and splintered bookcases.

Jon looked down at his blood-covered hand, then went sprawling across the floor as Hill smashed a chair across his back. He stood up, unsteady, pressing his hand against the wound again. *Losing too much blood.*

Hill kept coming.

Jon managed to evade each strike until a boot caught him square in the chest, sending him into the wall. He blinked a few times. The room wouldn't stop spinning.

Hill approached with his sword held high.

I need to move. Jon's body didn't respond.

Some Cortek men had returned, throwing trays and books and furniture—whatever they could grab.

Jon took advantage of the distraction and steadied himself, then attacked with a new-found ferocity.

With Hill defending from two fronts, Jon landed a few blows. The advance and rapid attack turned the battle in Jon's favor. *I've got you now, fobmuck.* He spun and slammed his blade hard on Hill's arm.

Hill screamed and dropped his sword. Blood gushed from a deep wound above the elbow.

Expecting a retreat, Jon dropped his guard.

Quick as lightning, Hill advanced, planting his dagger in Jon's stomach.

Jon felt no pain, just shock and horror at seeing the dagger protruding from his stomach. He pushed Hill away and the dagger went with him.

Hill's left arm still gushed blood, but he managed to stab one of the Cortek men who came too close.

Jon dropped his sword, intense pain registering in earnest now. *Don't pass out. Don't pass out.*

Hill tackled him, pinning him to the floor.

Don't pass out. Warm, salty sweat dripped into Jon's mouth as Hill hovered above him. He spat.

"Your time has come, Gardner," Hill said. His slurred words and dilated pupils told Jon he was close to passing out, too. He reached for the axe at Jon's waist.

Hill was heavy, and it was hard to breathe. Jon lifted a shaking hand to the other man's face and flipped the trigger on his bracer. With an audible *click,* the hidden spring-blade struck through Hill's chin, into his mouth, and out his left ear. A waterfall of blood showered Jon's face.

Hill's ear-splitting wail filled the room. He bolted upright, extracting himself from Jon's brace-blade. A bloody trail followed him as he staggered out of the library.

Jon lay there, gasping in pain. The man Hill had stabbed lay on the floor not far from him, still moving. *Not dead.* He tried to get to his feet to help.

Another man ran to him, providing support. "Let me help. You're hurt."

Jon collapsed to the floor. His gut burned like hell. Looking down at it, he watched bright red blood flow from the wound. It was a clean cut but very deep. *Fatal, no doubt.* He felt someone attending to his injuries, putting heavy pressure on his stomach.

"Just let me die." He moaned. "You're wasting your time. It's over for me."

They continued their ministrations. He heard talking but couldn't make out the words. *Are they talking to me?* An old man knelt beside him.

Headmaster something-or-other. "You... your people... get the hell out." His words were punctuated with pained gasps. "They... will come back!"

Jon drifted in and out of consciousness. The men tried to lift him. "Ow!" It felt like someone stuck a white-hot branding iron in his open wound. He swatted at the hands of the medics—a feeble effort. *God, just let a man die in peace!* Leaning his head back, he focused on taking the next breath, then the next, his lungs inhaling, exhaling hot air like the bellows of a blacksmiths forge.

A voice roused him. "Go get it, now!" He passed out again.

Searing pain. He was lifted, this time onto a stretcher. Weak from the loss of blood, he opened his mouth to shout, but no sound came. *I'm dying.* "Stop, please," he whispered. "Save yourselves." He tried pushing them away, but his arms wouldn't move.

"Just be still," someone—*the old man?*—objected. "You'll die if we don't get this bleeding stopped. Try to relax. You'll be fine soon enough."

"Fine? I'm... all but... dead. No... point." He fought against their efforts to strap him to the stretcher but grew weaker with each breath. Unable to resist or even argue, he finally collapsed. The stretcher began to move, and he closed his eyes.

Hands lifted him onto a cold, hard table. *Must've passed out.* He tried to raise an arm to shield his eyes against the bright lights, but his arms were strapped to the table. *Or are they?*

Jon heard a bird singing. *A singing bird? Is this what dying feels like? I don't much care for birds.* The bird's song was like nothing he'd heard before, beautiful and soothing, warm and quiet. *Warm and quiet? No. I wish it would shut up. I can't think straight.* Shaking his head from side to side, he tried to keep the bleary, hazy feeling from overtaking him. Something covered his nose and mouth. He didn't have the strength to remove it. *What's that smell?* His pain subsided, not as intense as before. *I guess this is it, then. Only darkness remains for me. I did what I could. I tried. Malcolm lost his way.*

"I tried," he said aloud. "I'm sorry. I tried."

"Shhh," someone muttered. "Relax. Go to sleep."

Chapter 3
Jon

Jon woke with a start and sat straight up. "Ahhh!" he cried, immediately regretting the impulsive movement. A searing fire shot through his gut, and he froze, afraid to move again in any direction. *What the hell? Where...?*

His fight with the XLs replayed in his mind—the gruesome corpses, the killing, the fight with Hill, the fatal wound. *I should be dead. Am I dead?*

"Oh, I'm so sorry! I didn't mean to wake you." A short, middle-aged woman appeared at the open doorway, rushing to him. "Easy, young man," she said, supporting him with a strong hand. "You are very hurt."

He groaned as he laid back. "Where... Where am I?"

The woman, a nurse no doubt, smiled at him. "You're safe with us," she said, pulling the white sheet down to his knees. "Since you're awake, I might as well redress this now." He wore a lightweight shirt and trousers, each tied loosely with a thin cord. Lifting his shirt, she pulled the bandage away from his stomach with care and removed the soiled, foul-smelling gauze. After a close inspection of the wound, she stepped away to the supply cabinet.

A dozen or so neat, black stitches held together the angry pink gash in his stomach. *No wonder it hurts.* A clear, yellowish fluid seeped from the cut.

"You're our savior, you know," she said. Returning to his bedside, she proceeded to redress the wound. "It just won't do for us to lose you after all you've done for us. This is going to hurt."

Jon inhaled sharply through bared teeth—*ouch, yes, that hurts.* He was pretty sure *us* meant the Cortek. He didn't know much about these people other than public knowledge and gossip. They ran the schools, the medical facilities, and most of the factories in the colony. They kept to themselves and had strange customs and habits. The *savior* comment bothered him.

"I assure you, that wasn't my intention," he objected. "And *safe* is not a *location*," he added, pointing out her failure to answer his question.

The woman's smile disappeared. She seemed confused. *Or insulted?* "You didn't intend to save us?" Her smile returned, an expression that affected her entire face, from the creases in her eyes to the deep dimples in her cheeks. "So, was it your *intention* to get yourself skewered like a spit pig?" She chuckled. "Or killed even? Because you came close to doing that, too."

"No… I didn't mean… I don't want you to…"

The woman interrupted his clumsy attempt to explain. "I'm going to get Headmaster Barrow. Please keep still," she said, wagging her finger in his face. "Do *not* try to get up again." She stared at him, serious now. "Please."

When Jon realized she expected a response, he nodded.

The door closed behind her, and he inspected his surroundings. The small room contained nothing more than the elevated bed, the supply cabinet, and a small round table in one corner. She never did say *where* he was, but he guessed it must be the infirmary on the Core Campus. He'd been sure he'd taken a fatal wound. *Maybe I'm dead.*

His face itched. He rubbed his chin, feeling the stubble. *How long have I been here?*

The elderly, white-bearded headmaster entered the room with open arms. "Jon!" he exclaimed, "Our savior!"

"Please stop calling me that," Jon implored.

"As you wish," the man replied with a smile. "I was merely trying to convey our deep gratitude. The Cortek are truly indebted to you." He bowed his head, hand to heart, in the common Edyson greeting of respect. "I am Headmaster Barrow. We have met before, yes? You are Commander Jon Gardner."

"Yes, we met years ago, Headmaster," Jon replied. "I'm surprised you remember. And it seems you are *my* savior. My wounds were bad. I should be dead." He looked around the room. "Assuming this isn't some kind of bizarre afterlife."

He chuckled. "I promise, Commander, you are very much alive. Healing your wounds was the least we could do after your brave heroics. And call me Barrow, please. Would you like to sit up?"

"I tried that. It hurt. How many of your peop—" he cut the question short, startled when the bed began to hum and move, elevating his upper body.

"Relax, I'm just repositioning the bed so you can sit up," Barrow explained, then answered the unfinished question. "Those men killed forty-three. They killed every person they encountered, including women and children... No explanation... Few words at all other than vulgar oaths and obscenities. They just charged in through the gates and started killing."

Someone walked by the open door, catching Barrow's attention.

After a lengthy pause, the old man took a deep breath then continued with eyes grown misty, "But we didn't lose one person after you entered the campus. Even the man Hill injured in the library will make a full recovery. Your arrival was the distraction we needed to get everyone to a safe place."

"I wish I could've been here sooner."

"Young man, this is not your fault." Barrow patted Jon's arm. "Those men were overheard saying they came here under orders from the Legiant. We know who is to blame."

If I hadn't helped Malcolm take the palace and overthrow Wilcox, none of this would've happened. Jon forced the guilt that threatened to consume him down into his subconscious and said, "He may have it in his head to kill all of you. Here, at the factories, and anywhere else your people may be."

"We sent word for all Cortek to go into hiding. Factory production, education, medical care—all will surely be impacted by this hiatus. Even more so if Malcolm takes over. He wants the factories to produce weapons, you know."

Jon sighed. "And the Cortek can't do that. Your religion forbids it, right?"

"Not so much a religion as a moral obligation," Barrow corrected. "The Oath forbids it—an age-old commitment we take very seriously," he explained. "Our factories produce only materials that are essential for community health, safety, and development.

"I see," Jon said. "That's why he wants the Cortek out of the way. So, he can take over the factories?" He shook his head. "And that's exactly what'll happen now."

"So it seems," Barrow agreed, shaking his head. "It does not bode well for Edyson."

The woman from earlier returned with a tray of food and water. Barrow lifted a table from the side of the bed. It unfolded, coming to rest with a *click* in front of Jon. The woman set the tray on the table and left them alone again.

"Are you thirsty? Hungry?" Barrow asked.

"Both, actually," Jon admitted.

"A good sign," Barrow smiled. "I'm afraid it's only water and a bland meal, but this is your first solid food in three days. We need to—"

"Three days!" Jon interrupted. "I've been here for three days?"

"Yes. As you said, your injuries were grave. We had to keep you quiet and give those wounds some time to he—Slow down, son!" he said when Jon started guzzling the water. "Small sips. And eat slowly, or you'll make yourself sick."

Barrow stood to get another glass and helped himself to some water.

Eat slowly? A challenge under normal circumstances, even when he wasn't so hungry. He concentrated on over-chewing the food, then swallowed. *Yuck!*

Barrow laughed. "I told you it was bland."

"Is *this* what bland tastes like?" His empty stomach prevailed over the unpleasant taste and texture, and he took another bite. *At least eating slow won't be a problem.*

"There's something else you should know," Barrow continued. "Word of the campus massacre, as it's being called, has circulated throughout the capital. The official report says that a squader came to the Core Campus, went berserk, and slaughtered everyone inside. The Legiant's XL squaders were sent to save the Cortek, but they were overcome by this madman until the sole survivor, Hill, chased the gravely injured man off, barely surviving himself. Posters hang all over the capital with your picture, Jon, and the promise of a huge reward for anyone who turns you in. Dead or alive."

Jon took another awful bite. "We used to be friends, you know," he told Barrow. "Very good friends. He's not the person he used to be."

"Weak men and fools easily succumb to the wicked attraction of power," Barrow explained. "There's an old saying, 'Absolute power corrupts absolutely.' Your friend is just another victim to those temptations. He's obsessed with power and has crossed over into the self-destructive phase. The desire for more power, or the fear of losing the power he has gained, controls every decision he makes."

"Well said," Jon agreed.

"Hill's been appointed Commander of the Law Squad," Barrow said.

"So, he survived?"

"I'm afraid so. He hasn't been seen in public but my contacts in the palace tell me he's grossly disfigured." The old man grinned. "Missing an ear, they say." His smile disappeared and he patted Jon's hand, his expression grim. "But you, my friend, are a wanted man—considered deranged and dangerous. The reward is more than any bounty hunter could hope to make in a year. They're out in force searching for you. You're welcome to stay here with us as long as—"

Jon interrupted, "How do we stop him?" Recognizing the hesitation in Barrow's expression, he added, *"This will only get worse."*

"The Cortek can't interfere with Legiancy affairs," Barrow shushed Jon before he could interrupt again. "For now, you just need to focus on your recovery. We can talk more later." He took Jon's empty plate and secured the fold-up table, then lowered the bed down. "If you need assistance, press this button here." He pointed to a button on the bedrail. "Go ahead and try it."

Jon pushed the button. In short order, the woman appeared again.

"This is Yelena, one of our best medical attendants. And a dear friend." Barrow wrapped his arm around her shoulders, pulling her close with a gentle squeeze. "Her husband was among those killed in the courtyard."

"Oh." *And I was so rude to her.* "I'm sorry for your loss. Please, I don't want you to… You should be…" He tried to find a way to say she shouldn't spend her time taking care of him.

"Thank you."

Barrow gave Yelena another squeeze. "I told her the same, Commander. She should take some time off. But she refused."

"Working occupies my mind. I'd go crazy otherwise," she said.

"As you said." Barrow smiled. "Well, my dear, our friend Jon here is ready to rest again." Jon wanted to protest, but Barrow held up a finger at him. "Will you please fetch Canary?"

"Yes, certainly," she said and left the room.

"Canary?" Jon asked.

"A twerb, to help you relax and rest," Barrow explained.

"The bird. The singing," Jon recalled. "I thought twerbs were a myth."

"Oh, they are quite real, I assure you. And very useful." Yelena returned with a covered birdcage which she placed on the table in the corner. "You'll be resting again in no time." Barrow uncovered the cage, and the bird began its peaceful, exasperating song. "I'll be back to visit with you again soon."

It was not at all *soon* by Jon's reckoning. He measured the passing of days by the meals brought to him and guessed it had been at least two days since the headmaster's visit. *Maybe three?*

The attendants who brought his meals and helped him in and out of bed to the bathroom were kind enough, but all gave him the same, obviously scripted, response. "The headmaster will come for a visit soon."

Soon must have a different meaning to these people.

Most of the time, he was kept in a twerb-induced sleep. He'd gained strength and stamina with every visit to the bathroom and could now make the short trip down the hallway unaided, although never unaccompanied. Between the damn bird and the attendants who appeared at his door whenever he opened his eyes, he was never alone and awake at the same time.

He'd discovered the twerb didn't sing endlessly. When he woke and opened his eyes, the room would be completely silent. But as soon as it heard the tiniest noise, even the slightest rustle of covers, it'd begin to sing its hypnotic melody. Jon would instantly relax, then slip into oblivion. It infuriated him to be so helpless. A couple of times, he'd been alert long enough to press the attendant's button but never knew if anyone showed up or not.

"…wake up. Commander?" Barrow's voice came from somewhere above him. "It can't be comfortable down there."

Jon opened his eyes. He was lying face-up on the floor.

Barrow and several attendants looked down on him, full of grins, smirks and chuckles.

Damn bird. "It is not," he said. With a groan, he eased into a sitting position, wincing at the pain in his gut. He glanced in the corner. "I see that fobmucking bird is gone at last. I hope to never see, or *hear*, it again."

His comment drew another round of laughter from his audience.

"Okay folks, show's over. Back to work," Barrow ordered, crouching down to help Jon into a nearby chair. "Yes, young man. Our little Canary has served his purpose and is returned to his aviary. Fair warning, though, some find it difficult to sleep the first few nights without him."

"I'll be just fine," Jon said.

"No doubt," Barrow smiled. "I apologize for not coming sooner. I've been busy getting the Cortek who've been arriving from around the colony settled in. I hear your recovery is going well?"

"Still stiff, but I've been working on the drills and exercises with your attendants. They seem to be helping. I should be out of your hair soon. Where exactly am I, anyway?"

"You're in a back room at the Forest Inn, outside the city. It is owned and operated by the Cortek, although that's not commonly known." He winked. "I apologize for keeping you sequestered here, but this is a public inn, and we can't risk anyone recognizing you. Listen, Commander—"

Jon interrupted with a grin, "Not a commander anymore."

Barrow didn't comment, his expression dubious. "You have a high price on your head. Your features are too striking, and the images posted around the city too accurate, for you to risk going out in public."

"But—"

"Please, hear me out. I won't keep you here like a prisoner. But what is your plan? Where will you go? It'll be another week or two before you fully heal. And more important, you need a disguise... more of that facial hair." The old man grinned. "To hide your striking good looks."

Jon ignored the jibe and rubbed his face. "It itches. I hate it."

Barrow chuckled, then gestured toward the door. "Let's go, we're moving you to a guest room."

Jon would've liked to change into regular clothes first, but his eagerness to get out of the cramped room won out over the inappropriate attire.

Barrow talked as he led Jon down a long nondescript hallway with walls as smooth as polished metal. "Did you know a man named Bancroft? At the palace?" he asked.

"Yes. A good man. Often opposed Malc—the Legiant's—decisions and wasn't afraid to voice his opinion. I haven't seen him since he left to manage the mine in Southrock." He thought for a moment. "Died in a fire, right? That his son started? I went there on assignment to look for the son a few years ago." The memory of that trip came to him, still disturbing. *Hill and his brutal tactics.* It was the first time they'd gone out on assignment together—and the last.

"His son had nothing to do with the fire." Barrow shook his head, and his lips pressed together in a frown. "Bancroft was killed by order of the Legiant. I don't believe it was his intent for the whole family to die. Whoever he sent to do the deed botched it or went rogue. The fire was an attempt to cover the murders." He shook his head again. "It's a damn shame. The false accusation of the son was meant to cast suspicion from the Legiant."

"How do you know all of this?"

"The Cortek have scouts all over the colony." Barrow winked. "Just because we can't interfere, doesn't mean we can't be informed. When Bancroft was in the capital, he rallied a group of citizens who opposed the Legiant. That opposition was gaining some traction up until the fire that killed him and his family. After the fire, there were more *accidents* here in the capital."

"Can I find these people? Do you know who they are?"

"Our scout's contact with Bancroft's group was one of the casualties. There were others, but the club here disbanded. There are rumors of a splinter group reorganizing in Baytown, but I don't know if that's true. If it is, they may provide some support, especially if they learn the truth of what happened at the campus."

Barrow exhaled a long sigh, guiding him through a set of double doors. "The Legiant seemed eager to locate Bancroft's son, Zakary. Perhaps he suspects the boy has incriminating information? You might try to find him. I don't even know if he's alive. If he is, he may know nothing. He was only a child at the time." He shrugged. "Or maybe there's someone else in Southrock that Bancroft confided in? It's a longshot at best. Your friend, Covington, has become a master at concealing his misdeeds and covering his tracks."

"My *ex*-friend," Jon corrected. He smelled food and heard the clinking and clanking of dishes, pots and pans as they approached the dining hall.

"I'm sorry, it's not much to go on, I know." Barrow said as they passed by the dining hall. "Let's go on up to your room."

"I can't help feeling responsible for this mess. I should've seen it coming." Jon said, following Barrow up the stairs.

"No—"

"Spare your argument. I always knew he was obsessed with power and control. But I got so absorbed in planning and organizing the attack on the palace, I never thought once about what kind of leader he'd be." He paused, thinking back "He wouldn't even be Legiant if it weren't for me." *I must fix this.*

"You're forgetting. Wilcox was no prince, either."

"Nevertheless," John resolved, "I intend to do what I can to make amends."

His new room was spacious, with dark paneled walls and its own private bath. "You'll have your privacy here. Your meals will be brought up to you. Yelena and I will visit from time to time to see if you need anything."

"My clothes?" he asked, pulling at the loose-fitting gown. "These are comfortable, but..."

Barrow chuckled. "Someone will be here shortly with your belongings and some extra clothing."

His memory of the Southrock assignment to search for the boy had sparked a memory. "Do you think someone could get something from my room at the palace?" he asked.

"Depends what it is. Possibly."

"A piece of jewelry. A locket." He described it and told Barrow where to find it in his room. "I don't know if it'll help, so don't go to a lot of trouble."

"I'll see what we can do," Barrow promised.

When Barrow left, Jon stepped over to the washbasin and looked in a mirror for the first time since the day of the battle. He knew the hair on his head and face had grown, but was unprepared for the gruff, unshaven image in the mirror. It was thick and long, a stark contrast to the bare-faced, well-groomed style he preferred. He frowned. *Damn, you're ugly.*

He answered a knock on the door, and the attendant brought in his things.

"Your horse was brought to the stables. The rest of your things are with your saddle and tack in a private locker there," the young man explained.

Jon spent most of the next few days in the training room, under strict supervision, working on drills and aerobics to get his strength back. On the same day his stitches came out, Yelena took him to a large storeroom filled with all manner of supplies, inviting him to gather anything he would need.

He traveled light as a rule, but everything he owned was at the palace. When the woman left, he wandered around gathering essential gear and clothing, including a hooded rain slicker that would serve well to hide his face.

Barrow came into the room, eyeing the gear he'd placed on a table. "Find everything you need?"

"Yes, thank you. This is most generous." He pointed to the object Barrow carried. "What've you got there?"

"Ah, yes, this," he handed it to Jon. "A gift for you. We have a talented craftsman who makes these special travelpacks for our scouts. I trust you'll find it useful."

Jon inspected the finely crafted pack. The leather had been meticulously stamped and stitched in an intricate checkered pattern with various straps and rings so it could be hung, secured to a saddle, or carried like a backpack. "I don't like to accept elaborate gifts," Jon said, "but..." he smiled. "I really like this." He set the pack he'd found in the storeroom aside.

"There's more to it." Barrow opened the pack and showed Jon the concealed compartments in the lining. "As long as you don't over pack these pockets, their contents are secure and hidden from all but the most scrutinous inspection." He pulled some papers from one pocket and a stash of bills from another.

"Clever! My compliments to the craftsman."

Barrow put the cash back in the hidden pocket. "The money is yours to keep."

"Thank you, I will pay—"

"You'll do no such thing. I meant what I said. The Cortek are forever in your debt. This is nothing." He patted the bag. "Your weapons and the rest of your gear are at the stables. The stablemaster brought your horse to the stable in the aftermath of the attack. By the time the Law Squad arrived to investigate, they found the campus deserted except for the dead bodies. They assumed you'd fled with the Cortek."

Jon packed his gear into the bag. "So, it's safe for me to leave? Are they still keeping a close eye on the campus?"

"A close eye? The Law Squad is occupying the campus."

"What?"

"I'm afraid so. They removed the bodies, cleaned up the mess, then moved in like they owned the place. But we're safe enough here. Few know this inn is Cortek-operated. It's actually good to have them on the campus where we can keep an eye on them."

"Keep your friends close and your enemies closer, eh?"

"Exactly. The Legiant believes he's rid of us. Thinks we've fled beyond the borders of Edyson. We have scouts—and friends of the Cortek—everywhere. Even among the Law Squad."

Jon picked up the travelpack, and they exited the storeroom.

Barrow continued, "You may leave any time."

"Tonight?" Jon asked.

"As you wish," Barrow agreed. "I will meet you at midnight in the dining hall downstairs."

That night, when he and Barrow arrived at the stables, one of the grooms disappeared into a back room and returned with Jon's gear. Anything that needed repair had been fixed. Everything was clean, and his weapons had been sharpened and polished.

"Thank you again… for everything," Jon said, admiring the work. He strapped on his gear and weapons, feeling like himself again. *Except for all this hair.* He combed his fingers through the thick mane on his head.

"Come along, Jon," Barrow said, "let's get your horse."

"Gard," he corrected. "I will use the name Gard, Gard Johnson," he said.

"It suits you, I think. Here we are."

His horse stood at the hitching rail in the center of the stable yard, saddled and freshly shod. He strapped his new travelpack behind the saddle and bridled the gelding.

Barrow handed him a card made of a strange material. "This card will identify you as a friend of the Cortek," Barrow explained. "Keep it well hidden. Few citizens know what these are, but we keep a close account of them. We don't want them getting into the wrong hands. Bancroft was given one. His is still missing."

He turned the card over in Jon's hand. "This emblem is a universal symbol of the Cortek. Any place of business where you find this symbol will accept this card as payment for goods or services. The owners may be Cortek themselves, or they may simply be honorable citizens." He pointed to a stall door where the emblem had been etched into the wood. "The mark will not be prominent, but easily spotted if you know what to look for. If you use it at a place of business, be sure to deal only with the owner. Be extra cautious, now. We are quite selective about these associations, but in light of recent events, we can't be sure that all sentiments remain in our favor."

The stablehand opened the gate.

"While the campus remains occupied, you may contact me here. Oh… and…" Barrow patted his clothing and fished something out. "Your locket. Wasn't any trouble at all."

"Thank you." Jon said, taking the locket. He gestured the formal Edyson greeting, then mounted and rode through the open gate.

"Safe travels, Jon… Gard." Barrow called.

Jon waved backwards, then picked up the pace as soon as he exited the stableyard.

The cool of the evening and fresh air seeped into his bones, restoring his energy. The wound still bothered him, especially now, getting jostled about in the saddle, but it should be fully healed during the week-long journey. He followed the tree-lined road east until he spotted a narrow path leading north and rode into the woods in the dark of night. *Chasing a longshot.* He doubled back to find a trail that would get him around the city unnoticed to catch the road that led to Southrock.

Chapter 4
Zak

✳✳✳

It's so hot. Zak shifted his travelpack to air out the sweat on his back. He just wanted to get home. Shielding his eyes from the glare, he watched Monk, the one-armed climber he'd adopted—or who adopted him—scrambling around among the branches high above.

Monk loved these trips, but he hated them. It used to be a grand adventure--traipsing through the woods, gathering dead animals from the traps he'd set days before. *When I was twelve.* Not anymore. Pa had promised he could work in the mine when he turned sixteen, but two years was still a long way off.

As he stepped onto the road that led to Southrock, he heard people shouting. A cloud of smoke billowed over the trees in the direction of his family's farm, and he took off running... running... running…

✳✳✳

A slap on the back of his head startled Zak awake. He rubbed his head, glaring at the bartender who'd just hit him.

"Eh, kid!" the man said, nodding his head to the left. "That big ugly fella over there has been eyeing you for half an hour."

Zak blinked a couple of times to get the bartender's face to stop weaving around in front of him. "Yeah, what guy? Where?" He turned his head but didn't see anyone watching him. "And don't call me kid. I'm nobody's kid." He downed his ale and shoved the mug at the man. "I'll take another."

"No need to get all bent outta shape. Just thought you might like to know is all." The man pushed the topped-off mug across the counter and left him alone.

Zak stared at the mug. *How many is this? Five? Six?* His tastebuds were numb, and his mouth felt like he'd been drinking tepid bathwater. *Worst brew ever.* He took a drink anyway.

"Finding any answers at the bottom of that mug?"

Zak didn't look up. "What's it to you?" he said, taking another gulp.

"Nothing, really," the man said. "There was talk about a boy from around here looking for information." Leaning in closer, he whispered, "Something about a fire?" The door creaked open, and the stranger looked in that direction, speaking again in a normal tone. "Someone told me you were him, but they must've been mistaken. You're just a drunken fool."

Zak never saw the man's face, just his back as he exited the pub—dark cloak, a shadowy figure, all mysterious-like with a long sword strapped across his back. The stink of his breath still hung in the air. *Or is that my breath?* "Hey! I'm not a boy!" he yelled at the man's back.

That man wouldn't know any more about the fire than Zak had already discovered since he'd arrived in town two days ago anyway. *Or was it three?* He took another drink. *Still need to go see Gabe.* His head grew heavy, and he rested it on the counter. *I'll do that tomorr…*

※※※

The fire raged. Heat radiated from flames that rose ten meters or more with a flume of dark, black smoke rising above that. Zak tossed his pack by the roadside gate and ran toward the house. People swarmed all over the grounds, shouting orders, leading panicked animals away, and filling buckets with water to douse the flames. *Where's Ma and Pa?* Around and around the burning building he ran, searching and shouting for them above the chaos.

The intense blaze engulfed the wood-frame building. Efforts to put the fire out ceased as all hope of saving the building or anything in it was lost. Friends, neighbors, and other townspeople he didn't know surrounded his home, they watching and waiting for the fire to burn itself out.

Zak still hadn't found his family. "Pa! Ma! Where are you? Katy!" he yelled, over and over.

"No one's seen them," Gabe's pa said.

His ears heard the words, but still he refused to accept it. The fire still burned. "We need to keep looking for them," he cried. But they dragged him—

✳✳✳

The bartender nudged him awake again. "Time to go, kid."

Zak left the bar, banging into a few tables that were in the way. On the long, slow climb up the stairs, he tried to recall the short conversation with the stranger. Being called a *boy* bothered him more than *kid*. He was twenty-two, for god's sake.

His head hurt, and the room was spinning. He flopped down onto the thin mattress of the bed.

Clink, clink, clink...

The sound came from the floorboards, and he sat up to investigate. He scooped up the locket and, with his other hand, touched his shirt where his locket usually rested. It was still there, under his shirt. Startled, he looked around. *Where'd this come from? Did it fall off the bed?*

Zak fell back on the bed and stared at the ceiling, his mind racing. Too soon, the alcoholic fog returned. It felt like twenty men hammered at his brain, mining for a coherent thought. *Whack! Bang! Wham!* Wrapping the pillow around his head, he closed his eyes.

A light fell on Zak's face, so intense he could sense it through his closed eyelids. "Ohhh!" He opened his eyes and immediately closed them again to shut out the morning sun coming through the window. Shielding his eyes from the glare, he got up and stumbled into the bathroom.

The water he splashed on his haggard, bearded face didn't clear his head completely, but it helped. *Maybe only ten men pounding around in there now.* He stared at the depressing, pathetic image in the mirror. The chain hanging around his neck caught his attention, and he pulled the locket out from under his shirt. A memory tugged at his brain. *Something about the locket?* It had been a gift from Ma and Pa on his twelfth birthday. The family crest adorned the lid. He popped it open. The inscription inside read, *When all seems lost, seek out your sister. She lov—Wait!*

He rushed out of the bathroom and searched through the covers with his hands. *Maybe it was just a dream.* Then he searched the floor… under the bed… underneath the pill—*Here it is.* Sitting on the edge of the bed, he stared at a locket that was identical to the one he wore around his neck.

Almost identical. Fingers trembling, he fumbled to pry it open. After a few failed attempts, it opened and he read the inscription with blinking, watery eyes. *When all seems lost, seek out your brother. He loves you, no matter what.*

Closing his fist around his twin sister's locket, he recalled the days that followed the fire that killed his family. The bodies of his parents were discovered in the wine cellar. He'd overheard Gabe's father talking to some other men from town who said his parents had been murdered. They never found his sister's body but claimed her remains were burned to ashes by the intense blaze. A few days later, he learned he would be taken away to live in The Ravens with an aunt and uncle he'd never met.

Zak picked his hat up off the bed. It'd been pa's favorite—a fixture on his head for as long as Zak could remember. Running his fingers along the brim, he wondered again about the strange, leather-like material that he'd never been able to identify.

He stared out the window as his mind drifted back to those last days in Southrock. His aunt wouldn't let him bring his pet climber, Monk, with him. He'd cried, begged, and pleaded, but it didn't matter what *he* wanted. "That animal stays here," she'd demanded.

***

The morning of the funeral, he and Gabe's father took Monk into the woods, to the place Zak had found the climber years before.

"I thought you might be wanting this," Gabe's pa said, handing him the ball cap. "Found it in his locker at the mine."

Zak took the hat. "Thanks, Mr. Murfy."

"We need to be going now, son."

He put Monk in a tree and said, "Stay!" At that moment, the devastation, the grief, the reality of his situation over-whelmed him, and he dropped to his knees, weeping into his pa's hat.

Gabe's father had to drag him away.

Monk followed, jumping from tree to tree.

Despair turned to anger, and Zak screamed at him, "Go back!"

But Monk kept following.

"Stay! No!... Go back!..." he yelled. Again and again until the climber finally stopped.

***

His last sight of Monk—the sad, hurt, confused expression on his face—branded its place in Zak's memory forever after. He'd gone straight from there to the funeral, buried his parents and sister, and then left for The Ravens. That had been the second worst day of his life, and he'd hated his aunt ever since.

Zak stared out the window, eyes misty. After so many years, he'd finally made his first trip back to Southrock. *And I've spent most of that time drinking.*

That hadn't been the plan. But then again, he didn't have a plan. He kept telling himself he came here to investigate the fate of his family, to get the real story about what happened. But maybe this trip just gave him an excuse to escape The Ravens—a place he never wanted to visit again.

He'd asked around town about the fire to see if anyone remembered anything but had learned nothing—no real leads to follow, no information at all that would help him understand who murdered his parents or why.

Then Katy's locket appeared on the same night as that stranger. *Coincidence?* Some say there's no such thing.

The shaving knife he pulled out of his travelpack was almost as old and weathered as the pack itself. *Probably a good thing.* A few scrapes and nicks later, he didn't even recognize the man staring back from the mirror. He slipped on the cap and the reflection transformed into a striking likeness of his pa—the same slender, angular face, the pointed chin, even the widow's peak on his forehead. Not the eyes, though.

A few girls he'd known over the years had mentioned his eyes, using words like *soft,* or *kind* to describe them. With his mother's eyes eerily watching him from the mirror, he now understood what they meant. He stared at his reflection, thinking of his parents for longer than he'd allowed in years.

And his sister. *Could she be alive?* The thought had been lurking at the fringes of his mind since he'd opened the locket. *Is it possible?* This trip, which began as a quest to discover who killed his family—*or an excuse to leave The Ravens*—had taken an unexpected turn with a serious and far more urgent objective.

Dressing in fresh clothes, he decided to go out to Gabe's farm. It was a chore he'd been avoiding since arriving in Southrock but a visit long overdue. Despite the strange aversion he felt about seeing Gabe and his family, he couldn't put it off any longer. *They must know something.*

When he lived in Southrock as a kid, the town only had one establishment for each necessary profession—one butcher, one blacksmith, one cobbler, one inn—all situated along the road that ran through the center of town. Back in those days, a need for anything beyond the ordinary required a trip to the capital. Now, there appeared to be two or three shops competing for the same business. Stone-paved streets sprouted off the once-familiar main road with more pubs and specialty shops than could've been supported by the former population. *I wonder if they even travel to the capital anymore?*

Zak passed the open door of the Cortek office building. *Strange. This place should be bustling this time of day.* The Cortek not only managed labor relations for the mine, but they also dispensed permits for wood clearing, sold and distributed building materials, and offered many other services vital to a town of this size. His curiosity got the best of him, and he looked inside. The place had been ransacked. *Or vacated in a hurry?* Papers and debris littered the floor, and a few of the cupboard doors hung askew on broken hinges.

A woman noticed him standing at the door. "They just up and took off a week or so ago," she said. "No explanation whatsoever."

Nodding to the woman, he went to the pub next door and stepped inside. His head hurt. *I could use a drink.*

A portly woman wandered around the room, placing dirty mugs and plates onto a tray and wiping the tables. "Good morning. What can I get you?"

You're just a drunken fool. The stranger's words echoed in his head, unexpected and unwelcome. *Damn!* "Uh, nothing, thank you."

"Suit yourself." The woman shrugged and went back to her cleaning.

The road out of town to Gabe's farm was as familiar to him as the town was strange. Shaking the cobwebs from his mind, he focused on the present, wondering if he'd recognize Gabe after so long. *I doubt he'll recognize me.*

A pack of mongrels greeted him at the gate barking, howling, and jumping up on him. *That's different.* There were just as many dogs as he remembered, but these weren't the same dogs. Gabe had taught the old pack to behave, and certainly wouldn't let them jump all over people. *Gabe's been slacking off to let these dogs get so obnoxious.*

He knocked on the door. The dogs still barked and bayed in a feverish pitch around him. From inside, a man's muffled scream at the dogs did nothing to calm them. Still yelling, the man opened the door.

The dogs scattered out of boot range, but the deafening noise continued.

"Quiet down, you good-fer-nothin'… Can I help you?" the man shouted above the din of the pack. Gabe's pa looked older with less hair on his head, but otherwise the same.

"Mr. Murfy, it's me, Zak," he shouted back.

"Zak?" He peered at Zak's face over his reading glasses. "My god, boy! How you've grown! Come in! Come in! Let's get outta this racket."

"Thank you, Mr. Murfy. I wasn't sure you'd even remember me after all this time," Zak said, still shouting.

"Remember you? Of course, I do! I remember everything about those days before—" Closing the door on the barking dogs, he coughed or choked on something. After an awkward, extended pause, he cleared his throat. "And none of that *mister* crap. You're a grown man. Call me Murf."

Zak followed Murf into the kitchen. It smelled of sizzling bacon and fresh-baked bread, and his stomach growled. Gabe's mother pounded dough on the counter.

"Punkin! Would you look who's here!" Murf called out to his wife.

The pet name, the dogs barking outside, the furniture, the smell of the kitchen mixed with the scent of burned fireplace ashes and dried up mud from the barnyard—it all felt so familiar. He'd often heard folks talk about coming, going, or being *home*. It was a feeling he'd lost long ago. A ghost of understanding flitted through him, then quickly transitioned into sorrow and envy. *Not my home.*

Unlike her husband, Gabe's mom recognized him at once. "Oh, my word! Zak you've come home at last, my dear!" she exclaimed. She wiped flour-covered hands on her apron and gave him a warm hug.

Zak returned the hug with an awkward pat on her shoulder. He'd spent almost as much time with this family growing up as he had with his own and had truly loved this woman. But he was out of practice with this kind of affection. It felt strange and uncomfortable.

Maybe because they sent me away to live with relatives I'd never met instead of letting me stay here to grow up with Gabe. The unexpected thought exhumed from deep in his psyche came forth, like a dug-up corpse meant to stay buried forever. But it explained why he'd been avoiding this visit. Afraid to reveal the raw, bitter resentment he'd just uncovered, he held Gabe's mother in the awkward embrace a moment or two longer.

"Hungry?" Mrs. Murfy asked, with a catch in her throat. "I've got fresh bread in the oven."

Zak took a deep breath, pushing the unpleasant thought back into its grave, shallower now. Holding her out at arm's length, he replied with a wry smile, "What do you think?"

The two men sat at the table while she fluttered about in the kitchen. "Where's Gabe these days? How's he doing?" Zak asked.

Gabe's mom dropped a pan on the stove with a loud crash.

Murf's face fell into a frown, and he reached over to rest his hand on Zak's.

Still uncomfortable with the familiar touching, Zak leaned back in the chair and crossed his arms.

Tears pooled at the corners of Murf's eyes. "You didn't know? Of course, you couldn't have." He swallowed, clearing his throat. "Gabe died in a mining accident back when he was sixteen. Fell off one of the upper platforms late one night." He left the table to console his wife.

"No, I'm… I'm so sorry. I had no idea. I didn't…" Zak hadn't heard from anyone in Southrock since he left. Early on, he'd given letters to his uncle to post, but when no replies came back, he'd just stopped trying.

"As I said, you wouldn't know. It's a tough thing," Murf said, helping his wife bring the food. They sat with Zak at the table.

He and Gabe grew up running, jumping and climbing all over the scaffolds and skywalks of the mines. To think that Gabe would fall? *No way.* Zak couldn't imagine ever taking a fall like that himself, and Gabe was the most agile and athletic of all their friends.

"I apologize," Mrs. Murfy said, wiping her eyes on the dishtowel. "It happened many years ago. But seeing you… it just brings back all those memories…" Her eyes teared, and her face disappeared behind the towel again.

"I understand." He pushed his chair away from the table. "Perhaps I shouldn't've come."

"No, no!" she exclaimed. "Sit!" She patted the spot where his hand had been. "They're wonderful, happy memories. Truly. I'm delighted you're here."

Still uncomfortable, he resettled himself.

"Eat. Enjoy the bread and honey," she said. "We've much catching up to do."

Zak stayed longer than he'd wanted, sharing stories about his life since leaving Southrock. He left out the worst of it and even made up a few stories to cover the reality of how miserable he'd been.

After the meal, Zak's headache came back with a vengeance. *I need a drink.* Murf's slow, drawn-out way of speaking tested his patience. He'd never noticed it before, but back then he'd never talked much to Gabe's father. "I've really got to get going. I have an appointment to get to," he lied.

Murf stood. "I'm gonna walk the boy into town, Punkin."

Ack! So much for a clean getaway.

Murf opened the door, and the dogs resumed their cacophony. When the pack lost interest, Zak spoke first. "Mist—Murf," he corrected himself to avoid being interrupted. "I don't want to take up any more of your time."

"Nonsense, it's the least I could do, after everything that's happened," Murf said, dismissing his concern.

They strolled along at a pace that matched the man's unhurried, dawdling dialogue as he droned on about inconsequential things—the weather, the town, local gossip, how their village had grown and other things of little interest to Zak. As they neared town, Murf directed him to sit on a bench along the roadside.

"Listen, son, there's something you need to know." He heaved a heavy sigh and a lengthy pause followed.

That sounds ominous. Zak had been desperate to escape the monotonous small talk, but Murf's serious tone and grim expression, in contrast to his casual manner moments before, piqued his curiosity. He sat, bracing himself to endure the man a while longer. *Wish I had a drink.*

Murf exhaled, sitting next to him on the bench. "I'm sure you wondered why me and the missus didn't offer to take you in after the blaze, or why none of us ever wrote to see how you were doing."

Zak squirmed in his seat. "It's okay, Mr. Murfy. It was a long time ago."

Murf touched his arm, "Please don't interrupt, Zak," he said, waiting for Zak to meet his gaze. "Just listen. You need to hear this." Leaning back against the bench, he asked, "I'm guessing you've heard the blaze wasn't an accident, right?"

Zak nodded. "My family was murdered. I could never make sense of it. Why would anyone want to kill *them*?"

"I think your pa got messed up in some serious stuff." Murf paused again. "Sometimes, I'd see him talking with strangers from outta town, and passing papers back and forth. I'd always thought it could be mine business, you know, but they never met at the mine. It was always kinda secret-like."

"Are you saying Pa did something wrong?"

"No, no, Zak. Nothing bad, I'm sure." Murf apologized. "Your pa was a good man, an honest man." He smiled. "Anyways, that morning of the blaze—you remember how crazy it was—"

Zak nodded, shards of the memory flashed through his brain... flames and black smoke... people scrambling and shouting... animals panicking... his frenzied, futile search for his parents. The visions drowned out Murf's words. He shook his head and blinked a couple of times to clear the distraction.

"... your folks might be trapped inside? Well, a man, pretending to be helpful but really not helping at all, kept asking questions of folks. Especially about you. Where you were... has anybody seen you? Me and some others thought this guy was up to no good. Someone noticed him bolting down the road on his horse, like a caver outta hell, saddle bags flailing all over and dropping things along the way. Stuff from your house. I know because we picked up some of it. I'm thinking he stole everything he could grab and set that blaze to cover his tracks."

Zak had already learned more sitting on this bench than he had since arriving in Southrock. *Could Murf know something that might lead him to his sister? To the person who killed his family?* "Do you remember anything about this guy? What he looked like? Anything?"

Murf continued on in his slow drawl. "As I recall—it was a long time ago, you know—ugly looking fella, shorter than me, a big scar on his cheek. His eyes weren't the same color, I remember that cause others said so too. And he wore a crest on his sleeve... a white bird and a flower. You turned up soon after he left. We kept you inside the house till your uncle came. We made the funeral a real quick one, didn't make a big fuss over you. Your family was well thought of around here and we all wanted to protect you. Your uncle agreed not to post any letters, and no one here would contact or visit you. After that day, if anyone asked, they always said no one'd seen you since the fire." He leaned back.

Zak's recollection of those days was mostly a blur, marked by short scenes forever burned in his memory and relived since on many a restless night—and the occasional tavern bar top. Never having attended a funeral before or since, he wouldn't have noticed anything unusual about the ceremony. It did give him some solace to know why he'd never heard from anyone, yet some resentment remained. So much time had passed without a word. *Not even to tell me about Gabe!*

"I was only fourteen. Why would anyone be looking for me?" he asked himself but spoke the question aloud.

"Beats me," Murf replied. "We were focused on keeping you safe is all. Now and again, some outta towner would come by asking about you. That's how come I remember that crest, some of those men wore the same one. Not a decent man among them, neither," Murf noted. "But after a few years, the men stopped coming around at all."

"My sister? What about Katy? They say she died in the fire. Is that true?"

"Yes, it is thought she burned in the fire, but her body was never recovered."

Zak thought of his sister and his parents. Leaning his head back, he gazed up at the sky. Puffy white clouds floated by, oblivious to the storm of emotions battering at his soul.

Murf sighed. "Listen, Zak, I know this ain't easy to take in. But I, the missus too, we want you to know how hard it was for us to let you go away. We didn't know them relatives of yours at all. But you couldn't stay here. It wouldn't've been safe. Then when we lost Gabe..." He choked up and tears came to his eyes. "Oh, how we wanted to come see you then, or at least get word to you about what happened." Wiping his face on his sleeve, he tried to dry tears that wouldn't stop flowing. "'It was such a hard time."

Zak had never seen a grown man lose it like this, weeping out of control. "I'm... I'm sorry, Mr. Murfy... It's okay..." He didn't know what to do with his hands, they almost reached out of their own accord, but he couldn't bring himself to touch the man. With his own gut-wrenching emotions tied in a knot, he was afraid of turning into a sniveling basket case himself. So, he just waited.

"No," Murf said, wiping his face again. "*I'm* sorry. We're both sorry. Me 'n Gladys. We want you to know you got a place—a home—here, with us, any time. Long as you need. Days. Months. Years." He chuckled at Zak's wide-eyed reaction. "Well, you're always welcome. Will you at least stay with us now, while you're in town?"

"No," Zak replied, perhaps too curtly. "Thank you for the offer, but I'll be leaving soon anyway." Without giving Murf an opportunity to object, he stood and added, "Mr. Murf—Murf, please, thank Mrs. Murfy again for the food. It was delicious."

"I will, indeed," Murf recovered his composure, more like the man Zak remembered from his youth. "Where're you headed from here?" he asked.

"I need to find who killed my family. I can't go on not knowing." It wasn't a good answer, but it was the best he could give.

Murf stood, then pulled a small box out from under his jacket. "Here, take this. It's something that flower-bird guy dropped. I figure he must've took it from your house."

Zak took the box and bowed the Edyson greeting. "Thanks again for everything." He held up the box, but the gesture was intended to encompass all the man had shared with him that day and had done for him in the past.

"You take care, Zak."

Inspecting the cylindrical box, Zak smiled to himself. *One of Pa's trick boxes—no obvious lid or latch.* It could take hours to figure out how to open it. His head hurt too much to work on it now.

He exhaled, releasing some of the tension that gripped his chest and the anxiety that had been building in him since hearing of Gabe's death. As he watched Murf amble down the road, his hope to have some idea of what to do next dissolved. Rather than answering questions about who killed his family, his visit with the Murfys only raised a dozen more. It did explain the reasons behind his exile to The Ravens and could also be the reason his uncle had been so insistent that he learn to fight. Not just with his fists, either. The man had even arranged for Zak to learn to fight with weapons.

Sitting back down on the bench, he stashed the box in his travelpack for later and took out his drink flask, shaking it. *Damn! Empty.* He twisted off the cap and shook the last few drops onto his tongue.

You're just a drunken fool. Zak couldn't shake the stranger's words from his head. He looked up at the sun, then down the road toward Southrock. It was still early. *Too early.* If he went back into town now, he'd end up in the tavern drinking again.

An open field spread out across the road. Beyond that, trees marked the edge of the forest. He'd thought about Monk often over the years. His chances of actually finding the climber now were slim. *But what've I got to lose?*

Chapter 5
Apri

Apri sat on the edge of the bed in her cell feeling utterly dejected. She'd tried everything to escape. *Well, almost everything.*

The key hung on the wall by the door, far out of her reach. She'd tested every one of the cell bars multiple times. A few could be rotated, or moved up and down, but not enough to be pulled out. Squeezing between them didn't work, either. That'd been a painful test. She still had scrapes and bruises from trying. At one point, she thought she'd be stuck for good.

Whenever anyone came with food or to change the chamber pot, neither happening as often as she would like, the procedure they used prevented any chance of her interfering with, or injuring, the person making the exchange. She'd even tried her telepathy trick a couple of times. Projecting things like *Give her key,* or *Open cell door.* But her subject just appeared confused and ignored the suggestion.

One last option had been in the back of her mind from the first day, to be used only as a last resort. Now, she was desperate enough to try it. She thought about Rrazmik, the old man who taught her to fight and survive on her own. Were it not for him, she may never have had the guts to leave Ararat, or if she had, she'd be dead already. *Or worse.*

Her father had taken her to meet Rrazmik the day before her sixteenth birthday. He must've sensed her restlessness—she certainly talked often enough about leaving. All the other girls her age just wanted to get married and have babies. *Not for me.* Perhaps he thought the training would be enough to get the wanderlust out of her system. Or maybe it was his way of trying to keep her safe.

Her mother always thought she was taking dancing lessons. *Dancing lessons!* She shook her head. If her parents had known about a particular lesson, one that came a year or so after she first met Rrazmik, she doubted he would've lived to see another day.

✳✳✳

"You are woman. This is disadvantage," Rrazmik said. "Your opponents will be men, more often than not. You must not allow sex or modesty to cloud your judgment or control your actions in fight." Then, to her utter shock and embarrassment, he took off his clothes. All of them.

Apri was not a virgin at the time, but her sexual experience consisted of fumbling around in the dark with a partner just as naïve and nervous. Her cheeks flushed and she whirled around. "Rrazmik! What are you doing?"

"Turn around," he ordered. "You must learn not to be distracted. By anything." He held up his practice sword. "Attack, now!"

She faced him but couldn't attack. Fifty or sixty years her senior, his skin hung on his frame like a curtain, the parts that never saw the sun pale in comparison to his arms and face. A strong man for his age, and physically fit to be sure, but still old and wrinkled. And so hairy. All Aratian men were hairy, with facial hair, chest hair, back hair, nose hair. *But this...?*

She turned her back to him again. "Damn!" The Aratian expletive escaped her lips before she caught herself.

"Watch your language, young lady!" he chastised.

The image of his genitals still burned, branded in her brain. It hung between his legs, all pink and limp, surrounded by wiry, grey hair looking like a rotten, shriveled up root vegetable just pulled out of the ground.

"Ahhh! Rrazmik, you are evil!" she said, squeezing her eyes shut and stomping her feet in fury.

"Turn around and fight." Rrazmik ordered, slapping her butt with the flat of his practice sword. "Now!"

She fought poorly, her strikes feeble and weak. Her only conscious thoughts were to avoid looking at him and to keep from hitting him in the wrong place. She failed on both accounts. Staring wide-eyed and horrified, she watched as Rrazmik dropped to his knees, grabbing his crotch.

"That will be all for today, my dear!" he rasped in a falsetto voice. A tear trickled down his weathered cheek.

Embarrassed, but thankful to have the lesson over, she turned her back on him while he dressed.

"That was pitiful," he said after recovering his normal voice. "We try again next time."

She should've known... it was just like him to prolong her suffering. On the walk home, Apri realized she would have to endure these lessons until she figured out how to get past her humiliation and disgust. Ugh, all that saggy skin and hair, he looks like a wild, hairy, ugly beast.

That's when the idea came to her to stop thinking of him as Rrazmik or even as a person. Could she convince her brain that she fought against an animal? A non-human opponent?

At the next lesson, she noticed Rrazmik being more protective of his private parts. That alone boosted her confidence and determination, at least to a small degree. After a few minutes of sparring, she tried her trick and fought the non-human beast. The strategy worked, and she won Rrazmik's praise, and a promise he would keep his clothes on from now on.

"I am not the man I once was," he said as he dressed. "You may still get distracted by... younger, more virile men." He shrugged, wagging his finger. "Perhaps if you do find yourself in such predicament, you will remember lesson and recover quickly."

***

A rough-looking woman came into the cell cave to change the chamber pot.

Damn! Disappointed that it wasn't the person she'd hoped would come, Apri pushed the used pot out the service opening as far as she could, then stepped back. The woman exchanged the pots and left. Retrieving the clean pot, she set it aside and sat on the bed in her cell.

Rrazmik's naked lesson hadn't been the worst of it, or the reason her father would've been angry enough to kill him. *That* happened in the next few sessions.

***

"Your turn," Rrazmik said.

"You want me to turn around?" she asked. From their first lesson, he'd insisted that they speak English—the language of Edyson. It'd been months since his words had tripped her up.

"It means you go next. To follow me. Strip."

"What?" She knew him well enough to know he wasn't joking. "No…" she said—not an objection but a statement of disbelief.

"Oh, yes, my dear. I am quite serious," he said. "There are many scenarios in which you might find yourself in such a situation. Turn around and face dummy, if that helps. Strip. Then pick up your weapon and fight.

It was the single most embarrassing moment of her life. She swiped at the dummy—an awkward and vain attempt. Being bare-ass naked consumed her every thought and action.

"Men, in general, do not have same discomfort being naked in front of others as do women. It is a disadvantage. All in your head. You must learn to master it."

It took three or four sessions to get her brain to think about something other than being naked. Just as she felt the insecurity fading and her confidence returning, Rrazmik started shouting sexual comments at her as she fought. Comments about her body, crude remarks about what he wanted to do to her, and with her. She pounded the dummy harder and harder. With each strike, his words became more vulgar until her anger seethed out of control. Turning around, she swung the practice sword hard, right at his head.

Rrazmik blocked the attack.

Mortified, she stood before him in shame and disbelief. She'd never felt such anger and repulsion. "I wanted to kill you."

"Anger is strongest of emotions," he said. "You can use it to your advantage in a fight. But do not let it consume you beyond all reason."

"I am sorry," she said.

"It is quite alright, my dear. It was my fault—and my intention—to drive you to it. Know this, taunting your opponent can be a wise tactic. Lead them to make poor decisions, to be more predictable, or more aggressive." He grinned. "It does seem that you have forgotten you stand before me stark naked."

She looked down and laughed.

"Get dressed," he said. "There is one more weapon you have at your disposal. It will be powerful against some, worthless against others. I can tell you about it, but I cannot teach you how to use it. It is something you must learn on your own."

"What weapon is that?" she asked, intrigued.

"Sex," he said. "Desire or lust might be better words. Some men, especially young men, are weak and gullible when it comes to sexual temptation. A man can be tricked to trust woman who pretends to be attracted to him."

∗∗∗

Rrazmik didn't spend much time on the subject, perhaps because of her age. Instead, he suggested that she hone that particular skill by observing others, and by paying attention during her own sexual encounters. Sex was never the same for her after that day. It became more like a sport, something to practice and refine, to strategize and improve upon—a game to be mastered, and her partners, opponents to be observed and evaluated. As a result, she tended to separate the act of sex from any personal feelings about her partner. She considered sex a sometimes pleasant, sometimes not, means to an end, using it at times to earn small favors, and at other times merely for her own pleasure.

This time would be different. *So much at stake.*

It'd been two weeks since Silas locked her up and she didn't want to be here when Damian returned. *You're done here...* he'd told her that night. Ominous words. He'd already saved her from certain death once. He wouldn't do that again.

And I must find Tina.

This was her last hope of escape. Several different men and women came to deliver food and change the chamber pot in her cell. Most ignored her when they came and went. But one young man had made eye contact and lingered a little longer than the others. It'd been days since she saw him last, and if he didn't come soon, she'd have to choose another. Laying on the cot, she waited for the meal delivery.

Apri woke to the sound of scraping metal on the floor and sprung from the cot. The boy was almost out the door. "Excuse me?" she said.

The kid stopped. "Yes?" His acne-riddled face turned red. He must be in his late teens, she guessed, perhaps early twenties.

"I was just wondering?" she said, innocent yet seductive.

"Wondering what?"

"I am here two weeks now. I feel so," she bit her lower lip, "dirty." *Come on, kid, look at me.* "Could you possibly get pail of water and cloth I could use to wash?" He met her eyes. *Yes! Good boy.* Her expression pleaded for his help.

"Ummm, I don't think…" he stammered. "I'm not s'pose…"

"What is your name?" she asked, running her hand along the bars, then pressing her body against them, close to where he stood.

"Samuel. My name's Samuel."

"Hmmm. Samuel. That is nice name," she said. "I only ask if you could put some water in bucket and slide it close to bars so I can wash, you know? I can use a piece of sheet from cot for a rag. Is that too much to ask?"

"I don't… I guess not," he said.

Yes! "Oh, that would be so wonderful! Oh, you have no idea!" Her mouth rounded, drawing out each of the 'o' sounds seductively.

He left.

She waited, praying no one else discovered what he was up to. After what felt like forever, he returned carrying a bucket of water.

"You step back over there, now," he said.

"Yes, of course," she said, obediently moving to the back of her cell. "You are not afraid of me, are you?"

He set the bucket next to the bars and stepped back. "They say you killed Jase."

"I did no such thing," she said, kneeling next to the bucket and dipping her hand in the water. "Oh, my. It is warm! And soap, too!" She gave him her most grateful smile.

"No trouble," he said and started out the door.

"You are not leaving, are you? Please stay and talk. It is lonely in here all by myself. Could you sit over there on stool? You will have to take bucket back anyway, yes?" His eyes watched her from the doorway with unconcealed lust.

"I suppose I could stay. For a little while." He sat on the stool against the far wall, facing her.

"Thank you, Samuel. That is so kind of you." Undoing the top buttons of her shirt, she loosened it over her shoulders just enough to reveal the curve of her breasts. "You do not think I could kill Jase, do you? He was big, strong guy, was he not?" Reaching for the rag, she soaped it up, the movement exposing one of her breasts. "Oops!" She looked his way, all shy and embarrassed, and covered herself.

Samuel wiggled around on the stool. His face got redder than ever and his hand twitched, moving toward his crotch. It stopped short to rest on his thigh.

Moving the sopping, soapy rag inside her shirt, she rubbed it on one breast, then the other. She closed her eyes and moaned in pleasure. "Oh, this feels so good."

"I should be going," he said, standing.

Too much. Turning her back to him, she pleaded, "No, please do not go. Where are you from, Samuel?"

It worked, he stayed. She toned down the seduction and made idle conversation with him to put him more at ease. Listening to his voice, she would create more sexual tension whenever he began to sound too casual. Using her telepathy, she popped in and out of his brain to read his thoughts, then used actions and words to drive him to the brink of arousal. At the point when his sexual desire dominated every other thought, she stayed in his head.

"Samuel?" she said, her voice deep and throaty.

"Mmmm?"

She stood with her back to him, her clothing loose and damp from reaching under it with the wet rag. "Do you think you could, maybe..." she glanced over her shoulder at him, dropping her shirt to her waist. "...wash my back?" It all came down to this moment.

"Uhhh." His thoughts were wild and feral—an obsessive, burning desire to copulate.

Perfect. She put one more thought in his head, hoping he was too far gone to reason it out. *Take the key. You don't want me to get it.* "Samuel?"

"Uhhh, yeah." Taking the key off the wall, he put it in his shirt pocket.

Yes! She jumped out of his head before he sensed her elation. "Samuel? Are you..." she bit her lower lip, "coming?" she asked, holding the rag out over her shoulder.

Apri made sure their hands touched when he took the rag from her. "Get it all soapy, will you?"

He knelt to soap the rag.

Wiggling her hips, she pushed her trousers down farther. "Rub, real hard, now," she said and stepped away from the cell, pushing backwards into the pressure. "Ohhh, yes, that feels good. Mmmm, Samuel, you smell so good." She squirmed to lower her pants, leaning against the bars again.

"I do?" The question caught in his throat. He rubbed her back, up and down.

Lifting her arms above her head, she grabbed the bars and pushed herself into his hand. "Harder, Samuel, harder."

He moaned.

"Mmmm, now do my front, will you?" She turned around.

Samuel stared at her bare breasts, then at her face.

"Come on, Samuel, please. I want..." she bit her lip. "Ohhh, I want..." Her hand rubbed his crotch through his trousers. "I want *you.*" Locking her eyes on his, she pulled his arms through the bars and around her naked waist. Her pants fell to the floor, and she moaned.

He didn't resist. Instead, he forced his body against hers, the bars between them.

"Samuel, Samuel, she said writhing against him. Can't you come in here? These bars, they hurt."

"No!" he backed off, stepping away, out of her reach. All her clothing had fallen to her feet, and he stared at her naked body.

Stepping backwards out of the pile of clothes, she pushed them away with her foot, then leaned against the bars. "It is okay. I understand. This is not allowed." She sighed. "Maybe we can figure some other way?" Pressing her body against the bars again, she extended her arms through. "Come on back over here, Samuel. I need to *feel* you again."

Unable to resist the invitation, he returned to her arms. When he was just close enough, she moaned, reached up, and ran her fingers through his curly, red hair. Then she smashed his head into the bars as hard as she could.

He dropped to the ground like a rock. His body fell backwards away from the cell, and he sprawled out, flat on his back. The key flew from his pocket and slid across the floor to rest against the back wall, far from her reach.

"Noooo!" she cried. With her back to the bars, she slid into a crumpled heap next to her clothes. "Damn!"

She wallowed in self-pity for a while, her mind recreating numerous alternative scenarios that wouldn't have ended in this failure.

Samuel hadn't moved, but he was still breathing. She watched his chest rise and fall, then glared at the key lying against the wall.

Pounding her fists and feet on the floor, she yelled again, "Damn!"

With her last hope of escape foiled, Apri dressed, resigned to her fate. The untouched food tray lay on the floor where Samuel had placed it. She took the tray and sat on the cot to eat.

Chapter 6
Zak

Jogging into the woods, Zak headed for the clearing beyond the creek where he'd abandoned Monk. A cool spring breeze blew from the east. The fresh, brisk air was absent the dusty, unnatural scents of town, and punctuated by the musky scent of rotting leaves that stirred underfoot. Zak took a deep breath, recalling his days of running through the thick brush, climbing trees with his sister, and trapping and hunting with his pa. He smiled, then laughed. This detour had already altered his mood, repressing the torturous memories uprooted by his talk with Murf. *Definitely worth it, even if I don't find Monk.*

With his arms outstretched for balance, he crossed over the creek on a fallen tree. The clearing was just ahead, but something felt wrong. *Too still… too quiet?* Zak froze on the other side of the creek, surveying in every direction around and ahead of him. *Nothing.*

Just as he relaxed and resumed his trek toward the clearing, the shrub beside him exploded in woody shrapnel, pelting him with a confetti of leaves and dirt. Zak ducked and backed up, shielding his eyes. His foot tangled on a root, and he dropped to his knees, then scrambled away, backing into a large tree trunk.

Frozen in place, he faced an adult forktoe. Its huge head waggled around on a snake-like neck, as if it wasn't quite sure of Zak's precise location. Its tiny arms were almost comical in contrast to the two long, spindly legs that stretched beneath its leathery-skinned body. Long talons sprouted from its bulbous toes, one by one. He'd always thought Pa's description of their length exaggerated, but those claws extended outward longer than seemed possible.

Zak took a quick look around. It appeared to be alone. "Easy there, big guy," he said, trying to sound calm. The forktoe stomped its feet a couple of times, talons tapping on the debris-littered ground. Multi-hued patterns danced across its bare skin in waves, as it changed color to blend into the forest surroundings. "I'll get outta your hair, buddy... er, outta your dry leathery skin. No need to get upset."

The beast took two large steps forward and craned its neck at Zak, screeching again—an awful, spine-chilling sound. He readied himself for the attack. From his position against the tree, he had two possible escape routes, to the right, or to the left. *Just pick one.*

The forktoe sprung at him and he lunged to his right... *Damn!*

It chose the same direction, launching into him, feet first. Being too close to the tree for it to catch him square, they still collided, and its talons raked Zak's side. He yelped as his body whipped around the tree from the force of the impact. His head slammed into the trunk. He couldn't see or hear anything.

He shook his head to clear his vision and dispel the ringing in his ears. Sounds were muffled and distant, and he was unsteady on his feet. He drew the knife from his belt.

The forktoe shrieked again. It was close, just on the other side of the tree.

A different shrill noise followed, a familiar squealy-screech.

Zak rubbed his eyes. *Monk?* Adrenaline pumping, he braced for another attack.

Monk's furry little legs hung tight to the beast's neck, and his tiny hand scratched and clawed at its eyes and face. With its vision blocked by the climber's limbs, the forktoe jerked its head up and down, up and down, shrieking wildly.

Monk held tight. His long, skinny tail flailing with each snaky swing of the thing's ugly head. But he was losing his grip.

Taking advantage of the diversion, Zak sprung toward them.

Using its long neck like a trebuchet, the forktoe sent Monk flying through the air, then twisted around to face him.

But Zak was already on it. His knife sliced halfway through its skinny neck.

Blood sprouted from the gash. No longer able to support its huge head, the forktoe's neck folded in two. Without another sound, it dropped straight to the ground in a heap.

Zak rested both hands on his knees, sucking in great lungfuls of air.

Monk emerged from the bushes, apparently unharmed. Jumping up on the dead animal, he bounced around and turned in circles, as if performing some kind of wild victory dance.

"Glad to see you, too, old friend!" He laughed, then slumped to the ground. His back and shoulder were on fire from being wrapped around the tree trunk, and the talon wound on his side bled, soaking into his shirt and pants. Taking off his travelpack, he inspected the damage. *Feels worse than it looks.* He dug in the pack for his med kit.

After dressing the injury, Zak examined the forktoe up close. Its body took on a neutral greyish-brown color, in contrast to the bright green foliage around it. *So, the chameleon trick died with it.* There were six talons, one at the end of each toe, the longest at least fifteen centimeters in length. Using his knife, Zak extracted them one-by-one, being careful not to slice his finger in the process. The part of the talon that went inside the animal's foot was thick and coarse, and long enough to use as a handle. The other end was razor-sharp—a formidable weapon.

He wrapped the sharp ends of the talons in a shirt from his pack. When he noticed the last one still tinged with his own blood, he grinned. Holding it at arm's length, he took a couple of practice swipes in the air.

"Ouch!" Grabbing his side, he sat on a tree stump to rest a while longer. Monk hopped into his lap, as if they'd not been apart all these years.

Zak rubbed on his ears, then sniffed and scrunched his nose. Monk fur was stiff, and he smelled like he'd been rolling around on dead animals. "Oh god, you stink," he said, pushing the climber off his lap. The climber's wide-eyed, tilted-head-sideways expression made him laugh again. "Stop it, will you?"

Tucking the last talon away, he fished out the puzzle box for a closer inspection, turning it over and over, around and around. *Come on, Pa, what's the trick here?* It might be the only one of Pa's boxes to survive the fire and he didn't want to destroy it. He held it to his ear and shook. *Something in there?* Tapping the box on his hand, he flipped it over a few times, then banged it against the trunk. *Nothing.*

Monk approached.

Zak leaned forward so the climber couldn't jump into his lap. "Sorry, little guy, but you really stink. I can smell you from—"

Monk slapped the box from his hand. It fell to the ground, and he tucked it under his arm and ran away.

"Hey, get back here!" Zak jumped up to give chase. "Ow!" His body, stiff from the brief rest, objected to the sudden movement. Hobbling off, he followed the climber who'd run in the direction of the creek. "Monk!"

Monk stood at the edge of the water, bouncing and screeching.

"Come on, now, give it back. This isn't a game," he said in his most serious tone, holding out his hand.

The climber kept up the antics, playing keep-away, whether Zak wanted to or not.

Zak came closer and tried to take the box from the agitated animal. Each time he grabbed for the box, Monk moved it away again, just out of his grasp. As they fought for the box, Zak recalled the game from his childhood. He found a rock and tossed it across the creek, then looked in the direction where the rock landed. "What's that?"

Startled, Monk looked too, dropping the box. It fell into the water at the creek's edge.

Zak snatched the box and stood up. "Hah! Gotcha!"

The box began to change in his hand, it was... *melting?* The strange material disintegrated, leaving a wet, sandy residue that oozed out of his hands. *So much for saving Pa's box.*

He shook the wet sandy material off the only remnant of the box that remained—a piece of paper—inspecting it as he wiped a hand on his shirt. The paper had a map of their farm and the surrounding woods, in precise detail, with words written in Pa's hand.

He turned the paper around a couple of times. *There's our house, the barn, the fort we built.* Pa'd written the word *Safe* next to two *X* marks on the map, one over the old barn. *The tack room, maybe?* The other one... He held it up, again, orienting it to his present location. "Come on, Monk. I know where this is."

Zak put the map in his pocket and hiked west of the creek another hundred meters or so until he began to recognize the area.

"Here we are. Home sweet home," he said with a sigh. He and Katy—and Monk—had spent hours and hours playing in this little clearing where they'd built a fort playhouse.

Like everything else in these woods—*except that forktoe*—the campsite was smaller than he remembered. They'd built the fort together over a few weekends to keep busy while they waited for the traps to do their job. He'd found Monk on the day they finished the playhouse.

✶✶✶

Pa sent him off to find a few small branches to put the finishing touches on the fort. As he searched for decent pieces of wood underneath a tree, a branch fell from above and hit him on the head. "Ouch!" Seeing nothing up in the tree, he picked up the fallen branch. Just the right size. Another branch fell, and this time he saw the little climber, way up in the tree.

"Pa. Come and look!"

Pa shaded his eyes from the sun glistening through the branches. "A climber?" He surveyed the other trees around them. "Strange it would be all alone," he said, squinting. "Is it missing an arm?"

"I think so," Zak said. "He threw branches down on me."

"Notice its big ears? They say a climber's hearing is far better than ours."

"Really?" The climber ventured down a few branches, watching Zak with the biggest, brightest eyes he'd ever seen. "Better than dogs?"

"So they say," Pa said. "He looks young. Maybe you've found a friend?" He took the branches from Zak, picked up a few more, then went back to work on the fort.

Zak stayed, watching the curious animal. "Wanna be friends?" he called out. With the first comical tilt of its head, Zak was determined to try.

The next day their veterinarian came to the farm, and Zak bombarded her with questions about climbers. The vet confirmed what his Pa had said about their hearing.

She explained they preferred a vegetarian diet but would eat just about anything.

"Some people keep climbers as pets," she told him. "They're real curious. If you want to make friends, just ignore it and go about your business. Once it realizes you're not a threat, I bet it'll come around."

Zak went out to the fort once or twice a week after that. He'd place food on the ground outside the fort, then play around. The climber would take the food and watch him, staying just out of reach. Zak didn't approach it, but he would talk, a one-way conversation about anything that came into his head. With each visit, the climber would come closer, as if anxious to investigate whatever he was doing. One dreary, drizzly day a few weeks later, Zak waited in the fort for the rain to stop, and the little guy finally came in.

Although he wanted to jump and shout, Zak contained his excitement to a non-threatening grin and squirm. The climber took a piece of fruit right out of Zak's hand and ate it, then sat back, watching, waiting for another piece.

✳✳✳

Zak had named him after a skinny, one-armed man in a robe that had come through town years before. Pa had called the man a monk.

"Our fort is gone," he said to Monk in an overly dramatic, sad voice. The structure had collapsed with forest vegetation encroaching on all sides. Two rotted posts jutted upwards, leaning sideways. Zak pulled out the map and checked it again. Monk jumped on his shoulder. "No, little buddy, you really need a bath bad." He pushed at the climber.

Monk coughed, nipped his ear, then darted away, farting in Zak's face as he left.

Zak swished his hand in front of his face to dispense the stink. "Dammit!" His ear bled some, but not much. *That's one annoying habit I didn't miss.*

According to the map, the fort had to be the location of one of the X marks. He knelt on the rotted floorboards, sweeping some of the dirt away. "Ouch!"

Tiny splinters had embedded in his palm, and he picked them out, one by one, with the point of his knife. Lopping off a branch from a nearby bush, he swept the rest of the dirt off the boards. With the handle of the knife, he banged on the floorboards one by one, stopping at one with a hollower sound.

The wood around the nails had rotted. He grabbed underneath the edge of the hollow-sounding board and pulled. It came off too easily, and he fell backwards, landing on his butt.

"Ow!" Pressing the bandage on his side, he waited for the pain to subside then inspected the metal lockbox he'd uncovered. Clearing away the debris from around the box, he tried prying it out of the ground. It wouldn't budge. *Just like Pa to make it difficult.* It could be stuck in the ground after years of erosion, or maybe it had one of Pa's tricky release mechanisms built into it. He sat back on his heels, dejected.

Monk came over and started playing with the combination padlock, banging it around.

"Yeah, I know, it's the only way in." Pushing the climber aside, he rubbed his hands together, then tried his birthdate, Ma's, Pa's. *Too obvious.* Tired, sore, and defeated, he slumped over and rested his forehead on the lockbox. "It could be anything," he said to Monk. Then he bolted up, crouching on his haunches again.

Monk flinched at the sudden movement and squeaked.

Zak gave the climber a little pat on the head. "Maybe, Monk, maybe," he muttered, trying another code, then another, and another, pulling on the lock after each attempt. He couldn't remember the exact date but knew the month and year.

Click. The lock gave when he tugged on it, just the tiniest bit, but more so than any time before.

Please. Using a rock as a hammer, he hit the rusty lock a few times and it fell open. "The date we finished building the fort," he said to Monk, unhooking the lock from the box. *Or maybe it was just a rusty lock.* The hinges were rusted too. He used the knife to pry at it, and the lid opened with a *crack* and a *creak*.

Inside, he found a small purse, a piece of paper, and a strange card. He set down the card and paper, opening the purse. *Forty credits.* "This'll pay for a couple more nights at least." Stashing the money in his pocket, he inspected the card. Made from a durable material of some kind, it was embossed with an unfamiliar symbol and some numbers.

Both sides of the paper were blank. Monk snatched it and jumped on Zak's shoulder, holding the paper like a grand prize.

"I swear, Monk, if you cough, fart or bite me right now I will—"

The climber waved the paper around in the air, and Zak saw something written on it. "Stop. Wait. Give that to me."

Being careful not to tear the paper as he pried it from the climber's tiny hand, he held it up to the sunlight. He recognized Pa's distinctive, meticulous handwriting. When he took the paper away from the light, the words disappeared. *That's one hell of a trick.* He did it again a couple times watching them appear and disappear before his eyes.

The paper listed some names that meant nothing to him. They could be related to old mine business, insignificant after all this time. *But in disappearing ink?* Putting it and the card into his travelpack, he threw the pack over his left shoulder so it wouldn't bang against the fresh wound.

"Ready to go, Monk?" The breeze had picked up, and the leaves in the trees above rustled. Occasional debris fell to the ground. From the direction of the wind and the smell it brought with it, there'd be rain by nightfall. "Rain coming."

He wasn't sure Monk would follow. But every time he checked he'd be there, following behind, sometimes right on his heels, other times farther off. But always there. *Just like the old days.*

Monk didn't go into the tavern through the front door. He'd been kicked out of too many places in the past. Zak stopped by the bar and ordered some food to take up to his room, including a small cup of vegetable stew for Monk. As much as he craved a mug of ale, he asked for water instead. *You're just a drunken fool.* The stranger's comment haunted him. *Am I?* Dismissing the thought, he opened the window and whistled for Monk. The first misty drops of rain had begun to fall.

Monk jumped in the window. Now soaking wet from the rain, he smelled worse than ever.

When the food came, Zak set his next to the bed and placed Monk's on the table by the door. "Eat up, bud. Then it's bath time."

Emptying his travelpack onto the bed, he reorganized the contents in between bites. Re-wrapping the forktoe talons, he tucked them down at the bottom of the pack. He'd look for some leather for a sheath so he could carry one or two of them on his belt.

When he finished his meal, he removed the bandage from his side to tend to the wound. Looking in the mirror, he craned his head around for a better view, then moved his arm and twisted his waist. It already felt a little better. He cleaned and redressed it, then refilled the washbasin with fresh, warm water.

Monk sat on the table licking his hand, then wiping it all around his face and head. Armed with soap from his travelpack, Zak coaxed Monk into his arms and carried him to the washbasin. At the sight of the water, the climber hung tight onto him with all three appendages, claws extended.

Zak peeled him off, limb-by-limb. "You used to like this, boy. Take it easy." He placed one leg into the warm water.

Monk's eyes widened. A climber's eyes were already large, a prominent feature on its small face, and Zak laughed at the comical expression. "Monk, those are gonna pop right outta your head!"

After another moment, he placed the other leg in the basin.

Finally, Monk lost the wild-eyed look and settled down, splashing the water around with his hand.

"Okay, okay, enough of that." He soaped the climber all over, emptied the basin, then rinsed him off. He inhaled deeply. "Much better, little buddy."

The climber jumped onto his chest, soaking wet.

"Aw, Monk!" Zak wrapped him in a towel and, holding the dripping animal at arm's length, carried him to the bed for a good rub-down. Still damp, Monk jumped out of the towel and settled on the end of the bed to resume his one-handed personal grooming routine.

The occasional gust of wind blew rain into the room. Zak shut the window He was determined to find the stranger from last night, but it was still too early to go down. Lying on the bed, he pulled his sister's locket out, turning it round and round in his fingers to pass the time.

Chapter 7
Zak

Cigarweed smoke hung in the tavern like a fog, catching the last light of the day from outside. The smoky, dusty beams of light made the place look even darker and dingier than before. Zak rubbed his nose. Some found the sweet, vanilla-y scent of the pipeweed favored by the miners to be pleasant. He did not. With a disapproving glare at the table of men smoking the weed, which was, of course, ignored, he bought a drink at the bar. He sat at a table against the opposite wall with a clear view of the door.

Determined not to drink as much tonight, he took small sips, watching the pub fill with rowdy, thirsty miners coming in off the day shift. Each time he heard the door creak open, he'd look up. Halfway through the first mug, he guzzled the ale all at once without a thought.

He stared into the empty mug. *You're just a drunken fool.*

A glass shattered, startling him out of his daze. Over at the bar, a drunk patron voiced a too-loud apology at the barkeep.

"Refill?" the barmaid asked. He pushed his empty mug toward her, and she filled it from a pitcher.

The door opened again. *Not him.*

"Looking for someone?"

He flinched, spilling his drink. Thinking to hide his discomfort, Zak stood and said, "Yes, for you, actually." It felt even more awkward standing next to the guy like that.

The man's calm composure was unsettling. *Like a damn shadow.* A little taller, and much bigger than Zak, he wore a thick leather vest and a longsword strapped to his back. Even without closer inspection, it'd be a good bet the man carried more weapons than just the sword. Dark, wavy hair fell to his shoulders, casting half his face in shadow. Piercing eyes studied Zak from a face covered by a full mustache and beard.

The man removed his scabbard and slid onto the bench across from him, raising a hand to get the barmaid's attention. Combing hair back from his face, he glanced at the mug on the table. "At it again, eh?"

Zak glared at the man and sat back down, taking a long swig of ale.

The stranger said nothing more. He accepted a mug from the barmaid, smiling his thanks as she filled it from a pitcher. Maintaining his indifference, he watched the other patrons, sipping his drink.

Although Zak tried to act just as nonchalant and aloof, his impatience won out. "Got any more trinkets for me?"

The man silently scrutinized him.

Zak stared back. *Why the hell is he looking at me like that?* He looked away, feeling like he'd just failed some kind of test.

"So, you found it?" the man finally replied. "I'm surprised you even noticed, given your condition last night."

Zak's first instinct was to launch across the table and grab the man by the collar. But he stopped himself, realizing the impulse was motivated by his own shame. Many a bar fight had begun in much the same manner. *You're just a drunken fool.* Letting the insult about his drinking slide, he set his mug on the table and asked, "Where did you get it? *How* did you get it?"

"That is not important—"

"Not *important?*" Zak interjected. He feared for his sister's safety. *If she's alive.* Raising his voice, he leaned forward and hammered his fist on the table. "Not important to *you,* maybe."

A few men sitting nearby glanced their way at the outburst.

The stranger raised his palms off the table. "Settle down... I'm not the enemy here."

And how the hell would I know that? The man's eyes pleaded with him not to make a scene. Still on edge, Zak leaned back.

"At least you seem to have recuperated from last night. I'm glad I caught you before you started round two. Or is it three?"

Zak clenched his jaw to avoid another outburst. *He might know something about my family, about my sister.*

"My name is Gard," the stranger said, dropping the condescending tone. "I hear you may be seeking information about a fire that happened here a decade or so ago. The fire that wiped out an entire family? *Your* family?"

His nerves and emotions were so raw, he had to make a conscious effort to stay calm. "It wasn't the *fire* that killed my family," Zak corrected.

"So, you know they were murdered. What else?"

"Not much beyond that," Zak admitted. "What's it to you?"

"Let's just say I have my own score to settle."

"With who?" Zak asked.

"That's not important."

"Again, with the *not important* shit? So far, all I'm hearing is that nothing is important." *Hell, this guy gets under my skin!* He managed to keep his temper in check. *I won't learn anything if he walks out.* "Why don't you tell me what *is* important?"

A brief smile crossed the man's lips, then disappeared. "Fair enough." The door creaked open, and he looked that way. "I knew your father when he lived in the capital. I was an agent with the Legiant's Law Squad back then."

"A squader?" This man didn't have the obnoxious, overbearing attitude typical of any squader he'd ever encountered. Arrogant enough, for sure, but a squader? *Unlikely.* "You said my pa lived in the capital?"

Gard nodded. "Yes. And Yes. Your father was a close friend and confidant of the Legiant when he lived in Edyson. I knew him then, a good man. He was appointed as director of the mines here in Southrock—a great honor," he said, pausing to take a drink. "You don't remember living in the capital? You were very young."

Zak shook his head. The man had his attention now. He'd never heard any of this before, not even from his parents.

"I only learned these details recently, myself, of what led to the fire. Several years after your family relocated here, rumors began circulating around the capital. Rumors about shady and unethical activities that traced back to the Legiant. The Legiant was convinced of a leak among his most trusted advisors. It took a year for his spies to track the source. The trail led them to your father."

"Pa?" *Did that make Pa a traitor?* "He didn't… wouldn't…"

"Some good people risked their lives trying to protect him, but ordinary citizens are no match for the Legiant and his ruthless interrogation methods."

Zak stared off. *Pa involved in colony espionage?*

"The Legiant was furious. His squaders were under too much scrutiny at the time and if they were caught, it would be a direct link back to him. So, he hired a bandit clan to deal with your father. The Legiant told these men that your father had a hidden cache of money, and a valuable artifact.

"They sent some low-life, with orders to kill your father and make it look like an accident. Maybe he got greedy and wanted time to search the premises. Or maybe something went wrong with his plan. Who knows? To cover the murders, he started the fire. Your parents were in the cellar, so the worst of the fire burned above them. There is no doubt they were murdered." Gard took another drink.

"A white dove holding a red rose?" Zak asked, though he already knew the answer. "Is that the mark of this bandit clan?"

Gard nodded. "The Dovetails, yes. The man must not've found any money or the artifact, or if he did, it was never turned in. You were marked as the only person who might know your father's secret hiding places. For years after the fire, many were sent to find you—the Legiant's agents, squaders, these bandits, other bounty hunters as well." He smiled, as if to himself. "But whoever protected you did a good job. Even the greediest of bounty hunters eventually stopped looking."

So, Mr. Murfy's concerns were well founded. The Ravens, where he'd been forced to spend his teenage years in seclusion, was a factory town far on the outskirts of the colony—a dreadful place for destitute people with nowhere else to go. Few ever went there on purpose. Aside from the letters that he now knew his uncle never posted, he'd never tried to connect with anyone from his past. Not until now. "Wait. Didn't you say *you* work for the Legiant? Have *you* been looking for me all this time?" Zak squinted in the dim light. *Are his eyes different colors?* Glancing around, he planned a quick escape.

Gard relaxed and leaned back, drink in hand. "Trust me, if I wanted to turn you in, we'd be halfway to the palace dungeons by now." He chugged the rest of the ale in his mug.

Since Zak just arrived in Southrock a couple days ago, that meant Gard had been tracking him before last night. *Maybe even before I came to town?* "Well, I have no idea where the thing you're look—"

The image of Pa's map with the mark above the tack room popped into his head. "...that artifact, or the money, could be. My pa didn't confide in me. I was just a kid."

"You remembered something," Gard accused, leaning forward. "What is it?"

Damn. Zak shrugged. "It's not important."

"Listen," Gard said. "We can work together, or you can go it alone, and I'll just follow you around. You've never noticed me before. Either way, I'll get what I want."

Those words bruised his ego. But what about today? *If he was tailing me this morning, he would've mentioned the forktoe.* Zak changed the subject. "Where'd you get the locket?"

"Ah, the locket," Gard repeated. "I got it from one of the Dovetails. But he wouldn't say where it came from. To be honest, I don't think he knew. It was many years ago. I recognized your family's crest, so I hung onto it."

Zak pulled it out of his pocket and fondled it, wondering whether to trust this man. *Not trust.* That wasn't possible. But *pretending* they were working together would be better than being stalked. Gard watched him, unreadable. *What* aren't *you telling me?*

"It was my sister, Katy's," he said. "You know, there's no proof she actually died in the fire."

The man's expression gave away nothing. "So I've heard."

"Is she alive?" Zak asked.

He shrugged. "I don't know. She might be. If so, she was—is—well hidden.

"Why did you leave?... And *don't* say it's not important."

Gard leaned forward, resting his arms on the table. "I fell out of favor with the Legiant. And I didn't leave on good terms, to say the least. My departure was," he paused, "messy." A cynical grin crossed his face. He finished his ale. "So, you see, we have something in common—we're both wanted men."

"Seems you left out some of the details."

He didn't elaborate.

Tight-lipped sucker. "Is the Legiant the person you need to settle the score with?"

Ignoring the question, Gard asked "What is it you remembered just now?"

"Noth—"

"Don't say *nothing*," Gard interrupted. "I know that isn't true."

Zak had to admit to himself that this man had the advantage over him on many levels—age, experience, stealth, strength, probably honor and integrity as well, if his instincts were on point. But the suspicious, guarded dialogue between them left many questions unanswered, and others unasked. He couldn't bring himself to trust the guy. Once Gard got what he wanted—the artifact, or whatever—what then? *Will he desert me? Or kill me, even?*

"I don't know what you're talking about," Zak said finally.

"So that's how it's going to be, then?"

Zak ignored him, taking another drink.

Without another word, Gard chugged the rest of his ale and left.

He sure likes to leave in a hurry. Fine. Good riddance. He stared at the empty seat across the table, recalling the map and what Gard's story had jogged in his memory.

✳✳✳

One afternoon, Pa came into the barn holding a small bundle, wrapped in a cloth. Ordinarily, Zak would've called out to him, but he acted like he didn't want anyone to see him, as if he were playing hide-and-seek. So, Zak kept quiet, watching from his vantage point up above in the hayloft. Pa disappeared into the tack room, stayed in there for several minutes during which Zak heard some scraping noises, then came out without the package, eyes searching the barn. Zak ducked behind the hay bales so he wouldn't be spotted until Pa left. When he heard the creak… slam of the barnyard gate, he scrambled down the ladder to search the tack room.

***

Zak couldn't have been very old at the time, maybe six or seven. He remembered nothing at all about his tack room search. *Probably because I didn't find anything.* The barn wasn't destroyed in the fire, he knew that, but it may have been torn down or remodeled.

Finishing his ale, he resisted the urge for another and went up to his room.

Monk screeched at him, and he opened the window to let the climber out. The rain alternated between a light sprinkle and short periods of a hard, steady downpour. But the wind had shifted, so it didn't blow into the room like before. The street outside his window was still and quiet.

He looked for a way to sneak out unnoticed. A narrow ledge, just within reach, jutted out from the wall below the window. It looked sturdy enough, and if he inched his way around, he could leap over to the roof of the building next door and make his escape. *If it isn't too slippery from the rain.*

Dousing the light, he sat on the edge of the bed and picked up his travelpack, pulling out the card he'd found in the lockbox. *Could this be the missing artifact?* The durable material was strange—flexible and waterproof, but not indestructible. In the dark, he felt the curious symbol embossed on the card. *Interesting, but valuable?* Putting the card back in he dug out the last of his jerky, and his hand touched the cloth-wrapped talons. *Now those are valuable.*

Setting his pack aside, he took his sister's locket and threaded it onto the chain around his neck. The two lockets clinked together, and he tucked them both underneath his shirt. *Where are you, Katy?*

An hour passed. Without lighting the lantern, he changed into dark clothing. Seeing no one on the street below, he slipped out the window and onto the narrow ledge. Rather than being slippery, as he expected, the rain had soaked the wood through and provided a secure footing. Shuffling his way along the wall and around the corner, he made the easy leap to the roof of the neighboring building. The shadow cast by the two-story inn provided cover as he snuck to the back of the building and peered over the edge into the mud-drenched alley below. A drainage pipe offered an easy, but slippery, descent to the deserted alley.

Being more familiar with the woods than with the town that had changed so much since his youth, he jogged into the trees on the other side of the alley, moving west. He doubted anyone would be out so late at night, especially in the rain, but he kept to the shadows. Gard's revelation about tracking him had his senses heightened.

"Ahhh!" he cried as Monk landed on his shoulder. "Monk! you scared the hell outta me!" Retracing the past few minutes in his head, he realized he'd heard the climber in the trees, but ignored what, to his ears, were just normal woodland sounds. *So much for being alert.*

The rain had let up some, but the ground was wet and sloppy with mud. Arriving at the familiar path that led to his family's farm, he crouched behind a hedgerow to survey the grounds. The barn still stood and, from this distance, appeared the same. The only noises or movement came from farm animals.

Dogs were a concern. Every farm had at least one but most, like the Murfys, had a pack of them. *The rain should help.* And Monk could help distract the dogs if they should venture out. *Assuming he remembers that trick after so long.*

Drawing his dagger, he circled around to the back side of the barn, crept out of the shadows, and snuck across the empty paddock that surrounded most of the barn. The horses were inside their stalls, staying out of the rain.

Entering the barn undisturbed, he made his way to where the tack room had been. It was dark, but he knew from the smell of the place that it wasn't a tack room anymore. He bumped into something near the door. Grain spilled onto the wood floor from the sack he'd just run into.

Hearing the muffled, but distinct sound, the horses started nickering and pawing at the stall doors.

"Eeeek!" Monk screeched.

Zak nearly jumped out of his skin. "Shhh!" Covering the climber's mouth with his free hand, he whispered, making eye contact, "No noise!"

Monk didn't usually react to farm animal noises, at least he didn't used to. Zak stood still, listening. *Just the horses.*

The climber still acted up, jumping from foot to foot on his shoulder, acting so panicky he was afraid to let go of him.

"What's got into you?" he whispered, surveying the dark room again. With his dagger in one hand and Monk's face in the other, he searched for a lantern.

"Need a light?"

Zak let go of Monk, who screeched again and jumped from his shoulder. He whirled around to face the threat, heart in his throat.

A hulking form stood at the door holding an unlit lantern, looking like the grim reaper. The hood of his slicker hid his face in shadow, and if he hadn't spoken, Zak might have attacked, or bolted. But from the smug, know-it-all, condescending tone, he knew the shadowy figure standing in the doorway. *That fobmucking squader.*

"You thought you could shake me so easy?" Gard asked. "You aren't as clever as you think."

Apparently not. Zak plopped onto a sack of grain, waiting for the adrenaline rush to subside.

"Cover that window so we can light this thing," Gard directed. "What're we looking for?"

Zak didn't argue or object to the command. Embarrassed at being bested, he resigned to his fate as the bumbling sidekick, at least for the time being. An empty grain sack served to cover the shuttered window. "I don't know. My pa used to hide things in this room."

Monk returned to his shoulder perch, quiet now. But he kept an eye on Gard.

"Things? What things?" Gard lit the lantern, adjusted it just bright enough to see a few feet, and carried it around the room, inspecting the floorboards, then along the walls.

Gard's tone and manner reminded him of his pa, if the guy wasn't scolding or berating him about something, he was giving pedantic instructions as if he was an idiot that didn't know how to tie his own shoes. "I said, I don't know!" His words echoed in the small room, provoking a sharp glance from the other man. Zak lowered his voice to a harsh whisper. "I saw him carry something in here once, wrapped in a cloth. Maybe it was nothing."

"Anything hidden under the floorboards could get wet," Gard said, exploring the room. "The outside walls can be damaged by animals or weather. That leaves one of these two walls," he indicated the inside walls, "or the ceiling," he said, raising the lantern upward. Setting the lantern down, he rearranged some of the feed bags to climb up for a closer look. "Ah, here we are. Come over here and hold this," he said, handing the lantern to Zak.

Zak saw nothing unusual.

"You see here, where these scuff marks are?" He pointed. "And again, over here?"

"Mm-hmm," Zak did see it now. There were some marks and splinters on both ends of one of the boards above, only notable when compared to all the other joints and gaps in the boards on the ceiling, which were absent of any such marks. Humiliated again, Zak realized he wouldn't have noticed if Gard hadn't pointed it out.

Gard lifted the wood slat then twisted it sideways and rested it on the other boards, revealing a hollow space between the tack room and the loft. Reaching inside, he pulled out a long, narrow, wooden box that just fit through the opening and handed it down to Zak. Replacing the board, he hopped off the pile of bags.

Zak set the lantern down and started to inspect the box.

"No time. We need to go." Dousing the lantern, Gard grabbed the box and tucked it under his arm.

"Hey!" Zak objected, but Gard was already out the door. He followed Gard into the barn and back outside into the paddock. "What, the—" Zak tripped over an unconscious—*or dead?*—man lying next to the barn door.

"Oh," Gard explained, "that's the night watch. Must've been on his rounds. Or maybe he heard you making all that racket and came to investigate. He'll wake up with a hell of a headache. Let's go."

They slipped out of the barn. The rain came down, hard and steady. Dogs started barking, the sound moving in their direction.

"Damn!" Gard said.

"I've got this," Zak said. "Monk, decoy!" he snapped at the climber and pointed toward the baying dogs. Monk sprinted away. *I hope this works.* If not, the dogs would be on them in seconds. The barking escalated, then faded off, moving away from them.

"Now *that's* useful," Gard said. The diversion took the dogs away on a chase, the ruckus also drawing the attention of a few horses who came out of the barn, nickering and prancing around in the muddy paddock.

Zak followed Gard to the hedgerow where he'd hid earlier, then on into the woods, until they were well away from the road. Gard crouched to the ground with his back to the rain, and Zak sat on a nearby rock.

"Listen," Gard said, "we need to get out of here as soon as—" he whirled around, dagger drawn.

Alarmed by Gard's sudden movement, Zak jumped up.

Monk bounded out of the trees nearby, then stopped short, watching Gard. He screeched—a loud, piercing sound.

Gard sheathed his weapon. "That animal is going to get killed if it keeps doing that."

"His name's Monk," Zak said.

Sitting on a nearby log, Monk kept his eyes on Gard until he put away the knife. Then, he relaxed and began picking at his soaking wet fur.

Gard shook his head. "As I said, we need to get out of here. There are curious people lurking about, asking questions." Gard started to pry the box open with his dagger, but Zak grabbed it from him.

"It's a puzzle box, you just have to find the trigger," Zak explained, turning the box around and over, inspecting it.

"No time." Gard snatched the box, dropped it to the ground, and stomped on it. Splinters flew everywhere. From the box remnants, he extracted some papers and a thick stack of money wrapped in a cloth. He handed everything to Zak. "Here, put this in your pack," he ordered.

Zak investigated the contents. Wrapped in the cloth was more money than he'd ever seen all in one place. "Look at all this mon—"

Gard slapped at Zak's hands, and everything fell to the wet ground. "No *time*. Just put it in your pack and let's go."

"Did you *have* to do that? Everything's all muddy now!" Zak griped. He bent over to pick the stuff up, then followed Gard back to town. *I could really use a drink.*

Covering the same route through the woods he'd taken earlier, Gard stopped when they were as close as they could get to the alley behind the inn without being seen. "Wait here." Gard disappeared into the dark for a few minutes, then returned. "Come with me."

Zak followed him to another unconscious man lying on the ground in some bushes. *Really? Another one?*

"This one followed you from the inn. He won't be waking up at all," Gard said. "Take his legs. Help me hide him."

They moved the body farther into the woods then jogged down the alley to the back of the inn.

"Can you have that animal go somewhere until we're out of town?" Gard asked. "The fewer people who see it the better."

"His name's Monk," Zak said again under his breath, giving the climber a gentle pat. He directed him away with a *Go, play!* hand motion.

Instead of taking the alley entrance to the rooms, Gard went to the delivery door of the bar and knocked. The door opened and the bartender stood aside to let them in, closing the door behind them.

"Thanks for your help," Gard said, handing the man a wad of money.

"Just get out of here." The bartender nodded to the corner where he'd stashed Zak's gear.

What? My stuff is here? Zak hustled over to the pile, doing a quick inventory to make sure everything was there. He picked it up, ready to tear into Gard about it, but he was already gone. Instead, he glared at the bartender, who shrugged and opened the hand holding the money.

Zak pulled his flask out of his travelpack. "Can you at least fill this?" he asked. "Surely there is enough there—"

"Sorry, bar's closed." The barkeep shoved him out the door and shut it in his face. Zak suspected Gard had a hand in *that* as well.

The man on duty at the stable dozed in a chair. Gard nudged him with his boot, and he woke with a start. "My apologies sirs," he said, stretching all four limbs.

"We have business in The Ravens and need to get an early start," Gard said. They each handed him their call tickets.

"The Ravens, eh?" He glanced at the tickets. "I don't know why you'd—" he stopped mid-sentence. "I'll go get them mounts."

The man went into the back of the barn and was gone a long while—too long. *What could be taking so long?*

"Come on," Gard said.

He followed Gard into the barn. Empty. *Where'd the guy go?*

"Did you put your real name on that ticket?" Gard asked.

"No," Zak said. "I've been using my uncle's name for years."

"Get your horse, we're leaving."

Zak haltered his gelding, Durka, and led him to the hitching rail, passing Gard who stood in the barn aisle, staring back and forth at two bay horses. "What's wrong?"

"They look alike," Gard said.

"No, they don't. That one has a wider blaze. *That* one has a thinner face and a longer forelo—Wait, are you saying you don't know which one is yours?"

"I have a bay gelding with a blaze," Gard said, sort-of admitting he didn't know *which* of the two bay horses was his.

Zak looked inside each horse's stall. "*This* one's yours." He pointed at the one with the wider blaze and walked off, shaking his head.

They tacked up in a rush. Zak took some extra leather pieces that hung near the barn door on his way out and stashed them in his travelpack.

Gard led them south, toward The Ravens.

Zak stared ahead at the man's dark silhouette. *So, no thanks at all for keeping you from being branded a horse thief?* He hated being ordered around, and he hated the man's infuriating habit of pointing out his mistakes. *And that arrangement with the barkeep? How could he possibly have known how this night would end?*

As they left town, Monk suddenly leaped for Zak's shoulder from a low-hanging branch. Durka took a wild sidestep, and Zak grabbed the horn to keep from falling off. Missing his target, Monk landed on his feet in the middle of the wet road. He screeched his displeasure.

"Serves you right, Monk, Durka's not used to you, yet," Zak scolded.

"Everything okay back there?" Gard turned around.

I'd like to wipe that snarky grin off your face. Zak shifted his saddle back to center. *If only I could get Monk to spook* his *horse.* That thought put him in a better mood.

The one thing that bothered Zak most, though, more than anything—he did *not* want to go back to The Ravens. The years he'd lived there were awful, and if that wasn't enough, the trek out to the far reaches of the colony would take weeks. But as much as he wanted to say something, to raise an objection, to suggest that they go some other direction—*any* other direction—he kept his mouth shut.

Were those men following me? Or him? What else hasn't he told me? Based on Gard's attitude, he knew the former squader—*if that's who he is*—was wary of their unwitting alliance. *He doesn't need me.* But, at least for the time being, Zak needed him. So, he rode on in silence, in the pouring rain, wondering what business the man could possibly have in that dreadful place.

Chapter 8
Zak

Gard stopped his horse in the middle of a bridge and looked past Zak, back toward town. They'd been moving at a moderate pace, and with the heavy rain, all evidence of their passing would be swept away in short order on the hard-packed road.

"Follow me, and be careful," he said. "Leave no sign that we changed course." Exiting the bridge on the far side, he guided the bay gelding down the steep embankment of rocks and gravel.

Monk jumped from behind Zak where he'd been resting and bounded down the slope and over to the stream to get a drink.

Once Gard reached the bottom, Zak took the same rocky route. "Are we not going to The Ravens, then?" he asked, as his horse picked its way down the short, slippery incline.

"No, of course not," Gard said with a chuckle.

What's funny? It was the first time the man had been anything but dead serious.

"What? You don't want to go to The Ravens?" Gard asked.

"Oh." Zak chuckled. "Was it that obvious? I hate that place."

"It is the armpit of the colony, to be sure," Gard agreed. "No, we need to find the Dovetails." His horse jerked its nose toward the stream.

He dismounted and led his horse to the stream for a drink, "Maybe they have the artifact and don't know it. Or maybe they know something about your sister."

Zak stayed on his horse, tossing his canteen to Gard to refill while Durka drank.

After riding through the streambed for a short time, Gard turned north. Once away from the noise of the rushing water, he said, "Their camp is on the other side of the capital, so we'll need to circle back around Southrock. We'll stay off the main road until we're closer to the capital and the traffic picks up."

"I used to hunt and trap in these woods," Zak said, "Spent more daylight hours out here than at home. I can lead the way until we're on the other side."

To his surprise, Gard relinquished the lead to him. Then, he asked, "How'd you know this was my horse?"

Zak assumed he'd forgotten about that. "The other horse had been shod within the past week. I assumed you've been on the road longer than that."

"Huh. Yes."

Monk scampered out of the trees next to them and Durka jumped sideways. Zak reached down and gave the gelding's neck a pat, "You really need to get used to that, boy."

With their proximity to Southrock increasing the risk of being discovered, the next few hours were spent riding in silence. Zak took a wide berth around town, avoiding popular watering holes and hunting sheds scattered about in the woods. It stopped raining, the sun peeked out from behind puffy white clouds, and the air was scented with the mustiness of the rain-soaked ground.

Hours later, Zak couldn't get his mind off his empty flask. After another unsatisfying sip of water, his stomach grumbled. *We'll need to eat.* He pulled his crossbow from its scabbard and carried it across his chest.

A furry quisler vaulted among the trees above, he took aim but didn't shoot. A short while later, a couple of long-eared barrits darted across the meadow as they passed, but he didn't bother with them, either. Gard would keep riding at least until sundown, no doubt. *There's still time.*

At dusk, he heard the familiar *toodle-ooo, toodle-ooo* from a flock of turbeasts, preparing to roost for the night. Zak whistled at Gard to stop, but he kept moving. *Dammit, fobmuck, stop already.* He whistled again. Still Gard didn't stop. Zak didn't want to yell and spook the turbeasts, so he trotted up ahead.

"Hey, hold up, will you? Didn't you hear me?" he asked.

"What, no," Gard said, "what is it? I didn't hear anything."

"Just wait here," Zak said.

"Wait for what?"

Why bother explaining? Zak rode back, hoping the turbeasts hadn't been disturbed. *Idiot.*

Dropping Durka to a walk, he approached the place where he'd heard the noise. They were still there. Monk took his place in the saddle as he dismounted, grabbing the reins to keep the horse still. *Just like old times.* Zak hid behind some bushes, then raised the crossbow and fired. The flock scattered, but his aim was true. He emerged from the brush, claimed his prize, then tied the dead turbeast to his saddle. The whole episode took but a few minutes, and he trotted back to where Gard waited.

"Well, you may be good for something after all," Gard said with a snarky grin. "I haven't eaten since breakfast yesterday."

That night, while Zak prepared and cooked the turbeast, Gard inspected the contents of the box they'd found in the barn. Besides the money, there were some papers with reports and evidence about the Legiant's illicit dealings and unlawful activities.

"I bet this money was for paying off informants," Gard said, skimming through the papers. "This information is too old to pursue now." He tossed the papers into the fire.

Zak watched the papers burn. *Just like our house, more of Pa's hard work going up in flames.*

Gard divided the money into several equal-sized stacks, giving one to Zak. "Don't waste it," he said.

What's that supposed to mean? Zak reached for his travelpack. "Waste it on what?"

Gard shot him a look but didn't explain. He split the other stacks among various compartments in his travelpack. The pack looked ordinary, if somewhat fancier than most, but with hidden pockets crafted to allow just enough room to stash papers or money inside the lining. When Gard finished, Zak inspected the pack. If he hadn't just seen Gard hide the money, he'd never know it was in there. "Clever trick."

"A gift," Gard bragged with a smile, then settled into his bedroll with his back to the fire. He slept almost immediately.

Zak spread out his bedroll, but he wasn't sleepy. He spent some time fashioning a talon sheath using the leather he took from the stable barn. The result wasn't pretty, but it would attach to his belt and keep the sharp end of the talon safely tucked away. *It'll do for now.*

The turbeast wasn't sitting well on his stomach, and his head was splitting. He went for his flask, then remembered it was empty. *Damn!* He glared at Gard's back. The man's snoring didn't help, either.

A short walk away from the campsite soothed his head and gut marginally. He climbed under the blankets and stared up at the stars, thinking of his sister.

Monk soon joined him, curling up in a ball on his chest, and he stroked the climber, waiting for weariness to overtake his discomfort.

The next morning, they continued their off-road trek. It started raining again, and as if the dismal weather wasn't enough to put him in a foul mood, Gard's frequent condescending comments etched at Zak's last nerve. *Does he think I've never traveled on horseback before?*

"Be careful," Gard said, pointing at the trails winding up the slopes ahead of them. "The rain can wash away the path along these steep slopes."

"Thanks for the warning. In all the years I've been hunting and trapping around Southrock and The Ravens, I've never ridden on a trail in the rain."

"I just don't want to have to fish you out of that river down there when your horse loses its footing," Gard said.

They rode single file on the trail. The rain fell in sheets now, and although they were within a couple meters of each other, they had to shout to be heard. "Give me *some* credit," Zak shouted back. "I'm not an idiot."

A crack of thunder erupted above, ending their bickering exchange. The immediate flash of lightning that followed prickled Zak's skin with its electric charge. Durka flinched beneath him.

Gard's horse spooked and reared up, its hind legs sinking in the thick mud. The gelding kicked out to get free, then panicked, bucking and twisting on the narrow path.

Gard fought to get his mount under control.

"Look out!" Zak yelled. The horse skidded close to the steep edge of the trail.

"Settle down." Gard said, then shouted, "Whoa! *Whoa!*"

The horse slipped again, one hoof going over the edge of the cliff this time. Gard attempted to bail, but at the same moment, the horse whirled and staggered, fighting for purchase on the rain-drenched trail. The sudden change of direction launched Gard off, over the ledge, and he tumbled down the embankment toward the river.

Zak jumped off his horse, peering over the edge of the trail. "Gard?!" He watched Gard careen down the steep incline in stops and starts, trying to stop his momentum with extended arms and legs. Every effort offered but a brief reprieve before he started tumbling again.

"Gard!" he yelled again, as his dark form rolled out of sight behind an outcropping of rock. The downpour had subsided enough to allow the faint sound of Gard's groan to reach Zak. He moved up the trail, his eyes followed the sound until he spotted the man on a ledge above the rushing river, stuck in some bushes. *At least he didn't go in the river. Who'd be fishing who out then?*

Monk scampered down the slope in Gard's direction.

Zak led the horses up to where the path widened and tied them to some trees. He untied the ropes from both saddles, looking over his shoulder at the distance Gard had fallen. Even tied together, the two ropes might not be long enough. *I hope this works.*

He stood above Gard's position. *Too far.* Using as little of the rope's length as possible, he secured it to the closest tree, then scaled his way down to Gard, sloshing and skidding on the mucky terrain. It was a quick descent, but he ran out of rope about four meters from where Gard waited, caught in the bushes that saved him from the turbulent waters below.

"Are you okay?"

"I think so, but I'm trapped in this damned tanglevine!" Gard replied. "I lost my axe somewhere on the way down. Do you have a knife?"

"No, but—"

"You didn't bring a knife!?" Gard yelled.

"That's it! Stop treating me like a brainless idiot or I swear I'll climb right back up there and leave you here to rot," Zak said. Before Gard could respond, he added, "Be careful what you say right now, or I'll show you just how serious I am."

Gard's expression was defiant, but at least he kept his mouth shut.

"I have this." Zak held up the forktoe talon.

"Toss it here!"

"It's too sharp. If you catch it wrong…" He whistled for Monk who climbed up from somewhere below. "Take this… to him… down there," he pointed to Gard, and placed the handle of the talon in the climber's hand.

Monk took the talon and pointed it in Gard's direction.

"Yes! Take it to him!" Zak ordered.

Monk screeched in reply, then turned and leaped down the slope. Zak flinched away from the climber's wild swing of the talon, but it grazed his forehead.

"Dammit, Monk!" Zak wiped his forehead. "You could've poked my eye out!" *Just a scratch.*

Landing near Gard, Monk lurched backwards, and the ledge gave way under his feet.

Zak held his breath. *Don't drop it!*

Catching his balance, the climber scurried over to Gard, waving the talon back and forth.

"Give me that. I'll take it from here." he said, grabbing the weapon from the careless animal.

Monk gave Gard what can only be described as a dirty look and scampered up the cliff.

"He doesn't like you," Zak said.

The talon cut through the shrub like a hot knife through butter. After a dozen or so swipes, Gard extracted himself from the tanglevine. His clothes were caked with mud, one spot particularly dark and—*Not mud.*

"That doesn't look good," Zak said, indicating the fresh blood soaking through Gard's shirt.

Gard pulled up his shirt to check it out. All Zak could see from his vantage was a lot of blood. "Must've caught it on my axe or a sharp rock on the way down."

From the gash on his eyebrow, the left side of his face took a blow as well, not much blood, but it was already beginning to bruise and swell. There were other nicks, cuts, and scrapes on his face, neck and arms but the hip injury looked to be the worst of it.

"Can you climb up to where I am? I ran out of rope." Zak asked. He stretched out his hand.

Gard stood, then teetered on the rim of the ledge. "Whoa!" Regaining his balance, he pressed on the wound at his hip.

"Try using the talon as a spike. Make a handhold," Zak suggested.

Gard nodded. Jumping as high as he could on his good leg, he drove the talon deep into the cliff.

"Can't do *that* with a knife," Zak couldn't help making that observation aloud.

Gard scoffed at the boast, then worked his way up the slope. The distance wasn't far but to Zak, the climb seemed to take forever. When Gard was within reach, Zak helped him up until they clung to the side of the cliff beside each other.

They climbed a few more meters side-by-side pointing out hand and footholds to each other along the way.

With enough slack in the rope now, Zak tied the end around Gard's waist, then advanced upwards ahead of him. There were enough natural crevices and vegetation for him to scale the cliff without using the rope, so it hung loose between him and the cliff.

Gard, on the other hand, relied heavily on the rope and the talon. His progress was slow and laborious.

The storm that had subsided to a drizzle when Zak first scaled the cliff, resumed its deluge. Thick, heavy raindrops pounded his back, drenching the rope, and making the ascent more treacherous.

Gard struggled. Each upward advance took more time and effort than the last.

"Doing okay?" Zak called down, not sure Gard heard him over the noise of the storm. "Gard?"

"Fine. Keep… going," he wheezed.

"You don't sound fine," Zak muttered, but not loud enough for Gard to hear. "Almost there!" he said, finding another handhold and pulling himself up.

The rope suddenly broke free and whipped past him, hissing like a snake. Mud splattered into his eyes and debris from above fell around him.

Gard yelped.

Zak made a mad grab for the rope, just as it jerked to an abrupt stop. Rubbing mud from his eyes, he looked up and tugged firmly on the rope. It seemed to be secure now. *But for how long?* Below him, Gard hung onto the rope with both hands with his arms stretched above his head and his back against the cliff.

"What the hell was that!" Gard shouted.

"The rope must've come loose. Can you speed it up? I don't know how long this will hold."

Gard said something, but Zak couldn't make it out. *Better keep your mouth shut.*

Gard turned himself around with some effort and resumed his climb.

Zak scrambled the rest of the way to the top, where he discovered the tree he'd used to secure the rope had uprooted, then lodged itself in some rocks and thick brush at the edge of the cliff. He grabbed the rope and pulled Gard the rest of the way up the slope, then helped him lean against a large boulder while he retrieved the ropes.

"That could've been a disaster!" Zak said, pointing at the uprooted tree.

Monk popped up onto the trail dragging something behind him.

"And here I thought he didn't like you," he said. "Look! He found your axe!" Zak took the axe from the climber and brought it over to Gard.

"Thank you kindly, little one," Gard addressed Monk directly with a mocking bow, then winced, grabbing his side.

Gard's mount still hadn't settled completely, and since the rain had stopped its deluge, they left the horses tied and trudged on up the trail to rest and regroup.

"I could sure use a drink," Zak said, pounding his feet to release some of the mud from his boots. He faced Gard and looked back at the horses who were both acting up now—snorting, shifting, and pawing at the ground.

"You *don't* need a drink. What you need is—" Gard's expression changed from irritated to deadly serious. He stood up, his wide-eyed gaze staring at something behind Zak.

Zak whirled around. A grear stood on the trail ahead—a big one. Monk stood between them facing the two men, oblivious to the danger.

"Monk! Run!" Zak yelled.

The climber turned, squealed, and scurried off into the trees, leaving a trail of excrement in his wake.

The grear roared—a guttural, menacing sound—and plodded toward them.

The two men backed away, putting more distance between them and the beast.

Zak glanced around. There was more space here, near the top of the hill, but not enough to get the horses past the beast.

Especially not with them freaking out like they are. The trail crested up ahead. *No telling what's beyond the ridge.* He glanced back down the trail, the way they had come. *Go back?* The trail was too narrow, and the horses too spooky. And with a grear chasing them? *Bad idea.* They'd end up in the river *with* the horses. *If the grear didn't catch us first.*

"I don't see a way out. What's the plan?" Zak asked.

"You draw its attention, and I'll flank it from the other side."

"So, I'm the bait? And you're going to do what? Flank it from *what* side? There's no room!"

"Right. You need to make room so I can get around it."

Zak glared at him. *Is he serious?*

"Well, *I* can't distract it, I'm injured." Gard barked. "If we attack it head on together, it'll kill us both." The squader used that unemotional, soldier-voice Zak had come to despise. "Do you have a better plan?"

He's serious. "What are you going to do?" Zak asked.

"I don't know," Gard said. He had his axe in one hand, and still held the talon in the other. "You'll need something longer than that," he said, eying Zak's knife. "Go get my short sword."

Zak ran to Gard's horse, dancing around it to avoid getting stomped on, and returned with Gard's sword. It'd been a while since his training, and he'd only held a real sword a couple of times. It felt good in his hand, and along with the adrenaline rush it produced, helped subdue his fear, if only by a small degree.

The grear stood about three meters tall—a hairy beast with huge, rock-hard arms the size of tree trunks.

This is insane. Zak thought a trip down the cliff right now might not be such a bad idea.

The grear took another hulking step forward.

"Now!" Gard commanded.

Zak hesitated. *I'll go when I'm good and ready.* Taking a deep breath, he tightened his grip on the sword and charged.

He recalled what he knew about grears. Not very intelligent, they relied on their immense bulk and strength in a fight. They had a high tolerance for pain and didn't back down once engaged. They were known to ignore serious injuries, even amputations. This would be a fight to the death. *Hopefully its death, not mine.*

Zak ran directly at the animal, screaming and waving his arms.

The grear trudged toward him.

Just as it took a swipe with its massive arm, Zak came to a dead stop. Its arm whizzed by in front of him, so close he felt the breeze as it passed. While the grear was off balance, he slashed its paw twice with the sword.

With a roar, it pulled its arm back in pain, then charged at him again.

Zak dove over a sweeping paw.

The creature's arm whacked against the side of the hill. Jagged rocks flew in all directions.

Zak ran at it again, slicing its leg and side, then darted away, out of reach.

The grear howled, facing him again.

Zak noticed Gard moving around to the other side of the animal, closing in.

A clap of thunder and flash of lightning distracted the grear. It changed direction, going after Gard.

"Hey! Ugly! Over here!" Zak shouted, jumping up and down and waving his arms. But it ignored him and kept advancing on Gard.

The grear raised its arm again, this time aiming for Gard.

Gard rolled out of the way.

The beast's paw landed on a large rock behind him and shattered it into pebbles. It raised an arm for another strike.

Gard was no match for the grear, not after his barrel ride down the cliff. And nothing could survive a direct hit from one of those massive arms. *Need a diversion.* Zak ran at the beast, dove between its giant legs and slashed the sword up through its underside, ripping open a huge gash.

The grear wailed at the fresh injury and raised a leg to stomp him.

Zak scrambled away, barely escaping the crushing foot. But it caught him with a grand swipe of its arm that sent him flying into a nearby tree.

The impact knocked the wind out of him, and he closed his eyes to focus on taking his next breath. And the next. Four or five gulps of air later, his head felt like it might explode. He opened his eyes. The world was upside down. *No. It's me that's upside down.* His leg had caught in a tanglevine, and he hung high up in the tree.

Struggling to free himself made it worse. The vine tightened around his leg with each movement. Looking down, or up to him, he saw the sword lying next to his hat at the base of the tree. *Not good.*

Monk screeched and jumped into the tree, pulling at the vine.

"Get out of here Monk! Go!" Zak yelled, but the climber didn't listen.

The grear closed in, moving as if in slow motion, one sluggish step after another.

From his upside-down perspective, Zak saw Gard flying out of nowhere, axe raised over his head. He drove the axe into the grear's skull.

The creature howled, falling forward into the tree that had Zak trapped.

The branch broke, and the vines loosened from around Zak's leg. He fell from the tree, sliding down the beast's back and landing hard, upside down, in the mud. Stumbling to his feet, he darted away, tripping a few times in his haste to put distance between him and the grear.

Gard tugged at the axe, trying to free it from where it wedged deep in the animal's skull.

The grear stood up.

Gard let go of the axe and fell to the ground with a muddy splash, clambering away on hands and feet to stand beside Zak.

"What can survive a wound like that?" Gard asked.

Zak shrugged. "Apparently, a grear."

"I'm used to… battling… people, not… wild animals." Gard said as he pressed a hand against his side.

"It will die eventually, but it's going to be more dangerous and unpredictable until then," Zak said, realizing Gard was spent. "Give me the talon. We need to finish it off."

He charged at the giant. Spinning away from its sweeping paw, he stabbed the talon deep in its side.

The creature groaned and swatted downward with its arm—a feeble effort.

Skidding again between its legs, Zak jumped up to face it from behind.

Dazed and confused, the animal followed his movement, bending over to look between its own legs. Gard's axe fell out of its head, and a stream of blood gushed onto the ground.

Zak jabbed the talon into the creature's bulbous eye and twisted.

The grear lurched up, howling. It staggered forward and tripped over the fallen tree. Blind and bleeding, unable to regain its footing, it toppled over the tree and down the cliff on the other side.

The ground trembled with each impact as the grear tumbled downward. A splash, heard even above the pounding rain, marked its passage into the waters of the rapid, swollen river.

Monk screeched. A tree near the cliff's edge had fallen over, and he was stuck under some branches.

Zak pulled him out of the debris. "Gotcha!"

The tree's roots gave way, sucking the ground around Zak's feet down the cliff. He yelped, reaching out for something that wasn't part of the tree.

Gard caught the hood of his slicker and pulled him away from the edge of the collapsing cliff. The two fell backwards, landing in the mud, drenched, exhausted, and gasping for air. *Well, that was fun.*

Zak stood first. Gard was covered in mud from head to toe. "Do I look as bad as you?" he asked, helping Gard to his feet.

"Worse," Gard said, laughing. "Ow." He grabbed his side.

Stomping his feet and brushing at his clothes didn't help. The gooey, clay-like mud stuck to Zak, and it was everywhere. *Even in places it shouldn't be.* The unexpected discomfort had him walking bowlegged for a few steps. He tried shaking his arms, but it was no use. *A shower would be nice.* He picked up his hat and Gard's sword, then extended his arms in the pouring rain, hoping to wash away the worst of it.

Gard nodded at Monk. "How is it *he's* not slimy with this stuff?"

As if in response, the climber shook his soaked body all over and what little mud he wore flew off his coat.

"Maybe because he wasn't rolling around in it," Zak said.

The horses were still agitated from the commotion, so they led them on foot up the trail. The downhill side was less treacherous, and they found a rocky outcropping that would keep them both out of the rain for the night. It would be crowded with all their gear, but at least they would stay dry.

Zak unsaddled the horses and hobbled them in a small clearing nearby where they could graze. Noticing a pile of fresh grear scat, he looked around in the fading light. *Hope that was the only one.* He returned to Gard, who'd stripped off his muddy clothes and had a med kit out, dressing his wound.

"It must be my axe that did this," he said, showing Zak the gash. "Cut's too clean to be a rock."

Zak noticed the wound on the other side of Gard's stomach—a dark pink scar. "What happened there?" he asked. "

"Oh, that." Gard shrugged. He moistened a cloth with water that dripped from above. "Something to do with that score I have to settle."

Zak tossed his hat inside and stripped. Standing naked in the rain, he washed the worst of the mud from his body.

Gard picked up the rough-looking ball cap and checked it out.

"It was my pa's," Zak said, and grinned. "When I first started wearing it, I did it just to irritate my aunt. She *hated* it." He shivered. "Whoo. Cold." Crossing his arms, he rubbed them, more for warmth than to get clean.

Gard tossed him a towel.

"After a while I got to knowing why Pa wore it all the time," he said. "It's comfortable. Keeps the sun," he held a palm out, "and the rain, off my head. And it's practically indestructible."

Gard set the cap aside. "Listen, kid…"

Zak stiffened. *Here we go.* Gard's expression reminded him of when Pa was about to scold him for something he did wrong.

"Zak," the squader corrected. "I know you think I'm patronizing. Maybe so, but that's just me. Don't take it personal." He finished bandaging the injury. "You can hold your own in a fight, I'll give you that." He winced as he put salve on his wound.

"I... uhhh... thank you?" Zak said, "I think?"

Gard laughed. "Ow!" he pressed a hand on the newly-dressed wound. "You see, there I go. Can't even give a man a decent compliment." Shaking his head, he waved his hand with flair, palm up. "Thank you, Zak, for saving my life back there, and for having my back, even though I can be a real ass."

"Now, was that so hard?" Zak climbed inside, out of the rain, and nodded his head toward Monk. "And it wasn't just me."

Gard looked at the climber who was busy licking his genitals, then laid back on his bedroll. "Don't push it."

Zak dressed, then pulled out some of the leftover turbeast he'd cooked to a crisp last night, tossing some to Gard. "It's all we've got." Chewing on the charred meat, he watched the rain pour off the top of the ledge. It wasn't long before Gard's snores echoed through their little hideaway.

He laughed, remembering how Pa used to snore. *Maybe even louder.* After years of camping together, the noise had become somewhat of a comfort to him. He'd wake up in the dark, in the middle of the night, hear the familiar sound, then drift off to sleep again.

Gard's snoring got louder with each breath. *I don't think I can get used to this.* Zak scooted into his bedroll and wrapped his arms around his head to cover his ears. *I need a drink.* Eventually, exhaustion won out and he slept.

The rain had stopped sometime during the night, and Zak woke to a bright, crisp morning.

Gard sighed, moaned and groaned as they packed their gear.

"Sore this morning?" Zak asked.

"Let's head for the main road," Gard said, ignoring the question. "We should be close enough to the capital now. I could use a good meal. And a real bed."

They rode alongside the swollen river until it wound away to the north. Conversations overheard when they stopped at a tavern for lunch reminded them of Landing Day, only a few weeks away.

"That explains the traffic," Gard said. "Suppliers are bringing things in for the holiday."

They spent the next few nights at one of the many roadhouses that also served meals, a refreshing change from the rainy days on the trail. The bed rest and hot meals seemed to help speed Gard's recovery. By the time they reached the outskirts of the city, he'd stopped groaning every time he mounted or dismounted.

The road had widened with each klick, graduating from dirt to the hard-packed gravel they rode on now. As they rounded a bend, Edyson City came into view. Wood-framed buildings were sprinkled here and there, but most of the structures inside and outside the gates were constructed of the flexclay panels manufactured in The Ravens—flat sheets of durable material produced by mixing clay with the flexsand from the mine in Southrock. With so much of the reddish-toned flexclay, most of it unpainted, Zak had to look up at the position of the sun to be convinced it was midday and not sunset.

Below them, the road became an even wider, stone-paved avenue as it wound its way through the tenements and businesses of Outer Southgate. The buildings were tall and short, wide and narrow, with less and less space between them the closer they came to the city gates. The streets were crowded with people, bustling about on some business or other. *And the noise!* Horses, wagons, carriages, people talking, people shouting, dogs barking, children playing. Zak wondered how anyone ever got used to all this racket.

The gates were open and the sentries on duty seemed to pay little attention to the travelers flooding back and forth. Monk drew a few stares and comments, but he wasn't too much of a spectacle.

Zak followed Gard as he fell in with the flow of riders and vehicles passing through the gates into the colony of Edyson's capital city.

Chapter 9
Zak

"I'll be out late. We'll get supplies in the morning," Gard said, tossing his travelpack onto the bed closest to the door.

Zak crossed to the window, throwing his pack onto the far bed as he went. The corner room Gard had rented near Westgate was cleaner than the last two places, but the view wasn't much different. *Buildings are a little taller, maybe.* The alley was dark and quiet now that the sun had set.

Monk joined him at the window.

"Keep that climber out of sight," Gard ordered.

Zak gave the climber's head a pat. "His name's Monk," he said between gritted teeth. *For the umpteenth time.*

Gard's expression, reflected in the window, shot like an arrow into his back. *Same to you, fobmuck.* The man's casual, sometimes even likeable, disposition from the trail had evaporated when they entered the city. No more idle conversation. Even his posture had changed, stiff and tense, eyes shifting side-to-side, watching for God-knows-what.

Just go already. The chance to be free of Gard's criticism and judging eyes, even for a short time, dangled, like a carrot to a hungry pony.

"Get something to eat and stay out of trouble," the squader ordered, then went out the door.

"Get something to eat and stay out of trouble," Zak mocked to Monk in an imitation of Gard's gruff voice.

Monk cocked his head sideways and squeaked.

"I know." Zak said. "He can be *such* a jerk."

The capital had a city-wide water and sewer system, and their room included a private bath with hot water and a shower, a luxury Zak hadn't enjoyed since leaving his uncle's place. Washing the days of trail dirt and grime down the drain, he wrapped a towel around his waist then cleaned his dirty clothes in the sink.

"Your turn," he said to Monk. He glanced at Gard's pack on the bed, with a fleeting thought to clean his dirty clothes, too. *Better not. Somehow, someway, the good deed would turn out bad for me.* He patted the surface of the water in the washbasin. "Come on, Monk."

This time, the climber jumped into the warm water and splashed around with glee.

"Don't forget to use the soap," Zak said, tossing the bar into the sink.

Thankful to have some time to himself, he dressed in the only clean, dry clothes he had left and opened the window.

Hearing the window open, Monk ran soaking wet across the beds, jumping onto the sill. Zak dried him with his towel, noticing a few patches of fur missing. He plucked at his coat near one of the patches. It didn't seem to be falling out. "You're looking a bit rangy, buddy. Don't be scratching so much."

Monk ignored him and bounded out the window onto the eave below. He'd been skittish since they entered the gates, and glanced around nervously, then began scratching and biting at his fur. *He won't go far.*

Zak found his flask and went downstairs to have dinner.

The pub was packed, not an empty table in sight. Seated patrons waved and called out to the frenzied servers. *It'll take forever to get a drink in here.* After six days of putting up with Gard and a wad of money to spend, he didn't want to wait, taking a newly vacated seat at the bar.

The first shot of whiskey went down in one gulp, smooth and satisfying, and he pushed the empty glass back to the bartender for another. Digging the flask out of his pocket, he waved it in the air and set it on the bar. "This too."

Zak felt himself relax for the first time in days as the ever-present need for a drink melted away—an infernal itch finally scratched. The drink warmed his bones and soothed his mind. His thoughts wandered in that mellow, pacified state until they snagged on his traveling companion's annoying split personalities. The tolerable, sometimes even pleasant, person who shared stories about his travels around the colony, versus the grouchy, condescending squader whose only words were barked orders. *Like a mad dog.* He chuckled. *Gard-dog.*

Whenever the man took on his *Gard-dog* persona, Zak found himself following his orders without objection. Strange, since he hated being bossed around. But with Gard, he'd settled into the subordinate role, and it felt as natural as... *as this drink in my hand.*

Zak savored the burn as the liquid slid down his throat and into his gut. When he put the glass down, it tipped over and spilled onto the scarred, wooden bar top. He stared at the beads of amber, sad he'd wasted it. So sad. And angry. Angry at himself for not doing more to find his sister. *Why did I let so many years go by?*

Maybe Gard-dog will find her. That'd be nice. Maybe he already did?

The bartender interrupted his hopeful thought. "Another?"

"Ummm, yeah," he replied, wondering how many he'd had already. *You're just a drunken fool.* "Make that an ale," he said. *Damn. Maybe I should order some food.* He looked around, but the tables were still packed. *I'm not hungry anyway.*

One of the servers came up to the bar with a tray of empty glasses—an older woman. *But good looking.* Listening to her recite her drink order to the bartender, his eyes drifted to her ample breasts bulging from the bodice of a tight-fitting blouse. Another itch that needs scratching. *I'd like to bury my face in tho—*

"What're you looking at?" the woman asked, her expression more annoyed than intrigued.

Zak grinned, then burped. *Oops!*

Grey eyes rolled upwards as she retrieved the tray of drink refills, then left to serve her thirsty customers.

He raised his mug to her back, watching the curve of her body, the sway of her hips, the firm ass. His own ass squirmed of its own accord on the stool. *How long has it been, anyway?*

He shook his head, pushing those thoughts away. *Her hair reminds me of...* his thoughts suddenly shifted to his sister. *Katy.* If she's still alive, and he'd taken so long to find her? *Will she ever forgive me?* He doubted he'd ever forgive himself.

He turned back around to the bar and ordered another drink.

His head wilted between his shoulders, and he thought of the soft bed in his room. He glanced in the direction of the staircase. Enticing, but the distance required more action than he could muster. *I'll just rest here a moment.* His head sagged to the bar top.

"Hey! Boy!" he felt a smack on the back of his head.

"Ow!" Zak lifted his head and rubbed at the sting, looking around in confusion. *Where...? Oh, yeah...* He raised the mug with a wobbly hand to the blurry face in front of him. "Another—"

"No more. Time for you to go."

"Okay. Okay. No need to get nasty." Zak turned on the stool and bumped into the man next to him, who spilled his drink. "Kid! What the hell?!" the man slurred.

Obviously drunk.

"You owe me a drink," the man said.

"The hell I do," Zak argued. "You're the one who spilled it, not me. And I'm not a kid!"

The man slugged him in the face. Zak dodged the next hit, and the other guy landed on the ground when his fist didn't connect with anything.

"Break it up, you two," the bartender yelled. "You. Get outta here," he said, nodding to Zak.

"I didn't start it," Zak argued.

The bartender gave him a stern look.

Stay out of trouble... The thought squelched the angry reply on his tongue. Instead, he raised his hands in the air and walked away.

"Wait! You forgot something." The bartender came to the end of the counter, holding out his flask.

Putting the flask in his pocket, Zak walked to the stairway, being careful not to bump into anyone else. Holding tight to the handrail, he climbed slowly, one step at a time. *These stairs are steep.* At the top of the second flight, he let go of the handrail, missed the last step, and lost his balance. His arms flapped a couple of times, and he tumbled all the way down to the landing.

"Who the hell pushed me!?" he shouted, squinting to get the landing above in focus. *Where the hell'd they go?* He didn't see anyone. *Fobmuck.*

Cautious and deliberate, he climbed again, then limped to his room and fell onto the bed...

Zak bolted upright in the bed, wiping cold water from his face. *What the—?* The bright shaft of sunlight from the window burned his eyes, and he raised his arm to block the glare.

Gard held an empty glass. "Get up!" he yelled. "You look like hell. What happened?"

Too loud, Gard-dog! "Ahhh, ow," Zak groaned as he rolled his legs over the side of the bed. "Ohhh... I... don't... I don't remember."

"You don't *remember*? Did you kill someone?"

"No!" *Is he serious? Killed someone?*

"I didn't kill anyone." He cradled his head in his hands.

"How do you know? You said you don't remember," Gard barked.

I've never killed anyone. The miners were back, hammering away in his head. "I'd remember *that*," he said.

"So, you remember what you didn't do, but not what you did? Get up. We're leaving."

I hate Gard-dog. Obscure memories of last night clouded Zak's brain. Sitting at the bar... a drunk man next to him... a woman's breasts... a fist in the face... His face hurt. His head hurt. He wanted to vomit. He wanted to lay back down on the bed and wait for the pain to go away. But Gard stood there, staring at him, as if he'd attack if Zak made one wrong move. *It's a wonder he's not growling at me.*

He summoned the will to stand. "Ow!" Pain in his left ankle shot up to his knee, and he dropped back down to the bed.

Gard made a noise that sounded much like a growl.

Zak pulled up his pant leg to investigate the source of the pain and discovered a long scrape on his shin, scabbed over now, above a bruised and swollen ankle. *Huh. How'd I get this?*

Spurred on by Gard's impatient hovering, he hobbled to the bathroom. The mirror gave evidence of his fist-in-the-face memory. Gently patting the puffy, swollen cheek, he tried to recall who hit him, or why. *No idea.* The eye above it, along with most of that side of his face, had turned various shades of yellow, purple and black. *But you should see the other guy,* he joked to himself and smiled, "Ow," he muttered. *No smiling. And no shave.*

Gard started blabbering on about how Zak drank too much, how much trouble he could get into, how his actions drew attention. *Blah, blah, blah. Shut up Gard-dog!* After splashing water on his face, he changed into one of the shirts hanging in the bathroom, noticing more scrapes and bruises on his arms and torso. *What the—?* A brief attempt to remember how that happened just made his head hurt.

Collecting the rest of his clothes from the bathroom, he stuffed them into his travelpack. *Where's my...?* He searched the bed and then the floor around it. "Have you seen—"

When he looked up, Gard was in the bathroom, holding his flask upside down, pouring the whiskey down the drain.

"Hey!" Zak complained.

Gard threw the empty flask out the open window and walked out of the room.

Fobmuck. Monk jumped onto his shoulder, and Zak picked up his hat, limping out on the bad ankle.

The streets were crowded as they made their way to the stable. His stomach reminded him he hadn't eaten dinner last night, and he stopped at a street vendor to get breakfast.

Their horses stood at the hitching rail beside the barn, already saddled. Each carried an extra-large, fully loaded saddlebag.

Zak followed Gard into the stable office, wandering around while Gard settled the account. An array of wanted posters decorated one entire wall—dozens of them, some tattered and faded as if they'd been hanging there for decades, others crisp and new, with every age and condition in between. *They must never take these down.* The display created a bizarre kind of wallpaper, so random and garish it could have been intentional.

Each poster included a picture or written description of the criminal, along with an account of the crime, and the reward. The largest poster, a recent one from the look of it, offering a reward more than triple any of the others. A dangerous, deranged man was wanted for going on a rampage at a school and killing forty-three civilians and nine squaders. The sketch depicted a clean-shaven man with shoulder-length, dark hair and a square jaw.

Gard finished his business and noticed him inspecting the posters. "Don't believe everything you read," he said, and pointed to one of the tattered, aged posters near the door as he exited.

Zak read the poster, an old one... *Zakary Bancroft...* he covered his audible reaction by faking a cough. The faded, outdated picture was horribly inaccurate and useless as a means of identification, even for fourteen-year-old Zak. The charge read... *for the arson of the Bancroft residence in Southrock resulting in the deaths of James, Angela, and Katrina Bancroft.*

He limped out of the office. Sure, he'd been told more than once men were looking for him, but the idea had been too absurd to take seriously. *Until now.* The poster made it very real.

"Coming?" The question jarred Zak from his contemplation, and Gard's irritated expression made him hasten his step, hop-skipping over to the horses.

Ouch! Putting weight on his foot in the stirrup was too painful, so he circled around to mount from the other side. With both feet dangling out of the stirrups, he followed behind Gard toward the city gates.

As they rode through Outer Westgate, Zak called out to Gard, "Did you find out anything? About my sister?"

Gard held up to ride abreast. "Nothing about you or your sister," he said. "Nothing new, anyway. But I did find out that the leader of the Dovetails comes here often. And he always stays at the palace."

They split apart as a carriage clattered by on the stone pavement.

"I was told he meets often, and in private, with the Legiant," Gard said after the carriage passed. "And he's coming here for Landing Day. Which means this clan leader, probably with his most trusted men, will be away from camp when we get there."

"But aren't they the ones with the information we need?" Zak asked.

"Not really," Gard replied. "Men like the Dovetails don't keep secrets. Too many windbags who like to boast. There'll be more than a few who know something, either because they were involved, or because they've heard others talk about it."

Zak hunched over in the saddle. *Not much to go on.* With hopes of finding his sister dashed, he felt trounced and beaten. *Why'd he have to toss out my whiskey?*

They traveled on the main road to Baytown, leaving the crowded streets of the city behind. Rolling foothills, lush and green from the recent rains, rose to the west, in the shadow of the

Broadwood Mountains. With every roadside inn full this close to Edyson, they spent their nights sleeping somewhere off the road.

Mostly, they rode in silence. Between his aching head and a stomach that threatened to heave with every movement the horse made, Zak didn't feel much like conversation anyway. The agonizing symptoms he'd been enduring, combined with the beating he'd taken last night with no memory of why or how, had him thinking that maybe he shouldn't drink so much. *Damned if I'd ever admit that to him, though.* He ate a sparse dinner, having no appetite and a splitting headache.

The next few days were monotonous, one day much like the next. As the time and distance from the city lengthened, Gard's alter-ego returned—the tolerable, somewhat congenial, travel companion who shared stories of the places he'd been and people he'd met around the colony. Not that he was particularly chatty, or that his stories gave away anything of his past or his reasons for being on the run, but at least he wasn't ordering Zak around or giving him riding lessons.

The few times they'd stopped at an inn to have a meal or spend the night had been grueling for Zak, and if it hadn't been for Gard's patronizing vigilance, he certainly would've given in to the temptation to drink. Gard didn't say anything—he didn't have to. He'd just sit there, nursing his one ale through an entire meal while Zak salivated in envious silence, drinking his vile soda. *Infuriating.*

By the fourth night on the road, the worst of his symptoms had subsided, although his craving for a drink continued to intensify with each new day. Without Gard's constant presence, and the fact that he had nothing more sinister than a canteen filled with water on him, he couldn't have resisted. Zak wondered how long it would take for that relentless need to go away. *And here I am thinking about it again.*

At least he should be able to sleep tonight without tossing and turning in constant discomfort. If only... He watched as Gard walked off to where the horses were hobbled. *You think maybe you could not snore tonight?*

A few minutes later Gard returned, carrying a sword in a worn, leather saddle-scabbard. "I assume you know how to use one of these?" he asked, tossing the weapon to Zak. "I mean, besides to poke an angry grear?"

Zak caught the sword mid-air, eying Gard.

Drawing the weapon from its scabbard, he inspected the blade. "Ummm, yes. My uncle made me learn." He dropped the scabbard and made a few swipes with the sword, feeling its weight and balance. "I got pretty good at it. But it's been a while. Never had a real sword, though, just the practice kind."

"It's yours," Gard said, then crawled into his bedroll with his back to the fire.

"Really?" Zak moved around, recalling those lessons from years ago. He swiped and parried, testing the feel of the weapon and practicing different techniques that came to him in a rush, as if his last lesson were but weeks past, not years. "Thanks!"

The squader gave a nonchalant, backward wave of his hand.

Zak stopped his swordplay and stared at Gard's back. *He's been carrying this extra sword since we left the city.* He replaced the sword in its scabbard. *I bet he meant to give it to me that morning, but then... he came to the room and I...* Swallowing his shame at that thought, he crawled into his bedroll, staring up at the stars. *It's a wonder he'll even talk to me.*

Monk crawled onto his chest and Zak stroked him, rubbing at the bare patches of fur, much to the climber's delight. Moments later, Gard's rumbling staccato resonated from across the fading campfire. Zak smiled, thinking back to that first sleepless night on the trail. So much had happened since then. He had to admit that if anyone could help him find his sister, and rescue her, Gard could. It was much later when he finally buried his head under the blankets to go to sleep.

A dewy mist blanketed the ground the next morning, moist air giving way to a muggy stillness around midday. At sundown they entered Meadowick—the largest town between Edyson and Baytown. Several roadside inns and other businesses that catered to travelers lined both sides of the main road, including restaurants, taverns, and a public stable. They boarded the horses, then went in search of an inn where they could get a room.

About halfway through town, Zak spotted a carriage in front of a fancy restaurant. "Look," he said, pointing across the road at a large sleeper-carriage with the Dovetail emblem painted on the side.

"I thought we might cross paths with them," Gard said.

"Should we—" Zak started to walk across the road.

"No," Gard interrupted, stopping him. "We'll have better luck dealing with the ones they left behind."

The next morning, they left Meadowick, traveling south on the main road, then east into the foothills. "We need to be on the alert now," Gard said, late one afternoon. They'd climbed out of the foothills into the shadow of the mountains and rode through a forest, lush with vegetation and tall, broad trees. "The Dovetails' cave is in this area somewhere. They'll have lookouts or patrols scouting around."

"Monk! Go. Watch," Zak said to the climber who dozed behind him. The climber woke and vaulted into a tree, then darted off ahead of them.

The rest of that day passed without seeing or hearing anyone. After dark, they stopped to camp in a thick grove of trees.

"No fire," Gard said. "We'll split the watch."

Gard took the first watch. The nights were cooler now that they were up in the foothills, and Zak snuggled into his bedroll, adding an extra blanket.

At some unknown hour in the middle of the night, Gard woke him for his watch. *I'd be awake, anyway,* he thought as he listened to Gard's monotonous wheezing.

"Where is the Dovetails' camp?" Zak asked the next morning.

"Don't know exactly," Gard admitted. "Only that it is in this general vicinity, in a complex of caves at the base of a mountain."

Zak sent Monk off to play sentry again, and the two men spread out, looking for signs of foot or horse traffic.

"What about that one?" Zak suggested, pointing at a boulder-riddled peak. "That mountain looks like it might have some caves in it."

Gard nodded, and they rode in that direction, stopping in the cover of some trees when they came close. A narrow trail had been cut into a steep incline and wound its way up towards the rocky mountain Zak had spotted.

"I don't like the looks of it," Gard said. "There's no cover at all on that trail. Let's circle around and see if we can find another way up."

Keeping to the trees, they rode around checking out other possible passages that would get them nearer to the base of the mountain. Settling on one approach that appeared to have the best cover, they settled in a secluded place nearby to wait for nightfall.

With no trail to follow, they'd have to pick their way in the dark through and around trees and thick brush, but with both moons out tonight it shouldn't be too treacherous.

"Dammit!" Zak jumped up, drawing his sword. Looking. Listening.

"What is it?" Gard drew also and pulled his axe.

"Monk just shouted a warning." He pointed, his adrenaline pumping. "Over there!"

Three armed men jogged toward them on foot.

"Go!" Gard yelled, and they ran for the horses.

A man and woman stepped out from behind the horses, swords drawn.

"Going somewhere?" the woman asked.

Two more men approached from the opposite direction. They were surrounded. *We're dead.*

"We don't want no trouble," Gard said. "We're just up here doing some hunting."

"Don't look like no hunters I ever seen," said one of the three men from the first group who'd just joined them. "What do you think, Blade?"

"Nope. Not hunters, I'd wager."

Zak spoke up, a plan formulating. "We just need to speak the truth," he said to Gard. "Actually, me and my friend, Garrett here, we heard about the Dovetails and were hoping we could join up."

"Why?" the first man asked.

"Well, we kinda got into some trou—"

"Zane, keep your mouth shut," Gard said, elbowing Zak in the ribs.

The man gave Gard a dirty look, "You were saying, Zane?"

"Well, we just need a safe place to hide out. We're real good fighters." He shrugged an apology to Gard.

"Boss said we need recruits," one of the men said.

"So he did," Blade said. "Bring them in. We'll hold them till the boss gets back from the city."

After being relieved of their weapons and gear, their hands were tied behind their backs. The first man led the group with Blade at his side, then the captives, each with an armed man on either side. The others followed behind, leading the two horses.

Zak congratulated himself as they were escorted to the base of the mountain he'd pointed out. Not only did he identify their hideout, but his quick thinking kept them from getting killed, at least for the time being.

They came to a small clearing that backed up to the side of the mountain. An array of caves of different shapes and sizes dotted the hillside. A few of the cave entrances had rope ladders dangling above or below them, but most had well-worn steps or paths leading to them, either from the clearing below, or from the mouth of another cave.

The horses were taken to the stables at the far end of the clearing. Four of the men escorted them to the largest of the cave entrances, a spacious cavern that appeared to be a public gathering place. Oil lanterns hung throughout the area occupied by a couple dozen men and women. The smell of food being prepared in an open kitchen area near the far wall filled the cavern.

Zak and Gard were led through a series of wood platforms and steps. Far in the back of the main cavern, a small cavity had been converted into a lockup cell. Another prisoner, a woman, sat on the floor, leaning against the back wall. Her green eyes watched as Blade unlocked the cell, untied their hands and shoved them inside.

"Here you go, Apri. Maybe you'll have more luck getting what you want, what you *neeeed*, from these two," Blade said, grinning at the woman.

The other men laughed.

"You two will stay locked up till the boss gets back," Blade said. "Be glad we're needing recruits, or you'd be dead already. Your cell mate, there, she's waiting for him, too, but her fate will be less…" he grinned at the woman again, "fortunate."

The others murmured agreement. Blade replaced the key on a peg hanging near the entrance as the four men exited.

The woman at the back of the cell still hadn't moved. Zak met her eyes. Their alluring greenish hue seemed to contrast with the challenging defiance of her stare. *Yikes! She's a prickly one.* He looked away, uncomfortable with the unabashed scrutiny.

A few rickety cots decorated the cell, one apparently being used by the woman, plus some dusty, tattered blankets. Pebbles and small stones littered the sandy floor… *and what is that awful smell?* In the far corner by the door, he spied the chamber pot. He covered his nose with the back of his hand.

Chapter 10
Zak

"They come to change it once a day," the woman said, noticing Zak's reaction. "Sometimes not even then."

"Always at the same time?" Gard asked, surveying everything inside and outside the cell, tugging and twisting on every bar.

"More or less, usually late in day when they bring food," she replied in an odd accent. "Forget about escaping. I am here three weeks. There is no way out." She stood and stretched.

The slightly built woman wore clothes that were decidedly masculine, and she moved like a nimble dancer, athletic and muscular, as if every motion were practiced and intentional. Her smooth skin seemed unnaturally pale, as if its pigments hungered for sunlight. Sparkly amber specks in her green eyes added a piercing intensity to every expression, to every look she shot his way. Her broad, prominent nose accentuated her features, giving her a somewhat captivating appeal. Zak had never seen, or heard, anyone even remotely like her.

Gard raised an eyebrow and faced the woman. "Is that so?"

"It is," she said, with a matter-of-fact expression that left no room for doubt.

Turning to inspect the cell lock, Zak grinned. *Take that, Gard-dog!* The mechanism and hinges looked strong and secure, and he saw nothing around that could be used for picking or prying at the lock.

Gard faced the woman, closed hand on heart, with a slight nod of his head, the standard Edyson greeting. "I am Gard, and this is Zak."

Zak mimicked the habitual greeting.

"I meant no disrespect, I assure you." Gard said. "You are from Ararat?" Zak had never heard of the place.

"Few know of Ararat," she said, lifting an eyebrow. "I am Apri."

"An unfortunate place to meet," Gard said, resuming his inspection. "We must find a way to escape."

"I will help any way I can," she said. "As that esh, Blade, said, my fate is set. If you can escape, I know these caves, I can get out. Also, I can help retrieve belongings they may have taken from you."

"Okay. Agreed," Gard said, "we work together."

"Wait, she's coming with us?" Zak asked.

"You have problem with this?"

"Uhhh…" Her intense, green-eyed gaze confounded him.

"Of course, he doesn't have a problem with it, right Zak?" Gard slapped Zak on the shoulder jarring him out of the trance.

"No," he said. "Not at all." He grinned. Suddenly warming to the idea of having a buffer, and an attractive one at that, between him and Gard.

Gard and the woman spent the next hour discussing their situation. Apri—*strange name*—explained the meal schedule, and her own attempts to escape, while Gard made comments and asked questions. Zak sat and listened, intrigued by the woman's odd accent, deep and guttural, sounding at times as if she had something caught in her throat that she couldn't quite clear. They spoke only about the Dovetails, the caves, and escape options. Neither shared information about why they were locked up or anything related to their respective personal situations.

Gard ran out of questions and had no escape ideas that she hadn't already tried, or at least considered. They fell silent.

"What did that guy mean about you getting what you need from us?" Zak asked.

"Yes," Gard said. "What *did* he mean by that?"

Apri's face turned red. "Ach!" Sitting on the bed, her hands hid her face, then she dropped them and looked down at her lap. "My last effort to escape," she said. "Poor Samuel."

Gard laughed.

"What'd I miss?" Zak asked.

"She tried to seduce him."

Apri's lips turned up in a brief, almost imperceptible smile. "At *that*, I succeeded," she said, then told them how she got this poor kid Samuel all hot and bothered, then knocked him out, only to have the key fly from his pocket and out of her reach.

Gard laughed again. "How'd you get him to take the key off the peg?"

She didn't laugh. "It was not difficult. Men are—" She didn't finish the thought, her eyes locked with Gard's and Zak sensed some kind of weird, silent exchange between them. Apri broke the contact first and looked at the exit. "Since then, only women, or one of Damian's boys, come here."

"Damian's boys?" Zak asked.

A squeal sounded from the doorway. Monk scrambled into the cell room, jumping up and down in glee.

"Monk!" Zak opened his arms. The climber squeezed through the bars, launching into his chest.

"You have climber?" Apri's reaction to Monk was different than most. She seemed pleased, delighted even.

"*A* climber," Zak said, feeling compelled to correct her speech. "I wouldn't say I have him. More like he has me," he massaged Monk's ears as he talked, "or we have each other?"

Apri laughed, a loud noise that echoed through the small cell room. "That makes sense." She approached Zak, lifting a finger for Monk to inspect before petting him. "He must have found an unguarded opening, there are many places he could get into caves," she said, "and climbers are common around here. Even if he were seen, he would be ignored, or chased away. What happened to his arm?"

"Don't know. He was like that when I found him."

To Monk she said, "You can get us out, little one, yes?" she said.

"What? No. He's not that smart," Zak said. "Pretty dumb, actually."

"He is smarter than you think," Apri said.

"How could you know that?" It bothered Zak that she'd think to know Monk better than him. "Watch," he said, pointing to the key hanging near the door. "Go get the key, Monk," he said in the training voice he used when giving commands to the climber.

Monk jumped down and cocked his head to the side, looking over to where Zak pointed.

Gard joined them. "Maybe he can do it? He seems to be listening, and he did bring that talon to me on the cliff."

Monk looked at Zak, then at the cell opening, "Go on Monk," he pointed at the key again.

Monk crept from the cell toward the exit. About halfway there, he stopped and looked back at Zak.

"Go on, get the key." Zak encouraged.

Monk bounded out the exit. "Come back," Zak shouted, whistling to the climber.

Monk bounded back in and through the cell bars, jumping on Zak.

Gard plopped onto the cot with a loud *harrumph* noise.

"See," Zak said. "Told you. He's not that smart."

"He is smarter than you think," Apri repeated. "But now is not best time. *The* best time," she said before Zak spoke up.

Zak rolled his eyes and sat on another cot.

Apri sat next to him, paying attention only to Monk, "Isn't that right, Monk," she said, "you are a very smart boy." She talked to and doted on the climber until she coaxed him over onto her own lap.

"He doesn't usually take to strangers," Zak said. "Actually, now that I think about it, he's never paid much attention to anyone else." He smiled at a long-ago memory. "Except our vet, he liked her a lot."

Apri inspected the bare patches on Monk's coat. "What happens with his fur? It comes out."

"I don't know, he keeps scratching at it," Zak said.

"Stupid animal," Gard muttered from the other cot.

Zak told Apri the story of how he met Monk and some of their history together. After that, the cell was quiet, aside from Apri's occasional soft prattle to the climber.

Monk screeched.

"Food comes," Apri said. "It is early today." She shoved the chamber pot as far out from the access slot as she could. "They take no chances."

"Hey, I've got an idea," Gard said. "Maybe if it's one of Damian's *boys?*" He nodded toward Zak, raising his eyebrows.

Apri laughed again, loud and boisterous, appraising Zak up and down. "You know," she said, "it may work. We should at least try, no?" She lay on the cot facing the wall, hiding Monk with her body.

Zak shook his head, confused.

The shuffle of footsteps announced someone's approach. Gard and Zak positioned themselves between Apri and the exit. A young man with a thin build and hair dyed purple, pranced into the room carrying a canteen, a tray of food and three clean chamber pots.

"Oh, my, who have we here?" the kid said in a high-pitched whine. "Hel*lo*, there, and what is *your* name?" He ogled Zak, much like Apri had done only moments before.

Gard choke-laughed.

Zak understood now.

"Oh, and look at you, getting all embarrassed," the kid said. "Aren't you just the bee's knees?" He made a lewd gesture with his tongue.

True to Apri's account of the exchange process, the newcomer placed the empty chamber pots on the floor near the exit, then the canteen and the full tray of food outside the opening at the opposite end of the cell, pushing them just within reach. One of them would have to lie on the floor and stretch to pull them into the cell.

"Scrreee…" Apri muffled Monk's squeal.

"What in hell's name is that noise?" the kid asked, trying to see around them at Apri lying on the bed.

"She's been making that noise since we got here," Gard said. "Whining and whimpering like a child. Don't you have somewhere else you can put us?"

Zak had to stifle a laugh. "Yes, please?" he begged, stepping to the bars and trying to act flirty. "It's very annoying."

"I sure as hell got somewhere I'd like to put *you*," he said to Zak, making another vulgar gesture. But he didn't come near the cell. "Sorry, boys, there ain't nowhere else."

He picked up the near-full chamber pot, and its contents sloshed over the rim. With a disgusted shriek, he gripped it with both hands. "I hate this job." he said, eyes glued to the pot. "There's extra food on the tray. Make it last. It's Landing Day. Big party going on tonight. You won't likely be seeing anyone at all tomorrow."

Purple-head carried the pot out at arm's length, flat-walking to avoid more spillage.

Gard chuckled. "Nice try, Zak. Appreciate the effort, sad as it was. But he wasn't coming anywhere near us."

"If you do not push bowl out far enough, they will not exchange it," Apri said, in between her chattering to Monk.

She spoke to Monk as she would to a small child, short sentences, easy words. Zak did the same sometimes, but the climber reacted differently to her. He bobbed his head, tilting it this way and that, making little squeaks, nods and changes of expression in response to her words.

It's almost like he knows what she's saying. Zak shook his head. *No. That's ridiculous.* He'd never been an observer, watching someone else have a conversation with Monk. *It's just my imagination.*

Gard pulled the food tray into the cell, and he and Zak started eating.

"Would you like to help?" Apri asked Monk. *Head bob.* "Let me show you." *Head tilt.* She carried Monk over to the cell door.

"Did he ever see you use key?" she asked Zak.

"*A* key. And yes," he mumbled, his mouth full of food.

She addressed Monk again, "We must open door," motioning to the cell door. She used a turn-key motion, then pointed to the lock saying, "Key. We need key. To open door."

Head tilt, screech, head bob.

Apri repeated the key motion and instructions several times.

Monk bounced up and down.

"No." She shook her head, then clasped his tiny hand in hers, calming him.

She can't know what he's thinking. "You're wasting your time," Zak told her.

"Shhh!" Apri scowled at him.

Raising his hands in surrender, he returned to his meal.

She repeated the key motion, using the same words over and over to the climber. After a minute or so, she sent him off.

Monk went through the cell bars and scampered over toward the exit, just like before, stopping to look at Apri a few times on the way. But this time he didn't exit, he stopped in front of the key, and looked up at it.

"Yes!" Apri shouted, clapping her hands, "Yes!" She looked at Zak, nodding toward Monk.

"Yes, Monk," he added, understanding the silent request. He set aside his food and joined her at the bars. "Good boy!"

Gard stopped eating, watching the exchange.

Monk jumped up. The single key lay flush against the wall, too high for him to grab. A couple of times, he touched it, and the key moved a little, but it wouldn't come off the hook.

"Dammit!" Gard's voice echoed in the cell room.

The sudden outburst spooked Monk, and he scampered out the exit.

Apri groaned, scowling at Gard.

Zak whistled, and the climber returned, wide eyes on Gard.

Apri spoke to him again, "Chair, Monk," she pointed to a three-legged stool that sat in the far corner, away from the door.

Head tilt.

"Give it up," Zak said.

Head bob, head tilt.

"No!" Gard said, "Leave them be! We have no other options. This has to work."

"Shhh!" Apri scowled at Gard. "It's alright, Monk," she said, distracting him from another flight attempt.

"Sorry," Gard apologized, then mouthed the words again to Zak. *This has to work.*

After another silent warning to Gard, Apri continued addressing the climber, "See chair? Use chair." She pointed at the stool and made a pushing motion with her hands. *Head tilt.* Monk moved toward the stool, then hesitated.

"Yes!" Zak and Apri said at once. "Use chair." Apri added.

Head bob. Monk scampered to the stool, got behind it and started pushing it to the other side of the room.

Gard commented, in a whisper this time "C'mon boy."

Monk had trouble pushing the heavy stool, especially difficult with only one arm. It kept falling over on the sandy, uneven ground. Zak and Apri voiced their support whenever he stopped. After getting it halfway across the floor, he seemed ready to give up.

Head scratch. Head tilt.

Their praise and encouragement escalated. "Don't give up, little buddy," Zak said.

Monk moved around to the other side of the stool and, after some inspection, grabbed one leg and dragged it the rest of the way to the entrance, placing it against the wall underneath the key. He climbed onto the stool. *Head bob.*

The three in the cell clapped and praised the climber.

It still took a few jumps, but the key was much closer, and he finally knocked it off the peg. Picking it up from the floor, he handed it to Apri through the cell bars.

She held the key in front of her, "You see, smarter than you think!" Handing the key to Zak, she made a big fuss over Monk, praising and thanking him for his success.

Zak opened the cell door.

"Wait!" She went back into the cell and started gathering small stones from the floor.

Now what? Already she's a problem. She arranged the stones on her cot and covered them with a blanket. *What the hell is she doing?*

"Good idea. Could buy us more time." Gard said. Following her lead, he placed sand and rocks on another cot and laid a blanket on top.

Zak figured it out and joined them, getting more rocks from outside the cell. When they finished, it sort of looked like people slept on the cots. *As long as you don't look too close.*

Apri grabbed food from the tray on the way out. "This way," she muttered with her mouth full.

Zak closed and locked the cell, smiling as he hung the key back on its peg. *They'll never figure out how we escaped.* "Right, buddy?" he said, with a pat for Monk who rode on his shoulder.

Monk stood, responding with a little *squeak-screech.*

The sound of musicians tuning instruments came from the direction of the cave entrance. Apri led them in the opposite direction, deeper into the cave. Widely spaced lanterns served more to guide the direction of travel than to light their way. The pathway varied, first a narrow path, then down to the sandy floor of a wide cave, then up to a one-way ledge and down to a wider, rocky trail.

"Few venture this far back, but be alert," Apri warned. "Everyone will be going to the party. We must *avoid* any who come this way," she emphasized the word *avoid* by stopping and turning around to face them. "We do not want anyone to come looking for them."

They continued on without incident, deeper into the cave, until Apri stopped at the end of a long footbridge suspended high above the cavern floor. "We cross here to other side," she said.

Zak stated the obvious, "It's too dark to see if anyone's coming."

"There's no other way across?" Gard asked.

"Only other way is too close to entrance," Apri replied.

"Okay then, we take our chances," Gard said.

Apri knelt, touching the rungs of the footbridge. She must've felt a vibration because she motioned for them to follow her up the path, away from the bridge. They hid in the shadows, behind an outcropping of rock, and soon heard voices coming from the bridge. The group exited the bridge, their voices trailing off in the direction of the entrance.

Returning to the bridge, Apri repeated the vibration test, then stepped onto it. The way was tricky. If they moved too fast the bridge rocked and swayed, making too much noise. Too slow escalated the risk of getting caught. She set a moderate pace and they followed, matching strides to keep the bridge sway and noise to a minimum. As they neared the other side, Zak heard more voices approaching the bridge.

Apri froze.

"Monk! Decoy!" Zak ordered to the climber, pointing in the direction of the voices.

Monk bounded off the bridge, turning toward the sound, and Apri launched into a full run.

Zak kept pace, listening to the commotion caused by Monk's antics.

The diversion was enough to get them off the bridge undetected. Apri led them up the trail, and they hid in the shadows.

The group discussed the encounter as they walked onto the bridge. "…one of them damn climbers..."

"How'd it get in here?" another asked.

"Who knows," the first man said. "Stupid pests. If you ask me, they sh…" Their voices faded away.

Zak wanted to yell out, *They're smarter than you think, fobmuck!* Just then, Monk came around the corner of their hiding place and jumped onto his chest. "Good job," he whispered, rubbing the climber's ears.

"There will be more people on this side," Apri said. "A few places we will need to go one by one. This is first. I will lead. When you lose sight of me, wait short time, then next one follows."

She left them, going past the bridge in the general direction of the cave entrance. They continued their stealthy passage from one hiding place to another, backtracking as necessary to avoid others on the pathway.

As they passed by another bridge that crossed to the opposite side of the cavern, Zak could just see the orange glow of the setting sun outside the wide mouth of the entrance. Apri took a side route off to the right, grabbed a lantern from a wall peg and darted around a corner into a secluded alcove.

She handed the lantern to Gard and crouched down, drawing a map in the sand. "We are here. Supply cave is here," she said. "It will be guarded. We do not want—"

"Is someone in here?" a man's voice echoed from the entrance to their hiding place. And their only exit. "Hello?"

Apri grabbed Zak by the shoulders and pulled him against her, positioning herself flat against the wall. Facing him, she grabbed his hips and shoved him back and forth against her. Zak caught on and went with the motion, his body blocking the man's view of Apri from the entrance.

Gard dimmed the lantern.

As the man stepped into the alcove, Apri made a whimpering noise and said, "That's it… ohhh… yeah…"

"Get out," Gard said as the man entered, "room's taken." Then, he raised his voice. "Hurry up, you two. I paid good money."

"You'll get your turn, big boy" Apri said in a soft, high-pitched voice.

Zak continued the humping, digging his face into Apri's neck and making fake sex noises he hoped were convincing enough to fool the intruder. He couldn't prevent the other, not so fake, reaction to their ruse. He tried to think of something to stop it, but it was hopeless. *How long has it been, anyway?*

The man held up his hands, "Okay! Sorry!" he laughed. "Didn't mean to interrupt! Happy Landing Day!" He turned around and walked back out.

Zak and Apri stopped moving but continued making the noises until they were sure he was gone.

"That was close," Gard said.

Zak still leaned against Apri. She shoved him away with both hands.

"Sorry, couldn't help it," he said with a grin.

"I should not speak so big," she said.

Big? Zak chuckled at the misuse of the word. "Loud," he corrected. Her voice did have a deep, resounding quality, even the tone she used now wasn't exactly quiet, although it didn't echo like before.

"Supply cave will have guard." She glanced at Zak. "*A* guard. But night shift just started. None will notice if we take him out."

She crouched to the floor again and finished drawing the map and explaining the entrance and layout of the supply cave. They discussed their strategy for getting past the guard, then exited the alcove.

Zak handed Monk to Apri and approached the guard at the supply cave.

"Who are you?"

"Name's Zane. I'm kinda new around here," Zak said. "Jannik sent me to get more wine for the party. Didn't he tell you?"

"Nobody told me nothing, as usual," the man said, standing to fish the ring of keys from his belt. He found the right key and inserted it into the lock.

Zak stood next to him at the door. "I guess you're gonna miss the party, then?"

"Yeah, I drew the short str—"

Gard came from behind and bashed the back of the man's head with a rock then dragged him to the chair, positioning him so it looked like he was asleep or passed out.

Gard turned the key and entered first. The contents of their packs had been dumped out onto a table and he started picking through it to separate his things from Zak's. "They took the money, but the rest, even our weapons, are still… What's this? Where did this come from?" He asked, holding the strange card Zak had found in the lockbox at the fort.

Zak grabbed the card and the other things of his from the table and stuffed everything into his pack. "It's nothing. I don't know what it is. I've had it a long time. A good luck charm." He doubted Gard would be fooled by his rambling explanation.

Apri came in, interrupting their discussion. "You found your gear? It should all be there, or most of it anyway. Damian is strict about stealing. Anyone who takes property without permission is punished. Informants are richly rewarded," she explained. She grabbed a short sword and a travelpack that hung on the wall. After a quick glance around the room, she grabbed a strange-looking vest that hung on another wall.

Relieved at the chance to ignore Gard, Zak walked to Apri to check out the vest. "Very unusual. What's this made of?" He rubbed the material between his fingers. The plates were dense and harder than leather, but lightweight. Pieces were stitched together in an odd, haphazard pattern.

"Tandorus hide." Backing away from him, she shrugged into it. It fit snugly around her torso.

"You have a tandorus-hide vest?" Gard approached her then, examining the strange material for himself. Zak noticed she didn't back away from *him*.

"My father is a tanner," she explained. "I made it myself from discarded scraps of hide." After affixing a sheath from her pack around the scabbard belt, she put it on and sheathed the sword. Opening the pack again, she pulled out an odd serpentine-shaped dagger.

"And a Rabukhan steel kris?" Gard exhaled a low whistle.

"It was gift," she said, handing it to Gard for a closer look. She grabbed a pack and started stuffing it with gear.

Gard returned the dagger and stuffed his own gear back into his pack.

"In here," she directed.

They followed her into a smaller alcove used for food storage and filled their packs with dry rations.

"Let's go." She hurried out without another word, taking a lantern from the table at the last. She didn't wait for them to follow.

"Stick with her. She doesn't need us anymore, but we need her to get out of here," Gard said, and rushed out to follow their guide.

Apri quickened her pace to a jog, retracing their inbound route. Music and laughter echoed through the cave, indicating the party had begun in earnest. She chose speed over stealth this time, and they followed her in single file without stopping until they got to the footbridge. After a brief check for movement, she leapt onto it. On the other side, she turned to the left, away from the cave entrance, slowing the pace as the way became more treacherous—dark and narrow, and slick in some spots. She lit the lantern, holding it in front of her.

"Let climber lead," she said.

"What?" Zak wasn't sure he heard her right.

"Let climber lead," she repeated. "He knows way to get out."

"You don't know the way?" Zak asked, "I thought you said you knew this place?"

He turned around to look at Gard.

Gard shrugged.

No support there. "Monk, go. Out. Get out," he said.

Monk took off, running in front of Apri.

"The air... it is fresh. There are exits back here," Apri said. "This is safer bet. We try this first."

The air did smell fresh rather than dank and musty, and Zak knew that meant there were places that led to the outside. But whether they'd find anything large enough and within reach was another story. "But maybe only climber-sized," he grumbled. *If this takes too long...* "We could get trapped back here."

Monk screeched with glee, then scrambled to the right and disappeared. They caught up to him at the opening, which must've been the way he came in.

"See!" The hole was much too small for them to use. "We should turn back. This is taking too long."

"No, keep going," Gard said. "This is just one place. There must be others."

Fobmucking Gard-dog. Zak called Monk back and coaxed him to lead them further on, deeper into the dark cave.

They passed a few more too-small cracks and openings until they came to one that looked big enough to crawl through. But it was high on the wall—more than three meters straight up from where they stood on the cave floor from the looks of it.

Apri stopped. "That looks big enough," she said.

"How will we get up there?" Zak asked. "Look, even Monk knows he can't scale that wall."

Monk sat in the middle of the path ahead watching them, having paid no attention to this particular opening.

Apri took off her pack and pulled out a length of rope. "Do you have more?" Gard gave her his rope and she tied the two pieces together, coiled it up, and threw it over her shoulder. "We can reach."

Gard stood next to the wall, and Zak realized what they planned. "Wait a minute," he said. "She could take off as soon as she climbs out."

"I could." Apri climbed up on Gard's shoulders like a circus acrobat. "But I will not."

"Her pack and her weapons are still here," Gard said. "She's not going anywhere."

"But you said—" Gard's glare told him to keep his mouth shut.

"I cannot reach," she said. Her hands rested on the sides of the opening, but she couldn't get enough grip to pull herself up. She looked down at Gard. "I need taller."

"Stand on my hands," Gard said to Apri, opening his hands at his shoulders, palms up.

Apri moved her feet, one at a time, to Gard's hands. He tested her weight for a few seconds then pushed up, giving her the extra height needed to climb out of the hole.

Zak watched the bottom of her boots disappear and sighed. *Will she or won't she?*

He saw Gard glance at Apri's gear on the ground, and knew he was thinking the same thing.

Chapter 11
Apri

Apri lifted herself through the opening into the moonlit night. *Freedom!* She took a moment to breathe in the cool mountain air and survey her surroundings. To think that only yesterday there'd been no hope of escape.

The closest trees were a short distance away, down a rocky incline. Slipping and sliding down the slope, she secured the rope to the nearest tree that looked strong enough to hold Gard's weight, then climbed back to the opening to check the length that remained. *Not enough.*

Next to the opening, she saw a crack between some rocks and kicked at the boulders on either side of it. *Might work.* Scrambling down to the tree again, she untied the rope, then found a branch to use as a wedge.

"You still there?" Gard shouted.

"Yes, couple more minutes," she replied, tying one end of the rope to the branch.

Even though Gard had defended her, she knew he'd be just as concerned about her leaving them stranded as Zak. The thought had crossed her mind, but only for an instant when they exited the supply cave. *So why do I stay?* True, without them she would still be rotting in that cell, but it was not like her to let an obligation overrule her better judgment. Yet, she had dismissed the idea of ditching them before they'd crossed the bridge. *At least for now.* She wouldn't leave them stranded down there.

Wedging the rope between the rocks, she braced the branch crosswise against the other side and tossed the loose end down into the opening.

"Test before you climb," she called down to them. The rope went taut and slack a few times and held firm.

"Monk, let's go." Apri heard Zak's invitation to the climber, and moments later, Monk popped out of the opening and scurried into the trees.

Zak squeezed through the opening next, and she worried it might be too small for Gard.

Poking his head into the hole, Zak called out to Gard, "You'd better strip down. It's gonna be a tight fit."

"Got it," he replied. "Sending up the gear next."

After four loads of packs and weapons, Gard came up, reaching both arms through the opening first. It took some twisting, wiggling, and contortion, to get his whole body through, but a few scrapes, bruises, and garment-tears later, he climbed out. Apri estimated it'd already taken about two hours to get this far, and they weren't free yet.

They suited up and reorganized their gear while Apri briefed them on their next objective. "Stable is on courtyard level below cave entrance," she explained. "I know not how many will be on duty tonight with party happening." She shrugged into her travelpack and buckled the front clasp. "Follow me."

The trek downhill to the barn was precarious—steep and rocky with loose pebbles and debris that slid out from underfoot without warning. After one falling rockslide that, to her relief, caused no alarm, she slowed the pace, testing each step before proceeding.

Other than the snorting and shuffling of horses, the barn was quiet as they approached from the back. Zak sent Monk off into the woods, then snuck around for a covert inspection of the barn while Gard and Apri waited.

"One man on duty," he reported upon returning.

"Okay, let's go," Gard said, leading them around to the right.

"Wait," Apri cautioned, holding a finger to her lips.

A woman's voice called out, "…muel? …Samuel, are you there?"

"In here," a man's voice came from inside the stable, then from the barn door. "Vicky? What're you doing here?"

"I heard this was your punishment for… that episode with the Aratian bitch."

"Oh god!" Apri whispered, leaning her back against the barn.

Gard chuckled, "Round two," he said.

"I brought this," the woman said.

"I *am* thirsty," Samuel replied.

"I'm so tired of hearing about how that bitch seduced you, as if she had some kind of magical powers."

Apri groaned, closing her eyes. *Poor Samuel!* When she opened her eyes, Gard and Zak were both grinning at her. "I am pleased to humor you," she muttered.

The woman walked into the stable, but they could still hear the conversation from their hiding place on the other side of the wall. "Tonight, Samuel, I'm gonna show you some real magic. You'll be forgetting all about her."

"Okay," Gard said, his expression serious now. "Here's the plan. We wait for them to get naked…" To his credit, he explained the plan without even cracking a smile.

Zak was not so discreet. He could not *stop* grinning. "Good plan," he said, raising an eyebrow at Apri.

Apri glared at him. But with his goofy expression, she couldn't keep a straight face. One corner of her lip curled upwards. "Agreed."

When the noise from inside shifted from words to moans and sighs, Gard said, "Now."

Sword drawn, Apri entered the barn, listening. She crept around a corner, following the sex sounds to one of the stalls with the top door open. The bottom half was closed but not latched.

Peeking over the door, she saw Samuel lying on a blanket that had been tossed on top of the bedding. The woman, Vicky, gyrated on top of him. Both were naked.

Apri pulled the door open.

"Holy shit!" Samuel yelled, pushing the woman off him.

"What the h—" The woman grabbed at the blanket to cover herself but couldn't wrest it out from under Samuel. She tried using some of the bedding straw instead.

Apri almost laughed aloud at the feeble attempt. Her feet stood on the clothes they'd discarded near the stall door.

"Hello, Samuel," she said, gesturing at the woman with her sword. "And… Vicky, is it?" She gave the woman a derisive grin. "I am the Aratian bitch. Nice to meet you."

The young woman couldn't be one of Damian's 'tails, or even a recruit. She shook with fear, eyes wide, her face and neck red. *Must be a servant.* Her hands attempted to cover her nakedness, but with no more success than before. Samuel covered his lower body with the blanket, gazing at Apri with undisguised adoration. *Poor Samuel.*

Apri called out, "Clear!"

Gard and Zak rushed in with ropes.

Vicky shrieked, scrambling to hide behind Samuel.

Zak started toward the girl.

Zak, really? Apri didn't think it a good idea for him to—

Gard reached out a hand to stop him. "I'll take her."

Vicky's eyes went wide with fear as Gard approached her, "No!" she cried.

Apri threw the girl's dress to him.

"Put it on," Gard ordered, tossing the dress at her.

While Zak bound Samuel, the girl tossed the dress over her head, frantically struggling to find the armholes and poke her head through the top.

Gard tied Vicky's hands, then bound the two captives together, back-to-back, gagging their mouths with cloth rags—dirty rags, from the look of them. Then the two men left the stall to get their horses.

"I am sorry, Samuel," Apri said, kneeling next to him. "If I am here when Damian returns, he will kill me. Prey for one of his vile hunting games, no doubt." She read understanding in his eyes, then gave him a peck on the cheek.

"You will take care of our Samuel, yes?" she said to Vicky. The girl nodded, her eyes wide as saucers. "He is a good man."

Apri stopped at the door and faced them. "Damian will not be too angry with you, Samuel," she told him. "At least two men should be on duty here tonight." *Not one sex-obsessed adolescent.* She shut the stall doors and walked back into the barn.

Inhaling deeply, she took in the smell of grain, musty old wood, manure and urine. Although she'd been given a private room in Damian's quarters and lived in reasonable comfort during her time here, she'd been no less a prisoner. Being in the barn now, without another person hovering around, making sure she behaved, reminded her again how much she missed her freedom.

"Dega!" she called out.

A throaty nicker sounded from a stall at the other end of the barn. The big, beautiful, blaze-adorned head of her chestnut mare popped out from a stall. Dega whinnied a loud greeting, pounding her hoof against the wooden door.

As she passed by the men leading their horses to the hitching rail, she asked Gard, "Are you attached to that gelding?"

"No," Zak said, "He definitely is not."

"You should take another. That one is injured." She pointed to a fresh cut and swelling on the horse's hock.

Gard inspected the wound on his mount's hind leg, then scanned the barn with a perplexed expression. Most of the horses had their heads out, watching their activity. With the Dovetails in the caves enjoying the night's festivities, few stalls were empty.

"You better pick one for him," Zak suggested.

Apri pointed to a big buckskin gelding, the one Kendall usually chose when they rode together. "That one."

Dega pawed at the door, and Apri jogged to her stall. From the dried sweat on the mare's back, she'd obviously been ridden, but she doubted anyone would choose her as a mount more than once. Dega could be an uncomfortable and challenging ride, especially for a person who sat a horse like they rode in a carriage, lethargic and immobile, expecting the horse to do all the work.

Leading Dega to the hitching rail, she found her saddle—its Aratian design making it easily distinguishable from the rest—and began tacking up. She finished at about the same time as Gard and mounted, situating herself in the familiar, comfortable seat.

Gard passed by her to take the lead, a sly grin on his face. "I do believe you've scarred that boy for life."

"Poor Samuel," she said to herself, taking up the rear behind Zak.

Music and laughter echoed from the mouth of the cave above, the party still going strong. As they exited the stable yard, Monk jumped from a tree to land on the rump of Zak's horse, startling Dega. Zak's mount took little notice of the extra passenger.

Apri laughed, a sound amplified by the pure joy of leaving the caves behind her. "You need to get used to that, Degajan," she said, stroking the mare's mane. "I bet he does it a lot."

"All the time," Zak acknowledged.

"Imagine them trying to discover how we got out!" she said to Zak's back. "Monk is good companion to have. His decoy trick saved us. You taught him that?"

Zak turned to face her. "Yep, a long time ago, actually." He rode off, following Gard at a brisk trot.

Gard took the well-worn trail toward Edyson. Odin lit up the night sky, but with so many tall trees around, it was too dark to risk moving any faster than a trot on the debris-riddled trail. Just as Apri began to question his choice of the most open and direct route for their escape, he stopped.

"We leave the trail here," he said. "Don't follow me. Choose a spot to exit the trail that won't leave a trace."

He cued his horse to jump over a fallen tree on the right, Zak exited next, and she followed from a different place. Once they were off the trail, Gard changed direction, leading them south.

They kept moving but at a slower pace, having to pick their way through the forest. Neither Gard nor Zak spoke, to her or to each other. Apri understood the need for quiet when they were near the caves, but it had been hours with no sign of pursuit. *Do they always ride in silence?* She dismissed that notion, sensing a tension between them that mounted with each klick like a tanned hide being stretched so thin it threatened to rip at any moment.

Not wanting to be the first to speak, Apri rode along behind them, staring at their backs. It was a grueling challenge for her to be quiet. She knew nothing about them, and the unspoken friction only added to the many questions she wanted to ask—about them, their relationship, about Edyson, where they were headed, the list went on and on. Her thoughts often drifted to Tina. *I need to find her.*

Several more hours passed, and she found herself making up conversations in her head to keep from talking. *So, why do you two travel together?* Her inner voice changed to a deep, gruff imitation of Gard. *We are secret lovers, running from our wives.* She coughed to cover a laugh. Of course, they were not gay. Zak had made his preference clear when they were in the alcove. And Gard? *Definitely not gay.*

Zak reminded her of many of the men, *boys*, she'd known growing up. Not that he looked anything like them, with his taller and leaner frame. *And that boyish face!* She imagined he could avoid shaving for a month and have nothing to show for it than downy stubble. But he had the same cocky, immature attitude as most of the boys she'd known. Insecure, too, and easily offended.

Yet the was something endearing about him, a familiarity she couldn't explain, and she'd already grown quite fond of him.

When she'd grabbed him in the caves to play that charade, it'd been uncomfortable for him. At first. And then it got too comfortable. Her smile faded, recalling her own discomfort. She'd felt awkward and embarrassed with Gard there, watching them.

Gard. She'd never met anyone like him before—tough, strong, and used to being in charge. *Except, perhaps, old Rrazmik.* At their first meeting back in the cell, there'd been an instant when their eyes locked, and in that brief exchange, she'd felt a sensation unlike any other. She couldn't explain it, nor could she dismiss it. That feeling, that man... *He is the reason I stay.* She stared at Gard's broad back. *Who are you?*

They rode through the night without a rest, taking only short breaks to stretch their legs and water the horses. Apri envied Monk, who had dozed behind Zak's saddle until dawn, then woke to cavort about in the trees without a care. Their pace didn't improve much in the daylight. With no trail to follow, they moved at a sluggish pace, and even had to backtrack a couple of times to find an easier, safer route.

By late afternoon, the two men still hadn't spoken more than a few words. Apri had to consciously focus on staying silent, and worried that in her weary state she'd make a sarcastic or insensitive comment that would start a feud. They'd come to a part of the woods that'd been harvested for lumber. Recently planted saplings, at least two for each raw stump of the broad, sawed-off trees competed for sunlight with the taller, older growth. Riding single file, the horses followed a narrow animal track by instinct more than by rider direction.

One... two... three... fifteen... twenty-one... Apri counted tree stumps while humming a tune to keep herself from dozing off.

Zak stopped his horse. "Where'd you hear that song?" He sounded angry.

Apri pulled on the reins but not quickly enough, and her horse ran into Zak's. Durka pinned his ears, and Dega jerked her head up, one rein flying over her neck to the wrong side.

Apri flicked the errant rein back over the mare's head, then backed her horse away from Zak's, her brain still processing his question. She wasn't even sure she heard him right. "I... I am... What?"

"That *song*," he demanded, "the one you were humming, how do you know it?"

"Uh…" With her mind so foggy from lack of sleep, the tune had gone right out of her head the second she stopped. She had to think about it. "Um... I think it was…"

Gard had dismounted and he broke into their conversation. "Song? What do you care about a song?" He sounded even angrier than Zak. "Where did you get that card?" Gard started untying the laces of Zak's travelpack.

Zak glared at him. "What're you doing?"

Gard took the pack and began rummaging through its contents.

Thankful for the diversion, Apri got off her horse. *I need to pee.* She threw her reins over a nearby branch and left the men. Monk followed her.

"Get out of my pack!" Zak yelled.

"*This* card!" Gard screamed back. Apri was well away from them now, but still heard the argument. "How long have you had this? And where'd you get it?"

"Give it back!"

"Where did it come from?" Gard sounded unreasonably angry, at least to her ears. She guessed the lack of sleep contributed to the intensity of their argument.

Monk crouched on the ground beside her. "So, you prefer to stay away when they get like this, too, eh, Monkjan?" she said to the climber. "I do not blame you."

Monk screeched and bounded away, as if in confirmation.

They all needed to get some rest, and so did the horses. She finished her business and returned to the men.

Gard had his back to her, but she saw the small card in his hand. "I've been tracking you for weeks. Where… *when* did you get this?!" He slammed the card down on a tree stump between him and Zak.

Zak grinned. "So, you're not such a great tracker, after all? Is that why you're so angry?" he asked. "It just so happens, I found it when we were in Southrock."

"Southrock?" the information seemed to surprise Gard out of his fury. "That day… when you went off into the woods?"

From Zak's smug, prideful expression, he relished this victory. *Gard really brings out the worst in—*

The unnatural rustling sound caught them all by surprise. All three instinctively reached for weapons.

"What's going on here?"

Even before turning to face the threat, Apri recognized the voice. *Damn!*

A group of men approached them from the direction of the trail they'd been avoiding all day. The loud argument must've drawn their attention.

"Apri?"

"Kendall!" Apri exclaimed. "Where are you coming from?" She wanted to sound casual but couldn't prevent apprehension from creeping into her tone. *Kendall? Really?*

Feeling her checks flush with the memory of their last, intimate, night together. Her heart raced, and she struggled to regain her composure as her brain scrambled to come up with a plausible explanation. Kendall was not gullible or stupid.

"Who are these two?" he asked, ignoring her question and gesturing to Zak and Gard.

She'd seen two of the other men with Kendall at the caves before, acknowledging them with a curt nod. They didn't act aggressive or threatening but held weapons at the ready. The others with them were young, unarmed, and assumed postures ranging from curiosity, to disinterest, to sheer exhaustion. Those would be the recruits.

"This is Gard, and Zak," she indicated each in turn. Damian asked me to escort them to Baytown."

"He asked *you* to be an escort? Who are they? And what business do they have in Baytown?" Kendall's tone was skeptical. "Damian gave you back your gear?" The men behind him started moving into position to surround them.

"Damian wouldn't let her go out alone," one of the men said.

At the same time, the other man said, "Why are *they* carrying wea—" that man's question was cut off by Gard's knife in his throat.

A couple of the boys let out startled cries. One ran off into the woods and two more followed. Apri couldn't bring herself to attack Kendall, so she approached the other man.

"I been wanting at you since that day Dam' let you off," the man said.

That's where she remembered this one, from her first encounter with the Dovetails. She'd faced him just before Damian stopped the fight.

She backed away from him, and he kept pace. His longsword had better reach, but it would be heavier. On any normal day, she could easily outmaneuver the older, heavyset man, but she was tired. *This has to be quick.*

He lunged, swinging hard at her head.

She blocked the hit with her short sword, but the force of the blow sent her to the ground.

Raising the sword high above his head, he came at her again.

Just as he brought the sword down, she rolled away, then sprung up and stabbed him through the chest.

The man screamed and dropped to the ground.

"You brave boys need to run off, now," she heard Gard say.

The two young recruits with Gard bled from numerous nicks and scratches, all harmless, superficial wounds. The weapons they'd picked up to join the fray lay at their feet. They ran off.

Kendall had Zak up against a tree, a knife at his throat.

Gard rushed over to them, barking a stern warning, "Drop the knife."

"Kendall, please! Do not hurt him!" Apri pleaded.

"Tell me what's going on here," Kendall demanded.

"Drop the knife!" Gard ordered again, stepping closer, his sword inches from Kendall's neck.

To Apri's relief, Kendall released his grip on Zak. He held on to the knife, though.

With his sword still pointed at Kendall, Gard backed off a pace but didn't order him to drop the knife again.

Zak let out a huge sigh and slid down the tree, resting on his haunches, then leaned his head back to rest against the trunk.

"Where'd that card come from? Whose is it?" Kendall asked, nodding toward the card Gard had thrown on the stump.

"You recognize the card?" Gard asked.

"I do," Kendall said. The two men regarded each other.

Apri shared a perplexed look with Zak.

Gard grinned. "You're Cortek." He dropped the threatening posture and began to wander around the clearing, gathering discarded weapons.

Kendall sheathed his knife, neither acknowledging nor denying Gard's allegation.

Apri exhaled a long breath, unaware she'd been holding it. *Cortek?*

Zak retrieved the weapons he'd lost in the skirmish. The sword he put away, but he kept a knife in his hand, watching Kendall.

Gard glared at Zak. "It just so happens the origin of that card is what we were discussing when we were interrupted. We need to get away from here. Would you care to join us? Kendall, is it?"

"I doubt I'll be welcome among the Dovetails after this," Kendall said, eying the two dead men. "Kendall Otero." He bowed the Edyson greeting.

Zak took the card and put it in his pack.

Apri mounted her horse while the men finished collecting the discarded weapons and anything else of value from the dead men.

Kendall approached, and she removed her foot from the stirrup so he could mount behind her. He reached around her to grab the reins and she relaxed into the warmth and comfort of the close contact. They rode from the clearing at a long trot.

"So, what's going on?" Kendall asked, his voice low enough that the others didn't hear.

"It is long story," she replied, her words slurred by a stifled yawn, "that starts with Jase getting killed."

"What?" he said, "You killed…"

Chapter 12
Apri

"Apri, wake up."

Roused by Kendall's nudge and his warm breath on her ear, Apri opened her eyes. Her neck was stiff as tanned tandorus hide, and her legs and butt were numb. *How long did I sleep?* The sun had set, but the moon phases were different here than in Ararat, so she couldn't be sure of the time. The winding trail descended more gradually than before. *Somewhere in the foothills.*

Kendall shook her again.

"Alright, alright, I am awake." She leaned forward in the saddle, putting as much space as she could between her and Kendall, then stretched her arms and legs. Her bones popped and cracked as tense muscles and tendons loosened around them.

"We're stopping for the night," he said, dismounting.

Apri took care of Dega while he gathered wood for a fire.

"I'll take first watch," Kendall said.

Gard seemed to hesitate, then accepted the offer. "Thanks."

Apri slid the saddle from Dega's back and the weary-eyed mare took a deep breath. "Yes, girl," she said quietly, patting the horse's neck, "a nice, long rest for you, too."

The babbling of a nearby stream explained Dega's wet muzzle and feet. The other horses were hobbled in a clearing nearby, and she led Dega to join them. The mare immediately dropped her head to graze.

Finding a sturdy piece of tree bark, Apri used it on the horse's back and flank, rubbing away the worst of the dirt and sweat. Caring for horses was a habit ingrained in her since childhood, not a bothersome chore so much as a welcome task that helped her relax and unwind after a long ride. When she finished with Dega, she went to each of the other two horses in turn, grooming them with the bark curry comb.

As she scrubbed Durka's flank, her mind wandered. *Tina, where are you? Why did Damian take you to the capital?... I'm still so tired, I could not have slept long... What is the story with Zak and Gard? ... What did they talk about while I slept?*

She rubbed at a spot of dried, dirty sweat on Durka's flank. "What did I miss, Durka?" she said to the horse. He turned his head toward her, and she stroked his nose. "You are not going to share?"

She shrugged it off. *I will find out or I will not. I must leave for Edyson tomorrow to find Tina anyway.* She finished with the grooming and grabbed her gear to join the men.

Gard and Zak were wrapped in their bedrolls with their backs to Kendall's fledgling fire. *Already asleep?* Monk, curled up on Zak's chest, watched her with half-open eyes. A couple of dead turbeasts lay on the ground. She was hungry, but too worn out to think about eating, much less preparing a meal.

"I need more sleep," she apologized to Kendall.

He nodded, stoking the fire. "Go ahead, I'll be here."

Apri crawled into her bedroll. The warm flames and crackling of the fire soon lulled her to sleep...

A noise startled Apri awake. She opened her eyes but heard nothing. Rising to rest on her forearms, she looked around.

Kendall sat across the fire, watching her. *Oh, no.* His eyes... that expression... *No.*

Gard snored again, a loud, gargley, growling sound, and she looked in his direction.

How does Zak sleep, lying right next to him? Then she noticed the blanket wrapped around his head, covering his ears. She smiled. *That's how.* Monk was not around.

"Wake you up?" Kendall asked. The unmistakable expression was gone from his face, but not from her memory.

She chuckled, avoiding eye contact. "Yes." Sliding out of her bedroll, she pulled on her boots. "Why don't you rest now," she offered, "if you can," she nodded toward Gard. "I'll take watch." Pointing to the cleaned and gutted turbeasts, she added, "And thank you for that."

"No trouble at all."

"Sweet dreams!" she mocked. *As if that's possible with all this racket.*

Apri took her canteen and left the snore zone. It was dark, but with a hint of daybreak soon to come. It felt good to be walking on two legs instead of sitting astride a horse for a change. A gentle breeze touched her face, brisk and refreshing. At the creek, she splashed water on her face and rubbed sand on her hands and arms until they were pink and clean.

Kendall. She'd never allowed any sexual relationship to be more than casual, always breaking it off at the first sign her partner might be getting serious. But the expression on Kendall's face when she woke suggested his feelings were more than casual. *Did I miss signs?* No. She sensed this was a new development, conceived by him during these weeks apart. *Or perhaps overnight, now that they were free of the caves?*

Monk jumped down from a tree and joined her.

"You really should warn person," she chided.

He squeaked and drank from the creek, then splashed at the water with his hand.

Apri filled her canteen and set it aside, inspecting the bare patches on Monk's coat. "My little Monkjan, what goes on here, hmmm?"

Since their first meeting in the cell, Apri had been enamored with the little climber, and curious. She'd always used her telepathic gift more often with animals than with people, with varying degrees of success. Dogs and horses were receptive, but skittish about it, especially at first. It didn't work at all with chickens, goats, and other small farm animals. With Monk, the connection had been immediate, and not only easier, but also more effective than with any animal she'd linked with before. *Except that first one.*

She slung the canteen over her shoulder and checked on the horses, gathering wood for the fire along the way. Monk scampered along beside her, picking up a stick, then discarding it in favor of another. When she stopped to gather some wild herbs, he screeched, hopping up and down, then ran off through the trees. He stopped up ahead and looked back at her, then squeaked and hopped up and down again.

"Okay, okay, I am coming!" she said, jogging to catch up to him.

"Oh, good find, Monkjan!" she said, ruffling his head. Using her shirt as a basket, she gathered some of the ripe, tasty berries.

By the time she returned to the campsite, Kendall slept, and Gard was quiet. *Probably woke himself up.* Adding more firewood, she stoked the fire, then prepped the meat with the herbs. While she waited for the flames to die down, she spitted the meat with the soaked green branches Kendall had placed next to them. Once the turbeast roasted above the hot coals, she started coffee brewing, then munched on berries, turning the meat now and then to keep it from burning.

The smell of the meat and coffee woke the men, one at a time, each commenting about their hunger. They talked while they ate but avoided any serious discussion.

Apri wanted to get on the road to Edyson as soon as possible to search for her friend. "I suppose I will start," she said. All three men looked at her as if she had just spoken Aratian. She had to mentally recall her words to convince herself otherwise.

"Start what?" Gard asked.

"To tell you how I came here, and where I go," she said. Gard and Zak stared off into the woods, or at the fire, avoiding eye contact with anyone, but they were listening. "Or do we just part ways here?"

"You're right," Gard said, "but I would like Zak to start." He glared at Zak, "where'd you get that card?"

Zak snapped back, "None of your b—"

"This again?" Apri interjected. "Do you forget how argument ended yesterday? Are you not friends, traveling together?"

"We're traveling together," Zak said, "but we are *not* friends."

"Well, I do not wish to travel with people who do not trust each other," Apri said, "or to worry about you two turning on each other again. I prefer to travel alone anyway." She started shoving things into her travelpack.

"How do you know that song you were humming on the trail yesterday?" Zak asked.

The unexpected question caused Apri to stop packing and look at him. His expression confused her—*Pain? Anger?* She'd remembered the tune yesterday, when he asked the first time, but then Gard interrupted and everything else happened, and she'd forgotten about it again. Yet Zak had not.

"There was young woman who lived in Damian's quarters, she sang it often," she said.

Zak jumped up, "What!? She's there?"

"No, no." Apri raised her hand. "No, he took her to capital. For Landing Day."

Zak sat back down.

Distant sounds seemed amplified in the silence that followed— the crackling of the fire, water rushing over rocks, the horses snorting and shuffling, birds twittering in the trees.

Zak glared at Gard. "I bet she was in that carriage… in Meadowick." He stared into the fire.

"His sister, Katrina" Gard explained. "They were separated over a decade ago. Until now, we didn't even know if she lived."

"You are her twin brother!" Apri said, "Of course!" She waited for Zak to look at her. "You have her eyes."

A trace of a smile crossed Zak's lips, and he wiped his face again.

"She was brought to caves many years ago," Apri explained. "She remembered fire. And being kidnapped. Damian said her family died in fire. He warned her not to speak of it or she may be killed, too. She was prisoner, but not mistreated or abused. Damian took me in to protect her from his own men. I thought it strange he would go to such trouble, but perhaps he came to care for her, in his own way."

Zak took a deep breath. "She was taken from our farm. A man, they say one of the Dovetails, killed my parents, burned our house, and took her. A man with a scar on his face... and eyes of two colors."

Apri and Kendall shared a look. "Jase." They spoke the name in unison.

"We were both prisoners alone in strange place. I knew her as Katrina, but called her Tina like everyone else. We became very close." Apri sipped her coffee, thinking of her friend.

She looked at Kendall. "Jase came to my room, caught me by surprise. He is dead now."

"You killed him?" Zak asked.

"No, not me… They think I killed him, but it was Ti—Katrina. I told her to tell no one. They locked me up. Next day, Damian took her to Edyson. I do not know why he took her or where she is now, but he said she would not be back."

Her heart went out to Zak. She could only imagine his anguish on hearing this news. "She is very dear to me," she said to him. "I want to find her, too."

"Your sister, she was already there when I joined the 'tails," Kendall told Zak. "Like Apri said, Damian—everyone—called her Tina. I thought her to be his servant, nothing more. I wish I'd known her true identity. You're James Bancroft's son?" he asked, studying Zak carefully. "I see the resemblance now. I knew your father well."

Zak sniffed. "Did you say you knew my father?" He rubbed his ear.

"He's the reason I became a scout," Kendall explained, "and why I joined up with the Dovetails."

Zak took a deep breath. "I need to go. I need to find her."

Apri sat cross-legged next to Zak and could sense his anxiety and frustration. She was worried about his sister, too.

Zak scratched at his ear again.

"That's unwise…" Gard said.

"Not a good idea," Kendall said at the same time. Before Zak could object, he explained, "You need information. If you go around asking about her, you could raise suspicion and get her, or yourself, into trouble."

"But…" Zak cut himself off, and turned to ask Apri "Do you hear that?" He poked a finger in his ear again and wiggled it around.

Apri shook her head. She didn't hear anything.

"Kendall's right, Zak," Gard said. "We need more information. Damian is friends with the Legiant. If he's involved—"

Ahhh!" Zak yelled. "Ow!" He keeled over, hands on his ears, crashing into Apri.

Apri jumped up, getting out of his way. "What is it?" she asked, confused. "He is upset?"

"No, it's not that," Kendall sprung to Zak's aid, grabbing at his hands, trying to pry them from his ears.

"Warm water!" Gard barked to Apri.

Zak screamed.

"Warm water! Now!" Gard ordered, tossing his coffee and throwing her the empty cup.

Apri caught the cup, pouring water into it from her canteen with shaking hands.

Zak's next scream was louder than the last.

She placed the cup on a rock near the hot coals using one of the spit branches. "What is wrong with him?"

Zak moaned, writhing against Kendall who tried to hold him still.

"It's an ear maggot. We need to get it out," Kendall said. "We can't do it with him thrashing around like this. Do we knock him out?"

A what? Ear maggot? She'd never heard of it. "Wait." Digging a med kit out of her pack, she found a tiny vial and dropped some of its liquid onto a cloth. "Here, put on face."

After a few seconds, Zak passed out.

"That smell. It's familiar," Gard said. He reached his hand out for the cup, wiggling his fingers. "The water, it can't be too hot."

Apri stuck in her finger to test it. *Ouch!* She added more water from her canteen then handed the cup to Gard.

"Which ear?" Kendall had Zak's head in his lap.

"The left," Apri said.

Kendall turned his head, and Gard poured some of the water into his ear.

"The maggot won't be able to breathe," Kendall explained. "We can pull it out when it comes up for air. Tweezers?"

"As long as it didn't go too deep," Gard added.

Apri handed Kendall the tweezers from her med kit.

"There it is," Kendall said a minute or so later.

"Be careful." Gard warned, as he moved in position to hold Zak's head still.

Kendall held the tweezers above Zak's ear, then slowly lowered them.

"There are nests of these things in moist, dark places," Gard explained. "Maybe he picked it up when Kendall had him up against that tree?"

The tweezers emerged from Zak's ear holding a fat, white maggot. It was still squirming when Kendall threw it into the fire.

"That is disgusting," Apri said, watching the thing sizzle and burn. "I never heard of this ear maggot."

"It's uncommon for one to get into a human ear, but it happens occasionally," Gard explained. "As long as you get it out quick enough, it does no harm."

Gard picked up the cloth and sniffed it. "Where have I…"

"It's a topical anesthetic. He should come out of it soon." Kendall placed a bedroll under Zak's head.

Apri packed away her med kit. *A maggot? Crawling around in my head?* The thought made her skin crawl. She twisted her head and cringed. *Creepy.*

A few minutes later Zak opened his eyes and sat up, groggy. "What happened?"

"Ear maggot," Gard said. "We got it out."

Zak picked at his ear again. "Ewww."

The men were quiet, sipping their coffee. *As if that did not just happen?* She couldn't stop thinking about that squishy, white maggot.

Zak broke the silence. "I found the card in the woods," he looked at Gard. "Mr. Murfy, my friend Gabe's father, gave me a box with a map. I found it along with a list with some names on it." He pulled the card out of his travelpack, set it on a rock, then dug in the pack again for the paper.

"It's blank," Gard said.

"It's not blank," Kendall said, taking it from Zak. Holding it up to the light, he read silently, then set the list aside. "A few of these people died in various accidents years ago, not long after the fire. They were members of a secret group who opposed the Legiant, but they disbanded. Some are in Baytown now and are meeting again. They may know where the others are."

Apri stared at the card. It looked like hers. So much so, that she had to check the pocket in her vest to make sure hers was still there. Making a quick decision, she pulled it out, "Ummm," she said, holding up the card. "I have one of those, too."

Gard leaned over and started digging into his own travelpack. "As do I," he said, holding his up. They looked at each other, curiosity mixed with amazement.

"I have one as well," he said. "I've known only a few non-Cortek who have a card. I can't tell you how unusual it is for three strangers, none Core-bound, to have come together in one place, all bearing those access cards," he said, shaking his head. "We know how Zak came by his. Would anyone else care to share?" He looked at Apri, then Gard.

Apri spoke first, "When I was twelve, a man came to village. He told my parents he wanted to recruit me, to go to school in Edyson. Why me? I do not know. But he volunteered to escort me. My mother, she would not agree. When the man left, I argued with my parents. But they refused to let me go. I ran from house and sat outside inn where he stayed. When I saw him, I begged him to take me, but he would not."

Picking up her card, she said, "He gave me this card and said if I still wanted to come when I was older, I could use for passage." She looked at Kendall, "I think I am too old now. But I found ship that accepted card to sail from Ararat. Even if it is too late for school, I must find way to pay him back."

"But how did you end up as Katrina's bodyguard?" Gard asked.

"On my way to Edyson, I met some of Damian's men. I was... persuaded... to return to caves with Damian."

Kendall laughed. "Word of that meeting spread through the caves like wildfire, let me tell you. She killed one man and injured two others before Damian came on the scene and ended the fight." He patted her shoulder.

Apri leaned away from him, uncomfortable with the praise and, even more so, the affection.

Ignoring her reticence, Kendall squeezed her shoulder. "She's quite the warrior." Picking up a stick, he poked at the fire. "Both my parents are Cortek. I grew up on the campus. Went to school there," he gazed fondly at Apri. "I took the oath at fourteen as is the custom for Core-born. On my first assignment at the palace, I served as an attendant for Zak's father, and after only a few months, he trusted me with his most sensitive business. But when he left Edyson to run the mine, I went back to the campus."

"I heard about the fire and the death of your parents," he said to Zak. "And of those other suspicious accidents in the city. I pleaded with the headmaster to give me an assignment that would help uncover the truth. There were rumors that the Dovetails were involved with the fire in Southrock, so he sent me here. It wasn't difficult to get recruited. I was the right age, with the right skills. I moved through the ranks until I became a recruiter myself."

"And that's how *I* came to be here," Kendall said, then looked at Gard.

Gard stared into the fire for several minutes. Then his eyes met hers, his expression intense. An unusual bond formed between them in that look. Tentative but persistent, like vines in the garden reaching for the sun. As he spoke, the bond strengthened, an invisible tether that neither could break.

"I was Commander of the Legiant's Law Squad, appointed to that post by Covington after the takeover. We grew up together, like brothers, but he changed after he became Legiant. Obsessed with power. Before long, we were at odds more often than not. A couple months ago, I discovered he'd sent his XLs to the Core Campus."

The violence and disregard for human life Gard described was unimaginable. Apri felt his pain, sensed his shame and guilt for helping his friend become the ruler of Edyson. Never had she been so compelled to reach out mentally to another person. She wanted to relieve his suffering, ease his internal struggle, comfort his heart. But fear of how he would perceive such an intimate intrusion stopped her.

"I was near dead when the last man gave up and ran out," Gard continued. "The Cortek took me in and patched me up." He stopped talking, his eyes still locked on hers.

Kendall coughed.

Apri broke the contact with Gard, wiping tears from her cheeks. She noticed Kendall and Zak exchange an odd look. Raw emotion pulsed through her. *Mine? His?* Their connection had felt so deep and personal, she had trouble separating her feelings from his. Staring into the fire, she inhaled deeply. Her senses needed a moment to rebound from the experience before she could focus on the conversation again.

"...stables." Zak spoke to Gard. "You're the squader in that wanted poster."

Gard nodded. "I disappeared, and the Cortek left the campus. The Legiancy named me responsible for the massacre, reporting that his men had been sent to save the Cortek. That lie gave him justification to release me as Commander of the Law Squad and expel me from the palace." He raised his hands. "Any of you could be instantly wealthy by turning me in."

Kendall shook his head. "There are different versions of that story floating around," he said, "many fabricated by the Legiant. After the massacre, the Cortek throughout Edyson were ordered to go into hiding. It happened fast, the Cortek vanished within a week... schools, hospitals, factories... everywhere. The vacancies are being covered by citizens, as best they can, but I've heard The Ravens is a mess with the Cortek gone. The factories aren't producing much of anything."

"That was Covington's plan all along, what caused him to send his squaders to the campus in the first place," Gard said. "He wanted the factories to mass-produce weapons, and the headmaster refused. I imagine he's anxious to restore order in The Ravens."

"Well, he'll have his hands full with that," Zak said. "If the Cortek are gone, The Ravens will be a war zone. I could never understand how they managed to keep factory workers from killing each other even then. The place is overrun with gangs and criminals. If workers aren't going to the factory every day? Aren't getting paid?..." He shrugged.

Kendall asked Gard, "You stayed on campus to recover?"

"For a few wee—" Gard interrupted himself "That's it! The odor... that stuff that knocked out Zak. They must've used it on me in the campus infirmary."

Kendall chuckled, "Yes, it's a common sedative among the Cortek."

"In Ararat, too," Apri added.

Gard grinned, "I try to avoid infirmaries and hospitals, as a general rule," he admitted, then finished his reply to Kendall's question. "I actually didn't stay on campus. I stayed at an inn outside Northgate. The Law Squad occupies the campus now."

"Well," Kendall said, "it seems we're all bound for Edyson. But I suggest we go to Baytown first. We can't hope to change anything without help."

That idea was disheartening. Apri couldn't keep her disappointment from showing. She wanted to go to Edyson immediately to find Katrina.

"I know how to get in touch with these people," Kendall said, referring to Zak's blank list of names, "and others like them. Their numbers have grown in recent months and with the news about this massacre, the missing Cortek, and the mess in The Ravens, they're gaining more support. They're still divided, but many are starting to talk seriously about taking action."

"I want to go to Edyson now," Zak said.

"Me too," Apri admitted.

"The people in Baytown may have word about your sister, or if not, they will know of others in Edyson who can find out," Kendall said. "Of course, you can go back alone now, but you'll have a better chance of finding her, and rescuing her, if you wait."

"I am not familiar with the city, and I know no one in Edyson. Do you?" Apri asked Zak.

Zak shook his head.

"They are right." Apri shook her head, disappointed. "I want to find her. Desperately. But even you and I together would have little chance to find her without help." She decided to let Zak make the decision. If he didn't agree, she would go to Edyson with him.

Zak reluctantly gave in, and they packed up for the journey to Baytown.

Chapter 13
Zak

Zak rode behind the horse Kendall and Apri shared, smiling to himself. Yesterday, Apri slept, cradled between Kendall's arms, almost from the moment they mounted. Now, after a full night's rest, she didn't seem to be enjoying his close proximity. Not at all. Perched erect in front of him, he watched her shift around in the saddle for the hundredth time. And Kendall didn't wrap his arms around her as he had the day before, either. Apri held the reins seated in front of him, and his arms hung like sausages by his side, limp and awkward.

Dega stumbled, and to keep from falling off, Kendall grabbed the saddle behind him rather than holding onto Apri. Zak laughed at the comical awkwardness of their behavior.

Monk jerked awake behind him and screeched at the sudden noise.

"What's so funny?" Kendall asked.

"Ummm… nothing," Zak replied.

To Apri, Kendall said, "There's a stable up ahead. I should be able to get a horse."

"Good," Apri replied curtly.

Zak laughed again, and Kendall shot him an irritated look.

Hey, don't look at me. She's your problem! I'm just enjoying the show back here.

When they rode out of the foothills, the main road to Baytown was busy with travelers returning from Landing Day festivities in the capital. While the increased traffic meant getting rooms for the night would be unlikely, it did give them a chance to catch up on news and gossip from Edyson.

They stopped at the first inn with a public stable. Kendall stayed back to see about getting a horse while the others went inside and found an empty table.

Kendall didn't look happy when he joined them.

"They did not have horse?" Apri asked.

"*A* horse," Zak muttered.

Kendall gave Apri an annoyed look. "I got a horse," he said. "It's not that."

Zak hid a grin behind his hand.

Kendall sat down on the bench next to Apri but didn't give a reason for his sour mood.

"What is it?" Zak finally asked.

The barmaid arrived with their drinks. Kendall waited for her to leave then leaned in, reaching for one of the mugs on the table. "The situation in Edyson is worse than I imagined." He leaned back on the bench. It seemed he wanted to say more, then decided against it. "Let's just eat and get out of here. I'll tell you later."

They ate in silence, listening to the conversations around them. The most frequent topic was the Legiant's announcement of his engagement. Most folks chattered excitedly about the news, happy to have a reason to visit the capital again so soon for another celebration.

"I knew it wouldn't be long before he took a bride," Gard said. "Not that he ever had any interest in female partners, but he needs an heir."

When they finished their meal, they left the pub and continued south, following Kendall, now mounted on his own horse—the buckskin gelding Gard had taken from the caves. Gard rode the new one.

Most of the other mounted travelers rode together in groups at a moderate pace, others moved slower, riding alongside wagons or carriages. Zak's group moved faster, slowing only to mingle among others on the road to gather what news they could before riding on. The unspoken urgency in Kendall's behavior since the inn had Zak on edge, anxious to find out what he knew. They quickened their pace around sundown, leaving the road after dark to camp for the night.

"I've known the stable owner for years," Kendall told them when they were settled. "He said a few weeks before Landing Day, the Legiancy started a smear campaign against the Cortek, spreading rumors and suspicions about treasonous activities." He sighed. "The disappearance of the Cortek, almost overnight, didn't help. He said the sudden exodus seemed to support the Legiant's claim that the Cortek went into exile after being confronted and challenged about their actions.

"All Cortek have been branded as criminals, with a reward offered to any citizen who turns them in," Kendall said. "He wouldn't take my card and told me not to try using it again. Anywhere. That's when I noticed he'd covered up the symbol."

"What symbol?" Zak asked.

"The symbol on the card. It's posted by establishments who are Core-friendly and will accept the card as payment for goods and services. You would only notice it if you knew what to look for, but he removed it anyway. That, in itself, is noteworthy... this man is not easily threatened or intimidated."

"Will he turn you in?" Apri asked.

"No," he said, then repeated when she appeared unconvinced, "No. But he told me to be careful—not to trust anyone."

"Really, there's no need to worry," he said, "Few know I'm Cortek." When Apri raised an eyebrow he said, "*You* didn't know, right?"

Apri's eyes flashed with irritation, and Zak chuckled at the instant change in her expression.

She glanced at Zak, then laughed herself.

Gard didn't get the joke and shot Zak an annoyed—*or jealous?*—look which only made him burst out laughing again.

Gard ignored him, asking the others. "Did you hear any details about the wedding? When the ceremony will take place? Anything about the bride?"

Zak laughed again. Watching these three people trying to ignore the obvious undercurrent of sexual tension between them had Zak in stitches. *Am I imagining this?* He rubbed his tearing eyes and sighed, then gathered his emotions to avoid another outburst. "I heard the Legiant announced he's engaged. Or would be soon. And that the wedding would be in a few months." The last he said with a straight face—almost.

Gard gave him another judgmental look and added, "I heard some say he hasn't even chosen a bride yet."

Zak looked at Apri who had been quiet since his outburst. *Is she upset? No. Maybe just tired. I'm tired.* He sighed again, drawing Kendall's attention this time.

"I doubt we'll discover anything more by stopping to chat with the people on the road," Kendall said. "Let's just get to Baytown as quick as possible. We'll get an early start tomorrow."

Gard and Kendall's conversation woke Zak up the next morning, and he started packing. He looked over at Apri who was still wrapped in her bedroll.

"Apri!" Kendall called out but she didn't move.

Zak stood over her. "Apri?" Her head rested on a sealed envelope. A pen lay next to her hand. He shook her. "Apri!"

She startled awake. "What?" Her hands went to her ears, pulling cotton out of them.

Zak laughed. "We're leaving, get up." He called out to Gard and Kendall, who were already packed up. "She had cotton in her ears!"

The men laughed.

"What is funny?" Apri asked. "I do not want ear maggot."

"They're only up in the hills," Zak said, "not down here."

"And it is extremely rare for one to get in your ear," Kendall said. "It never happens."

"It happened. To Zak," she argued. "It will *not* happen to me." Only Zak heard the last part. "I do not know how you can take it so lightly," she said to Zak, shoving her things in her pack and walking with him to the horses. "You did not see it. It was disgusting."

"Well, do what you want," he said, bumping against her. "I'll make sure and wake you in the mornings."

They arrived in Baytown a full day earlier than expected. Kendall led them to the waterfront district where they stabled the horses and rented rooms at an inn called *The Wet Whale*.

After a couple of drinks, they settled on a time to meet for dinner, then Kendall left with Gard to see about arranging for a meeting with his contacts.

Zak sat at the table with Apri, watching Gard's back as he and Kendall walked out of the pub. *See ya, Gard-dog.* The urgent need for another drink came on strong and sudden. He'd grown accustomed to using Gard, with his drink-nursing and constant judgment, to control his own drinking habit. He looked across the table at Apri, her glass still half-full of ale. He didn't trust himself to stay here, waiting for her to finish the drink.

"I've got to give Monk a bath," he said, sliding out of the seat. It was the only excuse he could think of.

"Hmmm?" Apri's attention was on the closed door the two men had just exited. She looked up at him. "Oh. Sure." She twirled the mug in front of her but didn't take a drink. "Okay."

Zak stopped at the bar, ordered a soda, and asked for some food scraps for Monk, then climbed the stairs to the room he shared with Gard.

Monk screeched when he opened the door, dancing and jumping around on the bed. After setting the food on the windowsill for Monk, he went to the bathroom and filled the wash basin with warm water.

Sitting on the bed, he dug through his pack for the soap, sipping on the unsatisfying soda. When Monk finished eating, he tossed the soap into the basin and Monk jumped in after it, splashing around and making all kinds of climber noises.

He ruffled the climber's head. "Be sure to wash behind your ears."

"He uses *that* soap?" Apri asked. She stood at the open door, pointing with an envelope she held in her hand.

"Yeah, he needs soap," Zak said. "He gets real dirty. And smelly."

Monk shook all over, then leaped onto Zak, soaking wet.

Apri's laughter filled the room as Zak held the dripping climber out at arm's length. "How many times do I have to tell you not to do that?"

Monk tilted his head and squeaked in reply.

"Can you...?" Zak asked Apri, nodding his head toward the window.

Apri maneuvered around him to open the window. Monk jumped from Zak's arms and out onto the sunny rooftop.

Zak dried himself with a towel. "Are you heading out?" he asked Apri.

"Oh, yes," she said. "I hope to find ship sailing to Ararat." She waved the envelope. "To take letter to my family."

"Mind if I tag along?" he asked.

"Not at all."

Zak had never been near the ocean before and was amazed by the size and variety of boats docked at the piers and anchored offshore—small fishing boats, huge sailing ships with multiple sails reaching up into the sky. Way down at the end he saw the large, flat barges that carried goods up and down the river. Beyond the boats, the ocean seemed to go on and on forever. "Wow, this is incredible!"

Not so much the smell coming from offshore, though, rancid salt, combined with… what?... *rotting fish?* Covering his nose, he asked Apri, indicating the people around them, "How can they stand this awful smell?" The putrid odor reminded him of the time his parents tried to get him to eat fish. He shuddered. *Phew.*

"You get used to it," Apri replied.

Zak glanced at her, skeptical.

"Think about it. Some of these people may not like smell of barn fully stocked with grain, or musty, moldy forest at end of rainy season." She paused, then added, "or flexsand mine like where you grew up. I bet it has distinct odor."

Zak thought about it and smiled, "It does, definitely. I suppose you're right." But then, after few minutes, he couldn't let it go. "Really? That smell doesn't bother you?"

"I think it smells great," Apri said, taking a deep breath and extending her arms wide. "Exciting," she spun around, "like an adventure is out there, calling to me."

A gust of wind came up and caught the brim of Zak's hat, blowing it off his head.

Apri ran to pick it up before it blew into the sea. She turned it over in her hand. "Where did you get this?" she asked.

"It was my pa's."

"It is tandorus hide," she said.

"What? You mean, like your vest?" He took the cap from her. "Doesn't feel anything like it."

"Different tanning process," she explained. "It is soaked in special liquid, then hide is stretched thin until it is soft and smooth. Like leather. But stronger."

He put it back on. "I always wondered. It's almost indestructible."

"Almost," she said. "Tandorus hide is rare and tanning process is long."

Apri had been scanning the boats docked along the piers as they walked. She stopped, shading her eyes from the glare, looking at a particular sailing ship. "I see ship I sailed from Ararat."

"Go ahead." Zak said. "I need to see a man about a horse." He laughed at Apri's expression. "Something my father used to say. I need to find a tree?" he tried, but when she still looked perplexed, he explained "I need to pee. I'll catch up with you. We can meet up over there." He pointed ahead to the wharf's center square.

Apri

Apri walked down the gangplank of *The Swift Lizzy,* the same ship she sailed from Ararat. The captain had promised to deliver her letter. During their short visit, she learned that the first mate had been fired right after her voyage. *Served him right, he was lazy, and mean.* She hadn't thought about that trip in months, so much had happened since. But being on board, seeing the captain, feeling the deck under her feet, the salty sea air, she'd been reminded her of the first time she truly realized the value of all those years in training with Rrazmik.

The first mate, Domingo, had been rude from the day she came on board, ordering her to stay in her cabin. *Passengers ain't allowed on deck,* he'd grumbled. But she'd been so seasick and staying inside the small, muggy cabin just made it worse. After others on the crew told her there was no such rule, she'd decided it'd be better for her own health to endure his boorish behavior rather than stay cooped up in the cabin. Domingo was just a bully, and he treated her no differently than the rest of the crew. If they could endure it, then so could she.

One evening, about a week after they set sail, she was on deck leaning against the rail, staring out at the endless ocean.

✱✱✱

"You just can't follow orders, can you?"

Startled, Apri turned around and faced Domingo, her back to the rail. "I... I needed some air, sir. I am not feeling well." Glancing around, she saw no one else and cursed herself for wandering so far forward. She attempted to walk around him, but he blocked her. "Excuse me," she said with a glare.

"You think you're a damn princess." he snarled. "A sweet thing like you shouldn't be traveling alone." He reached his hand toward her.

The rail pressed into her as she backed away. "Leave me alone." She couldn't keep the anger from her voice. Even to her ears it sounded like an order. But she was in no mood to placate this bully.

"Or what?" he asked, with a gruff laugh. "Or what?"

"Or you will regret it."

His face burned red with anger.

A young crewman, barely in his teens, interrupted. "Leave her be, 'Mingo." His high-pitched voice cracked. The crew mostly steered clear of Domingo, and this boy took a risk standing up to him. *Must be new.*

"Beat it, tar-boy," Domingo ordered.

The kid turned and trotted off.

Domingo leaned forward, placing his hands on the rail, with his arms on either side of her waist. "What's it gonna be, princess?" he asked, his face inches from hers. "This'll be a long voyage. It can be pleasant for you… or not." He grinned. "Your choice."

Apri kneed him in the groin. He was too close for her to cause much pain, but it caught him off guard, and he dropped a hand to his crotch. She stepped aside.

"Not so fast, sweetie." He grabbed her, his hand gripping her arm and holding it tight.

She twisted around, jabbing her elbow into his ribs, and swiping her other arm up at the same time to escape.

Domingo still held her arm firmly, but he was off balance. "What the..." he choked out in surprise.

She slammed her foot into his knee, hearing it pop out of joint.

Domingo screamed and grabbed the knee, falling to the deck.

"I choose pleasant," she said to him.

"You fobmucking bitch," he yelled at her, hands cradling his knee. "You broke my leg."

"I could have," she said. "But it is not broken." She heard a low whistle and the shuffling of feet.

The captain stood there with a few crew members.

"Captain," Domingo said, spying the witnesses at the same time, "the bitch broke my leg. For no reason. I told you she had no business being on deck."

"Not true, Captain, sir." The boy from earlier spoke up, quietly.

"Help him below deck and take the girl to her quarters," the captain ordered. "You," he pointed to the boy, "and you," he pointed to another man Apri knew to be his second mate, "with me. Now." He walked away with the other two in tow.

Apri followed her escort to her cabin.

She never saw Domingo on board again. Whether that was due to his injury or being confined to his quarters, no one ever said. And she didn't ask.

***

Kendall had suggested they dress nice for the meeting and the thought of wearing something other than trousers had her in a good mood. That, and the salty breeze coming from offshore that diffused the muggy weather they'd suffered on the road to Baytown. She strolled along the pier toward the river, browsing through a few of the shops.

As she neared the center square, she looked around for Zak and saw him tossing rocks into the ocean across the square. She headed in that direction.

Someone grabbed her from behind. Before she could react, she felt the tip of a knife at her side.

"Don't move bitch."

The voice was distinctive. She recognized it at once. "You wish to do this again, Domingo?" she threatened.

"Try anything and I'll name you as Cortek. Half this crowd will be all over you, wanting that bounty."

Apri looked around the crowded wharf. She could take Domingo. *But what if his threat is real. How many will come after me?* Her foreign appearance would not work in her favor. Deciding to wait before taking action, she glanced over to where she last saw Zak.

Zak

Zak turned around to look for Apri and spied her leaving the square with a haggard-looking man. Walking toward her, he stopped short when she shook her head almost imperceptibly and glanced downward. A glint of the knife the man held against her side flickered in the sun. Careful not to catch the man's notice, Zak followed them.

The man walked with a slight limp and didn't look particularly athletic. He'd seen her fight and knew she could take him out. *Why doesn't she do something?* He kept them in sight, staying close enough to come to her aid if necessary.

The man left the busy wharf district behind and took her down a dark, secluded street. Before Zak could confront them, Apri's captor called out to another man who dozed in the porch swing of a run-down building. "Jackson, I've got another one!"

The man stood, rubbing his eyes. "Domingo? What's that?"

Zak didn't hear the rest of the conversation and couldn't get closer without being noticed. Apri spoke to the men. Then Jackson opened the door, Domingo shoved her inside. Both men followed, shutting the door behind them.

Zak trotted up the street, then crossed to find a hiding place where he could see, or at least hear, what was happening inside. Creeping into a narrow alley next to the building, he heard their voices coming from an open window.

"…sure she's a geek?" one man asked.

"Gotta be." Something scraped across the floor. "Came here alone from Ararat a few months back. Captain treated her like a damn princess."

"Ow!" Apri's voice. "You are wrong! I am no Cortek."

"Then she leaves Baytown. Now, she suddenly shows up again?" he said. "Running for her life's my bet."

"Tie her up good. And stay here. I'll go get the squader."

Zak ducked behind some crates at the end of the alley and waited for the man to pass, then returned to his post.

"...don't matter. Them squaders is more likely to believe you are than you ain't. Consider it payback for getting me fired."

"You got *yourself* fired," Apri said. "Something wrong with your leg?"

Smack!

Zak flinched at the sound of a hand hitting flesh. He looked around, searching for a good-sized rock.

"My leg never healed right, bitch," Domingo said. "You're lucky there's a reward or I'd kill you right now."

Zak tossed the rock in front of the door. When he heard a commotion from inside, he raced to the door and slammed into it. The lock gave way on the second try and the door opened to reveal a man sprawled on the floor. Apri stood above him with a chair tied to her legs and a bloody knife in her hand.

"Thank you for distraction," she said. Slashing the ropes that bound her legs to the chair, she wiped the knife clean on the unconscious man's sleeve.

"Any time," he said.

Zak closed the splintered door behind them and headed back to *The Wet Whale*. The setting sun cast long shadows around the wharf as they approached the inn.

Chapter 14
Zak

Zak and Apri joined Gard and Kendall who were already seated at a table in the back.

"What happened to you?" Gard asked Apri.

Apri touched her lip. Zak hadn't noticed the swollen jaw until now, or the bruise on her face that had begun to show some color.

"I ran into an old friend," she said.

"You do seem to have the worst luck with that," Gard said.

Zak laughed.

The barmaid, a middle-aged, motherly woman, approached with a couple more mugs and eyed the injury, raising an eyebrow.

"It's nothing," she said. eyeing the barmaid.

"We'll have dinner, if you please. Whatever's the special," Kendall said to the woman.

"Yes, sir," she gave Apri's face a long look, frowned, then left.

"You met with your contacts?" Apri asked.

"There's a meeting later tonight," Kendall said. "They confirmed what we've heard about the hunt for Cortek. Apparently, the reward for their capture is causing many to be falsely accused."

Zak glanced at Apri, but she said nothing. *Not my story to tell.*

"The group uses sporting events as a cover," Kendall explained. "and there's a big wrestling match tonight on the wharf."

The barmaid returned to their table carrying a white cloth wrapped around ice, which she offered to Apri.

"Thank you," Apri said, then gingerly touched it to her swollen lip.

"You going to the match tonight?" the woman asked.

Kendall seemed perturbed by the intrusion.

"Take it from me," she said, not noticing Kendall's irritation, "put your money on Blakely, he's a beast. Just coming' up in the ranks, but I seen his last bout and he trounced his opponent."

"Thanks for the tip," Kendall said, "Will we see you there?" he asked.

"Naw, I got to work tonight. But I got my money on him." She winked, then left to serve another table.

"Well, that's not good. She might ask us about it tomorrow," Gard said.

"The club always sends a few members to watch the event," Kendall said. "They join the meeting afterwards to report the outcome and highlights." He regarded Apri. "Looks like your day was more eventful. What happened?"

"I ran into the first mate on ship I sailed from Ararat," she began. "Apparently, he got fired by captain after our voyage and blamed me."

"Was he right to blame you?" Kendall asked.

"No…" she muttered.

Kendall raised an eyebrow.

"Well, maybe," she admitted. "He was a drunk, a coward, and abusive to crew. He tried to treat me the same and I…"

The woman returned with their food and Apri didn't elaborate. The men ate while she continued her story. "He caught me off guard when I was looking for Zak and held a knife on me. Warned if I tried anything, he would scream and accuse me of being Cortek. He said many would pursue me for reward."

Gard asked Zak, "Where were you when this was happening?"

"He went to see man about horse—Ow!" Apri stifled a laugh, pressing the cloth to her lip.

Zak responded to the unspoken question from Gard and Kendall. "I had to pee!" He shrugged, then told them what had happened.

"Did you kill him?" Kendall asked Apri.

"No," she said. "I knocked him out good, though." She looked up at the men, each in turn. "Should he not know better, after the last time?"

The men laughed.

"He attacked you *because* of the last time," Gard told her.

Apri shook her head, her expression perplexed. "I am pleased to entertain you," she said, then resumed eating, placing the ice on her jaw between bites.

When she stopped eating, Zak asked, "You done?"

She pushed the plate toward him, and he shoveled her leftovers onto his plate for Monk. "I'm gonna go clean up. See you later," he said and went up to the room.

Monk greeted him at the door, making a racket when he saw the food.

"Quiet! You're disturbing the peace," Zak scolded, uncovering the plate.

Their clothes had been laundered and were folded in a neat pile on the nearest bed. Kendall told them at dinner they should dress their best for this meeting, and Zak had been too embarrassed to say he didn't have a *best* option. *At least now I can wear* clean *clothes.* He took a quick shower, shaved, and dressed. They wouldn't be leaving for the meeting for a few hours, so he laid on the bed to rest.

Zak startled awake when a pillow skidded across his face and fell to the floor. "Time to go," Gard said.

He hadn't meant to fall asleep, but the comfortable bed, warm shower, and his full stomach got the better of him. Zak looked Gard up and down. Unlike him, Gard *did* have a best option.

Gard faced a mirror and noticed Zak checking him out. "It's the jacket," he said, smoothing the back of his collar. He tugged on the lapel, then raked his hand through his dark hair, grinning at his image in the mirror. "Makes all the difference."

"Who're you trying to impress?" Zak teased. "Apri, maybe?"

"What?… No." Gard objected. "Kendall said—"

Zak laughed. *Hah! Struck a nerve there.*

"Grow up!" Gard said.

Zak picked up his own plain, drab jacket and followed Gard out the door. *This could be fun.*

Kendall exited the room he shared with Apri. "Something funny?" He wore a short, well-fitted vest over a long-sleeved white shirt. Even his boots were cleaned and polished. "What's funny?" he asked again.

"Nothing," Gard grumbled and changed the subject. "Thanks for getting our clothes cleaned."

"Yes, thanks," Zak added, "I worried I wouldn't have any—" he stopped and exhaled a whistle at Apri. "Wow, you clean up nice!" The transformation amazed him. She looked so... *female*. Her dress hugged her athletic form, and the shimmery blue color sparkled in the subdued light like a school of fish swimming in a shallow stream.

"Don't look so surprised," she replied, with a glance at Gard. "A lady never misses chance to dress up." Batting her eyes at Zak in mock flirtation, she twirled, her skirt billowing out around her.

She looked so different—beautiful and exotic. Maybe Zak overreacted a little, but for Gard to say nothing, not even the slightest compliment? *Definitely something there.* He elbowed Gard in the ribs as they followed Apri and Kendall down the hall. Gard didn't acknowledge the nudge.

The meeting wouldn't start for another hour but leaving early would give the appearance they were going to the wrestling match. Soon they were lost in the crowd of people going the same way. A few blocks from the venue, they walked away from the wharf down a side street. Kendall led, winding his way through dark streets and run-down tenements.

Entering a more affluent neighborhood of Baytown, they strolled along a wide avenue of paver-stones lined with flickering streetlights. Homes and businesses looked out above the wharf district and out onto the expanse of the bay beyond.

Music and laughter spilled out onto the street from a fancy-looking club. "We have some time to kill," Kendall suggested. "Let's go have a drink."

A drink sounds nice. Zak followed the others into the building. *Several drinks? Mmmm, even better.* Bright lights illuminated a dining area that buzzed with conversation and activity. Servers bustled between tables, dressed in white shirts and dark vests with the club's name embroidered above the pocket.

They took a table that had just been cleared and ordered drinks. Boisterous shouts from a separate room with gaming tables battled with the sound of musicians entertaining the diners in the main hall. A few couples twirled and swayed on the dance floor in front of the band.

The music changed to a mellow tune that sounded somewhat familiar. Apri swayed back and forth, her fingers drumming the table with the three-beat tempo of the waltz. Zak saw Kendall glance at Gard and nod almost imperceptibly toward Apri. Gard looked away.

Kendall stood and extended a hand to Apri.

Apri cast a brief frown in Gard's direction before then took Kendall's hand and rose from the table, graceful and beguiling. They walked off to the dance floor.

Apri made quite the impression—attractive, sultry, mysterious. *And flirtatious!* Although that seemed more natural than intentional. He shook his head, dispelling the thoughts, the images, that came into his head. *How long has it been, anyway?*

He knew his relationship with Apri would never lead in that direction. He could certainly appreciate her good looks, but they'd settled into a comfortable friendship. Thinking of her in a romantic or sexual way just felt awkward and wrong. Besides, she obviously had her sights set elsewhere.

Zak's attention shifted to Gard, sitting across from him. The poor guy would watch Apri and Kendall on the dance floor for a while, then look away. Moments later his eyes wandered right back to where they swirled around in each other's arms. *It's definitely over for you, my friend.* He grinned but kept his observation private. "What do you expect to come from this meeting?" he asked.

He wondered if Gard heard the question, but eventually he wrenched his eyes from the dance floor and replied, "I've been wondering that myself, I honestly don't know what to expect."

The server came with their drinks just as Kendall and Apri returned.

"What to expect of what?" Kendall asked. He read Gard's expression, "Oh, *that*," he replied, then took a long drink. "I don't know what to expect either. I've been out of contact with them for months, and so much has happened since. People are afraid. Very afraid. They're reluctant to do anything that might arouse suspicion."

"But they must realize this can't go on. The Legiant is corrupt and ruthless. And it's getting worse," Gard said.

"I think they know that. But these people aren't soldiers. They're just like these folks here," Kendall said, waving his mug in the air. "They have businesses to run and families to provide for and protect. Even if they support a change in leadership, they don't have the courage, the capacity, or the leadership to force a change. And they fear what'll happen if they try something and it fails." Taking another drink, he added, "And rightly so."

They sat in silence for a few moments digesting Kendall's words.

Zak watched Gard. *Take a drink already.* He regretted his drink-pacing plan. Gard was distracted and mostly ignored the drink in front of him. Zak twirled his mug, watching the liquid swirl around.

Gard slapped the table and Zak flinched. "We *must* convince them to take action," Gard said.

Kendall smiled, "Well, that's the plan." He raised his drink to a server for a refill.

Zak switched his pace to match Kendall's until they left for the meeting.

A half hour later, they approached a large, whitewashed mansion near the top of a hill. "This is the place," Kendall said, leading them up the steps of a wide, pillar-lined porch. "This family owns the largest shipping business in Baytown. They're highly respected and influential."

The door opened, and a servant greeted Kendall with a slight bow. "Follow me, Mr. Kendall, if you please," the man said. "Good to see you again."

"And you as well, Parker," Kendall replied.

The servant led them though the entry of the lushly furnished home still adorned with Landing Day decorations. *Good thing Kendall told us to dress nice.* At the back of the house, a large picture window looked out over the wharf and to the bay beyond. Only a few lights were visible from the buildings and streets below on this dark night, but Zak imagined the view on a moonlit night, or on a clear day, would be spectacular.

The servant opened a pair of double doors at the end of the window-room. The acrid smell of pipeweed drifted out of the room, mingled with the musty scent of old parchments and books. An unusual aroma, but not unpleasant—like wealth and power mixed with a touch of intellect, if such a thing had an odor.

As they entered the room, the men inside, and a few women, were engaged in a heated conversation.

"It's too risky," a man said. "The Legiant is too powerful." Murmurs from others suggested many in the room shared that concern.

"Yes, it *is* risky…" The man who stood near the door stopped mid-sentence. "Ah, here he is now. Kendall," he laid a hand on Kendall's shoulder, "I'm having difficulty convincing our friends here the gravity of our situation. I hope you have better luck."

"Thank you, Phillip," Kendall said. "And thank you all for your time..."

As Kendall spoke, Zak surveyed the room. A few people listened intently, nodding their heads in agreement now and then. Others carried on quiet conversations amongst themselves, seemingly skeptical. A couple of men at the back of the room weren't even paying attention.

Not a very dynamic speaker. Kendall's monotonous intonation and insipid style reminded Zak of the time he stood before his classmates sweating and stuttering his way through an oral book report. He'd avoided the humiliation ever since and gained an appreciation for people who excelled at public speaking. Kendall was not among them.

He listened as Kendall droned on, sharing more information with his audience about the Legiant and his corrupt activities.

At least he's not shaking.

"It is only going to get worse," Kendall said. "And more innocent people will die or have their lives ruined by his actions."

"How do we know these things you say are the truth?" a woman asked. "There are so many stories going around, about the Legiant, the Cortek. I'm not sure what to believe."

"Who do you think is spreading those stories? Casting doubt and suspicion?" Kendall asked.

"It could be *you*," another man said. "We don't know you… or your friends here."

Zak crossed his arms and shifted his stance. *He's losing them.*

"You say the Legiant was responsible for that massacre at the campus in Edyson, another said, "but I heard some squader went crazy and killed them all."

The group became agitated and divided. Murmurs and side conversations escalated and soon they were arguing with each other.

Kendall glanced at Zak with a look of desperation. *He can't be expecting* me *to—*

"You people have your heads in the sand!" Gard bellowed above the din.

The bickering ended, cut off like a snuffed candle. Gard's tone commanded attention, and his angry expression forced all in the room to silence. Even the two men in the back looked up.

This should be good.

Gard lowered his voice, but his next words were just as harsh. "Your fear has overtaken reason. And sanity."

Kendall took a step toward him, but Gard's defiant glare kept him at bay.

"Fear is the Legiant's most effective weapon. When fear rules our lives, we choose to believe whatever keeps us safe. But that safety is temporary at best." To Zak's surprise, Gard shared the story of the campus massacre with this group of strangers, in gruesome detail. "The truth is that power has corrupted this man that I once called my friend. The *only* option is to divest him of that power," he concluded, then stormed out of the room. The front door slammed shut, the sound echoing through the house.

Apri hurried after Gard, her heels beating a rhythmic staccato on the tile floor.

A few quiet murmurs broke the silence in the room.

"You talk about risk?" Kendall pointed at the door. "My friend just risked his own life sharing his story with you. *He* is the berserk squader the Legiant wishes to blame for that massacre."

"Friends, please," Phillip interjected, "let's be reasonable here..."

Phillip took lead of the discussion, then. Clearly a better orator than Kendall, he was quick to capture the emotion left in Gard's wake and use it to control and motivate his listeners. The men and women who'd been the most vocal skeptics earlier were among the first to voice their support. Others followed suit until every man and woman at the meeting agreed it was time to act.

They spent the next half hour talking about what action to take against the Legiant. Zak had little interest in the discussion and found himself wishing he'd left with Apri. *This is not helping me find Katy.*

In the end, they decided on a coup attempt, and felt it would have the best chance of success if executed on the day the Legiant was to be married. They would convene in the capital two weeks prior to the wedding date to make final plans. Many of those in attendance promised to make the trip to Edyson personally.

The doors opened and servers entered with drinks and refreshments. Conversations around Zak turned to the wrestling bout taking place that evening and other local sporting events and competitions. Zak was about to suggest to Kendall that they go find Gard and Apri, when two men entered to a round of applause and commotion. After the rowdy reception, the men gave a report on the outcome of the wrestling match.

Zak noticed Kendall sharing the list of camouflaged names with their host, Phillip. After a quiet conversation, he put the list back in his pocket, motioned to Zak, and they left the meeting together.

Gard and Apri were seated on a brick landscape fence across from the estate. *Don't they look cozy?* She leaned against him—she couldn't be any closer without sitting in his lap.

Kendall coughed.

Gard jumped up from the fence so quickly that Apri lost her balance, almost falling over before she caught herself. "Did it work?" he asked.

Kendall said, "It worked, they're on board." Then he said more seriously, "But you took a huge risk."

"You planned that?" Zak asked.

"No," Gard said, running fingers through his hair. "But we couldn't leave without their support. It wasn't going well, and it's all I could think of to win them over."

"You'll have to leave Baytown tonight," Kendall said. "I'm not sure we can trust everyone in that meeting. And someone on the staff may've overheard. The price on your head is too high to assume none will be tempted to turn you in. Apri and I can stay here until the wedding date is announced, then meet you in the city."

"No argument from me," Gard agreed.

As they made their way back to the inn, Kendall walked ahead telling Gard about what happened after he stormed out.

Apri looked like she wanted to argue, but she said nothing.

Zak nudged her. "You two looked rather chummy back there." He pursed his lips and made a kissing sound.

She rolled her eyes. "Grow up, Zak."

"We can't hope to pull this off without a few experienced fighters," Gard said.

Kendall shared what he'd learned from Phillip about others he knew to be Core-friendly and sympathetic to their cause. "Perhaps they can help. But he hasn't been in touch with these people in more than a year," Kendall said. "Take extra care before approaching or trusting anyone. I'll make some contacts in Edyson as well."

When Zak began this journey, whether it was a quest for revenge or an escape from The Ravens, the passage of time didn't matter. But now? *Every day I'm not searching for my sister is wasted time.* He thought about leaving straight for Edyson without them. But Apri was right, the capital was unfamiliar to him. *I shouldn't've spent the only night I was there at the bar getting drunk.* He wouldn't even know where to begin looking. If he tried on his own, he'd just waste more time aimlessly wandering around the city. *Or drinking.* It felt like he wore lead boots as he climbed the stairs to their rooms.

Monk bounced and chattered as Zak and Gard changed clothes and packed to leave.

Gard answered a knock at the door.

Apri stood at the door holding something in her hand. She slithered by Gard, brushing up against him as she went.

Gard backed away, but only the slightest bit. His eyes followed her as she moved across the room to Zak, handing him the small package. Apri's own attraction to Gard was as obvious as his pathetic attempt to dodge the sparks flying between them whenever they were together. *Get a room, already!*

"I brought you something, Zak," she said.

"Oh? For me?" He gave Gard a roguish grin.

A disgruntled *harrumph* came from the doorway as Gard turned to leave. "I'll be downstairs," he said.

"Good luck taming that one," Zak said to Apri.

She ignored the comment. "This is soap for Monk. The reason he loses fur is soap you use. It is too harsh."

"When did you—"

"When you went to…" Her forehead crinkled. "…to see horse?"

"To see a man about a horse," he corrected, "Thanks." He put the soap in his travelpack. "Let's go, Monk." The climber jumped on his shoulder. "I guess we'll be seeing you in Edyson."

"Safe travels." She reached up and stroked Monk's bristled little chin. "You be good Monkjan."

With so many visitors in town for the big wrestling match that night, they weren't the only late arrivals at the stable to collect their horses—a good time to slip away unnoticed. Zak watched Gard's dark shadow ahead of him as they rode out of Baytown in the dead of night. *Here we go again.*

Chapter 15
Apri

A few nights later, Apri walked with Kendall back to their room. They'd just left another lengthy and contentious meeting with the group in Baytown, with their exhaustive debating wildly diverse options of governing the colony. *What about the plan to get rid of Covington? Why do they not discuss that?* "All this talk about politics creates such conflict and divides the group when they should be united," she said to Kendall.

"Look at it this way," Kendall replied, "they've embraced the idea that how to rule Edyson after the takeover *is* open for debate. Doesn't that work in our favor? Their enthusiasm is evidence that they are committed to support the cause."

"Perhaps," she said. "It just seems they spend too much time worrying about what comes after instead of talking about what has to come before."

"In truth, they will have little to do with that," he said. "The action against the Legiant will not be their battle. We're not recruiting an army for military combat. This will be a covert operation involving a few skilled fighters intent on one objective alone... to capture, or kill, the Legiant with as few casualties as possible."

Kendall didn't seem to understand Apri's frustration or to take her concern seriously.

After an extended pause, Kendall said, "Listen, Apri, the odds are stacked against us. Chances of success are slim. If they weren't talking about how to rule Edyson after the current ruler is gone, the discussion would soon turn to how foolish it is to think we can actually pull this off."

"Exactly!"

He leaned away from her, hand on his chest, mocking her passionate response. Shaking his head, he chuckled. "It seems you are worrying about it enough for all of us."

The next day, news came from Edyson of the Legiant's wedding date—less than two months away.

"I say let's leave immediately," Kendall suggested.

"Yes!" Apri agreed, pleased at not having to attend another meeting.

After collecting their horses at the stables, they went to Phillip's business on the wharf to say goodbye and to leave instructions on how to contact Kendall when the members arrived at the capital.

The trip to Edyson would take the better part of three weeks, and Apri didn't look forward to the long road trip. Although she and Kendall had been sharing a room for the sake of convenience, they weren't sleeping together. He'd asked her about it a few times early on, but it always ended in an argument when she refused to explain. She thought about getting her own room, but they'd have no time to do anything but sleep on this trip. Enduring the awkward situation would be better than wasting what little money she had on a private room, especially with her future in Edyson so uncertain.

Apri struggled to understand the change herself. She liked Kendall, of course. They'd been intimate when she lived with the Dovetails, and quite frequently. But she'd always considered him to be a friend, and nothing more. But now, after that look he'd given her the first morning after their reunion, resuming their former affair would be cruel.

She'd always blamed Rrazmik for her inability to get terribly attached to another person. That, and being around so many complacent couples growing up. Couples who weren't necessarily unhappy, but not truly happy either. At least that's how it seemed to her. There'd been so much pressure to conform, to find a mate, to settle down and raise a family, but she wanted more from a relationship than just going through the motions to satisfy social convention.

She and Kendall had talked themselves out after only a couple of days on the road. They spent most nights in roadside inns, and even those were void of any worthwhile conversation. \A *life with him would be as boring as this road trip!*

They'd risen early again to weather warm and muggy, and traveled as fast as the horses could handle without breaking down. *Another day staring at Kendall's back, with nothing to do but reminisce.*

Throughout the long, tiresome days, she thought often of Gard. He was the first man with whom she felt a real connection—an attraction that went deeper than just the physical. It was a feeling that up to now she'd thought herself immune to. Her mind drifted back to that night in Baytown, when she'd followed him out of the house after his tirade.

✷✷✷

Gard walked out into the street with long, purposeful strides and she chased after him, calling his name.

He stopped and turned around, and she ran right into him. His arms wrapped around her to keep them both from falling.

For a heartbeat, she forgot about everything and everyone else... Kendall, Edyson, the Legiant, Katrina, those thoughtless people in the meeting room, even how clumsy it was to crash into him like that. In that moment, only one thing mattered—the feel of his arms around her.

He backed away, holding her at arm's length until she caught her balance.

Their eyes met, and she had to fight the urge to reach out to his mind. She broke eye contact before she lost that internal battle. "Are you alright?" she asked.

"I'm fine," he raked his fingers through his hair. "Those people... they just don't know..."

"Of course, they do not," she said. "How could they?"

Their eyes met again.

"Yes, how could they?" he repeated.

He crossed the street and sat on a low stone fence.

Sitting next to him, she edged closer, inch by inch. He felt tense as a bowstring, poised to release at any second. *Will that release bring him into my arms?* It seemed more likely he would flee from her, from the raw emotion they generated. She slid away.

He exhaled a sigh and relaxed. "It was unreal, what happened that day," he said. "I've seen men die. I've seen bodies scattered around the battlefield. This was different."

She listened, understanding his grief at witnessing the careless slaughter of those people. She wanted to hold him—this man who held himself responsible for every evil thing the Legiant did. But his compulsion to resist her, to keep his distance, formed an invisible barrier she would not cross.

"It is not your fault," she said after a quiet moment. "You could not have known." She eased herself closer, leaning into him for comfort.

"The first man I came to... he was still alive. Barely. He asked me to give a message to his son. Something about a secret. A secret that he and his wife, the boy's mother, had been keeping from him his whole life." Gard sighed again. "It seemed so important to him. That his son would get this message. I never even learned the man's name."

Apri reached out to stroke his arm, and this time, he didn't resist. "Perhaps there is still time for you to find him?" She sensed that delivering the stranger's message, this father's last wish, had become important to him. "You should not give up," she said.

His expression conveyed appreciation for her words. And something more?

Their eyes met again, and she looked into them, as deep as she could without entering his mind. He leaned into her.

She held her breath.

***

Then Kendall and Zak were there.

And now Gard was klicks away.

At least Kendall had given up trying to resume their sexual relationship, although the tension between them remained. Then again, they were both so tired of being on the road that the tension she felt could be as much from exhaustion and their mutual desire for the trip to be over. Relief swept over her when the walls of the capital came into view on the horizon.

The thick walls surrounding Edyson were at least ten meters high. *Is that to keep people in? Or out?* The cities of Ararat were not walled in, and with nothing to contain their borders they grew outwards, consuming more of the countryside over the years. Here, the buildings had almost no space between them. *And so tall!* If Apri didn't know better, she'd say they'd sprung upwards from being squashed so tightly together. The earthy, monochromatic tones, accentuated by the late afternoon sun, were also different from the elaborate and varied colors of the buildings in her homeland. The prevalence of flexclay gave the city a surreal, foreign quality.

And the people! So many people! Until coming to Edyson, she'd never considered how Aratians looked so much alike. But the culture shock she experienced in Baytown didn't compare to being here in the capital where the diverse physical features among the people accentuated the foreign atmosphere of the place.

Apri had dreamed of leaving Ararat, of sailing to the Edyson colony, for years. At times, she'd worried that being Aratian would set her apart, that she'd stand out as a stranger from a different land. She laughed. Everyone here looks different in some way. A man with white-blond hair and skin so light it was almost translucent walked alongside a dark-skinned woman with hair piled high in tiny braids that swirled in a nest on her head. A giggling young child with orange-red hair and a face full of freckles played in a courtyard.

The strange sights and sounds fueled her elation at being at the end of her long-delayed trek to Edyson. She kept asking questions of Kendall. "What is that sound?... Where is it coming from?... Where are all these people going?... How old is that building?...

What is that place?… What is that smell?…" She pelted him with an endless barrage of questions.

He answered them all cheerfully, even volunteering information she hadn't thought to ask about. For the first time since their reunion, she thought it possible they could get past the awkwardness that had infected their relationship like a bothersome parasite.

Apri finally thought to ask the most obvious question, "Where are we going?"

"Northgate," he replied. "We entered at Westgate."

"So, I suppose there is Southgate? And Eastgate?"

He laughed, "Yes, in fact there is!"

"Of course."

"Okay." he laughed again. "So maybe it's not the most creative, but it does help visitors keep their bearings. The city's divided into different districts. The district around each gate shares its name. So, we entered through Westgate—Outer Westgate first, then Inner Westgate on this side. We'll travel through a few other districts, most named after some noteworthy resident or politician from the past, on our way to Northgate. "I'd take a less direct route and show you more of the city, but it's getting late, and we need to reach our destination before dark."

"And our destination is…?" she asked.

"You'll see," he said.

Since Kendall didn't elaborate further, Apri resumed her litany of comments and questions about the city. "You seem to know much about this place," she observed.

They were riding single file down a narrow lane and Kendall turned around to face her. "I grew up here," he said.

"Hmmm, I suppose I never asked where you were from," she realized aloud.

"No, you never did," he said with a tone of disappointment.

She wanted to apologize. Not for never asking—that would just come off as insincere—but for not caring as much for him as, perhaps, he did for her. *How do I say that?* Unable to put her thoughts into words, she felt the awkwardness between them return.

They rode on in silence until they passed through the city gates and Apri's curiosity overcame her discomfort. "We are leaving city? Are you going to tell me where we go now?" she asked.

"No." Kendall replied. His response was so abrupt she thought he was still upset. But then he teased, "You really should learn to be more patient, you know."

"So I have been told," she admitted.

They followed the road out of Edyson until the buildings of Outer Northgate were behind them. Kendall picked up the pace, leading her down a narrow dirt road that led north. A large sign said *Forest Inn* with an arrow. A temporary-looking sign hung underneath it that read, *No Vacancy*. The road doubled back toward the city, and soon they were in the inn's courtyard.

"We're here, what do you think?" Kendall said.

"It is an inn. And the sign said *No Vacancy*. Why do we not stay in Edyson?"

"Ordinarily, I'd stay on the campus, in the city. But since the Law Squad has taken residence there, that's not an option. This is the next best thing."

A stablehand approached, and Kendall showed her his Cortek card.

"Welcome home," she said.

He dismounted and unlaced his pack from the back of his saddle. "They'll take care of the horses and stow any personal belongings you leave here with your tack in a private locker."

Apri unlaced her travelpack, slung it over her shoulder, and gave Dega a pat on the neck, rubbing the mare's sweaty ears. "You be good, now," she said.

"My name's Tarina," the stablehand said with a warm smile and a wink. "I'll give her a good rub down," she promised.

"Thank you, Tarina. I am Apri, and this is Dega," she said, giving the mare another pat on the neck. "We have been riding hard for almost three weeks. She deserves a good rest."

Apri watched the mare being led away, then followed Kendall into the inn. They entered a clean and spacious dining hall, much like those they'd stayed at on the road from Baytown. With one exception.

"So many children," she said.

"This place is housing the displaced Cortek. Many of these families were living on campus and others have come here from around the colony. This, or the campus anyway, is really where I grew up. It's all very familiar to me." After a few moments he added, "It's good to be home."

He stepped up to the clerk at the desk and handed her his card. "You'll need to show your card here. Do you have it?"

She retrieved it from the pocket of her vest.

"Thank you," the clerk said. "I'll be right back."

The dining hall was busy and some of the children ran around between tables, laughing and yelling. "They seem to be happy, anyway," she observed.

Kendall shrugged. "Heck, they're kids. They probably think it's a grand adventure."

The clerk returned, "Welcome back, sir. Your mother asked to be notified of your arrival. Can I tell her you're here?"

"Of course," he said, smiling. "Can you ask her to meet us in the dining hall?"

The woman nodded. "And you are Apri?" she asked.

"Yes." Apri didn't recall giving the woman her name. "Apri Balakian, from Ararat.

"I am Naomi. Welcome to the Forest Inn. Your recruiter has been advised of your arrival."

"My recruiter?"

Kendall answered, "The man who gave you the card."

How long have you had this card?" Naomi asked her as she handed their cards back.

"I was fourteen," she said, "so—"

Kendall raised an eyebrow. He'd been trying to discover her age since they first met. Not that she cared if he knew, but at some point, the secret had become a game between them—one she did not wish to lose.

With a grin at Kendall, she said, "a long time."

Naomi gave Kendall an odd look, then eyed Apri again. "Fourteen, you say?"

"What is it?" Kendall asked her.

"A long time, indeed," she said, smiling. "Before her recruiter became our headmaster."

"*Barrow* gave it to her?" Kendall asked.

"Yes, sir."

"Huh, imagine that," he said.

"And he insisted on coming here to greet her, as is the protocol," she said.

"That's quite fortunate, actually. I have some things to discuss with him. Now I won't have to worry about tracking him down."

"At any other time, you'd be greeted on campus," she explained to Apri. "But alas, we do what we must." The woman gave an exasperated look at the children running rampant in the dining hall.

Kendall laughed, "We'll be staying a while. I hope you have a room for Apri? I can stay with my parents."

Naomi gave Kendall an oddly sympathetic look, so brief he didn't seem to notice.

"I hope I do not intrude. I can stay in city if it is too much trouble," Apri volunteered.

"No trouble at all, dear," she said, taking a key off the wall next to the desk. "Here you go. Room two-twelve. Up the stairs, two flights, and to the right."

"Thank you." Her stomach grumbled. Other than chewing on some dried meat during their ride, she hadn't eaten since breakfast early that morning.

"Hungry?" Kendall asked.

"Starved," she admitted.

The food was served cafeteria-style. Following Kendall's example, she picked up a tray and slid it along, serving herself generous portions of food from the buffet. It smelled delicious, and her stomach growled again.

Kendall laughed. "There's that impatience again!" He gave his card to the server.

Apri did the same, and the server took both cards, went into a back room, then returned with them.

They sat at an empty table, away from the swarm of children. The food tasted as good as it smelled. *Or I am just hungry*.

"Mmmm, good," Apri muttered, drowning a mouthful with a drink of warm ale.

"Kendall!... Kendall? are you here?!" a woman's voice shouted from the doorway.

Kendall rolled his eyes, then raised his hand in the air. "Over here, mom," he yelled back to her.

She came to the table, and he gave his mother a huge grear hug, kissing her cheek. Tears streamed down her face, "My boy, you're home!" she cried.

"Yes, mom," he said, holding her at arm's length. "It's so good to see you!" He hugged her again.

"I've missed you so much," she said into his shoulder. "So much has happened."

Apri kept eating, eyes on her plate, uncomfortable to witness the emotional reunion.

"Mother, I'd like you to meet someone," he said, looking at Apri with misty eyes.

His mother tore her gaze from her son and greeted Apri with a broad grin. She had one of those smiles that lit up her whole face, crinkling her eyes and producing deep dimples in her cheeks.

"This is a good friend of mine, Apri Balakian. Would you please join us? Have you eaten? Something to drink?"

"Nice to meet you," Apri muttered.

His mother sat at their table, ogling her son. "No, I'm not hungry, but maybe some wine?"

Kendall left the table to get the wine, and his mother gave Apri her full attention, "*Balakian*, is it? You're Aratian?"

"Yes, I am. You know of Ararat?"

"Yes, but I've never been. Always wanted to, though. I am pleased to meet you." She reached out and put her hand on top of Apri's. "You may call me Yelena," she said with her beaming smile. "And thank you, Apri, for bringing my son home to me."

"I didn't really—" Apri felt a presence in her head and immediately blocked the mental contact. She glared at Yelena, but the woman's attention had turned to her son, who'd just returned with the wine. *Not her.*

Apri surveyed the room but saw no one paying particular attention to her. *Curious.* She'd never felt that kind of intrusion in her own thoughts, not at any time since her encounter with the pegafox. It didn't feel repulsive or unfriendly but was certainly foreign and invasive. Now she understood how others felt when she reached out to read their thoughts. And her reaction mirrored theirs. A mental block that translated as, *Get out of my head!*

"Mom, you're embarrassing her," Kendall said, pouring the wine.

"I don't care!" she said with such joy and gusto that Apri laughed aloud. Yelena picked up her glass and said, "Kenadz," using a common Aratian drinking salute. They touched glasses and drank.

"Is dad here?" Kendall asked.

His mother's smile and joyful demeanor disappeared, and she began weeping again. But these were not happy tears.

"What is it?"

"No one has told you?"

"No. Told me what? I've heard nothing," he said. When she didn't respond right away, fear crept into his voice, "Something about dad?"

"You heard about… the massacre?" The last two words were uttered with such grief that it could mean only one thing.

Apri inhaled sharply, hand covering her mouth.

"No!" Kendall exhaled.

"Your father… he was one of the first to die... He was… outside in the yard. They gave no warning… just came in the gate and started killing people," she said, wiping her tears. "Many more would've died if not for the squader who came to our rescue. An awful, awful day."

"Father is… dead?"

His mother broke down, and Kendall moved his chair to hers to hold her close, tears trailing down his face. "I am so sorry I wasn't here for you, Mom," he said quietly, his voice cracking with emotion, "for you both."

It took Yelena some time to recover. Kendall held her close, his own tears falling as he gently rubbed her back until she recovered enough to speak. "Don't be sorry. I thank heaven every day that you weren't here. To think I might've lost you both?" She began to cry again, and Kendall held her until her tears abated.

Apri cried with them, Gard's story replaying in her mind but now more personal, more real than ever. "I am so sorry for your loss," she said.

Kendall refilled their wine glasses. "Apri and I met the man who came to your rescue," he told his mother.

"What?… How?" The news seemed to help draw her out of her misery.

"It's a complicated story. And the reason we're here."

"I tended him during his recovery," Yelena said. "He's a very brave man, fighting those horrible squaders. All by himself!"

"Yes. A good man, indeed." Kendall finished his wine. "I need to get Apri sett—"

"Well, look what the kat dragged in!" The Aratian idiom was spoken by a spry, elderly man who walked up to their table, arms extended.

Kendall rose and greeted him with the Edyson gesture. "Headmaster Barrow! Good to see you."

Apri rose as well. Although much older, she recognized him as the man who'd visited her home those many years ago. Gratitude and relief swept over her. *I am here! I made it!* Followed by apprehension. *But is it too late? Am I too old?* Desperation set in, to think she might be turned away. After coming this far? She had to sit down to avoid passing out. *I want to stay.*

"I'm truly sorry about your father," Barrow said to Kendall, shaking his head. "A dreadful day."

"Thank you. I only found out myself just now," Kendall said. "About my father. But I actually heard of the attack firsthand."

Barrow raised a curious eyebrow.

Kendall turned his attention to Apri. "I ran into an acquaintance of yours." He extended a hand to her. "This is Apri Balakian of Ararat. She says she met you there as a young girl."

"Headmaster," Apri said, standing up again to greet him, "I am sure you do not recall. I was only fourteen, a long while ago. I apologize that it took so long to get here but things just… kept happening. If it is too late—"

"Oh poppycock," the old man interrupted. "It's never too late. And I *do* remember you. It wasn't often that I made the trip to Ararat," then added with a grin, "and I'm not *that* old."

Apri exhaled in a rush. "I am afraid if you told me it was too late, I would just hang around outside until you changed your mind," she said.

They laughed, but she was serious.

"I need to get Apri settled in," Kendall said. "Do you have time to meet tomorrow morning?" he asked Barrow. "We have much to discuss."

"Yes, I might have to move some things around." The old man seemed pensive. "I'll send you a time." He turned to leave, then faced them again. "Yelena, can you stop by and see me in an hour?"

Yelena nodded, appearing surprised by the invitation.

"Welcome to the home of the Cortek, Apri. Temporary home. I'm sorry we couldn't accommodate you on campus, but you'll be comfortable enough here. I hope I'll see you again soon." Barrow grasped her shoulder, then hurried away.

Kendall addressed his mother, "You have room for me at your place?"

"Yes, yes, of course! You get your friend settled." Yelena walked to the back.

"Please, Kendall" Apri said, "I can find my room." She nodded toward his mother and shrugged her travelpack over her shoulder. "We've seen enough of each other, no? Go be with your mother!" she ordered.

"Thanks," he said. "Meet you in the dining hall for breakfast tomorrow morning? Half past five?"

"Yes. Thank you for bringing me here, Kendall, truly. You cannot know how much it means to me." She hugged him, whispering in his ear, "And I am so sorry about your father."

"He was a good man." When they broke apart his eyes were misty again.

"Go," she said, pushing him toward the door.

Dropping her pack on the bed in her room, she undressed, looking forward to a long, hot shower. She found soap, shampoo, and fresh, clean towels. *And hot water!* The soap had a soothing scent that helped her relax. Focusing on the strange aroma kept her mind from wandering in countless directions.

Stepping from the shower, she wrapped a towel around her wet head and dressed for bed. Suddenly very sleepy, she fell onto the bed and crawled under the covers.

"Mmmm." *There must be something in that soap.*

Chapter 16
Apri

Apri woke early, still a little bleary-eyed but well rested. The skin on her face felt tight and warm, the mirror revealing a slight tinge of sunburn on her nose and cheeks. The weeks on the road had darkened her skin to a deep tan, not unusual for her, but a change after spending so much time inside at the caves. Her dark hair fell to well below her shoulders, framing her face in a tangled mess. Attacking it with a wet brush, she tamed it straight, then dressed and went down to the dining hall. *I need coffee!*

The dining room teemed with children again.

"Good morning, young Apri," Naomi greeted her cheerfully. "Can I get you some breakfast?"

"No breakfast, but… coffee?" she asked hopefully.

"Sure, hon." She stopped an older man who was rushing by. "Jay, I'd like you to meet someone."

The man stopped, wiping his hands on the apron tied at his waist. "Oh?"

"This is a new recruit. Apri. Of Ararat."

"Ararat, eh?" he said, bowing the Edyson greeting gesture. "Never been there myself. Welcome."

"Can you get her some coffee?" Naomi asked.

"A coffee drinker, of course. Come along with me, young lady." Placing a hand on Apri's back, he escorted her to the bar. "You drink it black, I assume?" He went behind the bar and poured some coffee into a cup.

She nodded, taking out her card.

"No." He waved his hand. "No charge for coffee. I'm afraid it isn't an Aratian roast," he apologized, serving her the mug.

"I do miss a strong brew," she admitted, sipping the coffee. "Mmmm. But this is just fine," she said, smiling. "Thank you, Jay. So good to meet you."

"You, too." A loud crash from behind startled her, and she almost spilt her coffee. Two children had run into each other, and the contents of their trays skittered across the floor. The younger girl began to cry.

"Gotta go!" Jay said with a sigh.

Apri placed her coffee on the bar and went to help clean up the mess.

"Please, you don't have to—" Jay protested.

"I have nothing better to do, and I hate being idle," she said. Kneeling to the level of the crying girl, she asked, "What is your name?"

The girl stopped crying and looked up. Red curls fell back from her face revealing freckle-faced cheeks wet with tears. "El," she said shyly.

"Hello, El," Apri said, making the Edyson greeting gesture. "My name is Apri. It is nice to meet you. How old are you?"

Blue eyes regarded Apri with an intent gaze. The girl held up her hand and raised three fingers, then four.

"Oh, my. A big girl!"

Jay handed a towel to Apri for wiping the floor while he gathered the far-flung bowls and utensils.

"Well, we will get this mess cleaned up, yes?" she said to El. "Things like this happen. It was accident. You are okay?"

The girl nodded.

A woman approached, smiling appreciation to Apri. "I apologize, Jay," she said, helping with the cleanup, then took the young girl by the hand, "Come along, Elenza."

The girl glanced back at Apri as she walked to the buffet line with her mother.

Apri gave the girl a little wave, then retrieved her mug from the bar and wandered out to the stables to check on Dega.

The mare munched on her breakfast looking quite content. No longer stiff and matted with sweat, her coat was just a bit dusty from rolling around in the straw. Apri entered the stall and checked her hooves. *Picked clean. Nice!*

The stablehand came to the stall door. "Hello, again, Apri."

"Hi, Tarina," Apri replied, still holding the mare's hoof in her hand. She dropped it, embarrassed to be caught checking the girl's work. "I do not mean to—"

"Oh, don't worry about it. I'd do the same myself."

Apri leaned into the mare, smiling. "I do love this girl. We are together since her birth."

Tarina grinned, "Would you like to meet *my* baby?" she said.

"Of course!" Apri said.

Tarina took her to the stall of a large bay gelding. "I raised him from a foal, too."

As they wandered around the stables together trading horse stories, the stablehand, Tarina, would pause at the occasional stall and introduce its equine resident. Inside the spacious tack room, Tarina showed Apri to her private locker and explained how to use her card to unlock it.

"So organized!" Apri observed. She looked into her mug. *Empty.* "Oh, my, what time is it?" she asked.

"Maybe about half past five?" Tarina guessed.

As she stepped from the tack room, Kendall's mother called out, "Apri! Apri? Are you here?"

"Ah, there you are, girl. I've got such good news!"

"Sorry, I lost track of time," Apri apologized. "Is Kendall waiting?"

"No, no. He had some other business and asked me to meet you instead. Have you had breakfast?"

"No, I was waiting for him," Apri said. "Tarina, it was nice visiting with you. Perhaps we could go riding together sometime?"

Tarina beamed. "I'd like that. Yes, let's do." she said. "I'd love to hear more about Ararat."

"I could use another cup of coffee," Apri said as she walked with Yelena to the dining hall. "I'm still a bit groggy from last night."

"You must've used the seda-soap," Yelena said.

Apri rubbed her arm. A trace of the scent still lingered on her skin. "I *knew* that soap had something in it. You said you have news?"

"Yes, but let's get some food and sit."

They found a table in the back, away from the hubbub and noise. Yelena seemed about to burst with her news, but she waited until Apri sat and gave her full attention.

"I've been assigned as your sponsor!"

"My sponsor?"

"Yes, all new recruits are assigned a sponsor to guide them through their first year at the campus."

"Oh, I see," Apri said. "My sponsor." Her attempt to sound enthusiastic failed. *Kendall's mother? This will be awkward.*

"Yes, by Headmaster Barrow, himself."

"Oh?"

"You aren't happy?" Yelena asked. "I know you and Kendall aren't a couple, if that's what's got you all hot and bothered." Yelena chuckled at the relief in Apri's expression. "I've always been fascinated by Aratian history," she explained. "He thought it'd be a good match, that's all."

"Oh." Apri relaxed. *Perhaps that explains her exuberance. She cannot be this bubbly all the time, right?*

"I asked Headmaster Barrow why he chose you as a recruit."

"I always wondered about that myself," Apri admitted.

"He said when he recruited anywhere outside of Edyson—which wasn't often—he'd talk to the priests, librarians, and teachers about the young people in the community."

Apri laughed, "I am sure my name was at the top of their list." She'd been a curious student, always asking questions and challenging beliefs, especially when it came to the origin of Ararat. And the other colonies, too. So much mystery with only vague and confusing answers. Like, "We come from the stars…" *What does that mean?* Mother had dismissed her interest. *Nothing you need to worry about, Aprijan,* she'd say. But Father encouraged her to ask questions, to do her own research for answers. *Don't accept ignorance as others do,* he'd told her. She took his advice, but even so, learned very little. Eventually, she just gave up trying.

Apri had missed some of Yelena's conversation by her reminiscing. "…asking questions, and challenging the answers, since you were very young. He wanted to recruit you, but your parents wouldn't let you go."

"My mother said no, of course. She just wanted me to get married and have babies like every other girl in Ararat. My father would have brought me to Edyson himself, if he could be away for so long. But he would not let his daughter to go away with man he did not know."

Sipping her coffee, Apri watched the children running around the hall. Missing that opportunity had been devastating for her. "When I did not grow out of my desire for adventure, Father took me to a man in the village, an ex-soldier or mercenary. I learned from him how to fight and defend myself. I would have run away, tried to get here on my own, were it not for old Rrazmik. When he became sick, I stayed to be his caretaker until he died."

With her long-anticipated goal of reaching the campus realized, precious memories of those days and the sequence of events that led her here, washed over her. She sighed. "That is when I left to come here," she said, smiling at Yelena.

Yelena reached across the table and put a hand on her arm. "You were lucky to have such a mentor."

"The combat training was useful, of course, but he taught me much more than just how to fight. I already owe him my life many times over." *Rrazmik… Do you see? I am here!*

When they finished breakfast, Yelena's face split into her wide, face-altering grin. "Ordinarily, new recruits are much younger than you," she said, raising a finger to ward off any interruption. "*Ordinarily*, new recruits start their education on the campus. *Ordinarily*, new recruits are assigned a *young* Cortek sponsor." Standing, she gathered her tableware, and Apri did the same. "But these are not *ordinary* times, and you are no *ordinary* recruit."

They carried their plates to Jay at the bar.

"And I'm no *ordinary* sponsor!" She laughed.

The noise from the children in the dining hall absorbed Apri's boisterous laughter, a release of anxiety, mixed with sheer joy. "I do not doubt that," she said.

"So, let's begin this *extraordinary* adventure together, shall we?" Yelena locked arms with Apri and escorted her through the back door of the dining hall to a private room furnished with a few comfy, stuffed chairs.

"Let's get to know each other a bit," Yelena began. "Why don't you start by telling me about your encounter with the pegafox?"

Apri managed to find the chair before falling to the floor. No words had ever stunned her more than that question from Yelena, and it set off a torrential storm in her head. She'd spent so many years suppressing that memory, trying to convince herself it didn't happen. It jolted her senses. And roused suspicion. *Maybe this is a test?* Did her parents tell Barrow about her story, and they wanted to find out if she still believed it? *How do I react to this?*

Apri felt a foreign presence in her head and recognized it as the same touch from the dining hall. Then came a vision of a pegafox—but not like an artist's rendition from a child's storybook. The image of the small, white-winged animal that appeared in her head was just as she remembered it, in every detail. *But the setting is different.* This vision came from someone else's experience.

Yelena watched her, nodding.

"It was you," Apri said, amazed.

"Yesterday? Yes." Yelena smiled. "But at that time, I just thought you were highly perceptive. I didn't realize you had the gift until I talked with Barrow after."

"Headmaster Barrow knew? About me?" Apri asked.

"Yes, he felt you in his head the day he met with your parents," she said. "Because he knew me and my story, he recognized the sensation immediately."

"Oh." Back then, Apri used to experiment with her gift from time to time, especially with strangers. She recalled Barrow's visit—remembered him sitting in the other room. *Of course.* He'd seen her lurking in the kitchen just after she reached out to his mind. *He knew!*

"You were one of the biggest regrets of his recruiting days, he told me," Yelena said. "He's very pleased you're here."

Apri shared her story of the pegafox with Yelena. She'd gone riding in the woods and took a bad fall. "I was knocked out, and when I woke, the pegafox hovered above me." The small, dog-like creature had silvery white fur and wings that spread out twice its length in either direction. "I felt it in my mind. It did not use words, but sensations and images, you know?"

Yelena nodded. "Mmm-hmm."

"I think it healed my head injury," Apri said, "and I always believed it to be the reason for my mental talent."

"And so it is," Yelena acknowledged. "You and I are proof that the legend of the pegafox is true—that they exist and can pass their telepathic gift to humans they encounter."

Apri relaxed into the back of her seat, absorbing the news, then recounted the days after her accident. "There were times I cried out to my parents when I was recovering, from my mind to theirs. But they closed their minds to me and refused to accept that I had been given special powers, or that I had seen a pegafox at all. I sensed their concern, their fear that the head injury had made me crazy. Maybe I even picked up that feeling from their thoughts? By the time I recovered, I had stopped talking about it. Afterwards, if anyone mentioned it, I just laughed along with them about my wild imagination. That is what they wanted to hear anyway. I tried sharing the story a few other times after that with close friends. But no one ever believed me."

"Well, I can assure you that it's very real. You, my dear, are a muse. As am I." Yelena patted Apri's knee. "And that's the real reason Barrow paired us up!"

With Yelena's guidance and encouragement over the next few weeks, Apri learned more about her gift than she'd ever discovered on her own. It was a welcome relief to have her ability confirmed as real after hiding it for so many years. Aspects of her gift that had confounded her in the past were explained or dispelled, one by one. Each tidbit of information, each of Yelena's explicit demonstrations or exercises, snapped into place for her like the missing piece of a puzzle.

"The reason you're comfortable and adept at projecting to animals is because their brains are simple," Yelena explained during one session. "They're reactionary, and how they react is determined by memories from their own experience. You project to them an image of a different outcome or experience, and they accept it without question. An animal wouldn't consider that a thought or sensation might not be their own. Most animals welcome, and even appreciate, the mental connection."

Apri had found the same to be true of animals. But after a few disastrous attempts to mentally connect with people, she'd given up trying. *Except for Katrina.*

Yelena helped her understand why. "Humans are complicated, especially when it comes to our brains. You can't just jump into a person's head and expect them not to notice the intrusion. Unless you're invited in, unless the contact is welcome, their automatic instinct will be to reject the invasion, and you will be blocked, just as you did to me yesterday. So, if your intention is to intrude secretly, you must be stealthy. Mimic their mindset. Think as they think. Ease into their head quietly, gently. The person must believe your thought is theirs."

One afternoon, she and Yelena joined a classroom of young children to experiment with what she had learned.

"Children are less complicated than adults. And less wary." Yelena said. "They're also easier to read... to interpret their thoughts. Very young children are so impressionable they seldom recognize a mental intruder." She pointed to a child. "See that boy over there? With the toy? I'm going to project for him to give the toy to another child."

Only seconds passed before the boy handed the toy to the girl next to him. Apri read the boy's confused and envious expression, as if he were thinking, *Why did I do that?*

"Notice how he already wants it back."

The boy was in a tug-of-war with the girl, the toy between them.

"Influencing a person to do something that goes against their nature, or their immediate desires, will not last. The more foreign the act is for them, the more likely they'll know the thought is not theirs. Now, why don't you try?"

Looking around the room, Apri brought to mind childish thoughts and desires. A girl sat on the floor, playing with a tea set. She wriggled and fidgeted with her legs squeezed together. Another girl stood nearby, eying the tea set. Recognizing the posture of the first girl, Apri reached out to her mind. *I need to go potty.*

The girl with the tea set eyed the other, wrapping her arms possessively around all the pieces in front of her.

Apri tried again. *It's just a stupid ol' tea set. I need to go potty.*

The girl pushed all the pieces away from her, stood up, and hurried to the bathroom.

Apri clapped her hands together, giggling.

"Success?" Yelena asked.

"Yes!"

They lingered a while longer. Apri practiced her skill until the children's playtime ended, and they were called back to their studies.

"Just remember what I said," Yelena warned, "children are easy. Don't go practicing on everyone. If others find out you're a muse, it can get downright awkward." She chuckled. "They even start worrying that their own thoughts were planted by you."

"You said Barrow knows you're a muse," Apri recalled. "What about Kendall?"

"Oh no, my dear, he has no idea." Yelena laughed. "And don't you go telling him either! I've been in that boy's head ever since he could put two words together."

Apri laughed.

"Truthfully, though, I don't try to manipulate him. Not anymore. But he's so familiar with my projection he doesn't even know when I'm in there, poking around." Yelena smiled. "It's different with people you're close to. You don't use your gift to control them. You use it to know them, to protect them, and to develop a stronger relationship than you'd have otherwise."

She sighed. "Besides my husband, Headmaster Barrow's the only one who knew my secret." Circling her arm around Apri's shoulders, she gave a little squeeze. "And now, you."

When they parted ways at the end of the hallway, Apri stopped, a memory tugging at her conscience. She watched Yelena hustle down the hallway in her usual bustling gait. *Another person, like me. Having to keep a secret for so—*

A secret? Could Yelena be the mother who'd kept a secret from her son? And Kendall? Is he the son Gard wanted—*needed*—to tell? Gard hadn't told her what the dying man said, what secret he wanted to share. But all the pieces fit. It had to be Kendall.

Chapter 17
Zak

"What do you mean? I can hold my own in a fight," Zak argued when Gard suggested they spend their evenings working on his fighting skills.

"Have you forgotten what happened with Kendall?" Gard reminded him. "You'd be dead now if he hadn't seen that card."

Having no defense against that, Zak gave in. *I'm not that bad, I'll show him.*

At their first training session that night, Gard disarmed him immediately... twice. In less than five minutes, his confidence was shattered. *So, maybe I'm not that good.*

The next few lessons were just as demoralizing… and painful. Night after night, he endured Gard's aggressive attacks and his patronizing, derisive comments. He'd pick his sword up off the ground again and again as Gard used some new maneuver he hadn't seen before to catch him off guard.

Monk disappeared whenever they fought. He didn't like the sparring, or any sport or game that involved physical contact for that matter. All the hitting, tackling, groaning, and grunting confused him. He'd return sometime after the fighting ended, approaching with caution and eying them both with a suspicious glare. No amount of coaxing on Zak's part would convince the little guy to come close until Zak slid into his bedroll. Then Monk would scamper over, find a comfy spot on the covers, and begin his nightly grooming ritual.

Unfortunately for Zak, no amount of blanket fluffing or repositioning would get him comfy at night. His suffering only escalated after Gard purchased two wooden practice swords from a woodsmith in one of the small towns they passed.

Even when he'd try one of the tactics Gard had used on him in practice, the infernal man would be one step ahead. He anticipated every move, and Zak would get slapped, jabbed, or stabbed as a result. *I feel like a bumbling fool.* New sores and bruises decorated his skin after each session, and he'd crawl into bed for a fitful night of tossing and turning with little sleep. But as much as he hated the humiliating bouts, he refused to quit. His initial reluctance had been replaced by an earnest desire to improve.

For more than a week they'd traveled east of Baytown in search of Kendall's contacts. An underlying fear and distrust percolated within each community. Even in the roadhouses where travelers outnumbered locals, suspicious looks and whispered conversations had him feeling like a criminal. So far, they'd tracked down two of Kendall's men. Both had acted anxious and fretful upon mention of the Baytown group. The first shut the door on them without a word. They caught the other, a farrier, in his barn. He didn't kick them out immediately but was obviously uncomfortable talking with them.

"Even this far from the capital, neighbors are turning on neighbors with false reports of alliance with the Cortek," he told them. "There are too many unscrupulous bastards looking for a quick buck. And squaders take every claim at face value." Shaking his head, he escorted them to the door. "I'm sorry, but I have to think of my family," he'd said. "I wish you the best, though. Truly."

After another disappointing day of travel, they finished their meal and Gard threw the wooden sword at Zak. He caught it and rose from his seat by the fire. Dejected, but unwilling to give up, he took a deep breath and prepared for his nightly beating.

"Are you ready to learn something?" Gard asked.

"Yes. Go ahead," he muttered. Raising the stick-sword, he pointed it at Gard.

"Zak!"

The harsh command compelled Zak to take his eyes off the sword that was about to whack him for the millionth time and look at Gard's face.

"Are you ready to *learn* something?" the squader asked again.

"Haven't I *been* learning?" he asked, exasperated.

"What do *you* think?"

Zak dropped the sword to his side. "I don't think I've learned a damn thing. Except how many different ways I can lose."

Gard chuckled. "That's because I haven't been teaching you anything."

"What?" *Not teaching me anything? Then what have we been doing all this time?* The squader's annoying commentary during their training only added to Zak's frustration.

"You can't teach a student who thinks he has nothing to learn," Gard said.

Zak attacked him then, angry at being subjected to another derisive, cynical comment.

Gard made a hop-skip maneuver, suddenly next to Zak instead of in front of him. He slapped Zak on the back with the wooden sword, then tripped him.

Zak fell to the ground face first. *Fobmucking Gard-dog.*

"Rule #1," Gard said. "Release all emotion. Anger, fear, hatred, contempt. These can control your actions... cause you to take risks you wouldn't otherwise... attack when you should retreat... or vice versa." Gard paced around Zak as he rose slowly from the ground. His voice had lost its usual sardonic tone. "Let all emotion go. Get it out of your head. Your only thought is survival, for yourself and those you wish to protect."

Zak faced Gard again. These weren't the mocking, taunting words he was used to hearing from the squader. *Is this just another of his tricks to catch me off guard?* He raised his sword.

"Deep breath," Gard said. "Forget about everything else. For these exercises, survival is not at risk, so think about victory instead. How can you win?"

Zak took a deep breath. "I can't," he said.

"*Good!*" Gard said. "Now, you are thinking, instead of just fighting. Attacking. *Losing*. But there is always a way to win." He shrugged. "Well, almost always. Except when there's not. Rule #2: Assess your opponent. What do you know about me, about how I fight, what are my weaknesses, my strengths?"

Gard circled.

Zak met him step for step but stayed out of reach and didn't attack.

Gard lunged at him.

He backed off. "I know you're an ass."

Gard chuckled. "Everyone you fight will be an ass. Knowing that doesn't help you win. What else?"

"You're good."

"Am I? Compared to who? How do you know I'm good? Maybe I'm not that good."

"You're better than me."

"*Yes!* That's a proven fact based on our previous encounters. A fact you can use to win."

"If you're better than me, how can I win?"

"Did you play sports when you were a kid? Get in fist fights? Did you ever win, or see someone else win, against an opponent who was better? How did they do it?"

"Strategy. Luck." Zak retreated again from another swift lunge. "Cheating."

"Cheating is a strategy in a fight for survival. And often a good one," Gard said.

"Rule #3: Assess your surroundings. What are your disadvantages? Anything around that you can use to your advantage? There'll be times when you're in a place that is more familiar to your opponent. Or you may have that advantage. Tonight, we're equal in that respect."

Gard kept pace with Zak, making harmless jabs and swipes. "You're already fighting better than every night before this. What's different?"

"We're talking."

"True. But do you know that the few times I've lunged at you tonight are the first that I've been the aggressor? That I've made the first move to attack you?"

"What? No." Zak thought back to the other nights. *How can that be true? I'm the one with all the bruises.*

Gard attacked, pounding the tip of his sword into Zak's chest.

The move took Zak by surprise. *Again.*

Gard leaned in till they were face to face, putting his weight on the sword. "Rule #4: Don't get distracted in the middle of a fight." He backed off.

Zak rubbed his chest. *Another bruise.*

"That's it for tonight. Think about how you can win and be prepared to execute your strategy next time. You're athletic, quick, and have good instincts. You could use some work on your grip and your arm strength. But you're your own worst enemy because you're not using this." He pointed at Zak's forehead, then punched a finger into it with each of his next words. "Not… at… all."

"Ow." Zak rubbed his head.

They spent the next night at an inn in Sweetdale. The aroma of freshly baked bread mixed with roasting meat greeted Zak before his eyes adjusted to the darkness inside the pub. He followed Gard to a table, looking forward to a real meal after a few days of nothing but dried meat and water.

The drinks came. Gard spoke little. Not that he was particularly chatty under normal circumstances, but he'd been exceptionally quiet since they broke camp that morning.

Halfway through the first mug of ale, Zak realized his Gard-paced drinking system had become a habit. *What'll I do when he's not around?* That thought kept his mind occupied for a while, until he started listening to a nearby conversation.

"... hear about that raid? The squaders at that wedding?" one man said.

*"*Yeah, I heard they took more 'n twenty people away," another man added.

"What a memory for the bride and groom, eh?" a woman said, full of sympathy.

The first man lowered his voice. Zak only heard a few words, "...didn't do nothing'… ex-boyfriend… them of being Cortek..."

"It's a shame, it is," the woman said. "Can't trust anyone these days."

When they finished their meal, Zak again noticed other diners eying them as they walked through the pub. A creepy feeling tingled at the back of his neck as they climbed the stairs to their room.

"We'll never find anyone willing to challenge the Legiant under these circumstances," Gard said the next morning as they rode out of Sweetdale. "We'd best ride straight to the capital and avoid public places until we're north of Southrock. Just being travelers from out of town with no business here draws unwanted attention."

"Maybe we can talk to Mr. Murfy in Southrock," Zak suggested. "I know he can be trusted."

Gard agreed.

Taking Gard's advice, Zak had spent most of his idle time thinking about how he could win their next bout. His only chance against the seasoned squader would be with tricks and diversion tactics. But not the same ones Gard had used on him. Those had proven too predictable. He'd have to be patient and wait for just the right moment, but he had one idea that might just work. *At least I have a plan this time.*

After dinner, he found the stick-swords and tossed one to Gard. *Let him be the aggressor,* he reminded himself.

"Well, aren't we eager tonight?" Gard said, accepting the challenge.

They danced around each other for half an hour. Gard made an occasional bluff move, which Zak blocked, then backed off. Gard tried to goad him into attacking, but Zak had set his mind to wait. He even ignored the jibes and snide remarks he now knew were intended to make him angry. A couple of times he even laughed when he realized how angry a particular comment would have made him before. Still, he did not attack. *What now, Gard-dog?*

"We could do this dance all night," Gard said.

"Indeed, we could," Zak replied. "If you drop from exhaustion first, does that mean I win?"

Gard attacked, but Zak's eyes rested on his center, near his navel, so he knew which direction to move. It was a trick he'd learned playing soccer as a kid but had forgotten until he put serious thought toward beating Gard. He caught the movements of Gard's sword arm with his peripheral vision and parried the strike, even managing a glancing blow of his own on Gard's off-arm.

"Where the hell did that come from?" Gard asked.

"Maybe you're a good teacher," Zak said. "Maybe I'm an even better student."

Zak charged, but his sword found nothing but air as he missed his mark again. Gard was too quick. *How the hell does he do that?* This time, though, Zak had planned an escape out of his attack in advance. So, instead of getting tripped and landing in the dirt, he spun around and faced Gard again, unscathed.

"Remember, keep your emotions in check. Don't get overconfident. It can be just as debilitating as anger."

Zak had to check an emotion, but it wasn't confidence. *Everything that man says annoys me!*

He attacked again. This time they sparred, back and forth—swipes, blocks, strikes, parries, jabs, deflections. Zak held his own, but he knew Gard was holding back. *He's just testing me.* They broke away and faced each other, pacing again. Both breathed heavily from the exertion of the scuffle. *Time for my secret weapon.*

Zak prepared to attack, then said, "I've been meaning to ask... Did we interrupt something the other night? Back in Baytown?"

"Interrupt? What?"

"You know, you and Apri?" As soon as he saw a change in Gard's expression, he attacked straight on, aiming to stab him in the chest.

Gard deflected the frontal blow, but Zak landed a hard jab in his side.

"Ooooh!" Gard moaned, doubling over and grabbing at his gut.

Zak backed off. He dropped the sword to his side, remembering Gard's injuries—the grear wound, and that other, awful-looking scar on his other side. *Which side did I hit?*

Gard attacked.

Once again, Zak had no time to react. Collapsing onto his back, Zak stared up at the squader's angry face.

"You've already forgotten Rule #4," Gard said, pressing the stick-sword sideways into Zak's throat. Then, he walked off into the woods, tossing the sword next to his travelpack as he left.

Zak didn't know if it was to take a piss or to cool off. *Or maybe I did hurt him?*

Rule #4? Zak picked a splinter out of his neck. *Don't get distracted. Damn!*

It was late when Gard came back.

Zak pretended to be asleep. *Best not to ask.*

Chapter 18
Zak

Gard suddenly reined in his horse, riding off the road into the thick brush. "Follow! And keep quiet!" His hushed tone carried no further than Zak's ears. "We're headed for an ambush."

Zak followed, looking around. *Where?* He didn't see anything, but he'd been traveling with Gard long enough to know not to question his instincts. He felt the adrenaline kick in, setting his nerves on edge.

"Two men followed us out of Mahogany," Gard said when they were well off the road. "They circled around on the other side after we crossed that stream." Gard nodded his head in the direction of the road, then dismounted. "Tie the horses. We go on foot from here."

They collected their weapons, and Monk jumped up to ride on Zak's shoulder.

Gard took the lead, keeping the road in sight. Fallen twigs and branches threatened to pop and crack with every step so they moved cautiously. Gard pointed at an outcropping of rocks across the road, then signaled for Zak to follow. He moved farther up the road, crossed, then doubled back. As they neared the outcropping—remnants of a long-ago rockslide—he heard a man's voice.

"Shouldn't they be here by now?"

"Quiet!" another man muttered. "They'll hear, you bonehead!"

"We can see way up the road. They can't hear."

"Maybe they stopped to take a piss. Just be quiet. They'll be along soon."

Gard motioned again for Zak to follow, and they edged along the base of the hill until they were out of earshot.

"I see no way to get to them except from the road," Gard said. "We'll have to go around the rocks and attack from the east. Try to get the jump on them before they have time to react." He looked at the climber. "We could use a diversion."

"Okay…" Zak agreed, "but this doesn't always go as planned." He pulled Monk off his shoulder.

Gard shrugged. "It'll work, or it won't. It's all we've got."

They moved back into position, as close as they could get without being seen.

Zak heard the men talking again but couldn't make out any words. He got Monk's attention and pointed in the direction of the ambushers.

From Monk's reaction, the climber heard them, too.

"Decoy!" he said quietly, making a wide circle with his arm, then back toward the hill, ending with his finger pointed at the hideout.

Monk tilted his head to one side, then the other.

"Decoy!" Zak said again, repeating the same arm movement.

Monk bounded off, moving out of their sight.

Moments later, he heard the clatter of falling rocks.

"What the hell?!" one of the men shouted.

Zak ran out onto the road with Gard, circling around the outcrop.

The ambushers faced the rock wall with their backs to the road, looking up. Both were armed and turned to face them.

Gard chose his man first, wasting no time to engage.

The other, a short, stocky man, attacked Zak with his longsword.

Zak blocked the hit, but almost lost his own sword from the force of the blow. The vibration shot up his arm and ended with a sharp twinge in his elbow. He moved to put both hands on his sword. *Too slow.*

His opponent came at him with a backhand swing.

Zak managed another one-handed block. But with his arm and hand still numb from the first strike, it was a weak attempt. He fell to the ground, losing his grip on the sword.

The man came at him again.

Zak grabbed a handful of dirt and threw it in the man's face.

His attacker staggered backwards, cursing and wiping his eyes with his free hand.

Springing to his feet, Zak picked up his sword with two hands and swung it with all his strength, aiming for his opponent's weapon.

The longsword flew from the man's hands.

Gard caught the sword by the hilt in mid-air. "Back, against the rock, both of you," he ordered.

Gard's opponent, also disarmed, bled from a nasty cut on his arm.

"I say we turn these two in as traitors. They look Cortek-friendly to me." Gard said, forcing the two men to the wall.

"What?" loudmouth said. "You guys are the geeks."

Zak held his elbow. It still stung from the hits he'd taken. "Do we *look* like geeks to you?"

The other man swallowed. "We were told—"

Gard cut him off, "You two even fight like Cortek," he looked at Zak, "don't they?"

"Sure do," Zak agreed.

"We aren't…" Zak's man objected. He spat a wad of muddy phlegm on the ground, wiping his face and eyes.

"But they don't look like geeks," Zak interjected.

Gard waved the two swords at the men. "You know that doesn't matter. I say we turn them in and get the cash."

"I like it better when we can turn in a whole group at once, like back in Sweetdale. These two aren't worth the trouble," Zak replied.

"Kill them, then? I doubt they'll be missed."

"No! We're just geek-hunters like you." Loudmouth's voice trembled. Zak thought he might just piss himself.

"We were told wrong. Please don't kill us," the other man begged.

"Take off your boots," Gard ordered.

"And your clothes," Zak added.

Monk jumped from the rock face above and landed between the two men who both jerked aside, startled.

"Move!" Gard yelled.

They scrambled to do as ordered.

Zak gathered up their gear and weapons and piled them on the ground next to Gard. "I'll go get the horses," he said.

His heart still raced from the fight. He replayed the short encounter in his head. *Did the nights of sparring help?* It was impossible to know if it was the training or simple survival instinct, but throwing that dirt probably saved his life. He flexed his sword arm a couple of times, feeling a trace of the twinge in his elbow.

On the way to retrieve their horses, he came across the ambusher's mounts and led all four horses back to the clearing.

"Look what I found!" he boasted.

The two men sat with their backs to the rock facing Gard and looking quite disappointed by Zak's discovery. Removing bridles and saddles, he left their tack on the ground along with their canteens. He and Gard divided the rest of the men's clothing and gear between their own packs, leaving the ambushers in their undergarments to fend for themselves. They mounted up and rode off with the other two horses in tow.

"We'll turn these two loose before nightfall," Gard called back to the two men. "I hope they can find their way home."

"You did good back there, kid." Gard said a few minutes later. His expression and tone bore no hint of mockery or condescension.

At the risk of blowing up Gard's ego, he admitted, "The training helped, I think."

"We'll work on your grip," Gard said. "There're some tricks and exercises that'll help."

Zak decided not to mention his Apri strategy, and he wouldn't tease Gard about her again, either. It felt too much like hitting below the belt, as if he broke some kind of unspoken man-code. *It'll be more fun teasing her about it anyway.*

Three days later, Zak and Gard entered Southrock. They rode abreast through town, then onto the road that would take them to the Murfy's farm.

"The Murfy's place was my second home growing up," Zak reminisced. "Their son, Gabe, was my best friend. We did everything together."

"Did he move away?" Gard asked.

"What?" asked Zak. "Who?"

"Their son? Why wouldn't we meet with him instead?"

"Oh, no," Zak explained, "He died a few years back. They say he fell from one of the scaffold walks. I only just heard about it when I was here last."

"You mean at the mine?" Gard asked.

The question surprised Zak. "Yes, at the mine." Zak had shared a few stories from his past as they traveled together these past few weeks, if only to pass the time. Seldom did Gard express any real interest. "Hard to believe, actually," he said. "We spent a lot of time climbing through that mine as kids. Never so much as a close call."

Gard looked in his direction, not at him, but beyond into the woods.

Zak turned to scan the trees but saw nothing. *What's he looking at?* When he turned back to ask, Gard had ridden on ahead. They spent the rest of the ride to the farm in silence.

Murf's pack of dogs started their barking and baying as soon as they rode through the gate. Monk squealed, then scrambled up to hitch a ride on the horse's rump. Durka had grown used to the climber's antics by now and didn't miss a step. The dogs, on the other hand, went crazy.

"Monk, decoy!" Zak yelled pointing in the direction of the dogs. He didn't want to listen to that racket again. Monk jumped down and led the dogs off on a wild chase through the fields.

Murf was at the barn using an axe to shave the bark off a tree trunk. "Zak? Hey! Welcome back, son!" Setting aside the axe and gloves, he walked over to greet them.

"Planting more hops?" Zak asked.

"Yep, I finally got a real good brew recipe. Could be my ticket outta the mines!" Murf called a young farmhand over to take care of their horses.

Gard addressed the farmhand, "Leave them tacked up, please.... maybe just water and feed?" Then he apologized to Mr. Murfy, "We can't stay long."

Murf looked disappointed but nodded to the farmhand.

"Mr. Murfy, this is my friend, Gard," Zak said.

"Murf, please," he insisted, bowing the Edyson greeting. "Pleased to meet you, sir."

Gard returned the gesture.

"The missus will be happy to see you again, Zak." Murf led them to the farmhouse. "Punkin! We have company!" he yelled as they entered. He almost closed the door on Monk who scampered inside behind them.

"Damn little pest," Murf said, which drew a chuckle from Gard.

"Sorry we can't stay longer," Zak apologized. "We need to be in Edyson for the wedding ceremony." Even though Zak trusted Murf, Gard had insisted they be evasive about getting information, rather than ask directly.

"Aye... Heard about that, but not much interested." Murf said with a disgusted snort. He raised an eyebrow at Zak. "I'm surprised you are."

"It's not the wedding," Gard interjected. "We heard there'll be work that pays well."

"No doubt," Murf replied. "Sure ain't none of that here."

"What do you mean?" Zak asked.

Mrs. Murfy came in. "Oh my, Zak!"

Zak gave the woman a hug and introduced Gard.

"You found your little climber! He's still such a cute thing," she said, reaching up to pet Monk.

The climber balked at first, but then accepted the woman's gentle stroke. Monk almost looked like his old self again. He'd stopped scratching, and the bare patches were growing back. *Thanks to Apri's special soap.*

"Ain't that funny?" Murf said to Gard. "Those two were inseparable when he was a kid. When that animal bounded in here after Zak, I didn't even think twice."

"Would y'all like something to drink?" Mrs. Murfy asked.

"Why don't you bring us out some of the new brew, Ma?" Murf suggested. "Like I said, best stuff I've produced yet," he bragged to Zak with a wink.

"So, what's going on here?" Zak wanted to get Murf back on subject. "Is it the mine?"

Murf looked confused, then remembered. "It really started way back when, well, after, you know, the fire, your folks…"

"Yes," Zak said, rolling his eyes. He'd forgotten the man's annoying penchant for longwinded storytelling.

His visible annoyance provoked a warning look from Gard. "What started?" he asked.

"It wasn't long after the fire, a new director shows up and starts changing things. All kinds of things. He's a real ass, that one.

Expecting everyone to work harder and faster. And don't care nothing about safety, either. More and more accidents been happening since he came on."

"Accidents?" Gard asked. "What kind of accidents?"

"All kinds," Murf said. "Carts running out of control, tools breaking, men so tired and working so hard they made stupid mistakes or break out in fights for no reason. Stuff like that."

Mrs. Murfy came in with a tray, serving the ale in darpact mugs, along with some bread and cheese. The special mugs were a sign that the brew had been fermented in darpact barrels.

"Mr. Murfy," Gard said after taking a drink. "This is truly excellent ale." He took another drink. "Seriously."

Murf smiled broadly. "Kind of you to say."

"Didn't I tell you, dear?" Mrs. Murfy said. "Everyone who tastes it says so, but he refuses to sell it to the pub."

"It ain't 'cause it's no good that I won't sell it, dear," Murf chided. "I told you that."

Zak fed a piece of the bread to Monk. "It's very good," he agreed. The dark, full-bodied taste was bold at first, followed by the sweet, spicy flavor of darpact that lingered on the tongue. He took another long swig. *I could drink a pitcher of this stuff!*

"So, you mentioned there isn't much work here in Southrock? Isn't that unusual?" Gard asked. "I mean, with the mine here there's always been plenty of work."

"Used to be, yeah," Murf said with a mouthful of bread. "But not no more. Not since that new director came on. First off, he went and replaced all the Cortek we lost with riff-raff who got no more sense than God gave a chicken. Then he'd go about blaming every accident on the good workers. Didn't matter whether they were responsible or not. He'd just fire them. Next thing you know, another good-for-nothing nobody comes into town to take their place." He shook his head.

"He's got the mine half-full of his own people now. And they got no idea what they're doing. Make matters worse, it started being pretty clear some of them accidents were staged just to get rid of workers and make room for more of his own."

Mrs. Murfy started talking when Murf stopped to take another bite. "That awful man and his crew's fixing to take over the whole town. Trying to bully businesses into closing their doors so's they can take over."

"Yep," Murf continued. "There's still enough of us old timers around hanging onto what we got, but no telling how much longer we can hold out. So many good folks just up and moved away. If it weren't for this farm, we'd be gone, too." He finished his ale.

Mrs. Murfy refilled his mug, and he stroked her arm. "Especially after our son, Gabe, was killed in one of them accidents."

"Zak told me about your son," Gard said. "That must've been a difficult time for you both. I'm sorry for your loss."

Gard's expression, his sympathy, seemed out of character for him. *Is he faking that?*

"Thank you, kindly. It was, it still is, difficult," Mrs. Murfy said, reaching over to touch Murf's shoulder.

Zak drained his drink. "Do you think Southrock will ever be the same?" he asked. He tried to ignore the evil glare from Gard as Mrs. Murfy refilled his mug.

"Not so long as that fobmuck director is running the mine." Murf said. "Some folks have complained. Even gone up to the capital. But nothing changes. Word is he's friendly with the Legiant." He shook his head again. "It's real bad. And the more folks that leave, the harder it is for the rest of us to keep trying to save it."

"It's a shame," Gard said, his voice full of compassion.

Zak eyed Gard suspiciously. *Why would he care? He's never even met these people before today.* He recalled Gard's outburst at the meeting in Baytown. *Was that an act, too?* Zak doubted the man even realized his duplicity. *Spending too much time around politicians, no doubt.*

Murf grunted. "It ain't your fault," he said. "It's that damn Legiant. He don't care nothing about no one but his own self." He lowered his voice. "And he's got folks so scared of getting killed or locked up for saying a cross word, ain't no one gonna go up against him."

Murf leaned back in his chair, looking so dejected and hopeless that Zak wanted to lighten the mood. He raised his mug high. "If the Legiant could get a taste of this ale, I guarantee he'd be serving it at his wedding!"

Everyone laughed. "He's not wrong," Gard said. "It's that good. How much do you have? I know a few pub owners in Edyson who might be interested in a barrel or two."

Murf smiled broadly "I got plenty out in the barn," he said. "I been keeping it to myself. If I sold it to our local pub, and that damn director got a taste of it? He'd surely find a way to take it all from me. And maybe my farm, too."

"Well, I tell you what," Gard said after some thought. "I'll see what I can do about finding someone in Edyson who'll buy this fine ale from you. Any pub would be happy to serve this... And just as happy to keep where it came from a secret." He raised his mug in a salute, then finished it.

Mrs. Murfy moved to refill the mug, but Gard waved her off.

"No, thank you, ma'am," he said, standing up. "We've got to get going."

Zak downed his half-full mug all at once without a glance at Gard. He stayed behind, giving Mrs. Murfy a hug and thank you before leaving the house. When he went outside, Gard was discussing the details of purchasing his ale with Murf should he find a buyer. Zak went to the barn to get the horses.

As they rode through Southrock, they skirted around the field where he and Gabe used to play soccer. Zak watched the kids running around, kicking the ball, and shouting to each other.

"We spent a lot of hours on that field," he told Gard. "Gabe was a good soccer player. Really good. Everyone thought he'd go pro," he recalled. "I wish he could've. I wish I'd never left here. Maybe he'd still be alive."

"Listen, kid," Gard said.

Zak turned to look at him, expecting a lecture about how it wasn't his fault... it was an accident... all the things people said at such times.

Gard seemed reluctant to continue.

"What is it?" Zak asked. "You've been acting strange since we got into town."

"There's something I need to tell you... about Gabe."

"Gabe?" Zak asked, confused. The horses ambled along, side by side, and he waited for a response. It would be dark soon, but Zak could make out Gard's face, which had the same distant look as when they were on the road to the Murfys. "What about him?"

"It wasn't an accident," Gard finally replied.

Zak blinked. *What?* He blinked again, unsure how to respond. *How could he know it wasn't an accident?* Perplexed, he looked down at the reins in his hand and tried to recall their past conversations. *Didn't he say he was here in Southrock, looking for me? After the fire?* With a confused shake of his head, he finally sputtered aloud, "What?"

Durka had stopped moving during Zak's rumination. Gard was up ahead and didn't hear the question. He urged the horse into a trot, shouting at Gard's back, "Did *you* kill him?"

"No... but I know who did." Gard said when he caught up. "His name is Thaddeus Hill, Commander of the Law Squad."

"The Commander of the Law Squad killed Gabe?"

"He wasn't Commander back then," Gard explained. "In fact, he'd been in prison just a few weeks prior for things he did when he was commander for the former Legiant. During his trial, even his own men testified against him. Covington released Hill from prison and appointed him as the leader of a new team within the Law Squad—the XLs. Southrock was his first assignment. He came here to get information about you, or about your father and his dealings."

"Like that list I found? And the Cortek card?" Zak asked.

"I suppose. I never could understand back then why he didn't just let it go... why he felt it was so important to find you. You were what, twelve, when this all went down?"

"Fourteen," Zak corrected.

"I think, maybe, it was personal... that Covington felt a fool for trusting your father for so many years, when almost the whole time he'd been plotting against him. Killing your father wasn't enough. He wanted to punish everyone he cared about."

"So, this guy killed Gabe? How do you know?"

"I was assigned to accompany Hill and brief him on the situation. And to and tell him what we knew, which wasn't much. We arrived late one evening and got a room, planning to start our investigation the next day. I woke late that night and Hill's bed was empty. I didn't know how long he'd been gone. Someone at the pub said he left for the mine with another person. I don't know if Gabe went with him willingly or by force. Hill must've thought he knew where you were."

"He didn't. He didn't know anything." Zak said. "Murf said only a couple of people in town knew where my aunt and uncle lived or even their names. But everyone knew me and Gabe were best friends."

"I came into the mine a couple levels below Hill. It was dark but I could see he had a man by the throat, holding him over the platform railing." Gard paused and looked at Zak. "I knew from stories I'd heard during his trial that he was cruel, but this was the first time I witnessed it for myself." His eyes glazed over. "When he saw me… he shoved the man over the edge and let go, never taking his eyes off me. The man is pure evil."

The horses had ambled to a halt in the middle of the road during Gard's narrative, waiting patiently for direction.

"I knew it wasn't an accident," Zak said, prodding his horse back into a walk. "So, this fobmuck Hill is Commander of the Law Squad now?"

"Last I heard," Gard said. "I refused to work with him... or with any of his team after that. Covington and I weren't seeing eye-to-eye already by then, but that was the breaking point for me. He didn't remove me as Commander, but we seldom spoke or even saw each other after that. Hill's squaders did all of the Legiant's dirty work, each assignment more brazen than the last. On the morning I heard they were sent to the Core Campus and rushed there as fast as I could."

Gard rubbed a palm on his gut. "I'd be dead, too, if that fight had taken place anywhere else."

"The Cortek are the only ones who know what really happened, and they've been forced into exile," Zak concluded.

"Exactly. The Cortek Headmaster, Barrow, said he would spread word through the capital that I died. Even so, the Legiant put out that reward," Gard said.

The account of Gabe's murder gave Zak another reason to hate Covington. And another name to add to his vengeful pursuit. *Thaddeus Hill.* Zak vowed to find and kill them both.

Zak and Gard arrived at Edyson City two days after Founder's Day. The weather had been hot and dry for weeks, and a film of fine road dust covered Zak's clothing. He'd taken to wearing a cloth over his nose and mouth to keep from breathing it in. When the dusty road gave way to the stone-paved avenue of Outer Southgate, Zak lowered the cloth and took a deep breath. He called to Monk who grabbed the stirrup and climbed up his leg, curling into a ball on the packs behind him.

"Do you know where we're going?" Zak asked.

"I know the place Kendall spoke of, yes," Gard replied. "It's on the other side of the city, in Northgate. We should be there in about an hour."

Zak slumped in the saddle, dejected. It felt like he'd been dragged in the dirt behind Gard all the way from Southrock. He wanted a warm bath, a real bed, and a full night's sleep. *Another hour?*

Gard chuckled. "You'll make it, kid."

The last time they were in the city, they rode from Southgate to Westgate, through street after street lined with tenements and businesses that looked very much the same. Zak recalled the crowds, the traffic, and the odors of the city, which ran the gamut from baking bread to the putrid scent of the sewer that ran beneath the street. The route to Northgate, on the other hand, took them into the heart of the city, away from the outer walls and through the more affluent districts near the palace.

"This is where all the major sports tournaments take place," Gard said, as they circled around Central Park.

The stadium rose above the grounds, casting a long shadow over the park. Zak thought of his friend, Gabe, again, and how he might've played there. *If only…*

The streets beyond the park were wider, the vehicles fancier, and the traffic lighter. Large mansions with immaculate open courtyards lined both sides of the street, becoming more lavish the closer they came to the palace. They passed a few building sites in various stages of construction, but all were vacant of any activity.

A high wall surrounded one side of Palace Avenue. Across from it were the most impressive mansions, apartments, and businesses Zak had seen yet. As they approached the elaborate wood and iron gates of the palace, they were closed tight with heavily armed guards on patrol.

"Is the palace always so…" Zak searched for the right word, "…uninviting?"

"Didn't used to be," Gard replied.

They boarded the horses at a stable within walking distance of the Inn at the Core, the place Kendall had recommended.

"We'll meet back here for dinner," Gard said, tossing his pack onto the closest bed without going in. "Don't get into any trouble," he ordered, with that condescending Gard-dog glare Zak had come to despise.

"Don't get into any trouble." Zak mimicked the command under his breath as he closed the door. Then he remembered his last night in Edyson and vowed not to drink too much.

Monk jumped off his shoulder with a screech, bouncing around the room.

Zak grinned. "I'm happy to be rid of him, too!" Sitting on the bed, he rummaged through his pack, digging around for the pouch that held his money.

Monk screeched again and jumped up next to Zak, inspecting each item as it was placed on the bed. Then he grabbed the pack, pulling it away from Zak.

"I don't need your help!" Zak yanked the pack away and turned his back on the climber.

Monk was undeterred, making every attempt to get at the pack until Zak spent more effort keeping him away than finding the pouch. He stood up, fighting Monk off from his shoulder, his back, his head. The two danced around the room playing keep-away, until Zak pulled out the money pouch.

"Here it is!" he exclaimed, holding it up and discarding the pack on the bed.

Monk jumped on the bed after it, victorious at having won the battle. He dug around in the pack, peering inside, then gave Zak a sideways look.

"Nothing in there for you, my friend." Zak held up the pouch. "I'll go get us some grub."

He opened the window, then noticed the near-empty bottle of Monk's special soap lying on the bed and picked it up. "We're gonna need more of this, too," he said, ruffling Monk's head. "Back soon!"

Chapter 19
Apri

"Come in," Yelena called out, responding to a knock at the door. She and Apri were in the middle of a history lesson.

The door opened. "Excuse me, I'm sorry to interrupt," the young girl said.

"Not to worry, dear," Yelena said. "What is it?"

"A message."

Yelena reached for the note.

"For Apri," she said with an apologetic expression.

Yelena raised an eyebrow and gestured toward Apri.

Apri accepted the paper from the girl and unfolded it, instantly recognizing Kendall's meticulous, block script. She hadn't seen him in more than a week. *Meet me at the dining hall. Gard's back.*

Staring at the note, she felt the prickly touch of goosebumps on her skin. *Gard's back!* She rubbed her arms up and down.

"Good news?" Yelena asked.

"It's Kendall," she told Yelena. "He wants to meet me in the dining hall."

"My dear, I've not known you long, but I know *that* reaction wasn't for Kendall."

Apri felt herself blush and touched her cheek. "Ummm, I..."

Yelena laughed. "Just go on," she said, waving her hand. "We can pick this up later."

"Thank you." She gave Yelena a quick hug. "I'll see you again soon!"

A few hours later, she and Kendall walked together to the Inn at the Core.

"I'm going to get a room," he said. "It'll be more convenient than going back and forth these next few days. You're welcome to use it if you want to stay in the city."

Before coming to the capital, she would've tried to read into his offer... *Does he want me to? Does he not? If I stay, what will he think that means?* But after spending this time apart, and now that she'd developed a close bond with his mother, it felt as if they had settled into a relationship more like family. With the awkwardness and second-guessing gone, she took his offer at face value. "I did not bring anything with me," she said.

"Me either, but it's not for tonight. I'll book it starting tomorrow until after the wedding. I just want to get a room before they're all gone." He held the door open for her. "Gard said he and Zak would meet us here for dinner."

Kendall left to make the reservation. The pub was crowded. She scanned the room looking for Gard, her senses heightened with the anticipation of seeing him again.

"Boo!"

A hand grabbed her shoulder, and she shot her arm upward, twisting around to face her attacker. Cocking her other hand back, she almost slapped Zak across the jaw.

"Hey!" Zak threw up his hands. "It's me!"

"Oh. Hello." She resumed her search of the pub. "You should not sneak up on person like that."

"On *a* person." He craned his head around in a dramatic imitation of her. "Hmm. Doesn't look like he's here yet," Zak said.

"Who?" she asked.

"Gard. And don't pretend that's not who you're looking for. I'm not stupid."

That is up for debate. "You look like you have been dragged across desert," she told him, then noticed the bottle he carried. "More soap for Monk?"

He held it up. "You nearly made me drop it. I had to run all over town looking for this."

"The veterin—"

"I know that *now,*" he interrupted. "The third different shop I went to, someone finally told me to try a vet. You could've mentioned where you got it. I mean, before just now."

She smiled, surprised by how much she enjoyed this banter. *This must be what it is like to have a sibling.*

"I planned to get cleaned up," he said, gesturing to his dusty clothing. "Now there's no time."

Her suppressed laugh came out as a snort. She took the bottle from him and read the label. "You spent much time to find it. So, it is working?"

"Yes," he admitted, then grinned. "You should see him! Come upstairs with me? I brought him some food."

She looked around again but didn't see Gard, and Kendall was still with the clerk.

"It'll only take a minute. Come on," Zak said.

Upstairs, Zak cracked open the door to his room, peeked inside, then backed out, easing it shut. "Shhh! Wait till you see this," he whispered. He shushed her again and, before she could say anything, positioned her in front of him, facing the door. "Open it... Be *quiet*!"

The door creaked, ever so slightly. Gard slept on the bed. Monk lay curled in a ball on his chest, also asleep, his little body rose and fall to the rhythm of Gard's snores. The sight warmed and excited her at the same time. It felt as if her last encounter with him in Baytown had happened only last night.

Zak pushed her into the room, following behind and making enough noise to wake Monk.

"Screeech!" Monk wailed.

Gard jolted up, and Monk flew off his chest, landing at her feet. Gard's eyes locked with hers.

For a split second, she sensed... *Joy? Desire? Lust?...* Definitely a pleasurable emotion. But then it was gone, replaced by the stoic, unreadable expression that reminded her so much of Rrazmik. She held his gaze as long as he allowed, conveying her own joy at seeing him again.

"You're late!" Zak said.

Gard combed his hair back from his face, "Fell asleep." He stood. "Hello again, Apri," he said with a brief nod without meeting her eyes. "Kendall is here?"

"Yes." The word came out as a raspy peep, and she cleared her throat. "Downstairs."

"Good." He straightened his shirt, then brushed past her to get to the door. "We should go."

Apri felt his breath on her face. *So close.*

"We'll be right down. I've got to feed Monk."

Gard left the room.

"...pri? Apri!"

Zak's voice disturbed her contemplation. "Hmmm?" She rubbed at the goosebumps on her arm. "Ohhh, Monkjan, look at you!"

Monk jumped up and down on the bed, screeching and spinning around as Zak dug in his pack for the food.

"If not for missing arm, I would not recognize him." She took a deep breath, still on edge after the close encounter with Gard.

Monk jumped into her arms.

"You are happy now, little one? Look at how beautiful and thick your fur has become!" She doted on him while Zak prepped the food.

"He likes you. It usually takes longer for him to get used to a person." Zak set the food on the small table between the two beds under the open window. "To find him sleeping on top of Gard? Didn't think I'd ever see that!"

Monk jumped out of her arms and bounded onto the table, inspecting each morsel with his eyes and nose, then tasting it with his tongue before devouring it.

"Maybe something spooked him?" Apri suggested.

"Must've." He looked around outside the window. "It's the only thing that makes any sense."

"Let's go," she said, trying not to sound too eager.

They found Gard and Kendall already deep in discussion at a small booth against the far wall. They stopped at the bar, and she listened to Zak flirt with a perky little barmaid while they waited for their drinks. Zak maneuvered ahead of her on the way to the table and slid onto the bench next to Kendall. He gestured with mock courtesy for her to sit across from him.

She sneered at him and slid in next to Gard.

Gard moved over as close to the wall as he could get but remained focused on his conversation with Kendall. "How many do you expect at the meeting tomorrow?" he asked.

The bench was too small for Gard to avoid physical contact with her, although he tried. He even twisted his upper body at an awkward angle to avoid the shoulder contact. But her hip and upper thigh tingled where they met with his under the table. The contact made him so obviously uncomfortable she had to resist the urge to tease him by sliding even closer.

Zak coughed, and she looked over the table at him. He nodded in Gard's direction and winked at her.

She rolled her eyes at him. *Such a child.*

"I've already met with Phillip and three others from Baytown who've been here since Tuesday. They're expecting four or five more to arrive later tonight," Kendall said. "What about you? Can we expect anyone from the south?"

"No. Too much fear. Everywhere we went there were stories about people falsely accused, detained, or arrested," Gard said, looking around them. "Some encouragement, but no support."

Kendall groaned. "I'm not surprised. It's the same here. So much suspicion... and fear. But I'm still working on some leads for…" He hesitated, glancing around. "…for the ceremony."

Zak's barmaid friend came with a tray of food. Apri watched the furtive interaction between them—Zak's subtle, but no doubt intentional, brush against her with his arm as she set down the tray, the blush of the young girl's cheeks, her backward glance as she left the table.

Zak kept his eyes on the girl till she turned around, then noticed Apri watching him. He shrugged, an impish smirk on his face.

Gard wriggled next to her, changing his position.

She slid over to the edge of her seat to give him more space.

Zak's foot nudged her under the table, his smirk transforming into a wide grin.

She ignored him, taking a drink. The tavern was packed with more people waiting at the door and outside. People talked and laughed, plates and silverware clinked and clanged, chairs scraped against the wood floor. The noise made it impossible to have a private conversation.

Kendall almost had to shout to be heard. "They say it's like a war zone in The Ravens. The factories are not producing... rival gangs fighting in the streets.... looting and ransacking. Freight carriers are refusing to go in or out with supplies."

"That explains those construction sites we passed today," Zak said. "Looks like they've been abandoned."

They stopped trying to converse and finished their meal, then went outside. The upper floors of the buildings around the inn glowed in the setting sun contrasting with the deeper shadows at street level. A gentle breeze carried away the heat of the day, promising a pleasant evening. A steady flow of people moved in the direction of the palace.

"Is something happening tonight?" Apri asked.

"Hey," Zak interjected, "if we're done here, I need to go get cleaned up."

"Let's meet here tomorrow night," Kendall said. "I've arranged for a meeting with someone who may know how to get into the palace."

Gard nodded, and Zak went back inside.

"I heard the Legiant is planning to present his bride tonight," Kendall said, looking in the direction of the palace. "They say she's a real beauty."

"I need to go there," Apri said, looking at the two men in turn.

"Can't," Kendall replied. "I've got to stay here to greet the others we're expecting from Baytown tonight."

She looked at Gard. It would be nice to have company, especially *his* company. "It is important," she said without emotion. Begging or flirting would not work with Gard, but he might respond to duty.

"Important? Why?" he asked.

"I will tell you on the way," she said, walking backwards, facing him.

He did not follow.

"What else do you have to do?" she goaded. "You already took a nap, so you cannot be tired."

Gard yielded.

She waited for him to catch up, being careful to keep her face from revealing her delight at the chance to spend time alone with him. "We will see you tomorrow, Kendall," she said.

She and Gard fell in with others who strolled down the street toward the palace.

"So, what is so important," Gard asked.

"I want to see bride who is supposed to be so beautiful. Are you not curious?"

"Curiosity? That's why you're dragging me down this street?"

I am not dragging you. And, she noted, he made no move to go back. But she would not tempt fate by pointing that out. "It is not far, and it is such a beautiful night. Is it not?"

They turned a corner, and she stopped. As if to punctuate her last statement, the palace came into view at the end of the street. The outer palace grounds in front of the entrance were adorned festively, with banners flying and lights ablaze. From their location, she could see through the open gates into the courtyard beyond. The palace tower stretched up, at least twice as high as any other building in Edyson. Behind it, Odin rose full, in red splendor, reflecting the last rays of the setting sun.

"Beautiful, indeed," Gard agreed. But his eyes were on her, not the view. *Or am I just imagining that?*

Fanfare announced the start of the ceremony. "Come on." She started jogging, eager to find a vantage point where she could see the bride.

Gard sprinted past her.

Following him through the gates to the inner grounds, she weaved in and out through the throng of people. It became too congested to run, but Gard hurried purposely on. *Of course! He knows this place.*

They got separated in the swarm of people. Apri searched for him, turning around in circles. Just as she began to worry she'd lost him, he took her hand. *Rough. Warm.* The feel of him overtook her senses.

He jerked her out of her reverie, pulling her along until he stopped underneath a large tree on the other side of the stage. They weren't far from the podium, but she couldn't see above the heads of those around her.

I need to see. Standing on her toes didn't help. The fanfare rang again. She jumped up and saw a carriage approaching from the palace. *I must see.*

"Ready?" Gard asked, and before she could reply, his hands were on her waist. He lifted her up high until she could just reach the bottom branch of the tree—a convenient perch where she could sit and watch the proceedings. She grabbed the branch and scrambled up, finding a safe spot, then smiled her appreciation down to Gard.

From her vantage point in the tree, she had a clear view of the podium. A detail of armed squaders kept those assembled back a good distance from the stage. It seemed an odd show of force for what should be a joyous social celebration. Other armed guards were scattered about, milling among the onlookers.

The Legiant stepped to the podium. Below her, Gard stiffened at the sight of his old friend. His hands clenched in tight fists.

An undercurrent of grumbles and groans resonated from the gathering, unobscured by the flutter of applause. Not the welcome reception she'd expect for the supreme leader of the colony. She observed the crowd more closely. The gathering seemed smaller than it should be considering the size of the city, and it lacked the eager anticipation of citizens about to get the first glimpse of their new Queen Legiant.

Raising a hand, it took but a second to silence the applause before Covington began. "My fellow citizens, I am honored to be with you here today on this mossst joyouss occasion." His high-pitched voice, accentuated by a shrill whistle when he spoke *s* sounds, seemed odd for such a stout, muscular man.

There were a few loud jeers from the crowd. Two squaders approached one of the more vocal men, taking him away. The man fought against his escorts, continuing his loud jeers and taunts, and disrupting those around him until one of the squaders slapped him hard with a gauntleted hand.

Covington didn't pause in his discourse, which to her ears sounded hurried and rehearsed. "It is with great pleasure I present to you, my fiancé. Soon to be your new queen. I am certain you will find her to be as beautiful and charming as have I, and as befits the Queen Legiant of Edyson."

Behind him, she could see the woman climbing the steps, escorted by a muscular, battle-scarred squader whose face looked horribly disfigured. The man blocked her view of the woman. For a man with such a rough-looking exterior, he treated the bride-to-be with gentle respect, matching his step to her slower cadence, one hand resting gently on top of hers. The squader led the woman to the podium where the Legiant waited, then backed away.

Apri gasped, "No!"

"What is it?" Gard looked up at her. "Apri?"

"Ladies and gentlemen, citizenss of Edysson," Covington announced, "I present your future queen, "Katrina Bancroft, of Ssouthrock."

"No!" Gard exclaimed under his breath, turning his attention back to the platform.

Chapter 20
Apri

Katrina! Apri projected. *Katrina! I am here.*

She felt the touch of her friend's thoughts, overwhelming fear most prevalent. The crowd applauded in earnest. Katrina's knees buckled, and she would've fallen had it not been for her squader escort who stepped up to catch her.

The girl's thoughts were a jumble of fearful recollections. Bits and pieces of her memory flashed in Apri's head, some confusing, some frightening. The images battered her senses until they settled on one particular incident. A memory so vivid and personal it felt as if it came from her own experience.

She was lying in a grand bed, naked. Covington plunged violently up and down on top of her, saturated in nasty sweat that dripped onto her face. His grunts and groans struck a strident discord to her own cries of pain.

Apri inhaled a great, gasping lungful of air.

Damian was there, too, whispering vulgar encouragement into Covington's ear. She was embarrassed, humiliated, disgusted. And it hurt… excruciating pain.

Apri gasped again. She lost her balance on the branch but caught herself just in time to avoid falling from the tree.

"Apri!" Gard's voice snapped her away from the contact. "Get down here. You're going to fall!"

"No! No. Not yet," she said, regaining her composure and securing her seat in the tree.

She projected again to her friend. *Do not think! Stop thinking, please! Think only of me!*

Katrina's eyes searched for her.

Do not look for me! Look at your citizens! You are their queen. You are beautiful. They adore you. You must be strong for them. You are their only hope for a brighter future. Give them that hope.

Katrina stood taller and lost the bewildered, fearful look. She focused on the people who stood before her in the courtyard, raising her hand in a wave that elicited another volley of applause and cheers. Clapping her hands together, she embraced the attention and scanned the crowd, making eye contact with different people. Resting her hands on her knees, she bent over to give a wave to the little children in the front row, then stood and waved high to the people in the back. She twisted this way and that, waving around to include everyone.

Yes! You are a natural! They love you! Apri projected with a feeling of pride and support. *I must go. Be strong. Be patient. We come to rescue you! Your brother is here, too.*

That news visibly buoyed Katrina's spirit and she transmitted that feeling of joy outward to those gathered to celebrate her engagement.

Apri noticed the squader who had led Katrina onto the platform staring at her with unabashed adoration and projected another thought to her friend. *Who is that man? The one who brought you to the stage?*

She felt her friend's disgust and fear.

You must put aside your fear. He adores you. Use that. She asked Gard, "Who is the squader standing beside her? Do you know him?"

"Hill." Gard stiffened again, hands flexing and unflexing in fists at his side.

"His *first* name?"

"Thaddeus Hill, Comman..."

Thaddeus Hill is his name. Encourage his adoration. Make him want you more than he wants to obey the Legiant. She felt Katrina's understanding. *Be strong.*

Gard was talking. "...to come down out of that tree? Look, they're taking her away now. Let's go."

He lifted his arms to help her out of the tree. She accepted his help but felt nothing. The elation of his touch and the joy of being with him were overshadowed by the disturbing and violent memory she'd just experienced as Katrina. Landing next to him, she backed away, then walked ahead of him as they moved with the crowd to the exit.

"Okay, so we know who the bride is now." Gard's body pressed against her back from the mass of people pushing and shoving their way to the exit. His quiet words came only to her ears. "Is that why you wanted to come?"

She nodded, not trusting herself to speak. She wanted to cry, to scream, to run away.

The image of a sweaty, naked, grotesque man flashed in her brain, and she shuddered. She couldn't shake the intense emotions and vivid images from her mind... fear... pain... humiliation.

No. Stop! That is Katrina's memory, she reminded herself again.

Slimy, prickly skin slid down her body. *Ewww!* She tried gritting her teeth and clenched her fists until her nails dug into her palm. Anything to get the images and sensations to stop.

They made it to the exit and out onto the street. As soon as the congestion cleared, she trudged ahead at a walk-run toward the inn. *What is happening to me?*

"April!"

Just keep moving.

"April!" Gard jogged ahead of her, touching her arm as he passed. "Slow down, what's wrong?" he asked, walking backwards in front of her.

She slowed to avoid running into him. To think that before tonight she'd been longing for his touch. Now it felt creepy... wrong. *Not wrong. He is Gard.* Her emotions were raw, her mind cluttered with conflicting thoughts and images. *I cannot do this.* She ducked around him and marched on.

I need Yelena. She will know what to do. Scanning the crowded street ahead, she dreaded the long walk back to the inn. *Will I go crazy before I make it back?*

"Wait... Just wait, please!" Gard ran ahead of her again.

Apri stopped, searching his face. *He is Gard... Gard.* "I need to go," she said.

"Stay." He stepped up to her, close enough to block her view of anything but him. "You can tell me what's wrong or not. But don't go. Let's get a drink."

She looked into his dark eyes and sensed his confusion. *I cannot tell you. You would never understand.*

"Try me," he said.

He heard that? Did I say it out loud? What is happening to me? Leaning into him, she muttered in a voice hoarse with emotion, "Oh, Gard, it was awful, so painful."

"Painful?" he repeated, wrapping his arms around her. "You mean because she has to marry Malcolm?"

Unprepared for the calming effect of his embrace, her body relaxed in his arms, and he held her tighter. She closed her eyes and forced herself to focus on him—the coarse feel of his beard on her forehead, the musky scent, the rhythm of his heartbeat against her ear. As she began to regain her composure, the images and feelings of Katrina's memory drifted from the forefront of her mind. Not far, but enough that she could separate the present from the memory. After taking a few deep breaths, she pressed her hands against his chest in a silent request for him to release her.

He let her push him away, but only enough so he could see her face. Calloused fingers rubbed the tears from her cheeks.

She wiped her face with both hands, embarrassed. *I've turned into a sniveling, blubbering child. What must he think of me?*

"Come on," he said. "Let's get that drink."

She took another look down the street toward Northgate. *So far.* Gard's presence held Katrina's memory at bay. *And he's here, now.*

She accepted the escort, but a torrent raged in her head over what she could, or should, tell him. Aside from Katrina, she'd never been successful at convincing anyone she had a special gift. *He will think I am crazy. Just like everyone else.*

Ultimately, she chose the more immediate solace and spent the rest of the short walk to the inn trying to figure out how to explain what had happened, and why she was so upset, without revealing her secret.

Gard led her to a booth in the pub. "I'll be right back." He backed away toward the bar, holding up a finger, then a palm, keeping watch on her, as if she might try to escape.

I should. She glanced at the exit. *That is one way out of this.* But she worried he might chase her down if she tried, and she didn't want that. *I do not even trust myself to stand right now.* Each time she let her mind drift, the explicit memory returned.

Gard slid onto the bench across from her, setting the drinks down on the table. He wrapped his fingers around her clenched fists. "Did something happen in the tree? Something painful? You nearly fell out of it."

I wish I did not use that word. She took a drink, watching him over the rim of her mug.

"And why did you ask about Hill?"

It still took some mental effort to separate Katrina's memory from what were her own real-life experiences. The interaction with Gard helped, but the dreadful encounter still felt intense and fresh. And very real. *Real for Katrina.* She pushed the incident to its rightful place in her mind for the umpteenth time.

"Painful was the wrong word, I apol—"

"Don't try to lie to me," he interrupted. "I saw the fear in your eyes. It was... is?... real."

Her eyes glazed over, clouding her vision. Her mind reached out for his of its own accord, feeling his frustration... his concern... and *something more?* His eyes widened, ever so slightly, and she backed out, ashamed for the intrusion into his thoughts. *Did he sense that?*

Whether he did or not, his gaze remained fixed on her. She doubted she could ever deceive those dark, imploring eyes. *Or would ever want to.* A tear trickled down her cheek and she brushed it away. "I cannot speak of it." Before he could protest, she added, "Not here."

He stood and took her hand, guiding her up the stairs to his room. When he unlocked the door, her last hope of avoiding this conversation with him dissolved. Zak wasn't there. Even Monk was gone.

She sat on the bed, dreading the consequences. *This will be it for us.*

Gard closed the door and sat next to her. He said nothing, but she could feel his eyes on her, waiting for her to begin.

Might as well just get it over with. "I have a gift."

Gard looked around, as if searching for a present. "A gift? For me?"

It was an attempt to lighten the mood, but she couldn't even smile. "Not that kind of gift." With her next words, she risked every chance of their relationship maturing beyond friendship. "A *mental* gift. I can read people's thoughts."

He leaned away from her, as if her words physically pushed him away. It was exactly the reaction she expected, and she braced for the ridicule she knew would follow.

"A mind-reader?"

She sensed no mocking or judgment in his tone. *He does not think I am crazy. At least not yet.*

"A muse," she corrected. Before he could say more, before he could ask any questions, she told him about her connection with Katrina, how they became close, learned to communicate with each other. "When I first heard about the wedding, I worried she might be the bride. That is why I had to go. To communicate, I must be close. It does not work otherwise."

Gard said nothing.

She couldn't blame him for being skeptical. This was no ordinary thing. She knew that better than anyone. But he had listened so far and didn't laugh or scoff at her. So, she forged ahead.

"I can read people's thoughts, and sometimes feel what they feel. But with Katrina tonight, it was different than any time before. I felt her fear as if it were my own. And she is very afraid."

"The pain? What was painful?" he asked.

She looked away from him.

"I'm sorry," he said. "I want to know, but you don't have to tell me."

"I will try." She took a deep breath and dropped her gaze, unable to tell this story while looking at him. It didn't reflect kindly on the man he'd once called a friend. "It was her memory of first time she shared a bed with the Legiant."

"Oh." Gard said, barely audible. He looked away then and stared out the window.

Apri told him everything—every disgusting detail. The memory was so fresh, the pain so real, a couple of times she caught herself saying I instead of she. Katrina had been a virgin, making it that much more heinous, more embarrassing, and more painful.

Overwhelmed by compassion for her friend, she wiped tears from her cheeks. *To have such a frightful, violent first experience was unimaginable.*

She forced herself to look at Gard. His face was still turned away, looking out the window. He combed his hair back with his fingers.

"You do not believe me?" She held her breath, dreading his next words.

Moments passed before he spoke. To Apri, it felt like an eternity.

"Believe you? Malcolm Covington hates women. It's not just a preference for male companionship, he truly *hates* women. What you've described is the only way he could possibly conceive a child. Yet you've never met him." He looked at her, his expression full of remorse. "How could I *not* believe you?"

He opened his arms, and she crumpled into his embrace, crying softly as raw emotion erupted inside her. But the dreadful memory soon gave way to other sensations, and she had to push away before she lost herself in the sheer maleness of him.

He let her go. *Did he feel it, too?*

"I'm so sorry," he said. "For you, and for Katrina."

"She is strong. Even so, she was close to giving up when I reached out to her. Almost suicidal. Her spirits rose when she felt my presence. I told her to be patient, to act as queen. To be savior to these people who need hope."

"So, I didn't imagine that change in her behavior? A timid mouse in one moment to a queen in the next? That was you?"

"No," she corrected. "I only made the suggestion. She did all the rest." She half-smiled, recalling her friend's unexpected talent. "I would have been a pile of mush in front of all those people!" Then she remembered something else. "And her escort? Hill?"

Gard nodded. "Scum of the world. A revolting excuse of a man."

"I told her to flirt with him," she said.

"You did what? Are you crazy? That man is worse than Malcolm!"

"He idolizes her. Did you not notice? I did not have to read his thoughts to know his mind. He could not take his eyes off her. Given a choice between protecting her and doing the Legiant's bidding, he may choose Katrina."

Gard chuckled. "Woman, you are wise beyond your years." He stood, holding his hand out to help her up from the bed.

When she stood, he didn't back away from the contact. They were so close she could feel the warmth of his body.

"What about me?" he asked. "Have you ever read my mind?"

She held her ground and met his gaze, fighting the urge to escape from... *from what? Joy? Ecstasy?* "No, I would not do that. Not to you. Not without invitation." Her shame returned as she recalled, "Except... just now... downstairs..."

"I see," he said, raising an eyebrow. "Well, you have my permission to do so again."

It felt as if they were locked together in the center of a whirlwind, its energy sucking them in, urgent and powerful, while everything beyond blurred to insignificance. Without hesitation, she reached out to touch his mind and sensed an intense, but unmistakable emotion. One she, herself, felt just as certainly. *He loves me!*

He abruptly rejected the contact, blocking her from his thoughts. But before the connection shattered, one other thought came to her mind. *His name is Jon.*

Gard—*Jon*—didn't push her away physically. Leaning into her, he pressed his lips to her forehead, then lifted her chin, stroking her cheek. The passion in his dark eyes brought her fully to the present. In that moment, she no longer felt any part of the Katrina-memory as her own.

The door opened, and they broke apart.

"Oh, sorry, did I interrupt something?" Zak asked with a wicked grin. "I can come back if..."

First to recover, Apri said, "No, not at all. I was just leaving, actually." She wanted to smack that silly-ass grin off his face. *I am glad I will not be here to endure his childish teasing.*

Gard had turned to face the window.

"Esh," she whispered to Zak as she left.

His laugh followed her down the stairs. Her heart pounded. Her head spun as she tried to make sense of everything that had happened.

Chapter 21
Apri

Apri woke to the knock at her door.

"Apri, it's Yelena. Are you there?"

She lay on the bed facing the wall still dressed in the clothes from yesterday. "Come in," she called without getting up.

Yelena bustled in. "I worried when I didn't see you at... Oh my, dear, are you sick?" Sitting on the bed, she pressed the back of her hand to Apri's cheek.

Apri sat up. Her desire to seek out Yelena to help understand Katrina's shared memory had become less urgent after her interaction with Jon. She'd tossed and turned through the night brooding over how to understand it. And whether she even wanted to try explaining it with the older woman.

Yelena's expression evolved from probing concern to full-on maternal. "What is it dear?"

"I do not know!" Apri cried and fell back onto the bed, covering her head with the blanket. *Please, just leave me alone.* The thought came unbidden, and she immediately regretted it. She did *not* want Yelena to leave.

"Tell me," Yelena said, grabbing the blanket from her hands and pulling Apri up again.

"Katrina..." she said, then paused, still undecided about what to share.

"Katrina?" Yelena asked. "The Legiant's fiancé? Everyone was talking about her at breakfast. Did you go to the ceremony last night? They say she is beautiful."

"Yes... She is. Beautiful." Of course, Yelena could help her understand and deal with the things that she felt last night but... *Am I embarrassed to talk about it?*

Yelena took her hand. "What is it, dear?"

Apri felt the woman's touch on her mind—not an intrusive probe, just a feeling of comfort and a nudge of support. It was so subtle. On any other day, the connection could easily have gone unnoticed, even by her. *She's good. I still have much to learn.* Shrugging her reluctance off, she told Yelena, "Katrina was... is my friend."

"You know Katrina Bancroft? But I heard she's from Southrock. How do you know her?"

Apri told Yelena how she and Katrina met. "We were—are—*very* close."

The implication was not missed by Yelena. "Oh... I see."

"At the palace, when they brought her out, I connected with her," Apri explained. "She shared a horrible memory with me. It was so intense, so real, Yelena, it felt like I was living it for real. As if it were happening to me, in that moment."

Talking about it brought the feelings back, though less intense and as Katrina's memory now. "I had to break off the connection. I could not endure it," she confessed, looking down into her lap. "I abandoned Katrina when she needed me most."

"You didn't abandon her, dear. You weren't there."

"After the ceremony ended and they took her away," Apri continued, "I had to keep reminding my... my brain?... that it was Katrina's memory, not my own."

Yelena took her hand and patted it gently. "When you share an intense, unforgettable memory, good or bad, especially with someone you care for, it is just..." Yelena's voice caught in her throat, "...just as you describe. As if it happened to you." Yelena stopped talking, her eyes wet. "The memory becomes a part of you. His pain—her pain—is your pain. Or joy. Or sorrow."

Apri realized Yelena spoke from her own experience. "Oh, Yelena. I..."

"It draws you closer. Closer than you can imagine." Yelena wiped a tear from her cheek. "It is a blessing and a curse, this gift of ours."

Yelena's face reflected the love, and the longing, for her late husband. The look reminded Apri of her own brief contact with

Jon. She hadn't been prepared for such emotional intensity, or for the mutual desire it exposed. *Is that love? Or something beyond love?*

"...Apri? Was there something else?" Yelena's voice drew Apri out of her introspection.

"I am sorry, I... no... Ummm..." Yelena could help her understand, she knew that. *But this is so personal, so intimate.*

"Tell me, dear," Yelena urged, "even if it's difficult. I had to discover this gift on my own, with no guidance. You don't have to."

"Gard... Jon, his name is Jon..."

Yelena nodded. "Yes, I know Jon, go on."

"You do?"

She nodded again, "I helped nurse him back to health after the massacre, remember? Please, go on."

"Oh, yes, I forgot that." Apri sighed. "Anyway, he was there when I... when this all happened with Katrina."

After a lengthy pause, Yelena prompted, "And?"

"I know you said we are not supposed to tell anyone. About the gift. But he noticed how it affected me. I tried to leave, but he would not let me go. I tried to think of something to explain what happened. But I could not. Or I did not want to lie to him. I don't know. But I told him." She stopped rambling and confessed again. Eyes on her lap, she repeated in a whisper, "I told him."

"And how did he react?"

She looked at Yelena. "Except for Katrina, any time I tried to explain this gift—to my parents or to a friend—they didn't believe me. They would say I imagined it. Or just laughed like it was a joke. I expected the same from him. But he believed me."

Yelena smiled. "I learned from Kendall of the bond developing between you and Jon."

"Kendall knew?"

"He didn't exactly *tell* me," Yelena said with a wink. "But he knew, deep down. He just refused to accept it until recently." She grinned. "I might've helped him with that," she said, putting a finger to her lips.

Apri laughed. She suddenly recalled Jon's story about the man whose last wish he still carried. *Kendall's father. Do I tell him? And betray Yelena's confidence?*

"So, he believed you. Then what?" Yelena asked.

"Hmmm?"

"What happened after you told him?"

"Oh." Apri felt her cheeks warm. "He invited me to connect with him. That is how I learned his true name. Then he blocked the contact—almost immediately."

"I see."

"What? What do you see?"

"People think they can control the contact," Yelena said. "As if they can put a thought in their head for the muse to read. But that only works if the muse is consciously focused on the same train of thought." She winked. "Whatever he had in his mind for you to know, you ignored it, searching elsewhere. That's why he blocked the contact. So, what did you discover?"

That he loves me. But she wasn't sure about that. It could be wishful thinking, and she couldn't bring herself to say it aloud. "That he cares for me," she said.

"And he knows your feelings for him," Yelena said, then raised a finger before Apri could protest. "It is a two-way street with an intimate connection. What you know, he knows." She raised her finger again. "Don't think you can hide your feelings from him any more than he can from you."

Apri hadn't considered that. Not at all. *Oh, bother.*

"I can't explain it, my dear, but you must trust me on this. When senses are heightened or when your relationship with the other person is profoundly intimate, this gift takes on a life of its own. One you can't control. You either go with it or break the connection."

"How is it that I learned his name?" Apri asked. "Always before, sensations and feelings, they are there, or I experience their memories, but not so much in specific words. But his name, it came to me so clear."

"A person can't hide their true identity from a muse, it is too deeply rooted in their psyche from the day they are born. The first thing you learn upon opening a link with a person is who they are. If they're acting, trying to hide their identity from you, you'll know instantly."

"Katrina," Apri whispered.

"Katrina?"

"She was introduced to me as Tina. I knew it was not her real name the first time we connected."

"Why don't you get cleaned up, dear?" Yelena stood. "Meet me in the dining hall in a half-hour? We can have a late breakfast."

"I suppose I have to eat. Thank you for coming, Yelena."

Apri left for the city after midday. Kendall's travelpack was on one of the beds in the room he'd rented for them yesterday. Tossing hers onto the far bed, she opened the window and looked out. Monk was perched on a ledge nearby, picking at a piece of fruit. He looked up at the sound, dropped the fruit, and scampered over into her room.

"Well, hello, my little Monkjan, how are you today?"

He jumped up and down on the bed, squeaking repeatedly.

"No, I have not seen him," she responded.

Continuing the chatter, the climber spun around a few times and raised his arm.

"I agree. Zak can be quite the gadabout sometimes."

She lay on the bed and continued her one-way conversation with the climber, petting him until he settled down and curled into a ball next to her. She fell asleep thinking of Katrina, trusting that her friend would find the courage and fortitude to survive a few more days.

Apri woke when Kendall opened the door.

"Oh, sorry, didn't know you were here," he apologized.

"It is okay. I did not mean to fall asleep." She noticed Monk was gone.

"I saw Gard. He told me about Katrina," Kendall said.

"Yes, I am afraid for her safety."

"Well, she has been introduced to all of Edyson as their new queen. Wouldn't that mean they intend to keep her safe?"

"I suppose so," she agreed. *Always the practical one.* "I hope the Legiant does not hurt her. Gard says he hates women." She recalled her quick exit when Zak barged in last night. "Does Zak know?"

"I don't think so. Gard didn't want to tell him. It would only enrage him further."

Apri pulled on the boots she'd discarded beside the bed, questioning that decision. *I would want to know.*

"Coming?" Kendall interrupted her thoughts.

"Coming." *I will talk to Jon. Zak needs to know.*

"I expect the meeting tonight to go late," Kendall said as they walked downstairs. "Can you take Gard and Zak to meet with Headmaster Barrow later?" he asked.

Apri nodded. "Sure."

"He'll meet you at the inn at thirteen hundred. There's a plan or map of the palace he wants to show Gard, and he's gathering information about the palace watch schedules." Kendall shook his head. "Barrow and I are treading a narrow path. We feel responsible to protect the people of Edyson, yet we must uphold the Cortek oath."

"I understand," she said. The oath—a sacred covenant of the Cortek people—had been covered by Yelena at one of their first lessons.

His expression changed, filled with anguish and regret. "You've no idea how much I want to help take that man down. He's hurt so many."

"Yes, he has. And none of this would be coming together without you, so you *are* helping." She stretched and slid off the bed. "Shall we go?"

They went to the pub and joined Jon at a table near the middle of the room. Zak sat at the bar, flirting with the barmaid again.

"We've got about an hour. The place is just down the street," Kendall said.

Jon didn't answer, at least not verbally. He might've nodded but she couldn't look at him. Not after last night. She sat across the table, next to Kendall.

She watched Zak with the barmaid. From the way those two acted, they'd already spent much time together, maybe even had been intimate. Unconcealed lust had replaced yesterday's innocent flirtation.

"At least she's keeping him occupied," Jon said.

Apri glanced at Jon. He was watching Zak at the bar with his ever-present, controlled expression. *But oh, how I can get lost in those eyes.* He met her gaze, and she felt that bond again, the same as last night. Not quite as intense, but just as real. He couldn't hide it from her. *Or he chooses not to.*

"What?" Kendall asked. "Oh, I see."

Zak returned with drinks, greeting them with a smug smile. "They're on the house."

"Found a friend, have you?" Kendall teased.

"Her name is Felicity." Zak gave Apri, and then Jon, a look that dared them to get in on the ridicule. Neither took the bait.

Kendall filled them in on the schedule for the evening, and they talked through dinner until it was time to leave.

"Which way are you going?" Zak asked as they walked outside.

Jon scowled at him.

"I'll catch up," he promised.

Kendall indicated the direction they were headed, and Zak scampered back to Felicity like a trained puppy.

"It's not far," Kendall said, explaining that a prominent businessman who owned buildings all over the city was hosting the meeting at a vacant property nearby. "Goldstein's latest project has been impacted severely by the situation in The Ravens," Kendall explained. "Construction has been suspended—shut down due to lack of materials. He's become more despondent and vocal in recent weeks. Some are worried he's treading on thin ice."

Zak caught up with them just before they turned into an alley.

A guard stood at the entrance to the building. Kendall gave his name and whispered something to the guard who unlocked the door to admit them.

The warehouse smelled of stale beer and felt twenty degrees warmer than outside. A bartender served drinks from behind a wood plank placed atop two barrels. A few men stood around conversing in quiet murmurs. Most looked their way when they came in.

One man approached them. "Kendall. And friends. Welcome," he said, nodding the Edyson greeting. "Sorry about the meager accommodations... and the smell." He winked at Apri. "It's the best I could do on short notice, times being what they are."

"Of course, we understand, Mr. Goldstein. These are the friends I told you about." Kendall introduced each of them in turn.

"It's nice to meet you and please, call me Arlen." He was a jovial man, but with a sharp, probing gaze that gave the impression he was sizing her up to determine her worth. "This way, please. Let's get you all something to drink." The man reminded Apri of her father.

She felt ashamed that she hadn't thought of her family in so long. *What would Father do if his business were threatened like this?* The thought gave her a new perspective of what these people were going through.

"Something wrong?" Jon asked as they followed the man to the makeshift bar.

She smiled. "He reminds me of my father."

Others joined the meeting over the next quarter hour until Arlen invited everyone to be seated. Zak, Jon and Apri remained standing while Kendall sat with the others at the table.

Arlen opened the meeting, "We shall not belabor this meeting with discussions about the wickedness, or the heartbreak, or the atrocities that are happening around the colony. We all know the situation is dire and that something must be done. What we discuss here this evening, my fellow citizens, would be considered treason by some, and certainly by the letter of the law. You're here because, like me, you believe our only recourse, the only way to restore Edyson to peace, order, and prosperity is to depose the Legiant and end his tyrannical rule." The men seated around the table nodded their support, some adding murmurs of agreement and consent.

Apri's motivation, her objective from the time she left the caves, had been to find and rescue Katrina. Until now, she hadn't considered the magnitude or significance of what they were preparing to do. This would be more than a rescue mission, with more at stake than her own life and Katrina's.

She shifted her stance, anxious to get out of the sweltering, smelly warehouse. She sensed Jon watching her. *What is this sudden hyper-sensitivity with him?* Fearing a connection that might be too powerful to break, or too revealing to others, she didn't look at him. Instead, she glanced at Zak who appeared distracted. He leaned against a support post with his arms crossed and his eyes on the door, like a child forced to sit in school when he wanted to go outside and play.

Goldstein continued, "…Kendall, who is here representing the Cortek. Although their oath forbids them from getting directly involved, they've agreed to help guide us through what we hope will be a leadership transition. We'll need their knowledge and understanding of the legal and historical precedent of the colony."

"Thank you, Arlen," Kendall began. "I must first remind each of you again of the risk you take in attending this meeting. As Arlen said, we're here because we all agree there is no other option. I thank each of you for your support in this time of great need."

Zak sighed dramatically, shifting his weight.

Jon elbowed him in the ribs.

"Everything we speak of tonight will be in vain if we don't succeed in taking the palace." He raised his hand to silence the murmuring. "I don't know any details of the mission, so don't ask. The palace must not be warned or the least bit suspicious of a pending attack. You must not speak of it, or anticipate it, or expect it. It'll be successful or it won't. Either way you'll hear the news… after it is over. For your own safety and for the safety of everyone involved, be patient. These meetings are to discuss, confer, and debate the future of Edyson politics, and to plan for a smooth transition in leadership, whatever form that may take."

Apri leaned toward Jon, and whispered, "We should leave now to meet Barrow."

Jon nudged Zak, and they left for the stables.

"Did you hear that?" Zak asked as they exited the alley. "Thanking those men for the risk they take? What risk? They are sitting in a meeting and talking. And here we are going to another meeting to talk some more. We need to find my sister. What of that?"

She and Jon exchanged a look. "Listen Zak," Jon said, "once the Legiant is deposed we'll have full access to the palace. We'll find her. You have my word."

"This is taking too long. We're wasting time."

Jon turned on him, barking a heated reply, "What d'you think we should do, Zak? Storm the palace? Just the three of us?"

Zak backed away from the onslaught.

"What's your plan, Zak? I'm all ears." Jon snapped.

Zak looked so dejected, Apri had to say something to diffuse the tension, even if it meant Jon might turn on her. "Listen, we are all on edge. It is understandable that Zak is impatient. We are so close."

Jon glared at her, still angry, and she gave him her best *Please calm down* expression.

"Yes, sorry," Zak said, holding up his hands, palms out.

We need to tell him. But even as she had that thought, she knew now was not the time.

The strained silence during the rest of their trip to the Forest Inn reminded Apri of their escape from the caves. She felt their anxiety and knew the tension between them would only get worse until this thing was settled, one way or another. In the meantime, conflict would be their only release.

Chapter 22
Apri

Apri breathed a sigh of relief when the inn came into view ahead. Tarina came out to greet them. "Hello, Apri," she called out.

"Tarina!" she replied, dismounting. "Good to see you again." They'd gone riding together a few times, and Apri counted Tarina among the few friends she'd made since coming to Edyson. "We won't be staying long. The horses can stay here," she said, tying Dega at the hitching rail.

"Oh, okay," she said. "I'll take them over to the water trough in a few minutes, in case they're thirsty."

"Thank you."

She led Zak and Gard into the empty dining hall. Naomi looked up from her task of cleaning tables and greeted her cheerfully, "Apri! How are you, sweetie?"

"I am good, Naomi," she replied. "We are here to meet with Headmaster Barrow."

"Headmaster Barrow? I haven't seen him. Are you sure?" She walked to the kitchen door and called out, "Jay, honey, come out here. Do you know anything about Barrow having a meeting here tonight?"

"Barrow?" The old man came out, scratching his head. "Apri, dear, how nice to see you again. Oh, I see you brought some friends. Can I get you folks something to drink?"

He fumbled under the bar for glasses.

"Jay, honey," Naomi said. "Barrow?"

"Barrow?" he repeated.

"Yes, dear, is he coming out?"

"Not that I know of," he said. "Dear."

Zak chuckled. He placed some coins on the bar.

"On the house," the man said, pushing the coins back and placing three full glasses on the bar.

"Jay?" Naomi nodded her head toward the back.

Jay rolled his eyes and winked at Apri. "I have customers to tend to," he said.

Naomi chastised him with a glare.

"Okay, okay. I'll go see what I can find out about Barrow." He tossed the bar towel over his shoulder, then pointed to the tap. "You all help yourself if you need a refill." He went into the kitchen, and Naomi returned to cleaning the dining hall.

"Help yourself?" Zak said, taking a drink. "This is the strangest pub I've ever seen. Empty at this hour? Free drinks?"

"You have your friends. I have mine," Apri said.

Jay came back in, mumbling, "Always the last to know. And this place a mess!"

"He is coming?" Naomi asked.

"Aye, that he is. On his way now," Jay said.

"On his way from where?" Zak asked.

Apri helped Naomi collect the last few glasses, plates and flatware scattered about on the tables.

"Oh, uh… from the back…" Jay stuttered.

"Don't mind him," Naomi interrupted, "he's scatterbrained sometimes." She pointed to her temple. "Headmaster Barrow is in the office. He'll be out soon to greet you."

A few minutes later, Headmaster Barrow emerged from behind the clerk's desk. "Ahhh, here we are. I apologize for my tardiness. I had to wait for this drawing." He held up a roll of paper and approached Jon. "J—Gard, it's been a while. So good to see you again."

"And you as well, Headmaster," Jon replied, "This is Zak, and I believe you've already met Apri?"

"Yes?" he seemed perplexed. "Ah, Kendall's friend, of course, yes. I hope you are enjoying your visit with us, my dear,"

"I am, very much, thank you." She had not seen the headmaster since that first day but was surprised he didn't remember her. *I thought I made more of an impression.*

He looked around, his gaze landing on a closed door. "Come along, you three, we have much to discuss."

They followed him into a storeroom piled high with extra furniture, boxes, and equipment. Closing the door behind them, Barrow held the rolled-up paper in his hand, scratching his head and scanning the tight space.

Jon moved around a few boxes and chairs, rearranging the clutter to uncover a flat surface on which Barrow could place the map.

"Thank you, son. Just what we need." He unrolled the map, and Jon and Zak held the edges to keep it from curling in on itself. "Let's get right to it, shall we?"

Jon nodded.

He pointed to a location on the map. "This here's the palace grounds," he said, then flipped the map around a couple of times. Satisfied with the orientation, he pointed again. "We are here." When Jon nodded again, he continued, "The sewer mains run underneath the streets and out underneath the city wall into the leech fields." Running his fingers along a couple of the streets from the palace outward, he explained, "There are two lines that run under the palace wall. This line, here, allows the most direct access to the palace from outside the wall, is farthest from the city gates, and would bring you into the grounds behind the palace tower.

"See here, these are street access grates," he said, pointing to the circles with an X in the center. "Counting from the wall: one, two, three, four… the fourth grate is inside the palace wall, behind the tower." Moving his finger on the map from the fourth grate, he tapped it on a point at the base of the tower. "Here is the back entrance to the tower. Always guarded. The Legiant's quarters are on the top floor."

"The sewer?" Zak asked. "We're planning to walk through sewage?"

"Do you have a better idea, Zak?" Jon's tone and expression conveyed more than his words.

Apri reached over and touched Jon's arm, wanting to avoid another pointless argument between the two men.

The men stared at each other.

"Zak?" Barrow interrupted the exchange. She thought he meant to diffuse the tension, until he asked, "Zakary Bancroft?"

Zak bristled. He looked at Barrow, then at Jon.

"It's okay, Zak, he's on our side," Jon said. "My apologies, Headmaster, I thought you knew."

"No, no, not your fault, son. I certainly should've made the connection. Just been so preoccupied." His expression changed, full of compassion. "I've not seen you since you, well, since your family... You were still in diapers then, I think. I'm so sorry about your parents. Good people. I knew your father well."

"Th—thanks," Zak said.

"Your sister, too, in such a wretched position, poor thing. I fear—"

"My sister?" Zak exclaimed. "What do you know of my sister?"

Apri and Jon exchanged glances, and Jon gave Barrow a disgruntled look.

"Oh, my," Barrow caught on. "I—I'm sorry, I thought you knew."

"Knew what?" he asked Jon, then Apri. "Knew what?"

"We only found out yesterday," she said, reaching out to touch his arm.

He backed away from the contact, "Tell me."

Jon shrugged a silent permission.

"We saw her yesterday, sh—"

"You saw her *yesterday*? And I have to hear about it from this old man?"

"Zak." Apri waited, hoping he would calm down. He didn't. *We should have told him.* "She's the Legiant's fiancé," she said finally. She looked at Jon, pleading for support.

"He introduced her last night at a public ceremony," Jon said. "She looked well, beautiful even."

Zak backed up. The closed door stopped his progress and he leaned against it heavily, snapping at Jon, "You think she is *well*? In the hands of that maniac and his men? You think they are treating her *well*?"

Jon studied the map. "She is alive. And we will rescue her."

"When? Who knows how much she's suffered already? How much longer must she be a prisoner? We need to do this now!" he shouted, slamming a fist into the door. "Tonight!"

"You know the plan," Jon said. "We wait for the wedding day." His tone left no room for debate. "Squaders will be spread thin, keeping order throughout the city. It's our best chance for success."

Perhaps he wanted to verbally smack some sense into Zak, to fracture the emotional turmoil that controlled his judgment. But Zak wasn't a disciplined soldier trained to follow the commands of his superior, so it didn't surprise her when he gave Jon a defiant scowl and left, slamming the door behind him.

Jon stared at the closed door.

You know that was your fault.

His expression changed, a silent apology.

She winced. Did I project that thought to him? If she did, it was unintentional.

"Oh, my. How unfortunate," Barrow said. "My apologies."

"He's a hothead," Jon said, "with a huge chip on his shoulder."

"Do you blame him?" Barrow's blue eyes glared at Jon. "Fate has not been kind to that boy."

Jon ignored the reprimand. "What else can you tell us?"

Barrow rolled up the map and handed it to Jon. "Here, take this. I have it on good authority that most of the squaders in the palace are unhappy and dissatisfied. But any dissension or even an innocent word of displeasure with their orders, or the situation, will land a squader in prison, or worse. Tensions are high among the Law Squad, but the Legiant's faithful are keeping mutiny at bay by fear. And torture. And God knows what else."

"So, you believe we have allies in the palace?" Jon asked.

"I have no doubt. But how many? Which ones? I can't say. You must treat all as enemies unless they act otherwise."

"We have some time and can use more help. Find out what you can about help from inside. We'll only get one chance at this." He addressed Apri, "We need to go after him. Make sure he stays out of trouble."

She nodded.

Barrow reached out to take her hand. "My dear Apri, I apologize for my greeting earlier. I didn't know how much that young man knew of your situation here. Yelena has been sharing with me your progress." He chuckled. "To be honest, she prattles on about you incessantly. I'm pleased you chose to make this journey after so many years."

"It is my honor to be here," she said, relieved and flattered to be acknowledged by the headmaster.

Barrow walked to the stables with them. "I wish you success. Be careful," he admonished. "I'll be sure to share anything I can find out about support from within the palace with Kendall."

Zak's horse was gone when they reached the stableyard.

"I was watering the horses and your friend took his and left in a hurry," Tarina said.

"Yes," Apri said. "Thank you, Tarina."

"One more thing," Barrow said as they mounted. "The sewer will be pitch dark. Take a lantern or it'll be slow going down there." Grinning, he added, "And something for the smell."

"Will do," Jon acknowledged. "And thank you for this." He held up the map, then gave a casual salute.

They rode to the city in haste and stabled the horses.

"Durka's here," Apri reported. *That is a good sign.*

They jogged over to the inn in hopes of finding Zak in the room, but no luck. Jon shut the door behind him.

Apri sat on the bed. "Will he do something stupid?" she wondered aloud. "Should we try to find him?"

He sat next to her, close. Their thighs and hips touched. "Where would we look?" he asked, raking fingers through his hair.

Was it only yesterday he'd tried so hard not to touch her? She avoided eye contact, her concern for Zak prevailing over other, more primal, desires.

"Listen, I know it's my fault he ran off like that."

She didn't respond.

"What was I supposed to do?"

"You have spent much time with him," she lashed out, exasperated. "You should know him by now. He hates authority, hates being told what to do or being made to feel foolish. Especially by you."

"Is it my fault he's such an immature child?" he barked back.

Her eyes met his in defiance, lips poised with an angry retort that went unspoken. In that moment, her anger evaporated. She couldn't look away, couldn't move away.

As he leaned into her, their eyes still locked, she felt the hint, the promise, of that remarkable, obsessive connection she felt yesterday.

He placed his arm behind her on the bed. Her skin burned where their bodies touched. "I'm sorry," he whispered.

Her body squirmed of its own accord, forcing itself into a firmer, more solid contact with his arm and shoulder. Then his mouth devoured hers as he drew her into a strong, welcome embrace.

Responding with the same fierce intensity, her hands searched for bare skin. They fumbled with buttons, snaps, and belts until their clothing lay scattered around them.

Their eyes met.

Never before had Apri used her gift in the act of sex. In fact, it'd never occurred to her to even try. Until now. *With him, it is the only way.* Without hesitation, she reached out with her mind, connecting with his and instantly reading every carnal, uncensored thought. To her shock and utter joy, she felt him in her head as well.

His eyes widened in surprise, and she thought she might lose him. But he stayed with her.

She didn't want to break the eye contact, afraid that might be what made this breathtaking mind link possible. But she wanted him, he wanted her. *If we do not get on with this, we may both come too soon.*

He laughed.

The throaty chuckle sounded in her ears and resonated in her head, stirring every sense within her. Anticipation overtook her apprehension, and she kissed him again, breaking the eye contact.

The link remained. Feeling his bare skin on her own, she pressed against him. *Hold me, closer, tighter.*

His arms wrapped around her like a vise in response to the unspoken request. He knew her most private, lustful desires and she, his. The give and take, the instant response to each other's needs, continued until they climaxed as one, their eyes and minds locking together in that final moment of ecstasy.

The mental connection faded as their bodies shuddered and trembled with the last remnants of their lovemaking. With every intimate thought laid bare, no words needed to be said. They fell asleep, legs and arms intertwined.

Apri woke to Jon's snoring—not as loud as those nights on the road to Baytown, but loud enough to wake her. It was still dark out, and Zak hadn't returned. *Or maybe he did? I do not care.*

Watching Jon as he slept, she touched his beard ever so slightly, not wanting to wake him. Most Aratian men wore full beards, but she typically preferred men with no facial hair. He turned over, facing away from her. Fearing Zak might return any minute—*okay, so I do care*—she resisted the temptation to touch his smooth, muscular back. *At least his back has no hair!*

Easing out of the bed, she dressed and padded barefoot to her room, boots in hand. Kendall had mentioned at dinner that he planned to stay there tonight, but he was still out. *Good!* Her travelpack was on the bed, and she rummaged around in it for the bottle of tonic she always carried. She held the bottle up to the light. *Empty.* Shoving it in her pack, she made a mental note to get it refilled in the morning, then lay down on the bed, tingling with the memory of—

Zak barged into her room without knocking. "Something's happened! At Kendall's meeting! Come on!"

Pulling on her boots, she followed Zak out of the room. Jon met them at the top of the stairs. They exchanged a glance. Without a second thought, she mentally projected to him that she didn't know any more than he did. They followed Zak down the stairs and ran down the street toward the warehouse.

Outside, Odin had risen to add its glow to the light of the streetlamps. They stopped at the end of the alley to the warehouse. EMTs hurried into the building carrying med kits. A few people stood around. Most of the women wept as their men consoled them. The warehouse door had been smashed off its hinges, and the guard lay unmoving on the street in a pool of blood.

"Kendall!" Apri screamed.

"No, April!" Jon tried to stop her, but she darted past him and ran inside.

EMTs darted around like ants disturbed from a hill, back and forth, back and forth. Apri scanned the chaos, hoping against hope.

Kendall lay motionless. He'd been stabbed through the chest. Blood still dripped from the wound, adding to the red puddle beneath him. The sight dragged a terrible sound from Apri's gut— a primal moan that vibrated through her bones and out her throat like the crescendo of thunder. She ran to him, falling to her knees and lifting his head onto her lap. Rocking slowly back and forth, she cried, "Kendall... oh god, nooo!"

Numerous smaller, less severe cuts decorated his body. She traced one of those with her finger. *I bet you told them nothing.*

She caressed his face, left untouched by his torturous attackers, then leaned over to press a kiss against his forehead. She had known him for months yet hadn't felt really close to him until they came here, and she met his... *Yelena! Oh, Yelena!* She raised up, her tears falling onto Kendall's face. *How will she ever bear this?*

Dazed by grief, she looked around, her ears registering only bits and pieces of the sounds in the warehouse.

"... men were tortured..." Jon spoke to a squader who had just arrived on the scene.

Someone gagged, then the sound of retching came from farther away.

"Your men did this!" a man shouted at another squader. "...murdered these unarmed men!"

Apri held Kendall, stroking his cheek. She caught Jon's attention, and grief poured from her mind. His expression filled with sympathy, and he walked toward her.

One of the EMTs draped a sheet over Kendall's body. "We'll need to take him soon," he said with a gentle touch on her shoulder.

"Not yet," she begged. With the sheet covering his injuries, he appeared to be sleeping. She kissed his cheek, then his forehead. The warmth had gone from them.

Zak stopped Jon, and they engaged in a heated argument. She didn't hear their words, but Zak's face was red with anger. He turned away and Jon tried to grab him. Zak shrugged him off and ran out the door.

The EMT still stood over her. "Ma'am?"

Jon came to her, then. "We need to go," he said, offering a hand to help her up.

She didn't want to leave.

He squatted beside her, taking her hands. "Apri?... There's nothing we can do for him now."

He helped her stand. Memories of Kendall flooded her thoughts, and she wept in the comfort of Jon's arms.

"We need to go," Jon's voice intruded, ever so gently. "I'm afraid Zak's going to do something stupid."

He took her hand, and she followed him, staggering a few steps as he hurried her out of the warehouse. The cool night air helped her recover. She pushed her grief to the back of her mind. *Later. Not now.*

"He overheard one of the witnesses describing the man who led the attack," Jon said, releasing her hand and quickening his pace. "It was Hill."

"What does he know of Hill?" she asked.

Jon didn't answer.

"What did you say to him?"

Still, he said nothing.

They sprinted up to his room. The door was ajar.

Monk startled awake, squealing when they entered.

"Oh, no." Jon said.

"Oh no, what?"

"Barrow's map. It's gone."

Chapter 23
Zak

His accusation that those men took no risks by just talking at a meeting couldn't have been more wrong. Zak's stomach churned from the brutality of it. Unarmed men who could've been arrested were slaughtered like... *like turbeasts before a Thanksgiving feast.* The gory, malicious scene escalated his fear for Katrina's safety.

And still Gard wants to wait? How long before this kind of violence, this blatant disregard for human life, turned on his sister*? I'm done waiting.*

He'd inspected Barrow's map under a streetlight near the stables. Now, urging Durka for more speed, he turned onto the road that led to the Forest Inn, then slowed to a walk. He searched the north side of the road for a path through the thick foliage. *Should've paid more attention when we came this way earlier.*

Just as the inn came into view ahead, he spied a narrow path leading into the forest and guided the horse onto it. The farther he travelled from the road, the more overgrown the pathway became until Durka had to drop his nose and pick his way along. With a fresh memory of Barrow's map, Zak used the location of the inn to keep his bearings, guiding the horse now and then in what he hoped would be the right direction. They broke through the thick brush into a clearing, and the city wall came into view.

"Come on, boy." He kicked Durka into a long, ground covering trot.

The map placed the sewer access in the ground near the wall, about halfway between Northgate and Eastgate. The forest had been cleared back, and with Odin setting in the northeast there should be enough light to find it without the need to search on foot. Urging his horse into a lope alongside the wall, he kept an eye out for the sewer access.

At the sound of rushing water, Zak looked up. *Damn!* The river was too close. *Must've missed it.* Turning around, he proceeded back at a trot, and then at a walk as he approached what seemed to be the right location. Moving back and forth in the cleared area, he finally found the access port hidden in shadows cast by the full moon.

A large, heavy-looking iron grate, about two meters across, covered the access hole. Littered with small rocks, branches, and dirt, the grate looked as if it hadn't been touched in years.

Vaulting from his horse, Zak inspected the grate up close, then immediately backed off from the unbearable stench. Inhaling deeply, he held his breath and returned, moving a few of the bigger rocks off the grate. He tried lifting it, but it wouldn't budge.

Expelling his breath, he stepped back from the putrid smell and surveyed his surroundings. The grate could be wedged in from years of neglect and erosion, or just too heavy for him to move. Either way, he needed something large and sturdy enough to use as a lever. Finding nothing suitable in the cleared area near the wall, he looked out past the horse into the forest beyond.

This is taking too long. He looked and listened for the inevitable approach of Gard and Apri. *If they catch up, it's over.*

Durka stomped his foot and snorted.

Durka! Yes!

Retrieving the rope from his saddle, he tied it to the grate, then uncoiled it as he retraced his steps back to the horse. *Too short.* He dropped the end of the rope and led the horse closer. Once he had enough slack, he tied the rope around Durka's neck.

"Okay, Durka, boy," he said, "let's do this." Facing the horse in the direction he felt had the best chance of dislodging the grate, he urged the gelding forward. Durka walked a few steps but stopped as soon as he felt the tension of the rope against his neck and chest.

"No, don't stop, Durk." He stood next to the horse to keep him from turning sideways, then reached behind and slapped his flank.

Durka lurched forward. The weight of the grate stopped him again, and he stepped back. His hoof landed on Zak's foot.

"Oww!"

Zak shoved the horse off his boot and looked back at the grate, still wedged solidly in the ground. He picked up a long stick.

"You gotta try harder Durk." Repositioning himself next to the horse, he tugged on the rein and smacked the horse's rump with the stick.

Durka surged forward.

Zak hit him again, just as the rope came taut.

The horse lurched, then leaned into the pressure, moving sideways against the heavy weight.

Zak pushed against the horse's shoulder, keeping him straight.

The grinding of metal on rocks reverberated through the air. He cringed. The noise echoed off the wall, shattering the silence of the calm night. *Too loud.*

One look back, and he knew he'd need more room. *No choice.* He encouraged the straining horse again, "Come on, Durk!" More scraping... then the *slurp-slurp* sound of debris falling into the hole. "Just a couple more steps, boy," he urged.

The horse took another step, then another.

Zak checked the grate again. "Good job, Durka!" He gave the horse a solid slap on the neck and Durka jumped. "No, no, easy boy," he said, stroking the horse's neck until he relaxed.

He drew his sword from the saddle scabbard and strapped a dagger around his lower leg.

Halfway to the grate, the disgusting smell hit him, and he turned back around. Retrieving the cloth he'd used to protect his face from the trail dust, he wrapped it tight around his nose and mouth and returned to the sewer access.

Concerned that the opening might not be big enough, he tried moving the grate himself, but it was too heavy. *Should've given it one more tug.* Not wanting to waste more time, he eased down into the opening, feet first, twisting this way and that.

Still unable to wiggle through, he climbed back out, faced a different direction and raised his arms above his head. His armpits scraped against the sides as his shoulders squeezed through, but he made it. Holding to the grate, he hung down into the opening, feet dangling, waiting for his eyes to adjust to the darkness.

With one hand, he grabbed the metal ladder mounted to the wall behind him, then twisted around to face it. Narrow slivers of light caught the moonlight coming in through the grate. The wide shaft was much like that of an open water well. *Except for the smell.* He began the descent downward, rung by rung, wondering about the depth of sewage he would have to walk—*or swim?*—through.

It was farther down than he expected, and darker than any darkness he could've imagined. Just as he thought about going back to try to fashion a torch out of something in his pack, he reached the line that stretched under the city wall. A dim spot of light came from what might be the first street access, and beyond that he thought he could see the second. *The old man said the fourth one would be on the palace grounds.* He could make his way through the sludge using those pinpoints of light for guidance.

The ladder ended. When he took the next dreaded step down, his foot felt a hard surface. With one foot and both hands on the ladder, he checked the width and firmness of the footing. Then, still gripping the ladder, he tested it with his full weight. *Feels solid enough.*

Sliding his foot toward the city side of the main he felt no give under his foot, so he stepped off the ladder. He ran his hands along the wall and slid his foot toward the faint light of the first street grate, then took a step. Several more times he did the slide-step maneuver, and discovered he stood on a fixed ledge, about a meter wide, set in the side wall above the sewage. *I hope this runs the whole way.*

About halfway to the first street grate, he heard running water and stopped, trying to determine the direction of the noise. Across from him, on the other side of the main, he heard the sucking and sloshing sound of waste as it made its way into the main trough. His face covering did little to protect his nose from the stench of the disturbed sewage below. *Of course, there are other lines feeding into this one.*

After only a few more steps forward, the ledge on his side ended and his hand felt the end of the side wall as well. *Another feeder line.* He could guess that the ledge started up again on the other side of the opening. *But how far ahead? Jump and pray?*

Deciding against that, he checked the size of the feeder opening. *Sure wish I had some light!* It felt like a large pipe, with a circumference a little less than he was tall. Facing the wall and blind from the darkness, he wrapped one hand around the edge and moved slowly into the pipe, first with one foot, then the other. His hands pressed against the sides for support.

The sound of rushing water came from somewhere upstream. *No!* As the sludge rushed closer and closer, Zak moved his hands upwards, then stretched his legs wide and put his feet as far up the sides as he could.

With his head and back pressed against the top of the opening, he held his breath as the sewage ran between his legs, sliding over his boots, and dropping into the main below. Careful to avoid slipping again, he inched around to the other side and reached with his foot for the ledge. It was there, right where he expected it to be. *Whew! Could've just jumped over here.*

The first street grate offered enough light from the streetlamps for him to assess the design of the underground sewer system. The ledge ran along both sides of the main line with a break wherever other lines fed into it. A bar hung from the ceiling above each feeder opening—a handlebar for stepping over to the other side. That *would've made the last crossing easier. And less messy.* A ladder provided access from his side of the ledge to the street grate above. At the location of each ladder, overhead bars were secured to the top of the main line for getting across to the opposite side. The main line gap required a hand-over-hand swinging maneuver to cross rather than the long step it took to pass the feeder lines.

Creeping down the line with more confidence, he ran his hand along the wall to feel for the incoming lines, using the overhead bar to cross the gaps on the ledge. About three quarters of the way to the third grate, his foot hit something on the ledge. He bent down to touch the blockage. It was about knee-high and felt slimy and gelatinous. *Ewww!* It covered the entire ledge, and, in the dark, he couldn't tell how far down the line it ran. *Damn!*

He retraced his steps to the second ladder, then used the upper holds to swing to the other side of the main. Encountering no obstructions between the second and third grates, he continued on the same side until he reached the fourth grate. The moon above shed enough light for him to see that the ledge on the other side was clear, so he crossed over. When he heard no sound from above, he mounted the ladder and climbed to the top.

The street grate was smaller and lighter than the access grate outside the wall and lifted easily out of its frame. He set the grate quietly beside the opening, then poked his head up and looked in the direction of the tower. The grate was in shadow, but moonlight illuminated most of the open ground between it and the back entrance to the palace, preventing a direct approach. One squader stood guard, about fifteen meters from his location. To the left of his position, a garden wall provided some cover. He ducked back inside, listening for an opportunity to make a run for the wall. At the sound of voices, he peeked out over the edge again.

"Hill? Late assignment?" The guard opened the door, blocking their view of Zak's position.

Zak scampered up out of the shaft, and over to the cover of the garden wall.

"Tell my men to wait for me here," Hill ordered. "They should arrive soon. I'm going to report to the Legiant."

"At this hour, I bet he's banging' that gorgeous fiancé—*Oohf! Ugh!*" *Thud.*

Zak bristled at the guard's comment. *Katrina.* He glanced around the corner.

The open door still blocked his view. "Fobmuck! Watch your mouth." Hill's voice trailed off inside.

"Ohhh, what the bloody 'ell?" the guard moaned. He lay on his back, his prone body holding the door open. Only his feet were visible from Zak's position.

After allowing some time for Hill to leave, Zak discarded the cloth on his face, then ran for the door.

The guard's nose bled, possibly broken. "Who the hell are you?"

Zak clubbed the guard hard across the side of his head with the hilt of his sword. The man slumped over, and Zak dragged him inside, propping him against the wall in a corner.

He stood in a small entry room. A staircase on his right led to the upper stories. A door, directly opposite the one he'd just entered, was closed. Shutting the outer door, he drew his dagger and darted up the stairs.

The few slivers of moonlight that filtered in through narrow windows cast most of the staircase in shadow. The stairs zigzagged upwards, with two flights between each floor. He bounded up the stairs. A low-wick oil lamp lit the landing, and he crept around the corner, then continued the stealthy pace, stopping when he heard voices on the top floor.

"...soon as Hill's gone, he's gonna call me back in there, you know."

Zak peered around the corner. Two squaders stood a few meters down the hallway in front of a pair of elaborately embellished double doors. He looked around. *Now what?*

"You know, he was asking about you. You outta think about it," the same man said.

"Not interest—"

Clang, clang, clang.

Zak cringed. The mop bucket he'd tossed clattered down the stairs, louder than expected.

"I'll go check it out. Probably some clumsy servant dropped it."

Zak heard the metallic rasp of a sword pulled from its scabbard. His sword hand twitched and a shiver crawled up his spine. He massaged his elbow recalling his injury during his last bout. Retreating down the stairs and around the first bend, he flattened his body against the wall and waited.

The tip of the guard's sword came into view... a flutter of cloth.

Zak leapt forward but overextended and his sword grated along the stone wall. *Damn!* The glancing blow across the guard's arm had little effect.

"Well, what have we here?" the guard asked, ignoring the scratch on his arm and dodging sideways to avoid Zak's next swipe. "And who might you be?"

Zak ducked and twisted sideways. The guard's blade missed him, but it came close enough that he felt its breath on his cheek. "Your worst nightmare," he warned.

The man outweighed him, and standing above him on the stairs had the height advantage as well. Zak backed down the steps, feeling for the landing that might help even the odds. Gard's voice surfaced in his frantic brain. *Deep breath, calm yourself, no wasted moves.*

Following him down, the guard chuckled under his breath. "Well, mister *nightmare,* get ready to go to sleep for good."

The man charged.

Zak froze for a heartbeat, then the instinct for survival kicked in and diffused his panic. He lifted his sword just in time to keep the guard from lopping off his head.

The concussion of the hit pushed him back a step. His awkward, two-handed block of the next blow twisted his left wrist. The pain shot up his arm and to his elbow, but it was more than just a twinge this time. *Ouch! Shit!*

The guard wore a cynical smile, showing no sign of stress or concern. *He's just playing with me.*

Clang! Retreat. *Clang!* Retreat.

Each strike was stronger and more powerful than the last. *Why doesn't he just kill me?* With his next step back, Zak's foot knocked the bucket, and it rolled sideways across the landing, clattering down the next stairwell.

The man glanced down the stairs behind Zak. *What's he looking at? The bucket?*

Clang! Ouch!

Stepping back again, he felt the end of the landing with the heel of his foot. *Oh god oh god oh god!*

The guard's fierce expression told Zak this next hit would be forceful enough to send him backwards down the stairs. The man's sword arced above his head.

Gard's training voice sounded in his brain, *Assess your surroundings.*

Zak raised his arm for another block. Then, just before the final strike made contact, he dropped his sword and ducked under the man's arm, diving onto the landing beside him.

With no resistance to stop his forward momentum, the guard teetered on the edge of the step, arms flapping like a crowing rooster.

Zak kicked the man's foot out from under him.

With a wild, futile attempt to grab onto something, the guard found nothing but air and toppled over. As he careened down the stairs, his head flopped into the mop bucket.

Thump. Clank! Thump. Clank!

He came to rest in a heap on the next landing, bucket-helm still firmly in place.

Zak grinned.

"That was clever," a voice said.

Startled, Zak looked up from where he still lay sprawled on the landing. The other squader held his sword inches from Zak's chest.

"Are you alone?"

Odd question. "Well, no," Zak said. "You're here."

The guard snorted. "I'd heard rumors about a possible attack. Is this it? One guy... one *kid*?" he asked, shaking his head. "Get up." He bent over to pick up Zak's sword, then offered a hand to help him off the floor.

Zak looked at the hand. *I'm not a kid!* In fact, the squader couldn't be that much older himself.

"Come on, get up." The squader wiggled his fingers.

Zak took the hand and stood, then reached to take his sword.

"Not a chance," the guard said, holding it away. "Hill could come out at any time. You are my prisoner." Grabbing Zak around the neck, he held the sword to his side. "What the hell is that—" The man sniffed. "Oh, kid, you smell bad. Like rolling-around-in-pig-shit bad."

He forced Zak to climb the stairs. "If Hill comes out, you will struggle to escape. Choose the right moment." The last point was driven home with a strong flex of the arm around his neck. "What's your name?"

"Zak?" he answered, confused.

"You're not sure?" the guard chuckled. "Great. I'm Baker. Just one of many who are fed up with this Legiant and his band of thugs. If this is it, if one—*small*—kid is our only chance at ending it, then I'm in," he said, flexing his arm again. "What d'you think, eh? We just doubled our chances." He laughed.

The man sounded deranged, but then having a madman on his side might not be such a bad thing. *Sure beats being dead.*

Hill didn't emerge before they came to the fancy doors on the top floor.

"Listen, kid," Baker spoke in his ear, a guttural whisper, "the two men inside are strong, skilled fighters. Vicious, ruthless killers."

"I know that."

"Do you?" Baker spat out the words, wetting Zak's ear. His arm tightened in a true chokehold, and he leaned in even closer, his voice menacing. "You would never try a stunt like this alone if you knew these men as I do. That trick you pulled on Crowell down there? These two would've seen it coming. They will not toy with you. You are nothing to them but shit to scrape off their boots." He released the vise-grip but still held Zak by the neck.

"Know this. Beyond some miracle of fate, we will not survive." He pounded on the door with the hilt of Zak's sword.

The door opened. "Who is this?" Hill growled, eyes on Zak.

"An intruder, Commander," Baker said to Hill, then, speaking louder. "He took out Crowell."

"Crowell?" A high tenor voice came from inside. "What'ss that, you ssay?

Hill opened the door wider and stepped back. "Bring him in."

Baker shoved him roughly into the room.

Zak's jaw clenched. His muscles flexed. His fingers itched for a weapon. The two men responsible for the death of his parents, for abducting his sister, for killing Gabe, *for ruining my life,* stood before him. He tried to lunge at them, but Baker held him fast. The *tick, tick, tick* of a clock sounded from somewhere, marking the seconds that passed as he waited for Baker to let him go.

"Sso, who is thiss young man?"

He expected a deep, booming voice from the stocky man, but he sounded more like a woman. *Except for that weird bird chirp.*

Covington raked his eyes over Zak, up and down, and licked his lips. "You say he killed Crowell? I liked Crowell," he said, as if talking about a dead pet.

"Not sure if he's dead. Unconscious at least." Baker cleared his throat. "Says his name's Zak."

Covington didn't hide his surprise. He looked at Hill, who showed no reaction, then back at Zak. "Zakary Bancroft?" he crooned. Studying Zak with a curious, questioning gaze, he walked to the wall and lifted a sword from its mount, then made a few practice moves. It was as if he wore the weapon, rather than carried it, as an extension of his arm that moved fluidly without conscious thought. "Yes, I do see the resemblance."

Baker's words echoed in Zak's head. *We will not survive.*

"Give him his weapon," Covington ordered.

Baker hesitated. "What?"

Zak swallowed the bile that rose in his throat. *Inhale. Exhale. Rule #1.* He released the anger, the hatred, the desire for revenge, all the emotion that drove him to this point. *Is fear an emotion?* He didn't think he could let that go. *Rule #2.* Swallowing again, he focused on his opponent who watched him with a brutish hunger.

"You dare to question me?" The Legiant spared a glance at Baker. "I said, give him his weapon."

Baker gave Zak his sword and backed off with his hands in the air.

Wasting no time, Covington attacked.

Aggressor. Egomaniac. Zak assumed the defensive, focusing on the other man's moves. His brain managed an unexpected shift in its perception. This fight would be a game to win or lose, just another sparring match, like those with Gard—not a life and death battle. That train of thought helped keep his fear and panic at bay.

Covington was barefoot, wearing only a nightshirt that hung loose around his considerable frame, whereas Zak wore a thick leather jerkin. *Advantage Zak?*

As if to answer the unspoken question, his opponent paid no heed to his ill-advised outfit and advanced, relentless in his attack, mounting charge after charge. Zak retreated backwards, his opponent leaving no opening for a counterattack.

Picking up a vase that toppled when he bumped into a table, Zak launched it at his opponent's head, then followed the vase's trajectory, sword first. He managed only to slice through the loose nightshirt.

Covington wasn't fooled by the distraction, and Zak came away from the clash with a deep cut in his left shoulder. The pain brought tears to his eyes. Warm blood dripped down his chest and torso. *Damn!*

The nightshirt hung precariously over the Legiant's right shoulder like a Halloween toga costume. Still, he paid it no mind. "Give up yet, boy? I hope not, I'm enjoying this," he said. "It's been a while since I've had such fun." He licked his lips. "I mean, *this* kind of fun. Your sister, she's a different kind of fun."

Zak seethed inside. *Deep breath.* He decided to continue his assault on the nightshirt and ran at the man. The gown dropped around Covington's feet, but he managed to skewer Zak again, his blade running all the way through his left side.

"Ahhh!" Zak moaned, grabbing his side and nearly passing out from the pain. He staggered backwards.

The Legiant stood in front of him, nearly naked. Blubbery skin bulged above the waistband of his undergarment. He made a run at Zak.

The forgotten gown tangled around his feet, and Covington tripped, falling flat on his face. His sword flew from his grasp and landed at Zak's feet.

Everything seemed to move in slow motion. Zak heard and sensed Hill coming after him from the other side of the room as he bent to pick up the sword. In excruciating pain, his pulse pounded in his ears.

A clash of metal came from behind as Baker engaged Hill.

Zak advanced toward the Legiant, a sword in each hand. Just putting one foot in front of the other took all his concentration.

His opponent stood and backed away.

A door opened, and Katrina stepped out into the room. "What is all the—"

Zak yelled at her, "Katrina! Go back!"

"Zak?"

Covington rushed to her, grabbing her before she could run.

The shrill sound of Katrina's scream rang in Zak's ears, filling him with dread.

The Legiant dragged her across the floor, then shoved her down until she knelt beside him. Wrapping her hair around his hand, he jerked her head sideways. "Drop your weapons," he yelled. "*Now!* Or I swear, I will break her pretty little neck."

Zak dropped the swords.

A crash and a heavy groan from the other side of the room drew his attention. Baker had landed hard against a wall. He slithered to the floor, still and silent.

Chapter 24
Apri

They found Zak's horse tethered to the grate. Gard dismounted to inspect the sewer access.

"Esh!" Apri scolded the absent Zak, jumping off to tend to Durka. From the abrasions on his chest, he had struggled some to get free. "Either the gelding calmed himself, or Zak has not been gone long." She clicked, coaxing the horse backwards to loosen the rope around his neck and chest.

"Wait." Jon said. "This is heavy. Can he move it a bit more?"

"I think so." She faced Durka away from the grate and rearranged the rope, so it didn't rub on the deeper cuts, then eased the horse forward until the rope was snug. "Ready?"

"Go."

Standing next to the horse's shoulder, Apri clucked and tugged on the reins, urging him to move forward. "C'mon boy, you can do it."

Durka eased into the pressure and took a step while she leaned into his shoulder for support. He took another step, and she heard the grate grinding over the ground behind them.

"That's good," Jon said.

Removing the rope from around Durka's neck, she coiled it up and slung it over her shoulder.

"We can send horses back. Dega knows the way," she said, unbridling Zak's horse. "Terina will recognize her and take them in." When she finished with Durka, she situated the tack on the other two horses for their riderless trip.

She and Jon geared up, including the lanterns and face coverings for the sewer.

Apri projected an image of the stables and fresh grain to all three horses with an extra promise of a good meal and rub down to Dega for good measure, then slapped her mare on the rump. The three horses trotted off.

Jon took the cloth for his face, and she tied hers on.

"Ugh!" Jon said, screwing up his face at the scent of the perfume she'd sprayed liberally on the cloth.

"Would you rather smell the sewer?"

"Maybe," he said, tying the cloth over his nose and mouth.

Jon gestured for her to go first, and she descended, lighting her lantern halfway down the ladder. The smell of the perfume mixed with the sewage was awful, like musky vomit. *Worse than without it.* Lifting the cloth from her nose, she sniffed. *Phew, no, not worse.* She covered her nose again, with a pang of regret for using her favorite perfume. *I will never wear* this *again.*

The lanterns shed plenty of light to see where they were going. They crept their way along the narrow ledge with Apri in the lead.

Something moved in the sewage below them, and she stopped. "Did you see that!?"

"No, I didn't see anything. Keep going."

As she passed the second grate, Apri held her lantern down, her eyes scanning the thick, murky sewage in the trough. "There," she pointed her sword, "did you see that?"

"Your mind is playing tricks on you, there's nothing dow—"

A dark, slimy, wormy creature came up out of the sewage ahead of them, its head rising almost to the ceiling. The thing reminded Apri of a gargantuan version of the earthworms she used to play with in their garden.

"Get back to the ladder!" Jon yelled, turning around.

Apri followed, hurrying toward the ladder at the second grate. She felt something grazing her back and looked over her shoulder. The worm's long tentacles reached out for her, and she sped up, jumping over the feeder line break without using the handhold.

"Go! Climb the ladder!" Jon ordered.

With both hands full, she had to drop her lantern to grab onto the ladder. It bounced off the ledge and clattered into the trough below, then flickered out. Near the top she turned around to face the sewer, wrapping one leg around the ladder for support.

Jon's lantern hung on a peg. He stood on the ledge, both hands on his sword.

Apri's heart raced. The worm, eight or nine meters long and about a meter thick, slithered at a slow pace on top of the raw sewage. Chunks of sewage dripped from its ugly, slimy head and plopped into the trough. Beady eyes looked at the lantern, then at the two of them. Wiry, long tentacles reached for Jon.

Her base instinct triggered, and Apri reached out with her mind. *There is no danger. These will not hurt me.* It was a habit she'd picked up long ago whenever she encountered an unfamiliar animal.

The creature hesitated, stopping just out of reach.

Jon held his sword up and prepared to attack. It reached for him again.

There is no danger. It means no harm. Apri sensed its concern, and fear, but not for itself.

The tentacles came within striking distance, and Jon recoiled, ready to strike.

"No!" Apri yelled aloud to Jon and mentally to the worm. Both stopped.

"What? It's coming at me."

The worm retracted its tentacles, its head turned to look up the line near the third grate.

Apri stepped down from the ladder, "Come, with me," she said. Taking the lantern from the wall, she retraced their steps back the way they had come.

"We're leaving?"

"I hope not," Apri said. "She is protecting clutch. It is somewhere up ahead."

The worm slunk down into the trough, following them but making no move to attack.

When they reached the first street access, Apri sheathed her sword and gave Jon the lantern. Grabbing the first bar, she swung hand-over-hand to the opposite ledge, crossing above the worm.

Jon followed, holding the lantern in his teeth.

Apri took the lantern and turned, moving again toward the palace. An undercurrent of concern still stirred in her head from the mama worm, but the fear had dissipated.

"We should be good on this side, I think," she said to Jon as he followed behind her.

"You think?"

She didn't respond.

"What about Zak? Did he get past this thing?"

"I do not know."

"Well, can you ask?"

Apri shook her head. "It does not work like that."

They passed the third grate, and the worm stopped, holding its position near the opposite ledge. At the fourth grate, they switched over to the ladder side of the ledge. Apri doused the lantern and hung it on a peg next to the ladder.

She looked up. "The grate is off," she said.

Jon climbed the ladder. "I don't see any guards," he called to her. "There should be." Looking down at her, he pointed to his right. "There's a fence for cover. I'll go first." He lifted himself out and disappeared.

Apri climbed up after him, peeked over the edge to get her bearings, then ran to the cover of the fence.

She heard a man's voice, "Where's the guard?"

Jon flattened against the fence, raising his arm to push her back as well. "That was close," he whispered.

"Hill told us to wait out here," another voice said.

Jon peered around the corner, held up five fingers, then drew his sword.

Apri unhooked the keeper on the kris at her waist.

"Hey, he's in here," a man shouted. "Asleep, the fob—. No. Not asleep." Swords were drawn.

"Now! Go!" Jon ordered.

She followed him at a trot. Two guards were still outside but faced the door unaware of the threat.

Jon took out one guard with a single thrust.

"Ahhh!" The man yelled and keeled over, blocking the entrance.

"Intruder!" Another man shouted from inside the room.

Jon sliced the back of the next guard's leg, leaving a deep gash. He crumbled to the ground, and Jon finished him off, slicing his throat with a knife. The man made a gurgling sound, then slumped over.

Only seconds had passed. When Apri came around the door, the two dead squaders blocked the entrance.

Walking over the corpses, she followed Jon into a small room, just as another man exited another door on the opposite wall. Two more men backed up the stairs facing Jon, swords drawn, and he went after them.

Apri felt movement behind her. She ducked, but not in time. Huge, hairy arms wrapped around her, pinning her arms at her side. The vise-like grip squeezed a yelp from her body.

The sound caught Jon's attention, and he turned to look.

"Be…hind you," she wheezed a warning as the two men on the stairs use the diversion to attack him.

She slammed her heel onto her captor's foot and bent over, shoving her weight to one side. The man lost his balance and toppled sideways, releasing her. She tumbled away from him. Her sword caught on his boot, and she lost it. She pulled the dagger from its sheath.

Her attacker lay sprawled on the ground, unarmed. He grabbed for her sword.

Stepping on the blade before he could lift it, she stabbed him in the neck.

Jon still fought one man. The other was unconscious, bleeding from a chest wound. Jon bled also, but she couldn't tell how seriously he was injured. He favored one leg, and his movements were sluggish. *But that could be deliberate.*

Apri picked up her sword just as the inner door burst open. More men rushed into the small room, and she turned to face them. The man who'd exited to sound the alarm ran by her to assist Jon's opponent. She faced five more men.

"Drop your weapon," one of them ordered.

With no hope against five armed guards, Apri dropped her sword and one of the men shoved it away with his boot. He grabbed her by the arm, relieving her of the dagger.

"Ahhh!" she turned to see Jon falling down the stairs, landing hard on the stone floor behind her. He didn't move.

A couple of the men knelt next to Jon, confiscating his weapons.

The man holding her pushed her roughly toward the other men on the stairs. "Take her upstairs to Hill. I'm sure he'll want to question her."

She watched Jon's motionless body as one of her captors searched her for weapons.

The man patted her all over, his hands probing and lingering longer than necessary in certain places.

Apri glared at him.

The guard smiled a putrid-smelling, toothless grin as he tucked her knife into his belt.

"This one's dead," the man kneeling next to Jon announced.

No! Her knees buckled. If the men didn't have such a firm hold on her, she would've crumbled to the floor. In a desperate attempt to prove the man wrong, she reached out for Jon's mind. *Nothing.*

"Let's go," one of her captors ordered, shoving her forward.

She tripped, falling to her knees.

The guard yanked her up by one arm and shoved her again.

Apri stood firm, like cold stone embedded in bedrock, and stared at Jon lying on the floor below. But after another jarring shove from the guard, she turned and plodded up the stairs between them, her vision blurred by a flood of tears.

"Get dressed." The muffled words came from within as they approached an open doorway on the top floor.

Stopping at the threshold, one of the men noisily cleared his throat.

"What now?" The harsh male voice sounded exasperated. After a few moments came an angry invitation, "Come in, if you must."

The two men exchanged worried looks.

As the door opened, Apri blinked rapidly to clear her vision. *This is not over yet.*

Covington stood near the center of the room straightening a knee-length robe around his obese frame. Katrina knelt at his side, dressed in a cotton nightgown, his hand holding her firmly by the shoulder. Hill held Zak upright by the throat. Blood dripped from the knife in his other hand.

"Stand up and tie this belt around me, won't you, my dear?" Covington said to Katrina.

"Yes, my liege." Katrina stood and did as asked, her eyes on Zak.

Zak's shirt had been sliced open. Blood flowed in rivulets from a couple of deep gashes on his side and shoulder. A myriad of fresh flesh wounds decorated his chest, neck, and face. He was conscious, but she guessed not for long. When he saw Apri, his eyes flashed with a flicker of recognition.

"Apri?" His voice was raspy, barely audible. "Got 'em all warmed up for you."

"Apri?!" Katrina and Covington spoke her name in unison.

"The Aratian bodyguard?" The Legiant eyed her with pure hatred, then immediately veiled his contempt with an expression of curiosity. "Damian said you were a brazen bitch." He licked his lips. "Well, you are just in time." He pulled Katrina close, arm around her waist, and ran his fingers seductively across her chin, then down to her breasts. "Maybe you can help me? I was trying to decide who to kill first. Her? Or him?" He grinned at her like a madman. "And now, there's you."

There wasn't a man in this room Apri could hope to influence with her gift. Least of all Covington. It would be impossible for her to think like him, to make him believe her thoughts were his. He was deranged and would recognize the intrusion immediately. So would Hill. And she could sense the fear in the two men that held her. *No help from these two cowards.*

She projected to Katrina. The girl's thoughts were hysterical, a mass of confusion and fear. *Katrina, listen to me. I know it is hard. Look at me! Be brave.*

Katrina looked at her. Through the panicky web of emotions and memories Apri could interpret only one pervasive, coherent thought—a revelation both shocking and unexpected. *Oh god.*

A brief, apologetic smile, meant only for Apri, crossed Katrina's face.

"I am thinking my beautiful fiancé, here," Covington said. "Would either of you like to give up the names of your co-conspirators to save her life?"

"No! Don't hurt her," Zak pleaded weakly. "I told you. I don't know any names. Ahh!" he screamed as Hill slowly made another deep incision across his chest.

"And I told you," Hill snarled, "we don't belei—What's this?" Using the edge of his knife, Hill caught a chain under Zak's shirt. "A necklace?" He cut the chain. It wrapped around the blade, and he tossed it toward the Legiant. "Something for you, my liege?"

"Hmmm... Pretty," he said, but made no move to pick it up. "So, no names, then?... Zak? A... Aratian Bitch?... No?" He lifted his sword to Katrina's neck.

"But, my liege, you just introduced her as your queen." Hill's expression did nothing to hide his obsession with Katrina. He reminded Apri of a stallion within scent of a mare in heat. Yet Covington didn't seem to notice.

Dragging Zak to the balcony, Hill shoved his upper body over the balustrade. A wide crimson trail of blood followed them.

Zak didn't resist. He may have passed out.

"This one already admitted he has no information. He is of no use to us," Hill said.

"No!" Katrina cried.

Malcolm slapped her. "Actually, I think this one first. She is weak. Unworthy to be my queen. We will tell the people she was assassinated." He put his sword to her throat. "By these two."

"I... uh..." Hill muttered. If Covington weren't so obsessed with himself, he surely would've seen the man's anguish and despair.

Tell him! Tell him now! Apri mentally shouted to Katrina.

Katrina looked at her.

Apri nodded encouragement. *Now!*

"I am pregnant." Katrina's quiet statement hung in the air, like a calm break in the midst of a frantic storm.

Covington dropped the sword from her throat. "What's that you say?"

Katrina cleared her throat and stood more erect. "I am pregnant. With your heir, my liege."

"My heir? Is it a boy?"

Apri projected to Katrina her response to that question.

"It is *your* child, my liege. What else could it be?" Katrina's intonation was perfect. Sweet and convincing. He would be too proud, and, hopefully, too ignorant not to believe her.

A commotion from the open door drew their attention as another pair of squaders entered. Behind them, Jon struggled between two others who held him firmly.

Jon! Her relief, and her love for him poured out from her mind to his. *I thought you were dead!* She sensed his irritation at her emotionally charged reaction. *I thought you were dead!* she relayed back to him in her own defense.

Not quite, he projected. *Be ready.*

She nodded.

"Another?" Hill bellowed from the balcony. "How many more have slipped through your defenses?" He was enraged, his accusation directed at every squader in the room. The two beside her shifted uncomfortably.

"This is it. It's all we need." Jon's voice sounded haughtily confident, considering the circumstances.

"Jon?" Covington stare. "No!"

"Malcolm." Jon said. "Good to see you again." His tone suggested that the seeing was anything but good.

"Gardner?" Hill seemed equally incredulous.

"Well, well, well. The prodigal son returns," the Legiant said. "And just in time. We are about to begin the—" he paused and grinned wickedly "proceedings." He gestured to Hill. "Let him go."

No! Apri reached out mentally. Nothing. No consciousness, no sense of being. *Zak! You need to wake up!* She remembered Yelena's lessons and tried mimicking his persona. *Hey! Wake up! I need to do something, or this fobmuck is gonna drop me.*

"Thaddeus, no! Please, I beg of you!" Katrina cried.

Hill froze.

Apri felt a sliver of awareness from Zak, so faint she could've imagined it. She kept prodding. *Wake up. I'm not ready to die. Katrina needs me.*

The Legiant's expression turned menacing, and he glared at Hill. "Thaddeus, is it?" He spoke the name with a cloying inflection. His next words were not an order, but an ominous threat. "Let..."

At that moment, Apri felt Zak become fully aware. She communicated as herself now, *Do something. Save yourself. Hill is right there. He will not expect—.*

"...him..." Covington's command echoed in the room, cutting her off.

Zak stayed with her. Her heart soared when she saw his eyes flicker, but she felt his consciousness fading. Then she sensed him in her head. *It's over for me... Save Katrina...* A faint smile touched his lips. *This is for...* He severed the connection.

"Go!"

Hill leaned forward.

Zak grabbed Hill's neck with both hands and gripped his legs around his torso.

"No!" Hill yelled and tried to push Zak off him. But with his momentum already leaning outward, he had no leverage. And no hope of saving himself. He toppled over the railing with Zak wrapped around him.

"No!" Apri's shocked exclamation went unheard over the wail from Katrina that drew her eyes off the empty balcony. The girl's legs buckled, and she collapsed like a rag doll.

As the remnants of Katrina's voice echoed through the room, Apri expelled the revulsion, contempt, and hatred she felt for the man who had hurt so many. Like a volcano spewing house-sized boulders, two words erupted from the depths of her soul in a silent, deafening command—*Kill him!*

The room exploded in chaos.

Suddenly released by her captors, Apri wrenched a sword from one of them and bolted toward Katrina. Other guards charged by her, reaching Covington first and brutally attacking him. She dove to the floor, skidding underneath the melee of grappling men for any part of Katrina she could grab. Finding a bare foot, she pulled on it, dragging the still unconscious girl across the floor until they were a safe distance from the fighting.

Apri stroked Katrina's face, then stood to face the fracas. More guards had arrived on the scene at some point after the fight broke out. Two of the newcomers had disarmed and detained her two captors. Another tended to the man against the wall who had regained consciousness. All eyes in the room were on Jon and Covington.

"So, my old friend, this is where it ends." Apri didn't recognize Jon's voice. *So evil.*

A few injured squaders littered the floor around them, victims of the Legiant's battle for his own life. A battle he had already lost. Blood gushed from several deep gashes on Malcolm's legs and upper body. He held his sword in a weak grip, dazedly following Jon who moved slowly around the wounded man, taunting.

"But first, how about a taste of your own medicine?" Jon raked the tip of his sword slowly across Covington's chest, slicing a shallow crevice from one nipple to the opposite hip.

Malcolm screamed and pissed himself.

End this! She projected the thought, hoping to snap Jon out of his vengeful lust. *You are better than this!* She felt a flash of recognition, then shame, before he blocked her projection.

Jon stabbed him through the heart, and he fell to the floor.

Katrina began to stir and moan, and Apri crouched down to tend to her.

Still dazed, Katrina rubbed her head where it had hit the floor. She searched the room. "Zak?"

"I am so sorry." Apri shook her head.

"No!" Katrina buried her head in her hands and cried.

"Come. Can you get up?" Helping the traumatized girl stand, Apri escorted her toward a door she hoped would lead to a bedroom.

Their progress was slow. Katrina moved as if in a trance, her hands clenching Apri's arm for support.

"The Legiant is dead," she heard one of the guards say with authority. "The Commander of the Law Squad is dead."

Whoops and cheers followed.

Katrina lurched beside her, the noise penetrating her trauma. Her fingers unclenched and now rested lightly on Apri's arm. Stopping suddenly, she stooped over to pick up Zak's discarded necklace from the floor. She hugged it to her chest.

The guard's voice rose above the cheering. "As Captain of the Palace Law Squad, in accordance with colony law, I am in command and hereby declare the colony of Edyson to be under Martial Law."

The men cheered again.

"My next, and last, official order as commander is to reinstate Jon Gardner as Commander of the Law Squad, effective immediately."

Through the closing door, Apri saw Jon accept the command with a curt nod. She released the rage, the fear, and the hostility that possessed her with a deep, cleansing breath. What remained was profound grief... for Zak... for Kendall... and for her two friends who had just lost all that remained of their family.

A memory came unexpectedly, nagging her as she followed Katrina down the hallway... Zak's last words—*This is for... ?* The name he projected had been unclear, but she caught the image of a young boy. *Why, Zak, would you owe that boy such a debt?*

Chapter 25
Apri

Apri returned from her visit to the campus infirmary and sat on the bed. A tornado of emotions whirled in her head. *What now?*

Monk leaped up next to her and danced around in a circle. She picked him up and wrapped both arms snugly around his little body.

He pushed against her with his one arm and both legs, but she held tight—he *hated* being hugged. When she finally let him go, he jumped up and down on the bed, screeching his annoyance.

Apri's eyes brimmed with tears. "I miss him too, Monkjan."

Collapsing on the bed, Monk offered his belly for a rub down. "Have it your way, you big baby."

He'd been outside her window at the inn when she went there to pick up her things those many weeks past. Jon had already checked out, but the climber was still there, waiting for Zak to return. She'd brought him back to stay with her at the campus.

Having his company helped fill the void of losing Zak and Kendall, but Monk still pined for Zak. At first, he'd been so desperate for her attention that he'd throw a fit whenever she left without him. He still acted like a spoiled three-year-old much of the time, but his little tantrums were fewer and less vocal lately. He seemed to be getting past his own grief from losing his friend.

The infirmary visit intruded viciously back into her thoughts, as did the recollection of rifling through her travelpack for her stash of morning-after tonic back on that fateful night—the night Kendall died… the night Zak raced off to save his sister… the night everything changed. The trivial concern of being out of tonic had slipped her mind in the chaos that followed. *Not so trivial now.*

Jon would have to be told, of course. *Oh god. Pregnant?* Apri wasn't ready to face her predicament head-on, much less think about *that* confrontation. So, she forced the concern to the back of her mind and dressed for her visit with Katrina at the palace.

"Let's go!" she called to Monk. "We cannot keep the queen waiting!"

Monk leaped onto her shoulder.

Yelena had volunteered to stay with Katrina to help her recover from all she'd been through, and the two women took to each other instantly. A couple weeks later, Yelena announced that she would be moving to the palace to live there indefinitely. At Katrina's insistence, Yelena would have her own suite on the top floor, now named the Queen's Quarters. Although Apri missed their company, she knew they needed each other far more than she needed them.

Katrina and Yelena had hosted a private, double funeral to honor Zak and Kendall. The ceremony was poignant and emotional, but with a theme of hope and promise and an underlying message that their loss wouldn't be in vain. The day after the funeral, Katrina appointed Yelena to a permanent position as head of the palace household.

Apri exited the campus building into the bright sun for the short walk to the palace. *Pregnant!* Her efforts to keep from thinking of her situation were futile. She recalled a conversation with Katrina a few days after the palace coup. They sat alone in Katrina's room and Apri felt compelled to broach a delicate subject.

***

"Katrina," Apri began, "you know that you have options, right?"

"Options? What options?"

"Your pregnancy," she said, "You do not have to do it, you know?"

"Don't have to… What are you trying to say?"

Yelena walked in, eying the two girls. "What's this about? You two look like you're up to something."

Katrina gestured at Apri, palm up. "I believe, Yelena, that my dear, pragmatic friend here, is trying to tell me that I can abort my child."

"Abort?! Apri! Why... What..." Yelena stammered.

Katrina smiled. "My dear Apri, you are my best friend in the whole world, but goodness gracious, why do you think I would want to do such a thing?"

"I just thought... under the circumstances... I, Ummm..."

Yelena scoffed, agitated. "Circumstances? Katrina has been through hell and back, to be sure. But should her unborn child suffer—die—because of... of circumstances?"

Katrina reached a hand out to calm Yelena. "Please. We are of one mind on this, Yelena. You can relax."

∗∗∗

At the time, Apri thought her suggestion had been perfectly reasonable. Why not put an end to such an unpleasant memory, especially when the alternative guaranteed you would have a lifelong reminder. *Pragmatic?* It was sensible. Yet both her friends had dismissed the idea, without hesitation, as ridiculous.

Apri entered the palace grounds where final preparations were underway for tomorrow's Legiant's Day ceremony. Jon, Headmaster Barrow, and a council of community leaders and business professionals from all over the colony had been sequestered for weeks discussing the future of Edyson's leadership and government. Rumors had been circulating that a new structure for governing the colony would be revealed on Legiant's Day. Inns and roadhouses within the city and outside its gates were filled to capacity, and the capital buzzed with excitement and anticipation.

Wherever Apri went, people recognized her, wanted to talk to her, wanted to be seen with her. Witnesses of the Legiant's assassination had shared their respective recollections of that night with friends and family, and soon the story took on a life of its own. After so much sharing by word of mouth, with embellishments and poetic license taken by each storyteller, there were now several different accounts circulating about that night, and none of them the whole truth. One even named her as the Legiant's killer. But in every version of the story, she was portrayed as the queen's champion, a real hero, always referred to as *Apri the Aratian.*

Apri didn't enjoy the notoriety, everyone seemed to know her on sight. Of course, having a climber as a frequent companion only added to the recognition and attraction.

The squader guarding the main entry nodded, opening the door. "Miss Apri, good day to you."

With a brief half-smile to the guard, she trotted up the stairs to Katrina's rooms.

Monk screeched at the sudden change in gait and jumped off. Preferring to climb the stairs on his own, he ran up ahead. When they reached the top floor, he jumped back onto her shoulder from the banister. After so many trips to the Queen's Quarters these past few weeks, this ascent routine of theirs had become an almost subconscious maneuver.

With no threat to her safety from within the palace, or from outside it for that matter, Katrina's rooms were not guarded. Apri entered without knocking, unexpectedly interrupting the queen in her sitting room as she entertained two guests.

"Oh, my, forgive me. I am so sorry to disturb you." She turned to leave.

"Apri, please, come in and meet the Murfys," Katrina said. "They were friends of my parents. Commander Gardner invited them for the festivities tomorrow."

Apri walked over to greet them.

"Is that…? Well, of course it is," the man said, looking at Monk. "That's Zak's climber!"

"Yes, Monk and I sort of adopted each other, after…" *Oh, my, do they know?*

"I told them about Zak," Katrina said. "They lost their son Gabe a few years back. He was Zak's best friend growing up."

Gabe? Zak's best friend. A ghost of a memory intruded. She shook it off. "I am sorry for your loss," she said.

"Thank you," the two said in unison.

"The Commander wanted to see the Murfys when they arrived, but he was busy, so I agreed to visit with them for a while. Speaking of which, he should be free by now, shall we?" Katrina stood and gestured to the door.

"It was very nice to meet you," Apri said.

"And you," Mrs. Murfy said, smiling. "We are so very thankful you were there to save our Katrina."

"I am sure that whatever story you heard was greatly exaggerated, but I am glad to have been there for her. She is a dear friend," she said, reaching for Katrina's hand.

"I believe Yelena is in her room, resting. It's a big day for her tomorrow," Katrina said.

"Her first major palace event." Apri laughed. "I doubt she is resting."

"You're probably right."

Apri went to Yelena's room and knocked.

"Come in."

As expected, she wasn't resting. A ledger sat in front of her on the bed and papers were strewn all around. From the look of her, Apri wondered if she'd slept at all in days.

"You really should get some rest," she told her friend.

Yelena looked up. "Apri, my dear! How good to see you. And I'll rest when this is over."

Apri sat in a chair. Monk jumped onto the bed, scattering papers everywhere.

"Get that climber out of here. He's messing everything up!"

Apri coaxed Monk out of the room and shut the door. Sitting back down, she silently watched Yelena... studying the book... picking up a paper... putting it down... picking up another...

Oh god. Pregnant. She needed to talk to Jon before she went back to the campus. *Maybe I should not tell him.* But trying to keep such a secret from him was a bad idea. Partly because it would gnaw at her until she drove herself crazy. But mostly because he would find out through their mental connection anyway, which had grown stronger and more habitual. If they were in the same room together, it took serious effort and concentration *not* to connect with him.

She'd always preferred a rip-the-bandage-off approach—just get it over with. *But this news? What do I say? How will he react?*

"How will who react? To what?" Yelena asked.

Apri had been so engrossed in her thoughts, she hadn't noticed Yelena's mental intrusion. Gently blocking Yelena's contact, she said, "You are good."

"As I've always told you... practice makes perfect. Now, tell me."

Apri took a deep breath, intending to tell her, but then exhaled without saying a word. She looked at Yelena.

Yelena watched her with an irritated expression, her work ignored for the moment. "Must I pry it out of you?"

"I... I am..." She looked again at Yelena.

"You are?... What?... Tired? Worried? Happy? Sad? Bored? Honey, I could go on guessing all—"

"Pregnant!" She buried her face in her hands, shaking her head. "I am pregnant." Hearing Yelena's laughter, she looked up, annoyed. "It is not funny."

"Oh, but, my dear, it is, a little. Have you ever heard the phrase, *What goes around, comes around*?"

"No, I have not. What has it to do with me being pregnant?"

"It has more to do with why I am amused."

She'd been hoping for reassurance or moral support from Yelena. Instead, the infernal woman wanted to play a guessing game.

"Never mind!" Apri stood up, intending to leave.

"Apri, my dear, you know that you have options, right?" Yelena said.

She turned around, "Options? Options for what? Why do you talk in riddles?"

"Options... with your pregnancy?" Yelena raised one eyebrow.

"What? I would never..." She fell back down into the chair. *What goes around, comes around.* "This is not the same thing."

"Isn't it? I can easily guess who *he* is, the person whose reaction you are so concerned about. Wouldn't it make things easier for everyone if you were *not* pregnant?"

She glared at Yelena, upset that she would choose this moment to interject one of her life lessons.

Yelena ignored her glare and went back to reorganizing the papers Monk had scattered about.

Is it the same thing? She knew what Yelena implied. *Whatever the circumstances, we are both pregnant, and that is the same.* She'd been so offended when Katrina called her pragmatic, yet she suggested aborting her pregnancy without any thought about emotions or beliefs, as if recommending she should toss out a new pair of shoes that were giving her blisters. She never considered what she, herself, might do in the same situation, or how she would feel about being pregnant under *any* circumstances. She hung her head, ashamed. "I should apologize."

"What? To Katrina? She loves you like a sister and knows you meant well. I'm sure she's forgotten about it already."

"What shall I do?"

"Tell him, of course."

"It will not be easy. He may not take the news well."

"Didn't say it would be easy." Yelena was rifling through her papers again, her tone emphatic. "But it's the right thing to do."

An hour later, Apri stood outside Jon's office on the second floor in the newly established council chambers. He'd been so busy—they both had. They'd not been together since the night after the funeral. *Has it been that long?* Her eagerness to see him battled with the dread of the news she had to share. Her hand trembled as she knocked on the door.

"Enter."

Breathe. She opened the door.

"Well, I'll be damned. If it isn't *Apri the Aratian*," he said with a warm smile. "To what do I owe this unexpected surprise?"

The comfortable, familiar bond they shared whenever they were in the same room linked immediately. But she kept that one particular thought far away from him at the back of her mind.

His skin was lighter from the weeks spent indoors, and paler still where his full beard and mustache used to be. His hair was groomed and cut back to shoulder length, and he wore a well-fitted Law Squad uniform. If it were possible for her to be more attracted to him, this new look would do it. But this handsome man, sitting behind a desk, perusing reports, with an expression that begged her to take him away from the drudgery, already had her heart and soul.

"I like the new look," she said.

He grazed fingers through his hair. "Oh, that, yes. Me, too. Never liked facial hair. It itches. All the time."

She laughed. *God, it is so good to be near him*. If she didn't keep her distance, she would lose herself and rush into his arms. "I see you are busy."

"Yes, preparing for tomorrow. Katrina was just here."

"I know, we've been missing each other. I need to see her, too, before I go." She hesitated, wondering how to start.

He looked at her, thoughtfully. "There's something I've been meaning to tell you."

"Oh? What's that?"

"Do you know that it was you? Who set everything in motion that night?"

Too wrapped up in her own predicament, she had to repeat his words in her head. Still unsure if she heard him right, she asked, "What was me?"

"You ordered the squaders to attack."

"I did not—" His serious expression and insistent thought cut her words short. "I remember being angry. And so filled with hate. That man was so vile," she said. "When those men let me go, I ran to Katrina."

"Every man who was there that night tells the same story. At the moment Hill and Zak… disappeared, they had only one thought. *Kill him.* Some explained it as a compulsion they couldn't ignore. Even Hill's men said the same, although the thought only confused them." He chuckled. "Your silent order even roused Baker out of unconsciousness."

"I was so… Zak…" Although stunned, Apri wouldn't doubt his word. She looked at the floor, trying to recall the sequence of events.

"The men holding me were on our side," he said. "I thought Zak was already dead, or I would've made a move sooner."

"He was barely alive when I came in," she said. "It would've been too late to save him."

"Oh." He didn't question how she knew that. "The Legiant's death would've come one way or another that night. I'm only telling you this because I believe you'd want to know—to help understand that gift of yours."

"Thank you for telling me. I wonder if I will ever understand it completely." Then she blurted out before she lost her nerve, "There is something I need to tell you, too."

"Of course. Why don't you come have a seat?" He stood and gestured to a chair next to the desk. "What is it?"

"Ummm…" She held up her hand. "No, I do not want to keep you."

Not wanting him to read her thoughts, her fear, she resisted the urge to connect with him mentally.

He stood at the chair he'd offered. She knew he felt her detachment, but he waited patiently for her to continue.

Her anxiety created an awkward tension. *Now or never.* She prepared herself to see and to feel his reaction. "I am pregnant."

Oh god. No! That was his first thought before he blocked her out. At first, she thought it no different from her own reaction to the news. But to be honest, she never once thought *No. Oh god,* yes, but not *No.* That was as much a revelation for herself as an understanding of his true feelings.

His brow furrowed. He said nothing for what seemed like forever. Then his expression changed to one of relief.

A flicker of hope rose within her.

"Yelena must be pleased," he said.

"Yelena?"

"Yes, after the loss of her son, to have a grandchild coming."

How can he think it is Kendall's child? She tried to read his expression without intruding on his thoughts. *Is he asking me to pretend it is not his? Or does he really believe it?* She felt sure it was the former, but she wouldn't challenge him. If he wished to avoid the obligation, she would honor that choice. "Yes, she is indeed," she said, very quietly.

He breathed a heavy sigh of relief, and, with that, she was even more convinced he knew the truth.

"Congratulations," he said with an almost-smile. "Does Katrina know yet?"

"No, that's why I'm looking for her."

"She'll be excited."

"No doubt." She laughed... or pretend-laughed anyway. It sounded forced. With the pretense set, she ventured a probe of his thoughts and found no obstruction, sensing only gratitude and relief.

It would take more time for her to get used to this idea before she could relax around him again. "I should let you get back to work," she said, turning to leave.

"You know you need to be on stage tomorrow? And the climber, too," he reminded her.

"Yes, I know," she said, still facing the door.

"Hey, if I have to be there, so do you."

"See you then," she waved backwards as she left.

She should be upset. If theirs was a normal relationship, she certainly would be. But she was strangely content with how it worked out. He didn't want the responsibility, especially right now. She understood and accepted that. She wanted to have his child, and he understood and accepted that. This seemed a reasonable compromise. *Pragmatic.* Smiling to herself, she jogged up the stairs.

Back on the fifth floor, Katrina was still out. Yelena sat on the couch in the sitting room with Monk dozing beside her.

Apri was prepared and blocked the contact this time, grinning when she felt the attempt.

"Okay, okay, smarty-pants," Yelena said. "So, what happened?"

"It seems congratulations are in order. For you, Grandma."

"For me? Grandma?" Her confused expression transitioned to comprehension. "He can't possibly think it's Kendall's."

"That is what he chooses to believe." She recounted the conversation with Jon.

"And you can accept this?" Yelena asked.

"I can and I do. Because I believe, with all my heart, that he knows it to be his. Am I crazy?"

Yelena smiled. "No, dear, you are not crazy. You're a muse." Yelena's expression turned solemn.

Apri felt a sudden awareness of what Yelena lost when her husband passed. She couldn't imagine going a single day without Jon. Even when they weren't together, the sense of him, knowing he'd always be there for her, was like an ever-present beacon lighting her way. An assurance that whatever obstacles and challenges she faced, she would get through it. He'd make sure of it. Yelena had that same connection with her Richard, and now he was gone, her beacon snuffed out.

"Can *you* accept this?" Apri asked Yelena, sincerely. "If it is too much—"

"Pretend that you carry my grandchild?" Yelena laughed through her tears. "I feel you are giving me a precious gift. I'd be honored to play along with this ridiculous ruse." She rubbed her eyes, "Under one condition."

"What condition?"

"That he or she will always be my grandchild, no matter what changes between the two of you."

"Agreed. Happily." They embraced.

"What did I miss? You two look like you're up to something," Katrina interrupted.

Yelena couldn't hide her tears. "Apri has news."

"News? Do tell."

Apri smiled. "I am pregnant."

Katrina went into a frenzy with congratulations and enthusiastic questions, which started all over again when she was told the child was Kendall's. "Now you will have two grandchildren!" she said to Yelena. "Because I insist that you be my child's grandmother as well. I can't accept Apri's child having a grandparent while mine has none!"

"Of course!" Yelena chuckled, still crying happily. "To think only weeks ago I thought I would live the rest of my days without a family. And now I shall have two grandchildren to spoil."

They laughed and talked about pregnancy, and babies, and all the wonderful things to come.

When they were talked out, Katrina said, "I have some less pleasant news." Her expression turned solemn. "After the Murfys met with the Commander, I escorted them to their room. Remember how I told you they lost their son, Gabe? Zak's best friend?"

Yelena nodded.

The nagging feeling returned to Apri at the mention of Zak's friend. *What is it about him?*

"Commander Gardner told them it wasn't an accident. Hill killed him..." Katrina choked up. "...when he was in Southrock trying to find Zak." She paused, inhaling deeply. "It is so sad. And he didn't even know where Zak was."

This is for Gabe. Zak's last words replayed in Apri's head. She recalled questioning Jon that night, about what Zak had against Hill. *He told Zak about Gabe.* "Huh."

Apri's vocal realization was not lost on Yelena, "What, dear?"

"Oh." *The woman misses nothing.* "It's just such a shame. How many lives have been lost, how many families forever changed by the actions of the Legiant and his men?"

Yelena slapped her knees and startled both girls out of their contemplation. "We have some work to do."

"We do?" Katrina asked.

"Yes. We're going to rewrite your speech for tomorrow's ceremony."

"I don't think the Commander and Headmaster Barrow will like that. They worked on my speech for days," Katrina said.

"Which is exactly why we aren't going to tell them." Yelena rubbed her hands together. "Let's go. No time to waste."

"I want no part of this conspiracy," Apri said, "Let's go Monkjan. I will see you both tomorrow."

Chapter 26
Apri

Apri stood with Jon on the platform where Katrina would address the gathering. Across from them on the other side sat the members of the leadership council. She estimated the crowd in the palace courtyard to be four or five times larger than on the day Katrina was first introduced to the citizens of Edyson.

Through her connection with Jon, she knew he was pleased. He and Barrow wanted the mood of today's event to be festive and uplifting, and they weren't disappointed. A feeling of celebration and anticipation exuded from all around. Palace squaders were on hand as necessary to manage such a gathering, but the two who stood in front of the platform were positioned there more for decoration than intimidation. Banners emblazoned with the Edyson seal fluttered above on the parapets while individuals wagged miniature likenesses to and fro among the crowd. The scent of pastries and treats from the street vendors mixed with the aroma of the meal being prepared in the palace kitchens and added to the sensory delight.

A cheer rose and spread through the crowd like a wave, a sign that the queen's open carriage had appeared to begin its meandering route from the palace to the platform. Although Apri couldn't see the carriage from her vantage point, its approach was no less evident by the volume of cheers that preceded it. She smiled, envisioning a regal Katrina, sitting atop the carriage and waving in grand parade style to the onlookers.

Every detail of the ceremony had been choreographed and orchestrated to entertain and impress the citizens of Edyson. Jon was dressed in an elaborate uniform, decorated with medals that glistened in the sun. In stark contrast to his resplendence, she wore the less ostentatious, but undoubtedly more comfortable, garb of *Apri the Aratian*, feeling just as ridiculous standing there in her tandorus-hide vest. Sitting on her shoulder excitedly surveying the crowd, Monk put the finishing touch on her exotic image.

She and Jon both despised the play-acting, but their objections had been overruled. They traded complaints and snide comments with each other, verbally and mentally, as they waited for the carriage to arrive.

Headmaster Barrow, dressed in his ceremonial headmaster cape, escorted Katrina to the podium, a calculated move to demonstrate that honor and trust had been fully restored to the Cortek.

Apri and Jon bowed.

Wearing a form-fitting gown that flattered her figure, Katrina gave them a wicked grin as she passed, enjoying their discomfort. A necklace with many-faceted jewels glittered around her neck—a compliment to the queen's tiara interlaced within the braid of her dark hair. The crowd roared as she and Barrow stepped up to the podium. She graciously bowed her head to Barrow, who then took his place beside Apri.

He grinned. "You two look—"

"Don't say it." Jon warned.

"My fellow citizens," Katrina began. The solar-powered PA system projected her voice so it could be heard throughout the grounds. "I stand before you today, in awe of this magnificent gathering to celebrate our newfound freedom from tyranny and oppression." Another roar from the throng. "I would like to tell you a story. One that I learned of only yesterday."

Apri felt the two men on either side of her bristle. *Thus begins the rewrite.* She smirked. *Nothing you two can do now but listen.*

"Gabriel Murfy was a young man I knew as a child in Southrock, before my abduction. He was my brother Zak's best friend back then…"

In two short sentences the grounds became quiet, all ears eager to hear this new story, one not heard by any before today. Yelena was a master speech writer, and Katrina's was the voice, and the history, that the citizens of Edyson wanted to hear. Together—Yelena's prose and Katrina's delivery—gripped the audience and held them captive.

"…at the hands of ex-commander Hill, by order of Legiant Malcolm Covington," Katrina continued. "He suffered the same fate as my own brother, Zakary Bancroft, as both of my parents, as Kendall Otero and his father, Richard. These are not the only innocent people to die needlessly at the hands of the former regime. These are just the few *I* knew. People *I* loved. There are stories like mine all over our colony." The last few words caught in her throat. Tears fell down her cheeks, and she paused.

The crowd was reverent as she continued in a soft, solemn voice. "To those of you who have suffered a loss from the insufferable abuse of power of this Legiant, or of the last, know this: I understand your pain. I know how you feel. And I promise you now… This. Will. Never. Happen. Again." Her delicate fist pounded the podium, her voice accelerating in crescendo, with each word.

A thunderous applause erupted from the crowd.

Her next words were forceful, in a voice Apri had never heard her use before. Loud, but not shrill. "In honor of all…" The words were drowned out in the cheers and applause, and she began again. "In honor of all those who gave their very lives for the greater good of Edyson and its citizens, we shall forever remember their sacrifice." More applause and cheering. "And we shall celebrate that sacrifice on this holiday each year, to be known from this day forward as… Memorial Day."

The crowd cheered their appreciation again as brightly colored *Memorial Day* banners unfurled throughout the grounds.

A minute or two passed as Katrina allowed the cheers to endure, then, using her loud voice again, she said, "I would like to introduce you to a couple of people to whom I owe, to whom we *all* owe, our deepest gratitude." The crowd grew quiet again. "By now you have heard stories of their heroics, of the night that they, along with my brother Zakary, put the welfare of Edyson above concern for their own safety and infiltrated the palace. Commander Jon Gardner…"

Jon stepped up to stand beside Katrina while the crowd applauded and cheered.

"…and Apri Balakian, of Ararat."

Apri took her place on Katrina's right.

Monk stood on his hind legs, screeching at the noise. He seemed to get the biggest applause of all.

Katrina took hold of Apri's hand and held it up, and Jon's, too, like a referee introducing a couple of boxers getting ready for a fight.

"Wave at them!" she scolded.

"I'm *not* going to wave," Jon said.

Apri gave a sad little wave, elbow bent at ninety degrees, hand moving back and forth at her waist. If she tried anything more than that, Monk would have nowhere to go other than to perch on her head.

Katrina put their hands down, "You two are insufferable. Go on back," she said in a harsh whisper.

Katrina then introduced Headmaster Barrow, and the rest of the proceedings involved him explaining the planned change in the government structure that would eliminate the position of Legiant and create three executive branches: the military, the legislative, and the royal family. Barrow explained briefly how the three branches would govern the people and police each other.

"It will take a few months to iron out the details and hold elections. Martial Law will remain in effect until the legislative council is elected and sworn in," Barrow explained.

"As our last order of business, I am pleased to announce that Commander Gardner has agreed to suspend the curfew in the capital for tonight only—" He paused to allow the cheers to subside, and stressed again, "For tonight only. The curfew will be enforced again as of tomorrow night."

"Enjoy your Memorial Day," he said. "May it be the first of many to come."

Barrow escorted Katrina back to the carriage and everyone on the podium followed, on foot, to the rear palace entrance.

Chapter 27
Jon

Jon untucked his shirt from his trousers, thankful to be free of the stiff, bedazzled uniform jacket and done with the pomp and circumstance of the day. It was best that he left the party when he did. He knew he'd take some heat from Barrow tomorrow, but he could only take so much of social events before he drank more than he should... or said something he shouldn't. Or both. He took a long swig from his mug, enjoying the smooth, earthy flavor of the ale.

Zak's rough-looking hat sat next to his discarded belt on the dressing table. Baker'd brought it to him after finding it lying in a corner on the stairwell. He picked up the hat, admiring the expertly-tanned leather—smooth and soft, yet strong and durable. *No wonder he wore it all the time!*

His mind drifted back to that evening after the grear battle when Zak stood outside their meager cove in the pouring rain, arms outstretched, washing the mud off his body. *I bet that wasn't the first time the kid took a shower in the rain.*

Zak! Jon wondered if he'd ever get past the guilt or quell the litany of what-if scenarios that played out in his head every time he thought of that young man. It wasn't the first time he'd lost a comrade, or a friend. But this loss lingered, as did his regret, more so than those that'd gone before. *What if I'd told him about Katrina? What if I'd acted sooner that night? What if I'd never gone looking for him in the first place?*

He propped the hat on his head and checked out his comical image in the mirror. *Too small.* After tucking the cap away in the back of a drawer, he picked up his mug and stepped onto the balcony. Looking out over the palace grounds and the capital city beyond, he raised his mug high. "Here's to you, Zak!" he said, then took another swig of Murfy's incredible brew.

At Jon's request, Murf had brought three barrels of his darpact ale with him from Southrock. The ale had been served for the first time at tonight's Memorial Day feast, receiving high praise from their guests, as he knew it would. Yelena wasted no time arranging an agreement to keep the palace supplied with the ale, insisting it be exclusively sold to the palace, and nowhere else. Headmaster Barrow overheard the negotiation and voiced his vehement objection to the monopoly, arguing that such a fine ale deserved to be available to more than just the privileged few. After much deliberation, and an assurance from Murf that he could meet the demand for both, Yelena agreed to share the exclusive distribution with the Cortek. So *Murfy's Ale,* as it would be known, would be served only at the palace, the Forest Inn and on the Core Campus.

Taking another drink, he felt the warmth of the liquid on his tongue. The luscious taste, the burn as it flowed down his throat, all set him to thinking about her again—*Apri*. He breathed deeply, smelling the scent of her that still lingered on his collar from their time on the dance floor. When she was in his arms, it was easy to forget others were around them. He only saw, only heard, only felt her, moving with him as one… in his arms, in his head, and in his heart.

Even when they weren't together, the sense of her was always there, at the edge of his awareness, poised and ready for him to turn his thoughts to her. *What is this thing that has taken such control of me? Love?* He hated that word. *So generic.* A label that described every normal, ordinary relationship from the beginning of time. *This is different.*

Of course, he knew the child was his. Kendall had told him when they were in Baytown that he and Apri weren't sleeping together. And, of course, she gave in to his desperate, panicked bail-out ploy. Somehow, she'd recognized he couldn't bear taking on that burden. Certainly not now, maybe not ever. There were no tears, no heated argument, no long, drawn-out discussion. It was an intuitive, unspoken arrangement—a mutually acceptable resolution that was settled silently, instinctively, in a few heartbeats.

That was the part of their relationship that transcended the average—the innate sense of what the other person desired most, and a compelling urge to fulfill that need. Perhaps it was that strange gift of hers that made what they had together so unusual. *It sure does make for the best sex ever.*

Apri's revelation about being a muse had shocked him. Not because it was hard for him to believe, but because it was the same secret the dying man in the courtyard wished to share with his son. He quickly dismissed his first thought that she could be that man's wife. Of course, that wasn't possible. But through discrete observation and deduction over the past few weeks, he'd figured out that the man's wife was Yelena and Kendall the son he'd promised to tell. He raised his mug again. "And to you, Kendall."

Laughter and music drifted from below. Apri had promised to join him later, after the party. *Sounds like it's still going strong. Why does she have to stay till the end?*

Pouring the last of the ale, he made a sad face as the final few drops fell into his mug. A lazy stupor sent his thoughts in wild directions. He leaned on the railing and looked out at the city, blinking a few times to clear the fog that clouded his eyes.

I'm going to be a father!?

Chapter 28
Advik

Advik Barrow re-filled his mug with Murf's exquisite ale. *This is it,* he promised himself. *Last mug.* But then, that's what he said the last time. He shrugged. Savoring another taste of the addictive brew, he surveyed the room over the rim of his mug.

He'd noticed Commander Gardner leaving the party earlier, grabbing a bottle of ale on his way out. *Probably for the best.* Jon had been in a sour mood all day, not surprising given his oft-mentioned distaste for social gatherings and political maneuvering. Yet it seemed there was more to it than that. Had he stayed much longer in that frame of mind, he might well have offended one or more members of the leadership council, inadvertently or intentionally.

Where would we be today without the selfless honor and courage of that young man? A shiver ran up his spine, and he took another sip of the smooth, warm ale.

In the weeks since that terrible day at the Core Campus, he'd spent much of his time studying the circumstances that brought Edyson to such a desperate state of anarchy and disorder, and what he and the Cortek, could've done, *should've* done, to prevent it. He'd vastly underestimated the extent of Covington's greed and thirst for power. At some point, the obsession within him overtook all reason and sanity. Did it happen after he became Legiant? Or was it there all along, festering inside like an abscess until it finally burst into the disease that ultimately consumed him?

He knew all of this, now. It's a simple thing to look back into the past and see the signs. But as Cortek Headmaster, it was his duty to recognize the threat to Edyson while it simmered—*before* it boiled and raged out of control. In this, he'd failed the citizens of his colony, the oathbound Cortek, and himself. He'd wallowed in misery for weeks after the massacre, fully intending to abdicate his position. Until he came to another dismal realization of his own incompetence—he'd failed to groom a suitable candidate to replace him as Headmaster.

Barrow spied Yelena with young Queen Katrina. Those two complimented each other like bread and butter. Like bacon and eggs. *How can I be hungry again? What time is it anyway?*

He well knew the value of having Yelena around. The woman has lost so much, yet she finds the strength and fortitude not just to survive, but to thrive, to forge ahead and get back from life what fate has taken from her. And she infects those around her with the same will, the same desire to move on, to learn from the past and make the best of the future.

Were it not for Yelena, he might still be floundering in despair and self-loathing. He thought back to that one evening when he was feeling particularly sorry for himself.

***

Yelena met him at the door to his rooms and followed him in without an invitation. "You need to snap out of it!" she scolded. Not just with her voice, but in his head as well.

He usually blocked her out when she tried that trick on him, but, on that day, he didn't have the willpower. "Get out," he told her, meaning out of the room and out of his head.

She didn't leave. Instead, she scoffed at him for abandoning his duty to the Cortek and to the citizens of Edyson.

He grumbled and complained about his unworthiness to serve, listing his many failures and shortcomings. They volleyed arguments back and forth. She listened to his doubts and degradation, and offered her introspective, muse-enlightened insight and support. It took hours—they talked long into the night.

With her help, he found his way out of the deep depression and vowed to atone for his failures and redeem his self-respect and integrity.

***

The first step toward recovery was complete, thanks to the unlikely threesome who delivered Edyson from its power-hungry Legiant.

The loss of Katrina's twin brother was regrettable. Stories of the rescue were being retold again and again, with each version more convincing at depicting Zakary Bancroft as a martyr for the people of Edyson. It was a story that would be forever written into the history of the colony.

The second step was underway, the establishment of a governmental structure that would not allow a single person or entity to hold a position of power over the welfare and future of Edyson. This stage would take much longer.

Step three... He watched Apri as she mingled with the palace guests. She'd changed from her battle garb into a sea-green gown with a bodice that hugged her slight frame and a full skirt that floated around her like ripples on a clear, fresh pond. She spent most of her time in Katrina's company yet didn't ignore other guests who begged for her attention. He noted how she and Yelena hovered around Katrina, always one or the other by her side lending their unique cerebral support and encouragement to help the queen through her first major social function.

Apri the Aratian. As a young girl she'd made quite the impression, and his intuition rarely missed the mark. *I'll have to wait and see how her relationship with the commander plays out, though.*

He chuckled, recalling the two of them on the dance floor. There wasn't an eye in the place that didn't wander in their direction to watch them dancing together. They moved together as if having no thought for any but each other. It was impossible not to notice the intense attraction, the sheer pleasure they enjoyed in each other's company. It was like watching young children at play, with not a care but for their own joy in that moment. It rekindled one's faith in humanity. And love.

When the two were not entwined together, they were like magnet and steel. Always standing a fair distance apart from each other, as if afraid they might not be able to separate if they came too close. He felt it whenever he stood between them, each would relax, his presence a welcome barrier—temporary relief from the powerful force that drew them to each other.

Perhaps it was their current obligations, or the uncertain future that drove them to resist the natural attraction. Both were struggling to settle into the new roles they had inadvertently carved out for themselves. Jon had his duties as commander to tend to, and Apri spent most of her time with Yelena or in the campus library, learning everything she could about the history of Edyson and the Cortek.

Advik scanned the Grand Ballroom, pleased with the festive atmosphere and the outcome of today's proceedings. The months to come would have their challenges, but he was up for it. He saw Murf sitting with his wife, caught his eye, and raised his mug in a salute.

Where was I? Ah, yes, step three. Even with her short time on campus, and the added complication of having a non-Cortek partner, Barrow was confident Apri would make a most suitable headmaster. *Much better than her predecessor.*

He drank the last of the ale from his mug, congratulating himself on convincing Yelena to let him in on the deal with Murfy. *My best work of the day!*

The End

From the Author:

I hope you enjoyed reading Cortek Exiled. The Oath of The Cortek series continues with Cortek Haven, scheduled for release in 2024. A sneak preview of the first chapter follows.

Please consider leaving a review on your preferred reading platform(s). Reviews help other readers find books they will love. Your feedback also helps me become a better writer and provides incentive and motivation to continue writing. Scan the QR code to leave comments on Amazon/Good Reads:

283

Additional links to get connected with Jacque Alanbery:

Jacque Alanbery Website →

← *Follow me on Facebook*

Cortek Haven
Oath of the Cortek Book 2
Chapter 1 - Apri

Apri reached across the desk and waved the letter at Jon's face. "She is gone!"

"Who's gone? Gone where?" Jon asked, grabbing the paper from her hand.

"If I knew *where*, I'd be going after her!" she yelled. "She is only thirteen."

"Excuse me, sir," one of Jon's men stood at the open door. "Sorry to disturb you, sir, but this came for you this morning."

Apri glared at the squader.

The man ignored her and spoke to his commander. "It has the campus seal. I thought it might be important."

Apri grabbed the envelope from him. "It is from her!" She broke the seal and began to read.

"Sir?"

"It's alright," Jon said. "Baker? Wait." Jon called the squader back.

"Sir?"

"Find Mistress Yelena and Prince Za..."

Apri didn't hear the rest of their exchange. The note, written in Kendra's hand, read the same as hers except… She blinked, reading the first word again to be sure. "How long has she known *this*?" she asked, her voice just above a whisper.

The guard said something to Jon, then left.

"Known what? What does it say?"

She handed him the letter, and he skimmed it. "Says the same thing as yours." He gave it back to her. "Almost exactly."

"When did you tell her?" Apri asked him.

"What are you talking about? Tell her what?"

"Your letter," she accused, pointing at the first word on the page. "It is addressed *Father*." She reached out to his thoughts but read only confusion.

"Oh, that." He was genuinely puzzled. "I didn't tell her. She knew."

"When?"

"When what? When did she know?" He raked his fingers through his hair. "She's known all along."

"All along?" Apri fell into the chair at Jon's desk. "How do I not know this? Why didn't you tell me?"

"I assumed you knew. She must've been four or five the first time she—You and I, we've never discussed it. I thought that was intentional, to avoid confusion, to keep the status quo, to protect Yelena?"

"Protect Yelena from what?" Yelena asked as she entered through the open door.

Jon ignored her and asked Apri, "How could you *not* know? Don't you, you know, get in her head? I've told her all along to keep it a secret. I never dreamed she could keep it from *you*."

"What's going on?" Yelena asked.

Apri took Jon's letter from the desk and handed it to Yelena, stabbing her finger at the first word.

"She *knows*?" Yelena looked at them each in turn, then returned to reading the letter.

"*You* know?" Jon asked Yelena. "I thought…" He combed his hair back again.

"She's run away?" Yelena exclaimed.

Jon would never have told Kendra voluntarily. Apri was sure of it. "How did she find out?"

"How?" Jon said. "You told me a person can't keep their true identity a secret from a muse, right? You could've warned me, by the way, and maybe she wouldn't have caught me off guard that first time."

Apri looked at Yelena who shook her head. Then she asked Jon, "What do you mean? Warned you about what?"

"That she's a muse, what do you think?"

"She is *not* a—" She stopped. Jon's expression dared her to argue that point. She looked at Yelena again.

"Well, that explains a lot," Yelena said bluntly.

Prince Zakary came to the door. "Commander? Permission to enter?"

"Granted, young Zakary," Jon said. "Please, come in and have a seat."

"Am I in trouble?" Zakary asked, eyeing the adults warily.

"No, not at all," Jon said. "Actually, we need your help with something."

Apri was still shaken by the revelation that her daughter was a muse, but there was no time to sort that out right now. She needed to find her daughter and bring her home, so she forced herself to listen to the conversation.

"…letter said she had someplace to go. As if she's been planning it or had some destination in mind. Do you know where she could be headed?" Jon asked.

Zakary and Kendra had grown up together and were as close as siblings. Apri doubted there would be anything Kendra wished for that Zakary wouldn't know. But he was a thoughtful, introspective young man, and loyal to a fault. He wouldn't want to get his friend in trouble.

"*Prince* Zakary," Yelena said with authority, "your friend might be in danger. It's important that you tell us anything you know that could help us find her."

Yelena had mentioned using his title lately to shift him into a more responsible frame of mind. And, of course, she could also be using some degree of mental influence on the unsuspecting young man.

His reluctance to speak dissolved. "She told me she heard something strange whenever she rode in the North Wood. Or *felt* something strange?"

"Where exactly?" Jon asked.

"Felt what?" Apri asked.

The questions came on top of each other, voiced with impatient fervor, and Zakary shifted in the chair. His eyes darted from Jon to Apri and back again.

Yelena shot her and Jon a warning look. "Zakary, were you ever riding with her when she felt it?"

"No, I don't like to ride much, not just for fun like she does. She goes all the time."

"Is there anyone she rides with who might know?"

"I don't know. Maybe someone at the stable? I think she mentioned something about the river once? Or across the river?" He paused and shook his head. "I don't always listen when she talks about her rides. Sometimes, I think she just makes things up to make it sound more exciting."

Jon chuckled.

This is not amusing, Apri warned him mentally.

Jon stood and grabbed his jacket from the coatrack. "Thank you, Zakary. You have been most helpful. Yelena, would you see that he gets back to his study group?"

"Let's go, young man," Yelena said, guiding him out of the room.

"Come on. Let's go find her," Jon said to Apri.

They rushed to the palace stables where two horses were saddled and waiting.

"I assume she keeps her horse at the campus stables?" Jon asked as they mounted.

Apri nodded.

"We'll stop there on the way out," he said, then rode away at a ground-covering trot.

Apri followed, her thoughts fixed on the shocking revelations about her daughter. Of course, she'd been communicating mentally with Kendra, as had Yelena, ever since she was a child. But all this time, she'd assumed it was *their* gift allowing the connection. *Yet, she's had the talent all along?* It couldn't have been bestowed by a chance encounter with a pegafox, as it had been with herself and Yelena. *Inherited? Is that possible?* Yelena's son, Kendall, hadn't inherited it, and from Yelena's reaction in Jon's office, Apri knew she'd been just as surprised.

She felt awful. So much time wasted. I could've been teaching my daughter about her special talent.

Her nails dug into her palm as she clenched her fists tightly over the reins. It was an age-old habit to get her brain to shift focus to the more immediate situation. Kendra was nearing her fourteenth birthday, the time when most Cortek-bred children became bound by oath to the Cortek way of life. Her letters said she didn't want to take the oath, but she didn't want to be a disappointment to her mother and grandmother.

How could I be so disconnected from my own daughter? She'd been utterly unaware of Kendra's burden—a pressure so great that the only way out was to run away. If Kendra had only said something. *Or if I would've said something to her! I'm such an awful mother!*

They stopped at the campus stables and found Elenza Suter in the barn grooming a horse. A few years older than Kendra, and already Core-bound, El shared Kendra's love of animals. They were about as close as two girls could be considering the five or six years that separated them—a significant difference at their age. Apri had already considered assigning El as Kendra's sponsor when she—*My daughter doesn't* want *to take the oath, yet I've already chosen her sponsor. I'm a horrible mother!*

Apri ran to Elenza, "El, have you seen Kendra this morning?"

"No. I just got here. What's wrong?" the girl asked.

"She's run off," Apri said with a frustrated sigh. "Do you know where she might have gone?"

"I don't, but..." she ran to one of the stalls and looked inside. "She can't have been gone long. Her mare always sh—poops in her stall before a ride. That pile looks pretty fresh."

"Thank you. That's something anyway. Keep an eye out, will you?" Apri ran back outside to where Jon waited.

"Yes, good luck!" El called out.

Apri mounted and they rode the short distance to Northgate. Jon increased speed as soon as the traffic thinned out, took the turn to the Northgate Roadhouse, then slowed to a walk at the narrow path that led into the North Wood. The thick underbrush forced them to drop their pace to a walk and ride single file.

Jon turned in the saddle. "So, you really didn't know she was a muse?" he asked, shaking his head. "And Yelena knows that she is *my* daughter?"

"Correct. It's all so messed up," she admitted. "When I next see Yelena, I know she's going to spout off some old saying about keeping secrets."

Jon chuckled. "I think I know just the one, too." He paused a moment, then quoted, "*Oh what a tangled web we weave...*"

Apri joined him to finish the quote, *"when first we practice to deceive. Yes, that's the one."* She asked him then, "How long have you known about Yelena?"

"Known what?"

"You talked about Kendra being a muse in front of Yelena without any hesitation."

"Did I ever tell you about the day of the massacre... about the dying man in the courtyard?"

"Yes, the one with the secret he asked you to share with his son." Of course, he'd told her. She'd been carrying a regret about it since before Kendra was born.

When they came to the cleared area next to the city wall, she rode next to Jon. "You never did tell me his secret, though."

"The man said, 'Tell my son his mother is a muse. That she can read his thoughts.' It was a strange, unbelievable message to me at the time, and I wasn't even sure I heard it right." He looked at her. "Until the day I learned *you're* a muse."

"I remember *that* day," she said with a smile. She considered it their anniversary—the day their relationship truly began.

He rolled his eyes. "As you remind me every year," he said. "Anyway, it wasn't a stretch to figure it out back then. You and Yelena were so close. Then, when she and the queen bonded so tightly, and so quickly?" he said.

"I've always regretted not telling you, but I couldn't bring myself to betray Yelena's trust, especially since Kendall was gone anyway. And you've known all along?"

He shrugged. "Ever since the first day I felt Kendra in my head, I've told her to keep it a secret... that I was her father. Because I didn't want Yelena to find out that Kendra wasn't really her granddaughter."

It was Apri's turn to laugh. "And Yelena has known *that* all along." She groaned.

"Now that I think about it, maybe Kendra thought it was about her being a muse? That she needed to keep *that* a secret," he said. "Or maybe she felt she had to, in order to keep the *other* secret? I don't know. It was all so very long ago. We haven't talked about it in years—the secret part, I mean."

"Oh, I am such a horrible mother! All of this time I should have been helping my daughter understand her gift."

"How could you *not* know?" he asked.

"I've been wondering that myself. To me, when I bond with Kendra, it feels exactly the same as with you, and you're not a muse. I guess I—we, myself *and* Yelena—assumed that it was *our* gift creating the bond."

They approached the river. The current was strong from snowmelt, and Jon had to raise his voice to be heard above the flowing water. "She wouldn't try to cross here. Let's head for the bridge." He shouted. "Do you *feel* anything?"

He was referring to Zakary's comment about Kendra feeling something strange. She shook her head.

The bridge was beyond the northwest corner of the city. Jon rode as fast as the terrain would allow, crossing the bridge and cantering down the narrow road, stopping when they were away from the noise of the river.

"Anything?" he asked.

Apri remained still, reaching out with her mind, listening, searching. She shook her head. "Nothing."

He looked around. "The North Wood goes in three directions from here."

The sound of horses came from the direction of the bridge. Jon pulled up, then put himself between her and the two approaching riders.

Such a man. Still, it made her feel special. She leaned over to see around him. "It's just Elenza," she said, then called out to them. "Did you find her?"

"No, sorry," Elenza said, then gestured to the other rider. "You know my sponsor, Hannah Burke? She's a trained tracker."

Apri nodded in greeting.

"So, after you left the stables, I remembered riding up here with Kendra. She wanted to explore in that direction," Elenza said, pointing east. "When it got late, I had to beg her to turn around. She got so mad. Wouldn't talk to me the whole way home."

Apri saw only trees. *Why east? There's nothing that way but more forest.*

"Anyways, if she did come this way, Hannah can help us find her."

"The ground is soft and muddy," Hannah said, inspecting the ground along the road. We should be able to see tracks if she rode through here. Spread out."

Elenza and Hannah rode south, back toward the bridge, while Apri and Jon went north.

"Still nothing?" Jon asked.

"Nothing," Apri said, frustrated.

"Try something else."

"What? What else should I try!" she snapped back. Concern for Kendra was getting the best of her.

He ignored the emotion. "It's just… something I do when I get stuck on a problem. Look at it from a different angle, a different approach. I don't know anything about your gift. Maybe instead of *listening,* call out to her? Talk to… I don't know, the forest?"

"It doesn't—"

"You have to forget about what you *think* you know," he interrupted. "Try *anything.* Try *everything.* You have nothing to lose by trying something different."

"Over here!" Elenza called out.

They galloped back toward the bridge.

"We found some tracks," Elenza said when they caught up, pointing to some hoofprint depressions leading off into the woods.

Hannah took the lead, looking for evidence of a rider passing through. As she rode, she would point out each sign she discovered to Elenza along the way.

It was a painfully slow process. Apri feared they would never catch up with Kendra if they didn't pick up the pace. She thought back on Jon's suggestion to try something different with her gift. She'd tried in the past connecting with a person who wasn't present, who wasn't visible to her. Often enough that she knew it wouldn't help to reach out to connect with her daughter. *Forget about what you think you know.*

She closed her eyes and reached out with her mind. *Kendra. Kendra! It is your mother. Where are you? Please! Come home.* She waited.

Nothing. She wiped tears from wet cheeks. Zakary had said Kendra felt, or heard, something strange. *Try anything.*

She reached out again. This time she didn't try to connect with her daughter or with anyone in particular. She just projected outward. To anywhere… to nowhere… to everywhere. *Please. Whoever you are, whatever you are. Send her back to me. She is young and confused. She is not ready. Please!* The last word she silently screamed with every ounce of emotion within her. *Still nothing.*

She turned around in the saddle to face Jon and shook her head to his silent question.

Kendra

Kendra stopped her horse and looked around. *Nooooo!* The fervent, insistent summons that had been driving her since she crossed over the bridge, guiding her deeper and deeper into the forest, had vanished. She was suddenly, and completely, alone. *Don't leave me!* She looked east, in the direction she'd been led, but saw only more trees, more brush, more forest. If she kept moving in that direction, without the intuitive guidance from whatever it was, or *who*ever it was, she would be lost before sundown.

"Arrrgh!" she screamed aloud. Her horse stomped, then stretched her nose out, pulling at the bit. "Take it easy, Velvet." She stroked the crest of the mare's neck, then pulled a twig from her mane. *Why did I choose to come this way?* She could've taken any other road out of Edyson—south to Baytown, east to Southrock and beyond to The Ravens or Casterly Lake. *Any* other direction, and she would not be sitting here staring at a dead end, with nowhere to go but backwards. She reached out again with her mind, but the irresistible urge to continue moving in a specific direction—the presence that had kept her company and made her feel safe and secure—had deserted her.

She looked to the south. She could ride that way to the river but the chance of finding a safe way across at this time of year was slim. She turned Velvet around. The mare snorted and pranced. Even if she couldn't exactly retrace the path back to the bridge, Velvet would know the way. She relaxed the reins and the mare charged off at a brisk, ground covering walk, head swinging like a pendulum side to side, moving as fast as she could without breaking gait.

Kendra sighed. "At least one of us is happy."

Cortek Haven
Oath of the Cortek Book 2
Coming 2024